THE OPUS

Andrea Clark

AuthorHouse™
1663 Liberty Drive
Bloomington, IN 47403
www.authorhouse.com
Phone: 1 (800) 839-8640

Published by AuthorHouse 02/19/2015

ISBN: 978-1-4969-6739-8 (sc)
ISBN: 978-1-4969-6740-4 (e)

Print information available on the last page.

This book is printed on acid-free paper.

Opus: the creative work by an individual.

PROLOGUE: THE Author

"So you see, I'm calling you because I know you can write it, Jackie." This stated in her firm, quiet way. "It needs to be written, even I know that, and I can't do it. That I also know." Then, hurriedly, "Could you at least see us getting together sometime, so Bobby can talk with you about it? Maybe then, you could think about writing it? Would that be possible?"

"Jeez, I don't know, Doreen. I'm just a reporter for a couple of local papers. I was never trained as a *serious* writer. I've mostly just bumbled along, teaching myself. Bobby's project sounds a little beyond me."

"Well, you're the only one he says he'll talk with about this. I suggested he look for a real writer, I mean someone who's written a book or something, you know, nothing against you, but he says no, he wants to talk with you about it, because you're a friend, and you are a real writer, which is true, you do write. Oh God, I'm babbling. I'm nervous about all this; he's making me a wreck." I could hear her taking a deep breath, then releasing it in a long, ragged sigh.

Finally, she continued, "Well, d'you think you could at least come over to talk with him about it for a couple of hours? Maybe that could help you decide if you're willing to work with him. How about you have Sunday dinner with us? Could you agree to that?"

"I don't know," I pondered. "Depends what you're having for dinner--I'm picky." Then, "Doreen, forget I said that; I'm just being sassy. I get like that when someone asks me to participate in an anxiety-producing, perhaps life-changing project. I guess I could come and talk. But only if you make it clear that there'll be no expectations, okay? If I think he's even beginning to think I'll commit to it, I'll boot out of there in a heartbeat, I swear."

"Oh, thanks loads, Jackie--he'll be so excited. This is great. I can't wait to tell him you're coming."

"Doreen, d'you see what you're doing? Sounds like you're starting already with the expectations. Could you just say I'm coming to have chicken or whatever with you and Bobby, and leave out the rest?"

"Okay, all right, Jackie," she agreed. "I'll tell him you've agreed to listen to him—just listen. I'm sorry, I can't help being excited. We'll see you Sunday at four. You know where we are, on the Harbor Point Road? About a mile and a half down on the left you'll see a blue mailbox with number 97 on it. If it snows before Sunday, we'll make sure the driveway's plowed. Oh, and watch out for Sharkey. He's part wolf, but real sweet. He's big and he loves everyone, so he's likely to jump in your car when you open the door. Just yell "Down" real firm and he'll stay away from you."

"Jeez, a wolf, for God's sake? I'm great with cats, but dogs and I don't always make it together, much less wolf-type dogs. Could you keep him in or something, at least until we get to know each other?"

"Oh, sure, we'll keep him in the shed," Doreen said, the anxiety now gone from her soft voice. "Just come, please."

This part of our conversation followed Doreen Parker's extensive explanation of a weird project her Husband Bobby had been involved in. This project had gone on for a couple of years, and involved an old lady from Milltown. Of course, it being such a small town, and no one being able to keep a secret, I knew Bobby had some dealings with an old lady from that area, but I wasn't sure of the details. Shortly before last Christmas, Bobby discovered some mysterious information about her long-deceased husband. The old lady had died shortly after she heard the news. Since her death, Bobby had been so depressed he couldn't stand himself, and because she loved him so much, it was getting harder and harder for Doreen to stand him either. Of course, she said, being Bobby, he's totally convinced himself that it's his fault she died. The old lady, Emma her name was, had been older than God—almost ninety.

Doreen and Bobby had agreed that maybe if he told the whole story to someone who was not involved, someone who might even put his experience in writing for him, he might feel better. He said he thought Emma might like that, which freaked Doreen out a bit. What did Emma have to say about it--she was dead for Godsakes. But she agreed, and for some not too clear reason, they had settled on me. Doreen thought that beyond merely the telling and the recording of it, it would make a great story.

"If he'd just think about it," she said. "What he's done for her and all, and think about working with you to write it all down in good order, not like it is now, which is just a jumble in his mind and a bunch of notes he's been writing down and cramming into a shoebox, all keeping him awake at night. He doesn't care if the writing ever gets published; he just has this need to talk about it, like go over it all with someone besides me." She sounded somewhat anxious. "I'm getting so sick of listening to it over and over. I want to scream at him, sometimes. He sort of lost one wife over this woman, you know."

"Yeah, I heard about that. Right after he started working for Emma, wasn't it?"

"A few months after. He started working for Emma two years ago this month, and Deb filed for divorce the end of that summer. We've only been married for two months. I love the guy to pieces, but if this keeps up much longer, I'm going around the bend, if you know what I mean. He cannot stop talking about it all--the husband, the money thing, how it all turned out."

"I heard the thing was finished some time ago," I said.

"After he first arranged for extra money to be sent to her, Bobby hoped he was done. But Emma wasn't satisfied. She felt that there was a lot more to the story. She needed more information than the firm in Portland could give her. She kept after Bobby until he and Thomas's old employee, Jonathan Brimmer, finally discovered the whole story.

"At first, even after she said she wanted to know it all, they didn't want to tell her. Finally, they were convinced she was ready to hear everything. Bobby told her, and a few weeks later, Emma died." Doreen sighed. "Their opus, she called the project. Their magnificent work. Bobby only wanted to help her. Instead, he feels he contributed to her death." Hoo, boy. Poor Doreen. I wouldn't want to be on the receiving end if Bobby Parker was riled. The Bobby I knew would stick with a thing like a turtle latched onto its prey; don't bother with him 'til he's done.

So there it was. "So you think my coming over for your great food will help this situation?" Doreen was the reputed queen of cuisine in Washington County.

"Jackie, you're not gonna believe this. Promise if I tell you, you'll still come. Promise."

"Sure, I'll come. I go anywhere in the County for a free meal, you gotta know that. What?"

"He says she's starting to haunt him--Emma, I mean. He's been up in the middle of the night for the last week--says she wakes him up and tells him she and Thomas won't rest proper until their story is written. He's a mess, I tell you. See what I mean? You need to come, Jackie, because if you don't I'm going to suggest he find a shrink. And you know him. He'll never go for that.

"Oh, and I forgot. He said to tell you even if the story never gets published, he'll pay you when he gets the money she left him."

"She left him money?"

"Quite a lot, he thinks. He's not too sure he is entitled to it, and it's going to take a long time to probate Emma's will, because from what I understand, the money is spread around. But he has a good lawyer, the guy was Emma's lawyer in Milltown, and he says Bobby will be very rich when they straighten it all out."

For once I was struck dumb. Me, write for real money? It wouldn't compute, somehow. I had always loved to write, beginning with schoolgirl journals, progressing to poems and stories which sometimes appeared in local papers, and lately, bi-monthly articles in two small local papers. For this last, I receive a few cents a word, so I guess you could call me a pro.

It had been my dream, too long ago to remember, to indulge in a novel, but with marriage, kids, and needing to support myself and my family with real lucre, I had given the dream up long ago. Oh, maybe when I was retired and my kids were on their own, I would get to real writing. But not in my present life. The way money went with me, if I did figure on being compensated for Bobby's story, he wouldn't get the money; that would be my dumb luck.

After what seemed like forever, I heard, "Jackie? You hang up? You still with me?"

"Yeah, Doreen, I'm here. I've gotta say, I'm a bit stunned. I never figured I could ever write anything worthwhile, or even better, make any real money writing. Who makes money doing what they really love to do? Wow, is all I can say. I'll see you Sunday at four. I still have a big need to think this over. Meantime, please, please tell me again, you won't absolutely count on me to do this."

That exchange took place on Tuesday, and I'll tell you honestly, I promptly put it right out of my head. Besides the enormity of the project, which probably sent me immediately into denial, there was the matter of writing an article for the Quoddy Sentinel, a miniscule bi-monthly paper published out of the tiny town of the same name in Washington County, Maine. The article was due by Friday of this week, and another for the Coastal Press in Cutler was due by next Monday. All of this, along with taking care of my old house with its archaic wood furnace, which is still going strong even if it is late March, and my two young munchkins. I was married for three years, a while ago. The products of that grisly coupling are Kristen, who's now seven and Stevie, who's five. Great products of a miserable marriage.

Stevie will start school in September, thank God. It was real hard for a few years there, since Big Steve, or B.S., as I prefer to call him, since he's so full of it his eyes are brown, took off and left me basically on the dole. I know where he is, but it's more peaceful for me to leave him there than to report him. The kids are fine, really, I love them more than life, but they're a heavy package of care. Stevie started in Headstart in September, which gives me a couple of mornings a week to increase my workload.

I also help Jim Darberry get out a monthly newsletter for his insurance company, and I clean his offices on Saturday afternoons. He pays me real cash, and gives me a few cords of hardwood to get through the cold season. With the small jobs, state aid, some food stamps and a few bucks of federal help with my backup oil furnace, I manage to feed the kids and keep them warm and in clean jeans and cheap sneakers.

Life's been pretty good, actually, since ol' B.S. left. He was worse than cockroaches to live with. I'm pretty easy-going. I more or less like to take life as it comes. He was always wanting something he couldn't get --more money, a bigger truck, more toys, more booze, more sex. Always reaching for the carrot, if you know what I mean. He had what I call a yearning streak. It could never be satisfied, and I'll tell you, I spent a lot of time trying. I had it with him after a while; I was always tense with him in my life.

The other thing was, having kids around drove him crazy, and I love having them with me all the time. He hated fatherhood. He still only sees his kids once or twice a year, and that much only because his mother wouldn't speak to him if he didn't. To make an endless story short, we just were not making it. So he left, and I've been more relaxed ever since. I''ve traded monetary support for a good night's sleep.

I also have Irv; he's my steady, a podiatrist from Sullivan. We've been spending Friday nights together for a few months now. He's sweet, and I think he would like our relationship to be more than it is, but I'm not ready to take it to another level. I like to dress up for someone one day a week, go out for a good meal, get a little swacked, have a little snuggle and maybe some more. Irv is pretty good in the sack, I must say. But I'm not ready to wake up next to a smelly body and bad breath every morning. I guess I appreciate privacy more than I thought.

I grew up in a house full of kids, and privacy was not something that was ever available. We were always tangled up in each other, in every way. I love them all and we get together on a regular basis, but I don't need to live that way. Me and the two kids—that's enough, and nice. But I won't discount wine coolers and good sex on Friday nights.

It was Sunday morning before I remembered my talk with Doreen. Little Steve woke me at five, wanting to eat and go, anywhere. He rises like the phoenix at dawn, a real dynamo, roaring around until he drops into bed at eight. Kristen, on the other hand, could sleep in until noon if I let her. I rolled out of bed, made sure Steve was dressed in clean clothes and happily plunked in front of a cartoon program with a cinnamon Pop-Tart until coffee was made. I retrieved the paper from under the porch where it always landed, having been tossed blithely from his car window by Abner the Bangor Daily deliveryman as he whizzed by at 3:00 a.m. I know, because I caught him one night when I was sewing, which I do when I can't sleep. I swear he never slowed down. It's a wonder he doesn't deliver my paper three doors down.

I was dunking a day-old coconut cruller in my coffee and listening to Stevie slurp his second breakfast of Oat Munchies while I read all the latest lousy news about the economy, the state, the country and the world in general. I happened to notice an article about an old lady who had died and left a load of cash to her 30-year-old lover, and how her kids were suing the guy for the estate.

"Shit."

"Don't shwear, Mommy," Stevie spit through his spoonful of cereal.

"Sorry, Stevie, I mean 'shoot'. I remembered I need to go somewhere this afternoon, and I was planning to stay put and catch up on bills and my reading today."

"You don't need to go. You can stay home with us if you want. I'll let you play my new computer game Grampa Gianni gave me."

"It's not that simple, Hon. I want to stay home, but I also want to go. I know it doesn't make sense, but that's the way it is. I can't explain it."

Steve looked up at me with those round brown eyes, and smiled. He was really adorable, olive skin and white teeth and blond hair, looked just like his dad. "You're a kook, Mom," he said.

"I know. Anyway, you'll have to go with Gramma Gianni for a couple of hours. You'll love that."

"Yeah!" His eyes lit up. "Grampa's helpin' me make a rifle out of applewood. It's boss!"

Five years old, he already speaks a foreign language. "I guess," I replied, not caring to learn yet another new word. If he looked happy, it must be positive. That was enough for me. "Kris will probably be bored, but them's the breaks."

"Gramma Gianni? No-o, Mumma. I wanna go to Jen's," my daughter whined from the bedroom.

"You have elephant's ears, my dear," I replied. "No argument, you go. Jen's next Sunday, promise"

Jen is my baby sister, and she and Kristen have a great time together. Jen is thirty-two, and she's never married or grown up.

She lives in a trailer and waits table at the Bluebird Restaurant in Machias. She's lots of fun, I must admit. Probably has something to do with lack of responsibility. I wouldn't know about that.

I can never please both kids at once, unless I take them and a sitter to the ten-screen theater in Bangor and let them each pick a movie. Kristen sees her movie with the sitter, and I go with Stevie to watch his pick of flicks. Then we go for Burger King and ice cream. We can only afford this once in a while, so I usually put up with one ornery kid if I want to see my family on Sundays. We alternate between Steve's parents, my sister's and my parents'.

I love Steve's mom and dad. They are so completely different from their son. I never could figure out how they raised him; he wasn't a bit like either of them. They were both, well, satisfied with their lives, and with each other. He was their only child, and probably their only disappointment. They never mentioned him to me, just asked that I continue to love them when we split. They were great with the kids, and I knew I could call Leena any time I needed to leave them for errands, or a date. Not so with Jen, who always needed a couple of days' notice at least, probably to shovel her clothes off the futon. Calling my parents was not an option, since they were visiting my dad's sister in Zephyrhills, Florida. So Gramma Gianni's it had to be.

I called at nine to make arrangements, cleaned the house for a couple of hours, did a few loads of laundry and arrived to drop the kids off at three, so I could have a little time to chat with Leena. Stevie disappeared to Grampa's basement workshop, and Kris reluctantly retired to the den to watch TV.

The house smelled great. Basil, oregano and lots of garlic mixed with wonderful French roast coffee and cinnamon from some luscious dessert. Leena Gianni made the best manicotti in Maine. I'd miss it. "I'll send some home with the kids, with the coffee cake. Don't worry, you won't go hungry," she assured me. I planted a kiss on her white-streaked black head, which was at least eight inches shorter than my mouth. She reached her short round arms up for a hug.

"Promise me another visit soon," she smiled, wrinkling her apple cheeks so far up that her gleaming black eyes almost disappeared. She waggled a rheumy, crooked index finger at me. "You're always working, now, no time for eating and some nice Chianti. You'll be sick, you don't relax, you," she said.

"Yeah, Ma, I know," I said over my shoulder as I dashed for the car. "See you at seven." I blew her a loud kiss.

"Why don't we keep the kids? We'll take them to school tomorrow," she yelled after me. "They have a change in the spare room. They'll be fine."

"Great idea. I'd love it. I can use the extra time," I hollered back. "Give them kisses and squeezes for me. Tell them I'll pick them up from school. Stevie has an appointment tomorrow at the doctor's and Kris needs to come. I don't have an after school sitter. It's for his shots. Just a checkup", I added, to placate Leena's suddenly worried look.

"Love you lots", I mouthed as I climbed into the car, throwing her another kiss. "See you soon."

It took me almost half an hour to get to Bobby and Doreen's small white house. True to her promise, they had not left old Sharkey the wolf to greet me at my car, but I did hear him announcing me from the small shed at the side of the house. Doreen's pleasant face greeted me from the kitchen window beside the back door. "Hi, come on in. I'm peeling carrots and potatoes. I hope Sharkey's yapping doesn't bother you. He'll stop after a few minutes. We have to give him credit. He's a great watchdog."

"It's not his bark that bugs me, it's the size of his bite," I grimaced as I pulled off my boots in the mudroom and came in to the kitchen. The large room was light and comfortable, with oak stained pine paneled walls, white tile counters and oak cabinets. The center of the room's wide pine floor contained a huge antique round oak table polished to a golden luster and placed over a colorful rug, hand-hooked with a Mayan design. There were herbs hanging from strings over the sink, and plants everywhere, and the aroma was marvelous. I was able to identify chicken roasting with garlic and thyme and basil, but my quivering nose couldn't place the other, more complex spicy and sweet odor.

"God, whatever I smell is wonderful. What is it? It smells like every good dessert I've ever eaten."

"Cinnamon raisin and pecan rolls and chocolate cheesecake, probably," Doreen said. "Take your coat off. Have a seat. Bobby will be down any minute. He's changing his shirt."

"Wow! I didn't know I'd be plied with such great goodies," I grinned.

"We thought we'd better treat you right, since you're the one who's going to get this problem straightened out. Or at least, you're willing to hear about it," she added hastily.

"Let's see if I'm able to do anything before you make that judgment. I get nervous when you start to talk about dumping all this responsibility on my attractive if narrow shoulders."

"Bobby's been so much better since you said you'd come," Doreen went on, ignoring my remark. "I really think that just getting it out is all he needs."

"Boy, I'm relieved you're here, Jack." I turned to see Bobby's large muscular frame in the doorway. He lumbered over and gave me a bear hug that about left me windless. I planted a kiss on his red-bearded cheek. "I don't know what I'd have done if you'd said no to all this," he added after releasing me.

"You know me, Bob. I'd probably never say no to you," I said. "Although, you realize I haven't said yes, either," I added. Bobby Parker and I had known each other all our lives. He was my brother's age, a few years older than I. His family lived just a few miles from mine, and had been almost as large.

Bobby was a hard worker, one of those guys who just plugs away at something until it's finished. He's pretty intelligent, I guess, but he didn't finish high school; he quit when his dad died, after his junior year. He had worked with his dad doing building and carpentry since he was about twelve, I think, and he married his first wife, Debra, when they were both seventeen and she was three months along. When he was in his twenties, he learned finish carpentry, special work like building cabinets, along with his other building and renovating work. He and Deb had three kids, now grown. Bobby had three grandkids, come to think of it.

Truthfully, I never much liked Deb. She and Bobby had a stormy relationship. Deb was a drinker and a screamer. Bobby yelled back at her just to make himself heard, I guess, because I hadn't heard him raise his voice since he started keeping company with Doreen Shanahan.

Deb left him over this thing with the old lady. She said since he was never around, she was going to find someone else to satisfy her needs. So far as I know, she did. I think Deb had been looking for an excuse to leave for years, and I don't think Bobby missed her much. I didn't miss her at all;

I much preferred Doreen, who was sweet and pretty, and cooked like the great chefs of Europe.

We finished every bite of Doreen's luscious dinner, including my pig-out of two pieces of cheesecake, then sat in the living room over coffee. "You gonna take notes?" Bobby asked brusquely. I realized he needed to begin talking about his adventures with Emma. "I guess so," I answered. "I'll get my recorder out of the car--how's that? Then I won't miss anything."

"Good idea," he said. "I'll go get the box." I retrieved the small recorder, inserted a fresh tape from the carrying case, and sat back to listen while Bobby produced his shoebox filled with notes jotted on small scraps of paper. "I been tryin' to write down stuff m'self", he said, "but it jest keeps goin' around in my head, and I can't organize it for shit."

Bobby began the procedure of unraveling the long saga of his relationship with Emma Manchester. At first, he referred to his scribbled notes from time to time, while I recorded and took some written notes. After an hour, as the excitement of telling his story mounted, his thoughts came faster and faster. Finally, I had to stop him.

"Enough, Bobby, hey. I can't take in any more right now, plus I don't have another tape with me. How much more is there, anyway?"

"Well, I'm act'ally only gettin' started. He pulled on his beard thoughtfully. "I would guess off-hand, there's quite some hours more to finish the whole story."

"Well, my brain can't take in any more," I said. "I'm bushed. I have to say, Bobby, I didn't think you could talk that much. You really must've been stressed out, keeping all that in." I smiled and winked at Doreen, because I knew he'd bugged her non-stop.

He glared at me under a bushy-browed frown. "I know, I been a shit to Doreen the past couple months. I keep blurtin' out bits of things about my time with Emma, but I can't seem to keep it straight. I drive her nuts, pushin' her t'help me make sense of it. It feels different, tellin' you. You're gonna write it all down right, so it's done. Then I can read it from start to finish when I need to, and keep it straight in my mind." He paused, pulling on his beard. I gotta admit, I don't really know why this whole thing with Emma has thrown me so much.

"She was like a grandmumma, y' know? She and I got really caught up in each other's lives. More than I have with my real kin, even. It's like I need this like people need a family album, or a diary. You know? The history of it, I guess you'd say. So gettin' it down is that, plus it's like gettin' a load off my back." He grinned. "So, Jack, you gonna do it?"

I could see this was going to take some serious time. I wanted to think about it. Bobby must have sensed that I had reservations, because he jumped in before I had a chance to open my mouth.

"I know this'll be hard, Jack, you with kids and work and all. But I can really make it worth your while. I'm prob'ly comin' into some real money. If I do, it could make your life different. You could write from home, like you always wanted. It may be more money than you or me ever seen. But, I gotta tell this right. I gotta get some peace over this. And you gotta help me, Jackie; you're the only one who can."

Part of this thing was still niggling me. "Doreen says this Emma is haunting you to finish this matter, Bobby. Do you think that will stop when we finish with your book?" I noted that "we" had slipped out of my mouth; I knew too well what that meant.

"Emma'll let me know when it's down jest right", he said. "Then she can rest in peace, and so can I."

He stopped at this point, because he realized Doreen and I were both looking at him with disbelief. "I realize this sounds crazy. But I swear on Grammie's old Bible it's all true. She is, or rather was, talkin' to me in the middle of the night. In my mind, like. I was wakin' up and hearin' her voice clear as if she was sittin' on my bed.

"She's already stopped buggin' me, though, since I told her I got you to at least listen to me. I promised her if you'd agree to do it, I'd keep goin' 'til she tells me we're done. I hope you can stick with it, Jack, 'cause if you don't, we're both in deep shit. Emma and me, I mean," he added, grinning. "Me with Doreen, and Emma with needin' me to finish the whole thing right."

Doreen sighed, and shook her head. "It better be over, and not take too long. I've given up a lot while you worked with her, Bob. It almost got to the point where I was jealous of that old lady, she took up so much of your time." She began to tear up and turned away. I guessed this was a serious thing between them. I also guessed I just better take Bobby at his word, for now.

"Okay, okay," I said. "I'm in. On one condition. I turn this story into a kind of novel, and you don't get whacked out over every little detail I don't get right. I promise I will stick to the story, mainly, but I need to know I can take a little license here." I looked at Bobby, then Doreen. "That okay with you guys?" They looked at each other for a brief moment, then both nodded vigorously.

"Also, let's take the project in bite-sized pieces. I'll come over and show you what I've written, then we can see where it goes from there. Don't worry about paying me. You can feed me. That make sense to you?"

I swear I could feel the relief in the room, like a wool blanket kicked off to relieve a summer night's heat. "Bobby, I promise I'll keep at it until you and I have something concrete to read over. Then we can begin to edit it together. I really can't say how long it will take."

Neither of them said a word. I couldn't wait. "So, are we gonna do this, Bobby?"

"Okay with me, as long as it's okay with Emma. It's her story, too." He sat quietly for a few minutes. We watched him, me at least wondering if he was going into a trance, roll his eyes back in his head or something. He just sat, looking like Bobby. Finally, "I got a feelin' it's fine that way," he stated firmly. "She wants it down, so whatever way we do it is fine with her."

I was finally getting excited. I did love to write, and this promised to be an interesting project.

1
The Meeting

ONE

Bobby had little desire to travel to Milltown again that week, but there seemed no getting around it. He was in the middle of building a room in the basement so the grandkids would have a place to stay when they came, and Deb would be off his back. He was preparing the room for paint, and had run out of primer halfway through one wall. It was Friday, and if he didn't finish priming today, the painting would interfere with the TV broadcast of the Giants' game he planned to get drunk in front of Sunday afternoon. He could have gone to Machias for the primer, but they didn't sell the brand he liked, and he knew Deb would be on his ass if it didn't look exactly the way she wanted it. It was worth driving a few more miles to keep her quiet.

Bobby was an ardent Giants' fan, and he and Joey Crawford, whose team was the Cowboys, watched the two teams play whenever they could, just so they could drink beer and rag on each other. If Bobby's team lost on Sunday, he would hear about it for the whole week. Joey would shut up if the

Cowboys lost their game the following week; then it may be Bobby's turn to gloat. They had been locked into this feud for years. They both loved it.

Not even Deb, who whined and complained every time it was Bobby's turn to host a game, could talk them out of it. Bobby and Joey drank beer, ate corn chips and salsa and microwaved pizza, kept the running stats of their favorites in a ratty spiral notebook and ignored her. When the kids were small, she took them and her complaints and headed for her friend Sissa's, leaving them to their gleeful rivalry. Now that the kids were grown, she would stomp up the stairs, slam the bedroom door, switch on her stereo and play her rock collection as loud as she could, until the game was over and Joey was gone.

Watching the game was definitely much more important than supplying a dank old basement with three coats of paint. Joey was ahead this season, and the Giants needed him to bring them back from their losing streak. If he missed the game because he was painting the damn basement, and they lost, he'd never forgive himself. He knew in his heart that Deb only wanted him to paint to divert him from his weekend pleasures.

He was coming out of the hardware with the primer when he noticed her across the street. The ground was early-spring slushy after mixed rain and snow, starting to freeze in the late afternoon's temperature drop. The old lady was carrying one of those stringy cotton bags stuffed with something, picking her way gingerly along the sidewalk. He registered her briefly, taking in the dark cloth coat, the bright blue flowered scarf tied around her head, her shoulders and back hunched against late March. It was cold and raw, and anyone who lived in northern Maine knew spring wasn't due to arrive for at least six weeks.

He threw the paint in the back of the truck, swung himself in and glanced at the clock on the dash. Four-thirty. If he booked it, he could drive the forty-two miles home, finish the room by eight or nine, and have enough time to relax a bit, maybe have a couple of beers and some hot dogs and beans. He was pulling the truck out into the street, whistling through his teeth at the thought of hot dogs, homemade beans and Bud, thinking they might even need to come before the work, when he saw her again, collapsed into a small dark bundle at the corner. It looked like she had tried to make the curb to cross the street, and had fallen back to the sidewalk. One foot in its short, fur-topped boot stuck off the curb, and her bag had landed in the gutter a few feet away. She wasn't moving, and there wasn't anyone else on the sidewalk, coming or going.

"Shit," he muttered.

His mind raced. If he used some of his precious time to help her, what would it matter? He could just check on her, make sure she was okay, then go to the State Police station and find a cop to get her home or wherever she needed to go. After all, what if she was really hurt? He shouldn't deal with that. He wasn't a doctor. Or he could just take off and leave her to whoever happened to come along. Someone was bound to come real soon.

The leaving thought bothered him right off. "That would be a real crappy thing to do", he decided instantly. He could take off and stop at the station. That option was tempting, since it wouldn't take much time. However, he knew all along what he was going to do. He'd do what he had to do, because he couldn't not do it. He parked the truck and walked over to her.

She looked up at him with startling blue eyes. "I'm afraid to move. I may be broken somewhere," she said faintly. Her voice was thin and reedy, emerging from a brittle old pipe. She was very old and very small; there wasn't much of her under the coat. The few inches of leg he could see between the boot and the coat were almost fleshless, covered with a tan stocking. Her other leg seemed to be pulled up under her. Her arms were both visible, hugged across her chest. "It's damn cold down here," she offered.

"I guess. What's with your other leg?" Bobby said.

"It's under me. It was up on the sidewalk, and I fell back and down on it," she replied. "Maybe it's broken, I can't really tell. It doesn't hurt very much. I think it's probably frozen."

"I'm gonna try to get you up, if it's all right with you," Bobby said. "Let's move everything real slow, and if you hurt too much, I'll get some help. How's that?"

"Sounds like a plan to me", she agreed.

TWO

Her full name was Emma Manchester. She was an eighty-seven year old widow and had lived in her house on Main Street her entire life. Just over two hours after her rescue, she was ensconced in a comfortable wingchair in her sitting room. Her leg was not broken. Bobby figured it was because she was so light. Her knee, which had been pretty badly sprained, was wrapped firmly in a wide bandage and propped up on a brocade hassock. A set of crutches leaned against one wing of the chair. The nurses and the on-call doctor at the small local hospital had known her well, and had fussed over her hastily and with much concern. They had bandaged the knee, warmed her with thick blankets, and supplied her with a hot cup of tea. She responded to their ministrations with warm smiles and quick humor.

While the doctor tended to Emma, Bobby gave up on hot dogs and beer, settling for a cheeseburger, fries and a coke from Burger King. Second best, but he had to see that she was delivered home. Emma had refused his offer to treat her to a burger, saying she never touched that fast food stuff. She would rather have some fish chowder when she got home, thank you very much.

Home was a large white frame house on the southern end of town, the last in a row of well-tended white houses. Emma's house wasn't as well cared for as the others. Many years had passed since it had seen fresh paint, and each of the eight faded, sagging blue shutters framing the front downstairs windows were missing slats.

As Bobby carried the old woman through the house to the front room, he noted that the interior of the house was also in varying stages of disrepair. Kitchen cabinets needed hardware and paint, and the pantry door was almost off its hinges. The dining room with its peeling wallpaper contained an ornate oak table and six beautifully carved, caned chairs which were settled on a large threadbare carpet, probably lovely when it was new, now so worn that the original pattern was no longer visible. The furnishings in the formal sitting room in the front of the double-parlored house were obviously not used as much as the room in which they sat. These consisted of a dated, stiff-looking brocade-covered sofa, two matching chairs, dark mahogany tables, and a newer, flowered carpet. Glassed doors closed it off from the narrow hall separating the two parlors.

The informal sitting room was worn, but comfortable, with a mantled fireplace, two deep wing chairs, a worn, deep blue velvet-covered sofa, and a collection of small tables that held various knickknacks and photos of a younger version of Emma in flowered dresses, with a tall, handsome, strongly-built man in his middle years, formally dressed in a dark suit, white shirt, striped tie and soft felt hat.

Emma noticed Bobby's eyes roaming around the room. "Pretty miserable old house, isn't it," she noted. "Used to be nice, back when my parents owned it. They bought all of the original furniture. Good pieces, bought to last. And last they have, since I am still using them, as you can see. I suppose I could have replaced them, or at least had the shabbiest pieces re-upholstered, but I never got around to it. Doesn't bother me, really. I have very little company, never use the formal parlor. Stiff, nasty stuff in there. Made so people don't stay long. Too uncomfortable. I am positive that's what my mother and father had in mind when they bought it." She chuckled.

"That is Thomas," she nodded toward the photos. "And me, of course. Thomas and I were married for twenty-three wonderful years. He died thirteen years ago next month. I miss him still." Her bright eyes gleamed with unshed tears.

Bobby picked up one of the photos. Emma had been quite pretty when she was younger. Dark, shining long hair, curled in the style of the day, a slim figure, athletic looking, and a bright, happy smile. And if what she said was true, she had married Thomas when she was in her early fifties. She was still pretty, he thought, looking at her. Soft, supple skin, long white hair pinned back in a knob on her neck and caught at the sides with ornate silver combs. She was very small and light, her muscular frame shrunken now. But, there were her eyes, so bright and blue, still youthful.

The old lady was nice enough, but he needed to get home. Deb would have a fit as it was. He had called her from the hospital, and she had yelled loud enough to be heard by the three or four people waiting with their end-of-week emergencies. "Yeah, sure, Bobby. You can sure think up good ones. An old lady, my ass. A beer at Jerry's, more'n likely. You better get your butt home right now. We're already eatin'." He had tried to reason with her, but no go. A worn-looking, middle-aged woman holding her swollen wrist had looked at him when he hung up, smiled wryly and shook her head. "Looks like you're in worse trouble than I am," she observed. She was probably right.

"Can I get you something before I go?" Bobby asked. "Food or a cuppa tea?" Then, thinking about the crutches, "You gonna be able to get around okay? You haven't had any practice on them sticks yet."

"I'll be fine. This is not the first time I have used these 'sticks', as you term them. I broke my leg a couple of years ago; fell off a ladder. That's the last time my roof was tended to. I never did finish replacing those tiles. Back hall still leaks." She looked at him intently. "You had better get yourself home, young man. Your wife will be wondering what happened to you. She might think you're off gallivanting around with some young thing."

"She's more likely to think I'm hangin' around with some young brew", he retorted. "I already tried to tell her what happened. She thinks I'm at Jerry's getting swacked." He shrugged his shoulders. "Hell with it. There's no winnin' with her." He stood and stretched. "I guess I'll be off, then, if you're okay. I'd like to see you manage them crutches a bit before I go, though."

Emma obliged him by rising from the chair, using her good leg for leverage. She grabbed the crutches, deftly inserted them under her arms and made her way fairly quickly toward the kitchen. "You see? I am fine," she tossed over her shoulder as she went.

"You convinced me," Bobby replied. "I can let m'self out. Get yourself some rest."

"Thank you, Bobby Parker. You're a nice man. I'm very pleased that it was you who picked me up. It's been a long time since I had such a good-looking date." She laughed as she waved him out.

THREE

Bobby was too busy dealing with the myriad events in his daily life to think about Emma for the next few days. Among them was Deb's long list of accusations when he got home, painting the basement on Saturday, the Sunday game, which he won, and the post-game celebration with Joey, who was despondent for all of ten minutes. Then he wanted to go to The Pizza Palace to get soused and bitch to everyone that the ol' Cowboys had let him down again. On Sunday night, there were Deb's whined complaints that he spent too much time with his friends and the TV, and not enough with her and Dicky, and because he had again wasted his weekend with Joey and the rest of his good-for-nothing friends, he had done a really crappy job of painting the basement. Thankfully, this last came when they were already in bed, and he was fried enough to be able to ignore her for once. In the midst of her whining, he turned his back on her and fell asleep.

Monday morning, there was work. He was building a kitchen extension onto Brud

Hassner's cabin. He had promised Brud that the project would be finished by the time Brud got married, which was in May. May third, to be exact. And nothing had gone right with this job since he had started it late last summer.

Brud, who was Walter Hassner's son, and ended up Brud instead of Junior, which he couldn't abide, had built the small cabin for himself ten years before. The tiny structure consisted of one room, with a half-loft for sleeping. Due to the toxic fumes emitted from the finishes he used on his canoes and custom-built furniture, his workshop needed to be a separate structure. He was a huge man, topping six feet and 300 pounds, and, since he did not cook, a kitchen had been unnecessary.

He ate his meals at Dot's, in Machias. "Meals" generally meant lunch every day, although he could be seen there for a late dinner one or two days a week. Dot served an all-you-can-eat lunch from 11 to 2, and Brud could eat. Dot regularly threatened to bar him from the place one of these days and scolded him because his food intake was putting her out of business. He would laugh, and remind her that he was probably her best advertisement. He'd sit in a booth in the window and shovel in three, maybe four large plates full of food at noon, Monday through Saturday. Sundays, he relied on friends or his mother to stock his empty larder. This daily feed, along with three or four pots of strong coffee and a couple six-packs of beer, constituted Brud's daily diet.

When he asked his long-time girl, Brittny Lacey, to marry him last June, she naturally wondered where they would live. Brud was then twenty-nine, and Brittny was just eighteen. They had gone together for four years. The first two they sneaked out, because Brittny's parents didn't allow her to date, much less screw her brains out every Saturday night. They wrongly assumed she was spending the nights with her girlfriend Suki. When Suki was faced with lying one rainy Saturday, she told all. The shit hit the fan. Faced with giving up Brud, Brittny warned her parents that if they stopped her from seeing the boy, she would do herself in. She meant it--just try it. Since it was a week before her 16th birthday, they reluctantly assented. Knowing Brittny, they probably had no choice.

Brud assumed they'd live in his place, since his workshop was there. She said she wouldn't put her foot through the door as his wife until he cleaned it up, furnished it properly and added a bathroom and a kitchen. The original cabin had been constructed without plumbing, since Brud had no use for running water. He showered at his parents' twice a week, drank from the water pump in the workshop, and used his 24 acres for his other needs. Since Brud was short on time but long on money, he contracted the work out to Bobby Parker. Because the couple did not want a fancy bathroom, they allowed Bobby to plan that space. Brittny would take care of the kitchen. Bobby started the job in early August, and had finished the bathroom and the basic plumbing for the kitchen by early October.

Building the kitchen was a different animal entirely. Brittny chose to make all of the initial decisions, since it was her first kitchen. Brud was fine with that. He never expected to spend any time in it except to eat. Bobby and Brittny discussed dimensions, cabinets, floor tile, and every other minute decision needed to build a room onto an existing house. The problem was, Brittny was just a kid, and she had no idea what she wanted.

Every time something was ordered that Brittny and Bobby had agreed on, by the time it had arrived she either hated it, or

Brud told her it cost too much. She bitched, or sulked and cried, and it went back. Every time Bobby measured off for a counter space or a closet, she changed her mind about the length, the width, or the height. By mid-November, the only concrete work consisted of a large rectangular box with a bright blue tarp over its frame to protect it from the weather. Bobby told the couple he needed to move indoors for the winter, and would resume the first of March, and Brittny had better make up her mind and not change it after that, because two months was not a long time to build a kitchen.

It was now late March, and he had the interior drywalled and had finished the roof. The counters had been marked off with relatively little difficulty, and the spaces decided for the appliances. Less expensive cabinets had been ordered, and the colors for the floor and the countertops had been chosen with only minor whining from Brittny. If she stayed away for a couple of weeks, he might finish the space on time.

He had picked up a load of plywood from A & B Supplies in Machias at six on Monday morning and was jouncing down Brud's dirt road when he thought about Emma.

He remembered her bright eyes, smiling up at him. "Wonder how she's makin' out," he thought. The old gal was eighty-seven, after all, and even if she could get around on the crutches, maybe she wasn't doing too well. He wondered if she had friends who could get food for her if she needed it. What if she should fall? Maybe no one would find her.

"What's the matter with me, anyway? She's been takin' up space on the good earth all these years, and she's taken care of herself pretty good, even after her husband died. 'Course she's okay."

Try as he would to push her aside, she continued to edge herself into his mind. Brittny never showed up to mewl and complain, so he was able to work with only his thoughts for company. There was Emma's house, for example, with its sagging shutters and peeling paint. He voiced these thoughts aloud from time to time, since no one was there to stop him. "Din't she say her roof still leaks?" or, "That pantry door is jest leanin', could fall and hurt her," and finally, "So what, you fool. What're you gonna do about all that? Like y'don't have enough t'do already, what with this job and all the things Deb wants you t'do around your own house."

Following this last thought, he laid off for a while, and worked.

He quit at five, and decided to call the old lady when he got home.

FOUR

Emma sounded really surprised to hear from him. And pleased. "Well, well, Bobby Parker. Never thought I'd hear a word from you again. I wondered how your Sunday game went. Did you win?"

"Yep, won the game and had some brews and pizza with ol' Joey. How're you doin', anyway?"

"I'm just fine. Feeling more like myself every day. Pastor James came from the church, and prayed over me. I can always use a bit of that. And my card club came yesterday and brought snacks, and I played a couple of rubbers with them. Neighbors and church people have dropped in. Word travels fast in a small town whenever some old lady gets laid up. They've been wonderful; supplied me with all kinds of goodies, more than I'll finish in a month."

"Rubbers?"

"Yes, games of bridge. Call them rubbers. It does sound silly, doesn't it? Like we're throwing boots around the table." She giggled.

"Sure does. Listen, Emma, I'm gonna be in Milltown Tuesday. Gotta pick up an order for this job I'm on. I thought I'd drop by if you're gonna be there. Check up on you, see how you're doin'."

"Ah-h. Don't trust me, hey? You think I'm really a mess, crawling around on the floor, starving...the old lady's fallen and she can't get up? That what you're thinking?"

Bobby was taken aback at her response. Boy, she could read his mind. He laughed. "Somethin' like that", he admitted. "I guess I'm outta line with that train of thought," he said somewhat sheepishly. "You sure sound fine to me."

"Well, I am. But I'd welcome your company any time, Bobby. Come when you can. I'll share some of my goodies with you."

Bobby arrived at eleven on Tuesday, and was greeted at the door by a smiling, apparently fully recovered Emma. She took his coat and sat him at the table in a kitchen which looked much more cheerful than when he had carried her through it two weeks ago. Emma had set the table with a red checked cloth and put out a plate of sandwiches, another of dessert squares, and a wicker basket filled with potato chips. White plates, red napkins in silver holders, and glasses of apple cider graced the two green plastic placemats. A low vase with dried flowers was placed jauntily in the center of the table. Bobby smelled something delicious on the stove.

"Well." He looked around. "I guess you're jest fine. Fine enough to make me whatever soup is brewin' there. Smells too good t'be true." Bobby was accustomed to Deb's idea of soup--a hastily opened can dumped in a bowl and heated in the microwave.

"Didn't make it. I don't cook. Haven't for years. Just throw food together on a plate, usually, or I might do some fresh haddock chowder if I really have a hankering for it. Janet Coombs, from the church, brought her chicken and cheese stew yesterday."

She dished him up a large bowl and brought it to him with an oversized spoon. "Here, eat up. Janet does cook, often and well. She brings me leftovers all the time. My friends and neighbors do very well by me, I must say." She perched on the chair facing him, watching as he shoveled the rich soup down, while she dished small spoonfuls daintily from her tiny cup.

Bobby followed the soup with two sandwiches, a bowl of chips and a lemon square. He drank two glasses of cider, and sat back, wiping his mouth with the napkin. "Wow. That was sure good."

"Does your wife feed you, Bobby?" Emma looked concerned. Bobby realized she meant the statement--she wasn't just pulling his leg. With her, he was beginning to realize, you never knew.

"Oh, sure. She feeds me. But it's just food, y'know. Not *real* food. She opens cans, defrosts microwave dinners, like that. If I'm still hungry, I fill in with fast food burgers and peanut butter sandwiches and pizza."

"Ahah." The old lady seemed to be taking this in. "I guess there are others in the world who don't like to cook. I did cook, and liked it more, when my Thomas was here. He so dearly loved to eat, and there's nothing like feeding a hungry man who appreciates his food." Emma smiled. "I don't cook for myself, because I don't eat much. A salad, a bowl of cereal with fruit, a nice piece of poached fish with a baked sweet potato, that's enough for me." She looked at his empty plate. "But I would love to feed a hungry man again," she mused longingly.

Bobby remembered Emma telling him that she still missed her husband. In his mind, thirteen years was a long time to yearn for a lost partner. It occurred to him he'd probably miss Deb for a week or so, if that long. She really got on a man's nerves. He imagined his feelings would include relief, perhaps even peace, if she left for good.

"You must've really loved your husband," he stated.

"We loved each other," she replied. "We were each other's best friend. We married too late to have children; never missed them, I must admit. If we had been younger, and the good Lord had blessed us with a few, we would have been all right with it, I'm sure. But the way it worked out, we were glad of it, if truth be known."

Bobby gazed around as she talked. Cupboards needed paint, the pantry door needed new hinges, the worn linoleum needed replacing and the room could use some bright paint and new curtains.

Emma became aware of his perusal of the old kitchen. "I have all I can do to keep the house clean, now, never mind thinking of cooking for myself or someone else. Norman Hoskins, my neighbor, drops in from time to time to fix anything that's broken beyond repair. He usually has just enough time to mend those things I can't do without, like my screen door, or that shelf over the sink that fell down last fall.

"I suspect I will die long before things ever get put back to their former condition. I don't mind much, any more. It used to frustrate me terribly to think that I couldn't keep house as well I once did. Then, after I broke my leg a few years back, I realized that climbing on ladders and mending closet doors were secondary to my real needs. Now, I'm much more concerned with getting other parts of my life in order, before I think about going over."

Bobby wasn't one to ask many questions. He preferred not to pry into someone else's life. He believed in live and let live. He was happy to answer any question someone asked of him, but he figured people would share what they wanted to share, without his poking into their privacy by asking foolish questions. So, although he discovered that he was somewhat curious about the "other parts" of Emma's life, he merely nodded when she finished.

"I been thinkin', maybe it would be good if I fixed a few things around here," he said. "Like, the things that could hurt you sooner or later. One example bein' that door." He pointed to the pantry. "It's lit'rally hangin' by one hinge. It could fall over any minute, and bang you good on the head." He grinned. "I realize you probly kin take good care of y'self, Miss Emma, but that door is beyond what you kin do, and it could hurt you."

He glanced around. "The floor ain't too good, either. You could trip, where there's holes in that lino."

"You're right, Bobby. I could. And yes, I would like you to fix things. But how can you do that when you live over in Quoddy? Your work, family and life are there."

"I could get over here once or twice a month. 'Specially when I finish that damn kitchen of Brud's, 'scuse my French." He was beginning to get excited about this. Why, he didn't know. But there it was. He wanted to help this old woman get her house back to its original condition, whatever that had been. He enjoyed her company. He didn't need any other reason just now.

"I'll be finished the first of May, if Brud's girlfriend leaves me alone. She wants 'er say in every nail I put in that wall, I swear. So 'til then, I'll only be able t' come by once in a while. But after, if it's okay with you, I c'd come, say, ev'ry other Sat'day or so. I'd show up early, since MLS supply here closes at noon sharp, and if I need anything, I gotta git it before then."

"You will expect to be paid, of course. I don't have much. I live on a limited income just now, but I can afford to pay a bit."

"You can pay for materials and feed me–-y'said you like to feed a hungry man. I kin get some hungry after workin' five or six hours straight." He wondered what she meant by "just now". She was eighty-seven, for God's sake. When were finances going to improve at her stage of life?

Emma stared at him. "You really want to do this? Fix up an old lady's house for virtually nothing?" Her eyes brightened. "Frankly, Bobby Parker, I would love it!"

Bobby grinned. "Then let's us say we got ourselves a deal, Miss Emma."

FIVE

It was three weeks after that Friday before Bobby was able to take the time to return to Emma's. The work at Brud's was progressing slowly in spite of Brittny's constant interference, but there had been a major snowstorm, and he needed to plow out his twelve regular customers twice each. Snow in early April was not unusual, but eight inches of snow, with the weather not cooperating to melt it right away, was. Usually a heavy spring storm was followed by a warm spell, and the snow was gone in a day or so.

The county's blueberry growers were anxious about their crop, even though the berries weren't harvested until late summer. Thousands of acres of wild low-bush blueberries were grown in Washington County, and a precise combination of cold, dry warmth and rain was necessary for full, sweet berries. A late April freeze was not the most ideal growing condition. Since Bobby and Deb maintained fifty acres of Parker family berry barrens, he had spent some anxious hours commiserating with fellow growers. The spring thaw had come three days before, so everyone was feeling somewhat relieved. He figured he could spare a day or two to work for the old lady.

"Knock, knock--you in there, Miss Emma?" Bobby said the words aloud because there was no bell that he could see, and the door stood partly open. He peered around the scarred oak frame into the kitchen.

Emma was sitting at the table, working diligently on a large piece of brightly colored cloth, with earphones set firmly on her head. A large black combination radio/CD player was on the floor beside her. She hummed and tapped her foot in rhythm to her private concert. Bobby grinned as he tiptoed to her side. He stood there a moment, wondering if she would have too severe a reaction to his presence if he touched her. She was pretty old, after all, and who knew how strong her heart was? Just as he was about to tap her shoulder, she snapped her head around.

"Bobby! Welcome. I'm so happy you're here." She grinned back at him. "I felt your presence in back of me. I'm so glad you could come on such a beautiful day." She pulled the headphones off, silenced the boom box, stuck a small sharp needle carefully in the cloth (which Bobby could now see was a small patterned quilt) and rose stiffly to greet him.

"I love to listen to the good crooners on headphones," she said. "Frankie, Tony Bennett, Vic Damone. I feel young again when they sing just to me, like that." She smiled sweetly, apparently still hearing the romantic music in her head. "That was Tony's album, "Live in Las Vegas". I have it on CD now. The tone is lovely. He's right there, serenading me."

Bobby suddenly found himself annoyed with her. "Anyone could have snuck in here and scared the bejesus out of you," he snapped, sounding sharper than he intended. "You oughtta keep your door locked."

"Oh? Do you keep yours locked?" Emma retorted, just as sharply.

"Nope, but then I'm more able to protect--"

"I have never found the need to lock my door or take the keys out of my car while I have lived here," she asserted. "And I'm not going to start now, just because I'm older than Methuselah. And, Bobby Parker," she added, "I would appreciate it if you did not act like my mother instead of my friend and low-paid handyman." She suddenly wrinkled her eyes at him, smiling broadly.

"I guess I been put in my place," Bobby replied sheepishly. In the future, he would need to remind himself that although Emma Manchester might seem old and helpless, she certainly did not feel that way. "Sorry, Miss Emma." Then, "And I'd appreciate it if you didn't call me down like a naughty schoolboy." He grinned at her in return, exaggerating it so his top and bottom teeth showed, clenched together in a mocking smirk.

Emma giggled. "Deal," she said. "We are a stubborn pair, I can see that", she said, adding, "Good that we both have a sense of the ridiculous."

"The door is open because spring is in the air today, and I couldn't keep it locked out," she explained as she carefully folded the quilt and put it on the sideboard, then bustled to the sink to fill a kettle of water. "Want a cup of tea before we make the list of repairs needed?"

He did, and noticed that her knee was completely mended as she spryly busied herself with cups and napkins and some cookies on a flowered plate.

"Spring always makes me feel two ways," Emma explained as she sat opposite him to have her tea. "I feel chipper--younger, you know? Of course you don't know, look at that young body, you can't be older than twenty-five, and so healthy it shoots sparks out of you like those old Roman candles. For ancient me, however, my bones don't ache as much—sap begins to run in me, like an old maple. I look forward to getting seeds into the pots to germinate, planning my spring garden and daily walks without falling and spraining a joint. My old body begins to warm and stretch to the sun."

She took a small sip of her tea. "Strangely, the other thing I feel...is such sadness." As the muscles of the old lady's face relaxed into her memories, she suddenly looked every year of her age. "Thomas died in April. April twenty-first, to be exact. Just as the world was waking and growing, Thomas went to sleep, and left me forever.

"I miss him every day", she added. "Are you happily married, Bobby?"

"I'm sure married. Happy? I don't know. What's that mean? Been with Deb over 20 years now. So you kin see, I ain't exactly 25, although I thank you for the compl'ment. I'm almost 39, be there just before Memorial Day. We got knocked up in high school and had our first kid a month after I turned 18. We got 3 kids, one still at home, Dicky, he's

17, a senior in high school. We're thinkin' he might even graduate. The others quit, haven't finished yet. Becka got knocked up when she was sixteen, married the kid and got two kids already and just turned twenty. Bess is eighteen and lives with anyone'll give her a bed and whatever goes with it." Bobby sighed involuntarily, thinking about his offspring.

"They're all pretty messed up," he added with a wry grin.

"Well." Emma sipped her tea, gazing at him intently over the delicate gold-painted rim of the cup. She noted his longish hair, the color of fall cornstalks, his ruddy, not-quite handsome face with its intense deep-set blue eyes, youthful roundness and full reddish beard. Bobby noticed her well-tended, buffed and filed nails, her gnarled, long fingers relaxing on the checked tablecloth.

"And do you love this Deb that you 'knocked up', produced three progeny with, and have co-habitated with for over two decades?"

Bobby smiled at the sound of Emma's delicate cultured voice echoing his words. "I don't think about it that much, tell you th'truth," Bobby answered. "We jest live, make it work from year t'year, make sure the kids have what they need, make it t'bed together once in a while, you know." He finished his large mug of tea and set it down firmly on the lace cloth. "It's just a life; I don't give it much thought", he repeated.

"Hmm." Emma peered at him curiously once more, then rose and cleared the cups. "Let's get to work before you need to leave," she said tersely. "The list is long and cumbersome. I feel you will scoot off after you realize the work necessary to put this old wreck of a house back together. But, I hope you don't," she added as she thumped a large yellow pad and two sharp pencils on the bare table.

SIX

The list was indeed long. It took most of the morning to discuss what was needed to return the ancient house to decent basic working order. Bobby and Emma began at the top and worked down, walking around the house, talking, looking, taking notes. The roof needed major repairs. To Bobby's mind it needed complete replacement, but Emma decided that a complete roof was beyond her means, so they decided on new shingles only where they were really damaged, and a bit of tarpaper and caulking in a few other places, especially around the chimney. The gutters needed cleaning and replacing, and it was decided to replace the original wood ones with plastic, since wood was so expensive these days.

Further outside repairs included replacement of rotted shingles over the second story in the front and on the sides, clapboard and trim where needed on the first floor, replacement of many of the original window frames and trim in lieu of completely new windows, repairing shutters and re-hanging them, painting everything and re-building the back stoop which had rotted to the point where Bobby worried that Emma might put her foot through one of the boards some dark night. She needed to step gingerly from the cement step to the door now, she admitted.

"And that's outside," Emma said, sighing deeply. "I'm afraid the inside will prove to be at least as bad, if not worse. Every room needs some care." She squinted at Bobby over her half-glasses. "Are you sure you want to begin this project, Bobby Parker? You may have taken a bigger bite than you bargained for, with me."

"My philosophy is take it one day at a time," Bobby answered. "We'll start with the outside, t'get it tight for the winter, then whatever we do, we do. If y'run out of cash, we stop. I do think it's important t'get that roof fixed right away, t'keep leaks out. And th'back stoop definitely needs fixin'. I'm plannin' to do that first thing, if it's all right with you. And," he added, "I will do that one inside job of re-hangin' your pantry door as soon as I can get to it.

"I think I kin be here next Friday. I'll git the supplies for the stoop today and rig up somethin' so's you can git from here to there, at least. We'll store th'stuff in th'barn and I'll finish it next week. Friday okay with you, Miss Emma? You got any pressin' engagement, throwin' a tea party that day or anything? We wouldn't want your busy social life t'be interrupted with all that bangin'." He peered at her and grinned.

"Actually, I had planned on having the mayor and the Reverend Hollyhock to tea with their wives that day," she retorted in an exaggeratedly Southern accent. (*to tee, with thaya wahves*). "But I shall inform them that I have something infinitely better (*bettah*) to do with my time than to dally with the likes (*lahks*) of them (*thee-em*). I have decided to call in my (*mah*) decorator to restore my entire manor to its original loveliness. My decorator (*decoratah*) and I cannot be disturbed in this important work. When it is complete, I shall invite the entire county to view its splendor. There, it has been decided (*Theyah, it has beein desahded*)." She waved her pencil wand-like, with a flourish, as she spoke.

Bobby roared. He laughed so hard he needed a paper towel from above the sink to blow his nose and wipe his eyes. "You're somethin' else, Miss Emma," he said when he could speak. "I ain't laughed like that since I can't say when."

"Back at you," Emma said. "Isn't that what the kids say nowadays? I haven't joked like that since Thomas died." She sighed. "The people around me are lovely, don't get me wrong, but they are all so adult, so serious, do you know what I mean? Few of them exhibit a sense of humor; even fewer have a sense of the ridiculous. Life, after all, is a bit absurd, don't you think?"

"Yeah, I think." Bobby stood by the sink a moment, looking at her. "I never had anyone in my life who took anything light. I hang with a couple of guys on the weekends, watch the games, drink some brew, but they ain't light. They're all drinkin' so's they don't have to think about the rest of their lives, you know? Like, take Joey; he's got a bitch of a wife, five years older than him, she's his third. You'd think he could pick someone could laugh once in a while instead a yellin' at everyone and haulin' off and beltin' him all the time." He shook his head. "No wonder we all wanna git drunk." He sighed.

"I gotta get to MLS and get those supplies," he said suddenly. He didn't want to start on his problems today. Moaning about his life would spoil the mood they had established, and he didn't want to lose that for a few hours, at least. "I'll be back in about an hour to fix that stoop."

As he drove, he found himself thinking about the unusual events of the morning. He listened to the radio for a few minutes, then shut it off. It annoyed him. Always playing that country western stuff, everyone cheating on everyone else, love lost, love misplaced, love unrequited. Love, shit. At least in his life. He sat for a minute outside Maine Lumber Supply.

That old Emma was a different thing, he thought. Here she was, so ancient and wrinkled he wondered how her insides were still working. He could almost see her old organs, shriveled and wrinkled like her face and neck, pale and barely doing their job. Her heart barely beating, her kidneys dribbling just a little fluid into her bladder..."Get off that, right now, you goon," he admonished himself. "You'll make yourself right sick."

Bobby had always been somewhat queasy around really old people. They seemed so damned fragile. Although he must say that Emma had surprised him when she fell. She had been there for at least fifteen minutes by the time he got to her, and although she was obviously hurt and cold, she certainly was still feisty. She hadn't uttered a word of complaint when he hoisted her tiny, bird-like body clad in its drooping wet wool coat and torn woolen stockings into the truck and drove her to the small local hospital. She had thanked him profusely for helping her, and she had maintained her sense of humor through the whole experience.

That was something, her sense of humor. Her quick mind certainly was not shriveled or wrinkled. She was as fast as he was, at least, with the quips and comic comebacks. Kept right up with the nurses and the aides who stopped to wish her well.

Also, she knew what she wanted. She was pretty well informed when she made choices for repairs on her house. "Make sure you don't spend a lot of money on shingles," she had stated. "I need a good solid product, not some fly-by-night thing that's the latest thing. And don't bother trying to match the color; grey is fine with me." And, "You be sure to get that pressure-treated lumber for the stoop. Lasts much longer; it will be here long after I'm gone."

He had to admit, that Miss Emma Manchester was one remarkable woman.

SEVEN

Bobby worked until after four. He was able to remove the old stoop, store the rotted wood in the shed, and put together enough of a platform so Emma could come and go fairly easily. Four cement blocks had to do for steps until he could get back, and he made sure that she could negotiate the steps before he left.

"You could use the front entrance," he said at one point, as he watched her step hesitatingly to the stoop.

"I have never, since I have lived in this house, used that entrance," Emma replied. "I don't think I even own a key for it. The lock must be firmly rusted shut after all this time."

Bobby raised his brows incredulously. "What? You've never used it? Even when your parents had company?" He knew that many older Mainers had formal social habits, and kept their "other" parlor closed and clean for Sunday and holiday visitors.

"My parents rarely had visitors, and even then they would come to the kitchen door, as we would," she replied. "They were very quiet, introverted people, and only admitted those they were very familiar with, like the pastor of their church, or members of their family." She paused, leaning on the weathered frame of the back door.

"It was a very small family, as I recall," she added. "There were a couple of ancient grand-uncles, brothers of my grandfather who died before I was born, and a daughter of one of them, who visited only once or twice with her stuffy husband.

"That about did it for family," she stated brusquely.

"So you were their only child?" Bobby returned.

"I was it, lock stock and barrel," Emily smiled. "It was rather a quiet life, as you can imagine." She paused, said "Hmm" and turned to go into the house. "Enough about that and everything else for today, Bobby. I'm headed for a much-needed nap before my supper. I've had more excitement today than I've had in a long time. Thank you for your help and your company, and I will see you whenever you are able to return."

She had the door partly closed when he said, "Prob'ly next Saturday. See you then, Mi--" With a quick wave, she slammed the door.

"Yes, ma'am, she's sure a different one," Bobby smiled to himself as he swung into the old truck.

Emma's house was a forty-five minute drive from Bobby's small blue-grey clapboard house on the north side of Quoddy. It was late afternoon, and the days were getting longer. He watched with delight as the sky darkened, the bottoms of the clouds turned blue-gray, and deep orange and rose shimmered on the horizon. The sky told him it would be another cool sunny day tomorrow. The sun would not warm the earth in early April, but it would bring a smidgen of cheer after the long frigid winter. Bobby switched on the radio to hear the local news. After ten minutes, he switched it off. "Nothin' but killin' and bad politics on any more," he grumbled. Emma crept into his mind again.

Why was he willing to work for her? He had that damned kitchen to finish; he was fully aware that following that project, many other jobs much closer to home were bound to come up. He hardly knew this old woman, yet he felt committed to fixing up her old wreck of a house. What was going on? Deb was already having a canary that he was traveling so far to work; Joey thought he was nuts.

All he knew was, he felt good when he was with the old lady. He felt comforted and comfortable, and that was not a usual feeling for Bobby when he was sober and in another's company. Emma was quiet, relaxed, and funny. He liked her mannerisms, her smile, her voice. He liked her. He grinned. "Surprises even me, f'r sure," he said aloud.

He wondered why she had so abruptly ended their conversation. She had stated that she was tired, but Bobby sensed it was more than that. He was sure it was that talk about Emma's family, probably something he had said that had triggered it. He was often the original foot-in-the-mouth idiot when it came to saying the wrong thing at the wrong time. But he had only mentioned something about the front entrance, and then asked if she had been her parents' only child, hadn't he? What the hell was wrong with that?

Suddenly he wanted a beer and a hot shower, and not necessarily in that order. "Let the old lady take care of herself, for now," he admonished himself. "I put in a long day, and I'm bushed." He switched on the radio again and searched until he found a song he could sing to, and roared the words in his off-key style, whistling when he came to phrases he couldn't remember.

When the song was done, he was bored with the music and switched it off. Maybe the old lady had been really lonely, he thought. Her parents had been, what did she say, introverted, but maybe she wasn't, and what she wanted was to fill the house with her friends, and run through the old place, yelling and laughing. He felt a bit sad, thinking of old Emma as a lithe, active young child, forced to live in a quiet, stern household while life outside went on without her.

It had not been that way for Bobby when he was young. He was his parents' fourth child, and had three brothers and two sisters. There had always been a crowd in their tiny house. His dad had built the three-room house for his new wife, and had added on a wing after the third child came, but there were no resources for any more additions in later years. Big Bob Parker, or Bunn, as he was called, had been a carpenter and handyman, as Bobby was now, and although there was always work, it did not pay a lot, and it took from the body. Bunn had developed severe arthritis in his early thirties, and work became harder as his muscles and joints tightened. It was tough for him to put food on the table, never mind worrying about more rooms for his children.

Bobby's mom Helen was a sweet person, quiet and accepting. She put up with her children and their friends, and fed them whenever she could. Every night, she boiled rags in large pots of water to wrap her husband's aching elbows and knees when he finished work. Bobby knew she had been pretty once, but too much work and worry had drained her beauty, leaving her grey and worn and too thin.

His Daddy had died when Bobby was sixteen. He was forty-six, and repairing a porch roof on Larry Hewlett's house in Machias. It had been raining for three days straight, and Helen had pleaded with Bunn to stay home; his joints were aching more than usual, and he didn't need money enough to work another day outdoors. Apparently Bunn had disagreed, not having had a history of ever listening to advice from anyone, and went off at seven-thirty as usual.

Helen received the call at ten-twenty. "I will always remember that time," she said, whenever talk of the day Bunn died came up. "The timer had just gone off for my bread, and I was bent over the oven fetchin' it out when the damn phone rang. I always answered the phone by three rings, but I had to let it ring one extra time to get that last loaf out." Bunn had slipped off the porch roof and broken his neck. He was dead when Larry's wife June reached him.

Bobby left school to work with his father's crew. He hadn't regretted leaving school. Working outside, using my body, is what I love to do, he thought. Inside was okay, but nothing beat being out in the spring or the fall, swinging a hammer, savoring the smell of new-cut pine or cedar, putting something together just right. It had been a good life, so far, he decided. Although he still missed working with his Dad.

Helen's life was not so difficult these days, with only her youngest boy, Darryl, still living at home. She worked at the Wal-Mart in Calais three days a week, and was able to travel to Pennsylvania and Vermont once or twice a year to see Pam and Trisha and their families, and to Oregon once in a while to see Walt, Bobby's oldest brother. Only last week he heard she was seeing a man from Calais, probably someone she worked with, a couple nights a week. Do her good, Bobby thought, to have someone in her life again. Helen was a great cook, and she had no one to keep a house for these days. Darryl worked as an electrician for a big company, and was not home more than four or five days a month. Bobby and Deb were usually there for dinner on Sundays with Dicky, and sometimes Becka and her young family, but Mumma always said she missed cooking for a crowd.

Thinking of his mother's good meals brought his own hunger to the fore. "I hope Deb has a decent dinner on tonight, for a change."

EIGHT

"Get your ass down here this minute and pick up your shit!!" Deb stood at the foot of the stairs, hands on her hips, feet planted on a denim jacket which had been dropped along with a book bag. A red and black flannel lined jacket was draped on the rail, with another book bag hanging from it, and a third jacket draped over the fourth step. The third book bag was not in sight.

"In a minute!" A muffled voice came from behind a closed door on the second floor. Laughter could be heard upstairs.

"NOW! This is not funny, you guys! Somebody's gonna break their freakin' neck trippin' over your shit. DICKY!! I MEAN IT!"

Bobby snapped the cap from his beer in the kitchen, took a deep pull and listened to his wife's howls. "Jeez, what a bitch," he muttered under his breath.

"Deb, keep it down, for crissakes," he said tersely. "I had a long day. Call the kid, for Godsake, don't holler at 'im like that. He won't do what you say jest because you raise your voice a few thousand decibels. You sound like a goddam fishwife!" He switched on the big screen TV in the living room and picked up the monthly satellite program guide. Before he had his rear comfortably settled in his cracked brown fake leather recliner, she had turned on him.

"You! About time you get home! Wastin' your freakin' time on some old broad in Milltown when you could be finishin' Brud's kitchen. A goddam hour away, for godsake. There's plenty of jobs here, why do you need to go all the way out there?"

Then, "And how about supper? Did you think that maybe since it's Friday I might have some plans? Maybe I wanted to go out or something. If I did, it's too late now, I got hungry an hour ago and ate a half a bag of corn chips with some sour cream and salsa. Now I got no appetite for supper. I hope you ate, because I ain't got an appetite for cookin', neither." She clomped into the kitchen on new chunky black platform shoes. He could hear her popping the cap from a beer. A few seconds later, she came back with the beer and an unopened bag of ridged potato chips, and threw herself onto the couch with her knees pulled up to her chest and her arms wrapped around them, one hand gripping the beer. She stared at the TV, surly and silent.

Bobby didn't bother to reply. He knew she would not listen to his answer, and if she did, she would have nothing but negative things to say about it. He knew there was no right thing to say. He had been through this many times before. As he drew deeply from his bottle, he glanced through half-closed eyes at his wife.

The first thing that struck him was her thinness. Deb wasn't just thin; she was narrow. She had a long narrow head, with high narrow cheekbones. Her pointed nose and pursed mouth were also narrow, as were her shoulders and hips. Her breasts were small and her waist seemed almost as wide as her hips, giving her a sleek, straight appearance. She looked like a greyhound, all sinew and wire, ready to jump up quickly even as she sat motionless.

He noticed also that she was wearing a freshly-pressed pair of black jeans and a cropped forest green chenille cowl-neck sweater. She wore earrings, too, dangling fake gold ones with green stones. They set off her short dark layered hair, dyed now, but her original color, almost black with deep red highlights. Her eyes were dramatized with shadow and mascara, and her lips and nails were painted a bluish-purple.

He had loved her hair once--loved the lean feel of her body. He had been hypnotized by the way she moved, like a panther, skulking around without a sound. Panther then, now a greyhound, he mused. He would put his hand on her hip, and she would begin to pulse against his touch. Later, he discovered that even while she slept, her body shifted constantly with almost unnoticed movements, as if her arteries were much wider than other peoples', allowing blood to flow like a river through her torso, causing endless fluctuation.

She excited the hell out of him, then. He couldn't keep his eyes, then his hands from her, and wanted her energy next to him every minute they were apart. She fed him something he needed, something he did not have in himself. He thirsted for her presence as if he had slogged through the Sahara for days without seeing an oasis. She had possessed him. He knew that, now. Because she needed him.

She needed his solidity, his sameness, his quiet acceptance. Before Bobby, everyone had left her. Her father had left before she was born. Her mother had left her when she was nine, to bury herself in need for any man who would have her for a while, and supply her with cheap wine. Her grandmother, who had given her some comfort in the form of a roof over her head and the basics for survival, had left her the night a massive embolism took her brain and her life. Debra was thirteen. She turned to her friends for comfort, mostly male friends, who satisfied her briefly with their bodies and their company, then left.

Bobby Parker and Debra Mangione met at a basketball game. She was fifteen; he had just turned sixteen. His father had died some months before, and he was working six days a week. Joey had persuaded him to take a rare Tuesday night off; they would eat at MacDonald's, then watch the local teams play. Deb was sitting with a friend, directly across the gym. Her wild energy bridged that wide space. She was dark and lithe and wild--he had never seen anyone like her. At halftime, he made his way to her. He informed her that they needed to be together. He felt crazy, because he had never taken that kind of risk with anyone. She smiled, exposing her small white pointed teeth. He was ready to die, right there.

Debra lived ten miles from him in Jonesboro; he hitched rides to be with her two or three days a week for the six months before he qualified for his driver's license. They necked on her porch, or watched TV and investigated each other's bodies while her grandfather slept. The first night he borrowed his brother's truck to take her out, she got pregnant.

The pregnancy was fine with Bobby. He would marry her and build her a small house on his parents' land. Deb had other plans. She would go to Boston when she was eighteen and become a supermodel, then do commercials and study acting, and have a star's career. Fame was her goal. She wasn't ready for baby poop and housecleaning. She wanted an abortion.

However, she also wanted Bobby Parker. She did her best to persuade him to move to Boston. The pair could work until she found the ideal modeling job. When she was famous, he would never need to work again; he could be her agent and they could go everywhere, even Europe. Then, maybe she would have a baby for him.

Trouble was, stubborn old Bobby would not go along with her plan. He would marry her and give her everything she needed, and according to him, what she didn't need was all that star stuff. They would be fine, together. They would make it because he would support her, and she could study acting or whatever later. Later--meaning after they had a couple of kids and got things together. So, because Debra had no money and no support for her dreams, she married Bobby. She left school, worked with him to build their little house, and had Bess just after her seventeenth birthday.

"You look nice, Deb," he offered as he ambled to the refrigerator for his second brew. "I didn't know you planned on me and you goin' out tonight. You never said nothin' to me about it this mornin'." Then, "You still wanna go somewhere? A movie, or the 'Claw, or somethin'? I'm game, I gotta git some food into my gut. All's I kin find is that chili you made, what, Monday?" He popped the beer cap into the trash and came to the door of the living room, which adjoined the kitchen.

Two rooms on the first level, and three small bedrooms and a bath upstairs made up the house. Bobby had wanted to build on a family room and a half bath downstairs some years before, but Deb stopped him. She wanted a new house, miles from her mother-in-law. Bobby's mother and brother lived a good two-acre distance from them, but Deb felt she was always being watched and judged.

"No goddam additions," she'd said firmly. "I want my own piece of land, back in Jonesboro. That's far enough away from old Pry-eye. We can sell the house the way it is. It's plenty big enough for a couple with a kid. I want my kids to grow up somewhere your mother ain't."

Bobby grinned. "Whatta y'say we go t'Pietro's in Calais? I could git some pasta there, you could get that salad you like, with the shrimps in it."

Now curled into a ball in a corner of the sofa, Deb glared at him. She had opened the bag of chips and was crunching them one at a time, taking infinitesimal sips at her beer between each chip.

"You want me to go out? Now that I don't even want to look at you, you want me to spend time sitting across from you at a booth? Forget it, asshole. You had your chance, and you freakin' blew it!" She threw the bag at him, scattering potato chips everywhere while she rose from the sofa. She put her thumb over the neck of the bottle, shaking it vigorously, and pointed it at him. Beer spurted wildly from the bottle, mostly wetting the recliner that sat placidly between Deb and Bobby, who had ducked behind it.

"Shit!" she exclaimed, and turned and went for the door, pulling her leather jacket from its hook in the hall. "I'm goin' out," she announced as she slammed the door behind her.

Dicky came thumping over the stairs with his two cohorts close behind him. "What the fuck's goin' on down here?" What he saw was chips all over the room, and the recliner dripping with wet stuff, which he figured must be beer, since that's what he smelled. "Dad? You okay?" then, "Jeez, what a mess. Mom do that?" He turned to his buddies. "My mom's a ball-buster," he remarked, shaking his head and grinning. Sam and Dusten stood in the hall, silent for once in their noisy young lives.

Bobby got up from behind the couch. "Yup. She's gone out." He didn't feel it was necessary to explain the whole thing to Dicky, since this or something like it happened at least once or twice a week. It was another verse to the same old tune, he figured, and Dicky knew this. "I'm goin' to Shanahan's for a pizza," he offered. "Want some?"

"I guess. You want pizza, guys?" The guys nodded. "Get a couple hamburg with extra cheese, and a couple quarts of Pepsi," Dicky offered. "You want the guys to chip in?" He looked at them to see if they had any money. Dustin, who was usually good for a few dollars, reached for his wallet.

"No, it's okay. My treat. I'll be back in a half hour." Bobby called and ordered the pizzas, then grabbed his denim jacket and headed for his truck. Shanahan's pizza wasn't half as good as Pietro's pasta, but he had to eat. Bad enough, he had to put up with Deb's temper, never mind the lack of food in the house, and needing to clean up the living room after her tantrum. He was not going hungry.

At Shanahan's, Doreen was boxing his pizzas. "Hey, Bobby Parker, how are you doing? Haven't seen you in a while." She smiled warmly at him.

Doreen was a couple of years older than Bobby, and had recently returned to Quoddy from New Hampshire, where she had worked as a cook in a large resort since graduation from the chef's program at the technical college in Calais. Her father had died a year before, and her mother, who owned the small restaurant, had suffered a heart attack last month. May Shanahan couldn't pay a full time person to do her job, so their only daughter had taken a leave from her job to run the place until her mother recovered enough to take over.

"I'm okay, Doreen. How's your mom?"

"She's actually doing quite well. I may be out of here long before I had planned. She wants to do more than she should, because she feels good, you know how that is? It's a part-time job just trying to keep her down." She rolled her eyes and laughed. Nice eyes, Bobby noticed. Round and blue-green, with long thick dark-blond lashes.

Doreen was as round as Deb was narrow, he mused. Not fat round, but solid and firm. Her skin looked great to touch, sort of like warm-white velvet. He also noticed that when she smiled, she showed round white teeth and a deep dimple in her left cheek. There was the promise of firm, high breasts under the red smock.

"That's good, Doreen," Bobby nodded. "You're a good daughter, givin' up a great job to come here to this jerkwater town t'take care of your mom's place.

"You're lookin' real good, too," he added, smiling back at her. "You was a real pretty girl, but you sure became a beautiful woman."

Doreen blushed a deep crimson. "God, Bobby, you're embarrassing me to death. But thank you," she added. "I haven't heard words that flattering in a very long time." Then, "You better get out of here before your pizza gets cold. Are you feeding your family tonight?"

"Just me and Dicky and a couple of his buds. Deb's out somewhere, and there wasn't anything else t'eat in the house." He didn't know why he was blabbing his business to this young woman. He never complained about Deb to anyone, even Joey.

Doreen peered at him, her eyes narrowed and darkened, like the sea when a sudden storm comes up. "Oh. Well, you better get the food home. You can heat it in a low oven for fifteen minutes; that will bring it right back." She put a large pie in the oven on a wooden spatula, then turned to Bobby, her hands on her ample hips. "You take good care of yourself, now, Bobby," she said. Bobby wanted to stay and talk some more. It felt good, being near Doreen. "Maybe I'll see you again before you go," he offered.

"Maybe so." Doreen smiled, her dimple just showing.

At the Irving convenience store, he picked up a six-pack of beer, a daily paper and bag of chips to replace the one Deb had flung. He also bought a half-gallon of butter pecan ice cream. Crummy diet, he thought, as he threw the plastic bag next to the pizza boxes on the seat beside him, but I want it. I want a whole pizza and the whole six and maybe even the whole box of ice cream.

The hell with it, he thought. At least once a week, for freaking years, he had asked Deb to get some decent food in the house. Maybe some potatoes, and green beans and carrots, and some bananas or even canned fruit. He wasn't that particular; he just want to eat a few vegetables or a piece of fruit once in a while.

"But then I have to cook it, for godsakes," Deb would whine. "You know how I hate to cook. I just can't be bothered."

"I don't care, I'll cook it," Bobby would reply. "Just put some edible food in the fridge."

But it was always microwave pizza, boxes of macaroni and cheese, cans of beans and packages of hot dogs. In August Deb relented and froze a few quarts of blueberries to serve over vanilla ice cream, and bought a couple dozen ears of fresh corn, which she made Bobby cook. That, with a lot of takeout, had been the diet Bobby and their children had lived on all his married life. "It's a wonder my kids aren't mutants or something," he muttered to himself.

He knew why the kids had grown into healthy young adults: his mumma fed them most of the time. Sundays and holidays, Bobby and his family, his brother and any other relative who happened to be in the vicinity crammed together around the huge table which took up the entire tiny dining area at one end of his mother's main room, and consumed enormous portions of boiled dinner or roast chicken with peas from the garden and home-made cranberry orange sauce, and new potatoes and turnip, and large fragrant fruit pies with cheddar cheese or real whipped cream for dessert. Some days, there were more people than the table could accommodate, and kids would spill out into the rest of the house, balancing full plates on end tables or their laps.

Deb often skipped these meals. If she did go, she complained that Helen served too much food, and everyone ate until it made her want to puke just being there. She would brood in front of the TV all afternoon, drinking coffee sombreros, eating popcorn from a large plastic bag, and sulking. Bobby knew the real reason she stayed away; she was afraid of his mother. Helen was good at those regular wifely things, like cooking and keeping a house clean, and putting clean clothes back in drawers every week instead of leaving piles of washed clothes heaped in with the dirty ones in the basement, so you never knew if your socks would still smell like dirty sneakers when you grabbed a pair last thing in the morning. Deb felt she couldn't do any of that, and get them right. So, why bother doing anything?

At first, Bobby listened to her, and held her, and told her it would be fine, she would learn after a while. He had assured her that she was a fine mother, and that he was happy with her and her cooking, and he didn't mind living in a house which was less than pristine. No one liked nasty neat, anyhow. As the years went on, and nothing changed, he held her less, and listened less, and gradually took over much of the care of his children or allowed his mother to intercede, since Deb didn't seem to care if they were clean, properly fed, or made to pick up their things and do their homework.

In short, much of her prophecy had been fulfilled. Deb was indeed a lax parent at best, and a poor housekeeper, and generally good for working sporadically, and then, only when she wanted a toy Bobby couldn't afford. There was the personal beauty salon, complete with sit-down dryer, exercise equipment, expensive cosmetics, gold jewelry. All of these were purchased on the TV shopping channels, which Debra watched religiously. They were things she could not do without, she informed him, things she needed to keep up her body, hair and youthful appearance. Although Bobby agreed that she should have anything she wanted, he also informed her he didn't make enough money to buy those things for her. However, he didn't mind her working for them. After some days spent glaring accusingly at him and moaning that he didn't love her enough to make her happy, she would reluctantly find a part-time job for a few months.

Her many temporary jobs included clerking in the Ben Franklin store in Machias, cashiering in the Shop'n'Save, or selling crafts at Flo's in Marshfield. There was always someone who was ready to hire her for three or four months at a low wage. Deb would pull herself out of bed at seven o'clock each morning, work for eight to ten hours a day, and save almost all that she made to buy those things she felt she could not do without. When there was enough money in her private account, she would quit.

She was always truthful to her employers, telling them that she would work her buns off for them, but when she had earned enough money, she'd be out of there. Although the people who had hired her over the years were fully aware that she would not stay after she had acquired her allotted cash, most of them actually rehired her many times, because they knew she would work really hard while she was there, and they could not always count on their employees to do that.

"She's nothin' but a pain in the butt," Bobby muttered as he drove home with his supper. He had forgotten long ago why he stayed with her. There were the kids to consider, he supposed, and she was fun to be with when she was in a rare good mood and ready to party. And, he had to admit, sex was still good. More than good, it was still exciting, and there was something to be said for that.

Doreen's sea-colored eyes drifted into his mind. He briefly wondered what it would be like to hold her, to touch her smooth firm skin. He had been faithful to Debra all of their married lives. His friends thought he was crazy, but he felt strongly that marriage meant one person for your life. You chose this person, you married her, you stayed with her until one of you died. That was it. Period.

Most of Bobby's friends did not share his philosophy. They preferred to wave their manhood freely whenever and at whomever they chose, and to suffer the consequences. They strongly urged Bobby to do the same. Bobby felt that whatever his friends did was their business, not his. He was not religious. In fact he had been to church only two times--to bury his father, and to marry Debra. His allegiance was not to God, but to himself and his beliefs. So, when Doreen Shanahan drifted into his thoughts on that cloudy April night as he drove home, he felt slightly adulterous. More than slightly, in fact. Because she was actually gorgeous, and he knew that she had caused a reaction in him that he had not felt since that long ago day at the Jonesboro game, when he spied Debra Mangione across the gym.

NINE

"Where do you want me to unload all this stuff?" Bobby called to Emma as he backed into her side yard. Emma was ready for him this time, since Bobby had called her earlier to announce that he would be by with a large load of roofing shingles. She stood on her small porch, wrapped in a heavy tweed wool cardigan against the brisk northerly breeze. Her hands were stuffed into deep pockets, and wisps of white hair escaped from their captive knot on her neck and blew around her small face.

"You certainly came loaded down," she remarked wryly. "I suppose you should just dump them at the end of the drive, just where the field begins. They'll be out of the way, there."

"Whatever you say, ma'am," Bobby replied. "I'll spread the tarp under 'em, and cover 'em when I finish for the day. You ready f'r all the noise this'll make?"

Emma waved her hand at him. "That will not pose a problem. My hearing is not all it should be, anyway, and I have plans to immerse myself in Englebert Humperdink and to finish that small quilt while you work." Then, "Would you like a cup of something hot before you start? Or some breakfast?"

"Nope, jest finished a couple cups of coffee, and a biscuit and egg thingy at Burger King; but I'd appreciate a cup of somethin' in a couple hours, if the offer still stands." He jumped from the truck, and as he was unloading a large blue tarp from the cab, he looked at her over his shoulder, one eyebrow cocked. "Englewho?"

"Engle*bert*--Humperdink, of course. A true crooner, in the manner of Frank and Jerry Vale and the ever-great Tony Bennett," she replied shortly. Then, "Do you ever eat anything that does not come from a fast food establishment?"

"Not very often," Bobby offered. "Deb ain't much in the cookin' department. Kraft macaroni and cheese is her best offerin'. She kin also perform miracles with Tony's microwave pizza on Friday nights, if she decides to stay home. Adds extra cheese or sausage, yknow? If not, I tend t'git real pizza from Shanahan's in Machias."

"Not a lot of fruit or vegetables in your diet, I assume," Emma mused.

"Fruit? What's that? Oh, I know. It's them little dried things in the cereal--raisins, I think they're called."

"Yes, it can be that," Emma grinned. "Or, you could actually eat an apple or a banana once in a while."

"Nope. They hardly ever get theirselves into this guy's mouth," Bobby quipped. "I do git apple pie once in a while at Mumma's, and I git t'have carrots or peas, or even sometimes a piece of fresh brocc'li from mumma's garden of a Sunday in summer. It's a wonder I'm still alive and kickin', considerin' the junk I eat," he mused, serious now.

"You are probably genetically endowed," Emma offered. "Some keep healthy, and live forever on a diet that seems very deficient," she added. "How have your children fared?"

This conversation was carried on between trips to unload armfuls of tarpaper and gray shingles to the rear of the driveway, where Bobby deposited them on the large tarp. As he worked, he wondered just why he was offering personal information to this woman he had only known for a few weeks. In the past, he had not cared to share information about his life with Deb and his children. Deb's household disabilities remained within his family; even his children kept silent on the subject of their life with Debra. The incident last Friday night was one of the first he and Dicky had shared with outsiders, and that only because Deb had probably forgotten that the two boys were upstairs. She usually planned her temper tantrums so that only he and their kids were affected by them.

His children had not fared at all well, he thought, and not just in the food department. However, he was not ready to share this with Emma. "Mumma's always fed us once or twice a week," he offered. "She loves a crowd f'dinner, any time, and we sure love her cookin'. She's a stickler for gettin' veget'bles into a body, and I guess we get enough fruit, too, in her pies and such. The kids're mostly grown now, anyways," he added. "Only one home's Dicky, and he more or less feeds himself, workin' for the LobstaClaw bussin' tables. He gits a free meal every day plus his pay."

Bobby retrieved the aluminum ladder from the truck and set it up on the east side of the house. The east and north sides had received the most damage from water and wind. He would replace these, and continue with the west side, completing as much as Emma's budget would allow.

"I'll get goin' on them shingles now, unless you got somethin' else you'd rather have me do."

"Shingles are the first priority with me," Emma said. "I'm on my way to my quilt and Englebert. Feel free to come in for anything you need. Please tap me on the shoulder, so I won't jump a foot when I see you."

As Bobby shingled, he thought about his life with Debra. He was aware that although her family did not talk about her, negative information had leaked into the community. Bobby's friends and their wives were generally not Deb's friends. They were fine with Bobby, but did not feel comfortable with Deb. They didn't like her because she snubbed them in town, and sneered at their choices of meals or the way they served them during those rare times she condescended to attend a party. They did not appreciate the fact that she usually sat quietly curled up in a corner, closed-mouthed while everyone else chatted, glaring at Bobby or snapping at her children if she felt they were not behaving properly. She did not offer to join a gathering, and would answer any questions directed to her with one or two curt words.

Early in their marriage, Bobby had tried to appease his wife, staying home when she refused to visit his family or childhood friends. He took her out alone, to a movie or dinner at the 'Claw, the local seafood restaurant. He enjoyed his wife's company then, even if it consisted mainly of complaints about him and the amount of money he made, whining about the birth and care of children and the ravages they had made on her perfect body, and deep sighs when she complained about her inability to go to New York or Los Angeles to make use of her God-given talents. He found if he attended to her needs, sympathized with her, listened to her without judgment, there was always glorious sex.

But Bobby was a warm, outgoing soul, and he missed the company of his friends and family. He began to go alone, or to take his children to social gatherings. Debra was incensed, and punished him for days after he had indulged in a gathering of the friends who missed him, by denying him her affection and participation in lovemaking. She cooked less than usual, and the house became even more slovenly. Sometimes, she would pack a bag and leave him to care for the children for days at a time, never telling him where she had gone.

When Debra felt Bobby had been punished long enough, she would come home, stock the kitchen with food, make the family a decent meal, offer him a beer, and snuggle up to him on the couch before dinner. She would smile, and share her electric energy with him, and they would make love long into the night. Bobby always forgave her, and welcomed her back to their bed. He felt miserable when she was gone, and full and happy when she came back. He never asked her where she went; he was afraid if he did, she would leave him for good. And *that*, he did not think he could bear. He could not be happy if he did not see his friends, and he figured that Deb's trips to god-knows-where were a fair trade-off, in the long run.

Joey Crawford, who had known his friend Bobby since they were in diapers, could not forgive Debra. He knew when she was gone, no matter how much Bobby tried to hide the fact. He also thought he knew who she went with, when she left.

Sissa Hedley had moved to Portland about five years after Bobby and Deb married. Sissa had become Debra's only friend, a sharp-tongued, sharp-nosed, sharp-eyed brassy blond who was nothing but trouble. She waited tables at the LobstaClaw for years, went through the local men like mercury, had at least 3 rumored abortions, then took off for richer territory. Joey tried to talk with Bobby about this early on, but Bobby would have none of it. Debra was his wife, and Sissa was her friend, and their problems were none of Joey's business, no matter if they were best friends. "If you're my friend, you'll leave matters alone," was all he would say.

Following Debra's third leaving, Joey declared, "Awright, Bobby, but you gotta know I ain't havin' nothin' to do with that bitch. Sandi and I don't want her around. You wanna stay with 'er, it's your problem, not ours. You and me's been friends forever, and I'd kill a bear f'you, but don't bring that bitch into my sight, I'm likely to smack her one in the keester."

When time had not ended the relationship that Sandi and Joey bet would be over long ago, and after Sandi had left Joey for parts unknown, and after Marie and he had their stormy two-year marriage, and after he married Adrienne, who beat him up on a regular basis, Joey softened enough to come to Bobby's to watch games. However, he never acknowledged Debra's presence other than emitting a few mumbled growls and glaring at her sideways from slitted eyes when she began to whine about the TV being too loud, or the game going into too long an overtime. Bobby had long suspected that if he and Debra split, his friends and family would rejoice. There was really nothing left they could call a marriage. Their kids were a mess; Dicky never talked to either of his parents, and both girls had moved out with no plan to return. Deb would visit Becka from time to time, or keep the grandkids overnight, but her relationship with her daughters was not good. Becka, the older girl, had moved out when she was sixteen to live with and later marry her long-time boyfriend Jared Longstreet. They produced two kids in just under two years, and struggled constantly to keep themselves financially solvent. Jared was a high school graduate, but work was hard to find in the county, and if Becka worked, they sacrificed precious funds to pay for daycare.

Deb hated Jared, of course, and did not approve of Bobby helping them out in any way. She figured if they were broke enough, Becka would leave him. Bobby liked the boy, and knew that they really loved each other, and that if they could both get out of here and get work in Bangor or Portland, they might make it. Without Deb's knowledge, he had started a nest egg to help them with relocation expenses. He hoped he could help them leave before next winter. He had warned them to be careful, not to make more babies until they got things together, and Becka had promised to make sure that they wouldn't. She was a good kid, quiet and soft, a small field mouse. She looked like Deb, same eyes and hair, but without the angles, and lacking her electrically charged energy. Bobby adored her. She was his first, and his favorite, and he had vowed he would never let her get hurt again.

Bess looked like Bobby, round and pink-cheeked with bright blue eyes and auburn hair, but was just like her mother. She could not have enough of anything, and had been like that always. Her dissatisfaction had led her into booze, drugs and very early sex. She had left home at fourteen and school when she was fifteen, and these days she was living in Calais with two young women and a guy, working at MacDonald's when she could. She was eighteen and looked 30. Bobby loved her, tried to talk with her or help her, but she could not be reached. All she wanted was money to satisfy her habits, so Bobby stopped supplying her with cash. He wished better for her and felt helpless. It was all he could do.

His boy was still home. Dicky was a pretty good kid, considering. At seventeen, he was tall and lean and dark, with a quiet, considering gaze. He sized up a situation, and seemed able to keep himself in his mother's good graces more than the girls had. He was the survivor. He had stayed in school, and would graduate in June, God and his teachers willing. He was not the best of students, but he did put a modicum of effort into completing his assignments and getting himself to school on time. Basketball had been his chief motivation. He ate and slept and lived the game, and he was fully aware that he could not play if his grades dropped below average. Bobby hoped Dicky would go to college some day. As far as Bobby could tell, the boy had kept away from beer and drugs, and had little interest in girls. He knew he could also thank basketball for at least the first two.

Dicky was the great unknown. He did not talk to his parents, even to fight or complain or sass back as the girls had. He mostly did what he was told; that was the extent of the relationship he had with Bobby and Debra. They had no idea what he thought, whether he had plans or dreams for his life, whom he hung with except for Sam Beckett or Dusten Thomas, friends he brought to the house.

Sam was his son's best friend, and came home from school with him almost every day. He was as non-committal as Dicky. They usually grabbed something from the fridge, went to Dicky's room for a few hours to study and play music, or spent their time in the side yard, shooting baskets into the ratty, frayed old net on Dicky's hoop. When Sam went home, Dicky returned to his room. Whatever part of himself Dicky shared with friends was not shared with Bobby or Debra. He usually took his meals at the restaurant, or piled a plate with leftovers from the refrigerator after Bobby and Deb had finished their meal. He did his chores, kept his room somewhat clean, sorted his laundry and washed it weekly, and took care of his old car with the money he earned at the 'Claw.

Deb had not grieved when her daughters left, nor had she tried to keep them from leaving. It was no wonder they didn't want to come home. They knew there was nothing waiting there for them. Bobby was aware that they loved him, but he was never there. He worked, he ate, he slept; that left him no time to care for them. He regretted that, but he had always figured it was a woman's job to take care of the house and kids. He needed to work, to supply the never-ending things needed by his growing family. He figured he would have time to spend with them when they were grown, and came for visits on Sundays, as he did with his mother. Now, they were grown, and they never came.

Bobby loved his work. Now, leaning on the north side of Emma's roof, looking up at the thick branches of a huge, still-bare oak arching over his head, he loved the feeling of his strong, muscular body balancing on the rough protruding shingles. He loved the repetitive movement of placing and stapling the tarpaper and new shingles with the gun, loved the feeling of the early spring breeze in his hair and on his face, bringing in April scents of the warmth to come mixed with the sharp tingling of the end of winter. Bobby knew he was meant to live out of doors, to be in the weather. No matter how cold or hot or rainsoaked he became, he always felt alive. This was the only place to be. He couldn't draw a complete breath when he was in a warm, crowded room. Most of his friends and family smoked, and this made it worse. He was forever seeking the coolness and space of a back porch, or the woods behind his house, or the shore near his mother's.

He also loved his kids. Bobby was sure that they had no idea how much he loved them. He certainly had not told them very often. He had spent countless hours at their cribsides when they were small, running his large calloused fingers gently over their incredibly soft hair and downy faces. He had taken them from their beds to cuddle them when thunder threatened, or they were disturbed by nightmares. He had comforted them when they fell, kissed their hurts, rocked them and sung to them in his off-tune, raspy way when they were tired and couldn't sleep, and fed them when their mother was not there.

One of his favorite things was to pile Dicky and Bess and Debra in his truck, and ride the county's back roads on a warm summer night, with Dicky cuddled next to him, Bess with her arm out the window, Becky and a couple of her friends in the back, singing and yelling at the wind. He would take them to Gardner's Lake to swim, then to Bridey's in Machias for ice cream, and never minded when they dripped on the truck's leather seat. He gave them quarters for A's on their report cards, then for C's, because at least they were passing, took them to the rodeo in Machias every year, and to the Bangor Mall at Christmas to see Santa and purchase small presents for each other and their friends.

These were wonderful times, but in the kaleidoscope of Bobby's life, they did not happen often. He was sorely afraid not frequently enough to save his children. All of them seemed so lost, and as much as he adored them, Bobby didn't know what to do to make their lives better. He could no longer cuddle and protect them from life's storms, nor would ice cream soothe their wounds.

As Bobby was finishing the first quarter of the north side of the large roof, he noticed the sun directly overhead. "Enough workin' for now," he stated firmly. "Enough workin', and enough worryin'. I need to eat somethin' and have a beer". He climbed down the ladder and strode toward the kitchen. "I swear, since I met this old woman, I have laughed more and worried more that I have in many a month. She is a caution to be with, but my mind is a constant worry and jumble. Nothin' is goin' smooth in my life these days."

TEN

"Grilled cheese and tuna with tomato all right with you, Bobby?" Emma queried as he lowered himself into a chair with a groan.

"Sure, anything's all right, long's a beer goes with it," he answered wearily.

"Beer coming up; your sandwich will take a couple of minutes, if you don't mind. I'm moving a mite slowly today." Emma smiled. "You sound like me. Your bones aching, are they?" She put a pat of butter in a small cast iron frying pan and turned on the burner under it. Large slices of white bread, thick slabs of cheddar cheese and a small glass bowl filled with tuna salad sat beside the stove, along with a large, ripe tomato. Bobby smelled onion; good, he loved tuna with onion. He also smelled a pungent cheesy smell coming from a small heavy pot on a back burner.

"Neighbors supply you with more stew?" he asked. "Whatever it is, smells great."

"You have a sensitive nose, my friend," Emma replied. "It's Mrs. Crider's broccoli and cheese soup, and it's a winner," she added. She turned and looked sharply at him. "Also, you have not answered my question. What is your moaning and groaning all about?" She placed a tall frosty glass of amber beer in front of him. Bobby took a long drink and sat back. "Hmmm. Good. Hits that right place."

He took another, then thought a moment before he answered her. "It's nothin', really," he said with a sigh. "Well, no, the pain seems more inner than outer, if you wanna know," he added. He shook his head. "You pick up every little thing, don't you, Miss Emma. I don't know what it is about you that makes me tell you the things I do, but my mouth gets goin' and it don't wanna stop, sometimes. I don't know if my prattlin' on bothers you or not. I better keep it in until I check with you. I'm not used to tellin' anyone my business." He sighed. "I don't know why I wanna tell you, I swear." He leaned forward, planting his elbows heavily on the table and resting his head in his hands as he watched her prepare lunch.

Emma glanced sideways at him as she toasted the sandwich, listening to him and nodding. She cut the sandwich in three pieces, put it on a flowered plate, added a slice of dill pickle and placed it in front of him. She poured two small bowls of the fragrant soup, gave him one and took the other to her place. She sat slowly and took up her spoon. Then she put it down and peered at him solemnly.

"Perhaps it's because it's about time you said some of those things," she mused. "I don't think you 'go on and on', as you say. To me, you are just sharing a part of yourself with a friend. That is what friends do," she added with a quick smile.

"Oh, that's what it is?" Bobby grinned as he took a huge bite of his sandwich. "Not my friends, they don't," he mumbled through his food.

"You can say anything you want to me, but please wait until your mouth is empty," Emma moaned, smiling.

Bobby swallowed. "Sorry; it jest came out. I's thinkin' that I would never say anythin' of a personal nature t'my friends. Or my wife, or my mumma. Forget it. I'd be laughed right past th'three mile limit."

"That's too bad, now, isn't it, Bobby," Emma said. "You miss out on a lot of comfort when you are not able to share sadnesses and angers with each other," she added. She placed her chin delicately in one palm and looked sadly at him across the table. She had apparently forgotten her soup. "I have not shared much since Thomas died, actually," she said. "I feel good usually, but there are things I would like to talk over with a friend from time to time." She took a few sips of the rich broth.

"Maybe, we could do this for each other," she added. "Wouldn't that be nice. Meantime, it's perfectly all right for you to share what is bothering you, Bobby, any time you wish. I may even pry, to poke it out of you." She smiled broadly. "Only when I think you really want to tell me, of course," she added.

Bobby finished the large sandwich in a few gulps. He spooned down generous mouthfuls of soup and finished his beer. Emma watched him with a satisfied smile as she sipped at her soup. They joked lightly with each other, and talked about her crooners and his country western favorites. After he had finished the soup, she cut him a large brownie from a pan on the counter, heated it in her microwave and topped it with a generous scoop of vanilla ice cream. She added a large glass of cold milk to wash down the dessert. While he finished his lunch, she made herself a cup of tea, took a small cube of brownie and joined him.

"That was great," Bobby sighed, sitting back in his chair. "Can't tell you when I last had a real lunch, sandwich and soup and all. And dessert. The best." He rubbed his full stomach briskly. "I'll need to work some hard to make up for that meal."

"As I have told you, I love to feed a hungry man," Emma smiled. "And you, I must say, are one of the hungriest I have seen."

Bobby laughed. "I guess I am. I'm always stokin' up the furnace, it seems. My mumma used to say she had to work over a week a month just t'put food in my mouth." He smiled at her. "It's about my kids, and Deb," he said. "The groanin' and moanin'," he added.

"Hmm." Emma nodded. "You want some tea?"

"Sure," he answered. She busied herself fetching a second thick white mug, filling the blue enamel teapot, pouring milk, fetching sugar. "Just jump in anywhere," she said.

Bobby filled Emma in on the thoughts he'd had all morning. He also told her about meeting Doreen Shanahan at the pizza place. Why he mentioned that, he hadn't a clue. It just popped out. He talked through three more cups of tea and two more brownies.

"I better git back to work or I'll eat more'n I'm worth," he said wryly. "It sure felt some good to heft all them heavy thoughts off my brain," he added. It had helped that Emma had listened to every word, not interrupting once except to fill his cup and cut him more brownies.

She regarded him intently. "Well, Bobby Parker, sounds like your life doesn't hold a lot of joy these days." She rose and began clearing the lunch dishes, stopping to gently rub his shoulder. At her light touch, Bobby suddenly felt like crying. He grabbed a paper towel and wiped his face quickly.

"Joy? What's that?" he said gruffly. "Seems I remember some of that once, but it's been a long spell. I feel dried out and old, most days, I gotta say." He rose and stretched. "Sort of like one o'them shriveled shingles I been throwin' off y'r roof."

"Maybe you need to make a few small changes in your life," Emma suggested hesitantly. "Perhaps you need to visit that young pizza woman again." Then, "I don't mean to meddle, Bobby. I have no business telling you how to lead your life. Don't pay any attention to me."

"Maybe more'n a few, and not so small," Bobby returned. "It's hard, though, I been goin' along like this for more years than I wanna to think about. Seems normal, somehow, like it's my rut and I'm sunk in it." He turned at the door. "I don't know why, but I don't mind you tellin' me what t'do. Maybe someone needs to do it."

He shook his head briskly back and forth and ran thick fingers through his coarse sandy hair. "Anyways, I'll work a couple more hours today, and come back tomorrow," he added. "I only got a few more days on Brud's job, and I ain't got nothin' big lined up yet, so I kin afford t'give you a few extra days, maybe in a week or two. I'd like t'git that roof safe before spring rains set in. Due any time, I'd say."

"Sounds good," Emma retorted. Her bright eyes crinkled with her smile. "One of these days, I'll tell you my story over many cups of tea."

"Fine with me," Bobby called as he closed the door gently behind him.

ELEVEN

The phone was ringing as Bobby came into the house. "Wait a minute, wait a minute," he muttered as he shrugged off his heavy sweater, hung it on its hook and threw his cap on the shelf by the door. "I'm comin', for Godsakes." He strode into the kitchen and grabbed the receiver from the wall. "Parker here," he said.

"Daddy?" Bess said hesitantly. She was crying.

"That you, Bess? What's up?" Bobby asked. "You okay?"

"No, Daddy, I'm not okay, I'm a mess," she sobbed hysterically. She began to wail, a thin keening that made Bobby's scalp tingle and hurt his teeth.

"Jesus, what th'hell's goin' on?" he yelled into the phone.

"Don't yell at me, Dad, I can't stand it when you yell," Bess wailed. "I called you because I couldn't think of anyone else t'call, that's all. If you're gonna yell, I'm gonna hang up."

Bobby took a deep breath, then another. His younger daughter had caused this reaction in him ever since she had moved out. He never knew what she would say, or where she would be when she contacted him or Deb. She had called them so drunk she couldn't talk, so drugged out she couldn't do anything but mumble incoherently. She had called from jail twice, from a man's apartment once. The man was threatening to kill her if she didn't open his bedroom door. Bobby dialed 9-1-1 and the police rescued her, that time. Panic rose in his throat whenever she called. After the third breath he answered her, calling up as much calm as he could muster.

"Okay, okay, baby, I need t'hear what's wrong. I won't yell again, I promise. Just don't hang up on me. I'm glad you called, I am. So what's botherin' you?" He hoped he sounded normal. Bess was a firecracker with a very short fuse; if he let it burn down, she would be gone in the flash, and he might not hear from her for months.

"I need you to come and see me, Daddy," she said. "I need you bad. Will you come?" She sounded so small, a lost child. Tears welled up in Bobby for the second time that day.

"Sure, Bess, y'know I will," he answered. "Where are you? D'you need me to come right away, or will it wait 'til tomorrow?"

"I guess it kin wait, if it's hard for you to come tonight," Bess answered, her voice teary and hesitant, but a bit calmer. "Is Mom there, or off somewhere?"

"She's gone for a while," Bobby affirmed. "I could come tonight, but I'm bone weary, you wanna know," he said. "Jest back from Milltown. Jest put my foot in the door, matter of fact. I'm starved and bushed, so you'd need t'wait 'til I get some food into me anyways."

"Figures, she's not there," Bess replied, sarcasm leaking into her voice. "She's never, never been there when she needs to be."

"Let's not git into that, Bess. Y'know your mom, I don't need t'discuss that shit with you right now. Where are you, anyways?"

"I'm in Calais, at a guy's. Donnie's. He's on Downes Street, right off Main, you know? Near the park. Three houses from the corner of Lincoln, upstair'. What time kin you come?"

"Is he hurtin' you? Who th'hell is 'e?" Bobby was losing patience again. Bess was with another man, and he was probably beating the crap out of her on a regular basis.

"Relax, Daddy, he's okay. He's married, got two kids. I came here yesterday 'cause I needed a place to go. He's a counselor at the Center, you know, where I went when the court sent me. His wife works there too, Thelma, she's the secretary. I went to see her yesterday. She said I could stay here for a couple days. They're okay."

Bobby did remember. Bess was ordered to complete two months of drug counseling some months before. Another nightmare. She finished the program, was clean for a short while, then had gradually lapsed into her former habits.

"Yuh, I remember. Okay, long's you're gonna be fine tonight, I'm gonna say I'll be there tomorrow mornin'. I guess about ten, t'be safe. Maybe a little before, but I doubt it. It's my sleepin' in day, and I need it. That be okay with you?"

"Fine, Daddy. See you then, 'bye." Bobby took the phone from his ear. He heard her yell at him. "What? What?"

"Thanks," she said softly.

Bobby stood for a moment with the dead receiver in his hand. He ran his fingers through his hair and sank heavily into the nearby recliner. It never ends, does it? He thought. Always someone in trouble, someone needing him to be there or someone leaving. Bottom line was, he couldn't count on anyone or anything these days. Deb off who knew where, Becka and Bess always in trouble, Dicky doing whatever he did with his life--for all Bobby knew, he was out causing trouble every night, knocking up every girl under sixteen in town. Where was he, anyway? God, he was hungry, and he needed some sleep. Lots of sleep. Maybe he'd never wake up. That thought didn't bother him much, just now.

He rested his head on the cracked, pillowed back of the large chair. The next thing he knew, Dicky was shaking him. "Hey Dad! Hey, wake up, you gonna eat tonight?"

"Hum..wha?" Bobby looked blearily up at his son. "What th'hell time is it?" he asked.

"Nine-fifteen," Dicky replied. "I been home since seven-thirty, waitin' for you to come back to life and figure out what we're eatin' tonight. There's nothin' in the kitchen, and I ain't got any money to eat out, spent it all on my car yesterday. I din't work today, so I din't get fed."

"Oh, yuh. I got in at seven, talked with your sister Bess a few minutes, then fell asleep. I was starvin' when I came in; I don't know if I can even get up from this chair, my body needs t'be fed that bad." He grinned at Dicky. "Let's go over t'the 'Claw and feed ourselves good," he suggested. "How's that sound to you?"

"Great idea, Dad, but one thing's keepin' us from that. The 'Claw closes the kitchen at nine tonight. It's only open for booze 'til eleven." Dicky grinned back. "So now what?"

"How 'bout pizza?" The word brought back the reddish blond hair of a certain dimple-cheeked woman. "We could eat at Shanahan's; I could use a beer, tell you the truth."

"Fine with me. If Ma was here, she'd say we was turnin' into pizza, we eat so much of it. Not that she feeds us any great stuff," he added wryly.

"That's for sure," Bobby agreed. "The way I see it, we got no choice. Nothin' else open, this time o'night. Frig healthy eatin', I want a couple beers and a huge pepperoni. Let's go."

As he was pulling on his jacket, he thought about Emma, and his promise to be at her house first thing tomorrow morning. He picked up the phone. "Gotta make one call b'fore we go," he told his son.

As they drove, Bobby couldn't help grinning to himself in the truck's darkened cab. Maybe Emma was right; maybe he needed to see that pizza woman again.

Doreen Shanahan was not there. The stocky, pimple-faced young man who had taken her place said she was off that night. Somewhere deep inside, Bobby registered disappointment, but it was so overwhelmed with hunger he hardly noticed. He and his son had a good time. Dicky actually talked to him, answering a couple of his questions. They had a lively conversation about Dicky's two loves, basketball and his car. Turned out, Dicky knew quite a bit about both. And, it also turned out that he had enough social finesse to ask Bobby about his two passions, football and work. Bobby enjoyed his time with his son, and was thoroughly surprised and pleased.

"Well, that was a good meal, wasn't it?" he said as they were pulling up to their small house.

"Yeah, I guess," Dicky returned, smiling over at him. "I gotta go call a few people. See y'later." He bounded to the house, whistling as he went. Bobby sat for a few minutes, his head resting on the seat of the truck, looking up at the chill, clear Maine night. Maybe his son was maturing, Bobby mused, growing into a decent man. That would be good. One kid he didn't need to lose sleep over. He stored their leftover pizza in the freezer, climbed the steep stairs, and fell into bed.

TWELVE

It was exactly ten o'clock when he knocked on the door of Donnie and Thelma Landish's apartment that Sunday morning. The weather was clear, sunny and cool, he had slept soundly for nine hours and was comfortably full after a huge breakfast of steak, eggs and pancakes consumed at the Friendly Restaurant in Perry on the way to Calais. Life seemed easier to handle this morning. He felt able to take whatever Bess would hand him today.

"I gotta tell you, Daddy, I may have AIDs, and I'm pregnant."

Bobby was not prepared for that. He stared incredulously at his young daughter. She was sitting on the edge of the Landish's worn brown velour sofa, white-knuckled hands gripping grey-covered knees. She looked worse than usual, her reddish hair tri-colored black, pink and some other color in between, her bitten nails haphazardly spotted with black polish, her formerly-white hooded sweatshirt torn and dirty, its broken zipper stuck halfway, exposing a vivid pink, once-clean halter top. The sole of one of her sneakers had ripped and was held together with a wide strip of silver duct-tape. She had showered recently, probably due to the kind intercession of the Landishes, and her exposed, pale face was hollow-eyed and weary-looking, devoid of the black-and-white makeup she usually wore. Bobby sat across from her in the other chair in the small room, his hands balled in his pockets. He wanted to touch her in the worst way, to hold and comfort her, but he was afraid he'd shake her.

"You clean?" he said.

"Sort of," she replied shakily. "I ain't done nothin' for a week or so, since I found out." She began to cry, tears streaming from her red-rimmed eyes down her pale cheeks. "That I'm pregnant, I mean. I don't wanna hurt the kid. I ain't even had coffee or Pepsi. Someone told me it's not good for a baby."

Bobby sighed and sat back, taking his hands from his pockets. "So tell me the whole thing, Bess. The whole, whole thing, the real thing, and don't leave nothin' out, or I'll find out somehow." Bess had a history of weaving the fabric of a story consisting of half-truths, accusing any person or situation that would excuse her from blame. No situation she found herself in was ever her fault.

"It isn't all my fault, Daddy," she began. "Derek--"

"That's not what I need to hear, Bess," Bobby yelled. "Just facts, not whether it's your fault or this guy Derek's fault or God's fault, for Chrissake. Just tell me what happened, and what you're gonna do about it." He rose.

"You're scaring me, Daddy—what're you gonna do-oo," Bess wailed and flinched, putting her hands to her face, warding off whatever might come.

"I'm havin' a hard time sittin' still. I ain't gonna do nothin' to you, for Godsakes. Jest tell me what's goin' on." Bobby stood, stuffed his hands back in his pockets and paced the small room. He was suffocating in the tiny space. "Let's go for a walk, honey," he said quietly. "I kin listen and think better when I'm outdoor' and movin'."

They walked while Bess talked. She had been living with two young women and a man for almost a year. One of the women had one child and was collecting food stamps and child support from the state of Maine. Her child lived with an aunt in New Hampshire, but the state had not been informed of that. The young man, Derek by name, held stop signs for the state road repair crews for seven dollars an hour. Bess and the other woman worked from time to time, waitressing or doing seasonal work, like digging clams or making Christmas wreaths at Guilford's. The woman who was bilking the state made a decent living selling marijuana to local high school kids and turning a trick now and then.

Among the four, they managed to put enough money together to eat, pay the rent on the two-bedroom apartment and buy enough beer, cheap wine and drugs to keep them fairly unconscious at least half of the time. Two months earlier, Bess and Derek had discovered they had feelings for each other. Until then, Derek had slept with Bess and the other two women with no sense of discrimination. When the other two women had begun to turn to each other for comfort more frequently, Derek, not being much "into the lezzie scene", began to offer exclusive time to Bess.

Three weeks ago, Derek got really sick. After two weeks of drinking over-the-counter cough medicine and taking fistfuls of aspirin for a fever, he was still coughing up blood. Nervous, Bess dragged him to the emergency room of the small local hospital. They discovered that twenty-two year old Derek had active AIDS virus, and a severe case of pneumonia. The attending physician suggested that the three women be tested for the virus, and asked Bess if she had been sleeping with him on a regular basis. Bess confirmed that she had, and the young doctor, noting her depleted condition, suggested she have a full examination. He discovered the pregnancy, then estimated at four or five weeks.

"He prob'ly caught me the first night I moved my stuff into his room," she sighed. They were sitting on a park bench, and Bobby was feeling less agitated after a long walk.

"I suppose it's stupid and useless to ask if you used any kind of protection," he said.

"We did, some nights, but you know, sometimes you just forget..." She absentmindedly chewed at a thumbnail as she looked down at her worn shoes. "It was prob'ly too late, anyways," she surmised. She looked at Bobby. "He could've told me about the AIDS, though, he musta known he was sick!" She paced in front of the bench. "It's not all my fault, he could've remembered t'use a rubber, y' know!"

Bobby looked at his daughter. "Bess", he said, "it ain't always someone else's fault when life ain't goin' the way y'want it to."

He suddenly felt very tired; his whole body ached to be somewhere else--anywhere else. He thought about Emma's big warm kitchen with its welcoming checkered cloth covered table. That was the place he wanted to be, drinking hot sweet tea and joking with her. Feeling safe.

But he wasn't there; he was sharing a park bench with his pregnant, sick daughter. "It's a lotta peoples' fault you're in this condition," he continued wearily. "It's your mom's and my fault because we didn't do a good enough job of raisin' you, and it's this asshole Derek's fault because he got sick and knocked up a kid with another kid, and it's your own damn fault because you ain't got enough ambition nor sense t'take proper care of yourself.

"Everyone's at fault, prob'ly even God," he continued. "So don't give me that shit no more that it's not your fault. It *is* your fault, and you are the only one's responsible for doin' somethin' about this."

"You mean I need to take care of everything?" Bess said, putting her hands over her small tense face. "I can't do that, Dad, I just can't...I'm scared, and I got nowhere to go. I can't go back t'Derek, and he ain't gonna take care of me or his kid, he already told me that. And Kitty and Cindy don't want me to live with them any more, they think I got AIDS and they're afraid I'll spit on them or somethin' and give it to them.

"Fuckin' bitches", she added vehemently.

Bobby ignored her foul language. "Well, I din't exactly say that," Bobby returned. "I can help you some, but we gotta figure what you want to do, and what's your next step.

"Y'seem to want to take care of y'self, keep yourself healthy I mean, because you're carryin' this kid," he added. "You thinkin' y'might want to keep it?"

Bess was. She told her father that she felt different, that she wanted to make herself more healthy because she was growing something inside her, and she felt this was very important. Bobby realized as she talked that this may have been the first time in her young life that Bess had ever given any thought to anything except herself, or shared this much of her emotional self with an adult, even her father, and that she had given this problem of carrying a child and being the mother of that child some serious consideration. He heard her through, then sat for a few minutes digesting her words.

His silence increased Bess' anxiety. "What're you gonna do, Dad? What am I gonna do?"

"I'm not exactly sure, Honey, but I'll find out about some things. One thing's pretty clear t'me; I think you need to go away somewheres safe, where you kin rest and git healthy and learn about yourself and what this whole baby and motherin' thing is all about. Maybe you're jest wantin' this now, because you ain't got nothin' else in your life. Maybe y'won't feel the same way in a few months, when you're as big as a house and th'kid's ready t'come, or when he's here. Or she. You're pretty messed up right now, y'know. Who knows how you'd feel if your head's clear and you've put on a few pounds.

"I guess what I'm sayin' is, let's take it a bit at a time; let's not make plans for y'r old age, for Godsakes." He smiled a bit at that, his mouth quirking up on one side. He looked at Bess, and realized she was doing the same thing.

He reached for her. She came to him at the same time, collapsing into his large warm hug. "I been so scared, Daddy," she whispered into his chest. "It's been awful."

"I know, baby...it ain't been too good for me, neither," he muttered gruffly into her hair. "Your mom and me, we been worried about you for a long time now."

Bess jerked her head up and pulled away. "Oh, yeah, that's why she's here now," she spat. "That's why she always comes when I need to see her or when I call her. Yeah, I can see how worried she is." She folded her arms across her chest and sank into the bench, her bottom lip in its characteristic pout. "She ain't no mom t'me," she stated firmly. "I hate her."

Bobby couldn't defend Debra; Bess was right. Funny, but his first thought was to defend Deb. It's what he always did. Give her the old 'you gotta love her because she's your mumma' speech. But he couldn't do it, this time. The words stuck in his throat.

"I guess it's been hard for you, havin' ol' Debra for a mumma," he said instead. "It's been hard for me a lot, havin' her for a wife," he added. "But you gotta know, it ain't all her fault, neither. Jest like this mess ain't all yours or someone else's. It's always a lot of things, makes up what a person is.

"Your mom had dreams when she was a kid. She wanted me to dream 'em with her, and I couldn't. So, I guess she gave 'em up, because she was too scared to go out and git what she wanted by herself. That jest happens, sometimes. And you kids had t'live with 'er. I had t'live with her. Mostly, she had t'live with herself. That ain't been an easy thing, either. So let's not tell her about this whole thing. Let's keep it to ourselves. Let's jest hope you ain't got AIDS and let's get you somewheres you can be comfortable while you decide what's gonna happen to you and this kid. How's that?"

Bess looked intently at him. "You mean that? You ain't gonna tell Mom?" She smiled fully, for the first time since he had seen her at the Landish's. Even her eyes crinkled. She was suddenly seventeen again. "Wow," she said. "That's awesome."

He grinned back at her. "She wouldn't be much help, we both know that," he said. "And frankly, I don't feel like puttin' up with day after day of crap comin' from her mouth about what you've gotten yourself into." He rose. "Let's go git some lunch, I'm hungry again," he stated, "and let's make some plans." Bess rose with him, gave him a quick spontaneous hug and agreed that she could eat, too.

Life for neither of them was good, Bobby thought as they walked slowly toward the small burger joint on Main Street. But, for right now, it was better.

THIRTEEN

The Landishes agreed to keep Bess for a week while he made more permanent arrangements for her. As soon as he got home, after he made sure Debra wasn't home (apparently, she was still away, since the house was in the same condition he had left it in that morning), he called the guidance director of the local high school and obtained the names of three places in southern Maine that specialized in the care of pregnant teens. Two of them were willing to accept her immediately, and agreed to keep her if her AIDS test was positive. One was in South Portland, the other in Bath.

He called to give Bess the information. She said a girl she knew had gone to Freedom House in South Portland and said the people were pretty nice. She said the other one, Ste. Anne's Retreat, was too religious, they made you pray all the time and you couldn't go out as much. Freedom House treated the girls more like adults.

Although Bobby raised an eyebrow at the thought of treating his wayward, heretofore irresponsible daughter as an adult, he didn't argue with her, because he thought it time she made a positive decision for herself. He arranged to take her to Portland the following Sunday, and called to register her at Freedom House. They would welcome her any time after noon, and gave him a list of clothing and personal items she would need. Bobby arranged to have their brochures and written information sent to Bess at the Landishes.

"Been quite a day," he muttered to himself as he sat at the old metal table in the kitchen with a cold beer in one hand and a leftover piece of cold pepperoni pizza in the other. Bobby was exhausted. He didn't want to think about anything. His life was a mess, and he wanted to go somewhere and sleep forever. But he couldn't, he knew that. Debra would come home, she always did, and he needed to decide what that meant for him. Dicky was still in school and needed at least one parent to stick around until he decided what he would do with his young life. Bess needed him to take her to South Portland next Sunday. As much as he yearned for escape, it was out of the question.

He decided that tonight, he would treat himself to sleep. Although it felt more like midnight, it was only six. Bobby had noticed a few of Debra's sleeping pills loose in the drawer of their bedside table last night when he had reached for the tube of liniment for his aching neck and shoulders. He would take a couple of those to make sure nothing woke him, even Debra's homecoming, should she decide to come back in the early morning hours. He would leave a note for Dicky so he wouldn't be disturbed; his son was working at the Claw tonight, and would be home soon. Tomorrow, he would work at Brud's. It shouldn't take him longer than three or four days to finish that job. Friday, he could go to Emma's. He hoped the weather would hold, so he could do some serious work on her roof.

He had a plan. He found a certain warm contentment welling up at the thought of spending a long stretch of time at Emma's. He smiled at the realization that her house was beginning to feel like home to him. That was it, he thought. He was going home, when he went there. Home not in the sense of a house, or a related family, but a welcoming.

That was strange, he mused. He got along well with his mother, spent a lot of time at the house he had been raised in. He ate Sunday dinners there, most weeks. But Helen was a somewhat distant, busy woman. She bustled around constantly, cooking, cleaning, baking, singing in her choir, bringing covered dishes to every sick or injured person in town. Time spent with his mother was time watching her move around like a worker ant, carrying something from place to place, never stopping to rest.

Bobby loved his mother, but he could not ever remember having an extended conversation with her. She would bustle around him while he talked, preparing a meal or sweeping the floor. When he paused, she would smile and drop a quick kiss on his head, patting him on the shoulder and saying "That's nice, Sweetie. Good to talk to you. You know I love you, Bobby." Then off she'd go, to deliver a package to someone in need.

Helen called everyone Sweetie. She was a nice woman who seemed to love everyone around her. Bobby appreciated the things she had done for him, his family and his siblings, but he also realized that she did not really hear what he said, nor did she offer him advice, as Emma had. He was in the process of discovering that this was something he had missed. Emma's periods of rapt attention shoveled filling of a sort into a deep, long-empty hole in his gut. The filling felt like a warm, thick custard, relaxing and comforting him.

"Bet she'd love to know she feels like custard," he grinned to himself. He took the last piece of pizza from the freezer, warmed it in the microwave, opened a beer, grabbed a pad of paper and munched on the pie while he wrote a note to Dicky. Exhausted, he lumbered up the stairs to a hot shower, two little pills and a long, well-deserved sleep.

FOURTEEN

With a minimum of complaint from the future queen of the manor, Bobby was able to finish the kitchen for Brud and Brittny at six o'clock the following Thursday, a few days before the wedding. He called Brud in from his shop at five, and Brud called Brittny at work to tell her it was finished, and that she needed to get her ass there pronto, to give her final okay to the work. Brittny arrived in fifteen minutes, spent what seemed forever inspecting every detail including the inside cabinet hinges, the corners of the installed Formica, and the grout between each four-inch tile in the work island, while the two men held their breath. Finally, she pronounced that she loved it. "Really, Bobby, it's cool." Bobby heaved a deep sigh, and grinned. Brud was standing beside him, and he could feel the big man's body sag with relief. This poor guy's really in for it with this broad, he thought.

At six-fifteen, Bobby dropped the final check from the job into the night slot at the bank and headed for Shanahan's. Doreen smiled at him from the oven in the rear of the restaurant. "Haven't seen you for a while, Bobby Parker," she offered. "Where you been?"

What a face, he thought. She was flushed with the heat from the large oven. Her cheeks were pink, her left dimple deep, her eyes bright green and sparkling. Wisps of hair that had escaped from the thick ponytail she caught it in to keep it from the pizza curled around her face. She boxed a large pie, wiped her hands with a towel hanging from a steel drawer and turned to talk with him. He felt shined on, as if the sun had suddenly come out to warm only him. Whew, he thought.

"Been finishin' a long, not-much-fun job," he said. "But it's as done as it's gonna get. How's your mumma?"

"She's been real good, better than expected," Doreen replied. "Thanks for asking, Bobby." Then, "What's your pleasure this evening?"

Bobby almost bit his tongue to keep from the word he wanted to say: You. In its stead, "Guess I'll try a large sausage and mushroom, extra cheese. I'm hungry; prob'ly finish it all m'self."

Doreen busied herself making the pie, taking phone calls from customers and selling the pizza she had prepared. She and Bobby chatted as she worked. Bobby felt very comfortable with her. She was beautiful, but she was also natural and friendly. She smiled easily, and moved gracefully. Again, he felt an overwhelming need to be closer to her, to feel her large warm body, to lose himself in her warmth.

"Doreen, what time do you get through here tonight?" he found himself asking.

"I should be able to leave by nine thirty. It's not too busy, not like a weekend. I'll be here 'til eleven tomorrow night," she replied. She looked quizzically at him, cocking one arched brow. "Why?"

"I don't really know why," Bobby said. "Deb ain't home yet, Dicky's workin' tonight, and I just don't want to go back to that empty house again. I'm feelin' pretty good havin' finished this job, kinda loose and relaxed, and I like talkin' to you. I don't feel like hangin' around here for another two hours, so I thought maybe if you didn't mind, we could take a ride and talk f'r a while after you git through. I'm in need of food and a long hot shower, but I kin come back f'you later." He grinned.

"I can't believe I'm askin' you this," he continued. "I am married, for what good it does me or her, and I got a kid still livin' at home, and I ain't never kept company with any other woman while Deb and me have been t'gether. And I prob'ly wouldn't be askin' you if it wasn't for that old lady." He paused, realizing Doreen was eying him suspiciously. "You must think I'm a loon," he finished with a sheepish smile.

"What old lady?" Doreen asked.

"If y'come for a ride, I kin tell you about her," Bobby replied. "If y'can't, well, y'can't, and I'd understand. Now, I gotta go. Here comes some people who want waitin' on, and I ain't takin' up any more of y'r time."

"Pick me up around ten," she said with a grin and a flash of both dimples.

"See y'then," Bobby left with his pizza and two bottles of beer, grinning broadly.

INTERLUDE: The Author

It's September already. Time really does fly, when you're having fun. That may be an old saw, but as most old sayings are, it's true. I deposited Little Steve in Headstart a week ago, Kris in third. I'm still working for the paper, but that's the only other job I have. The Opus, which was what we agreed to call Bobby's book, is taking up most of my working time. I'm not seeing Irv as much; he doesn't seem too upset about it. After all, Sullivan is quite a trek from Quoddy, especially when the snow is flying. So I missed a few weeks during the winter, and the summer's been busy, what with his family coming from Massachusetts and my needing to spend more time with the kids, and to meet with Bobby and Doreen a couple of times a month.

The work on the book is going so much more slowly than I expected. Bobby and Doreen decided they needed to read each chapter as it was completed, and Bobby couldn't help his urge to give me input on every word. He didn't mind so much that all the facts weren't just so when they pertained to him, but he did want Emma and his family to be represented as they were, and that took some discussion and time. It pissed me off for a while, but I am now used to it, and it's become part of the flow of the book, to write, edit, then meet with the Parkers.

Meanwhile, my kids actually spent time with Big Steve, in July. He and one of his bimbos (I shouldn't talk, since I'd once been a Bimbette of his) took over her family's camp on Cooper Lake for a couple of weeks, and invited the kids for a whole week. It wasn't bad; they came home dirty and full of mosquito and black fly bites, but well fed and seemingly happy. Stevie only fell off the boat twice, according to Kris, and his dad had actually made him wear a lifejacket. Perhaps the child was becoming a man. B.S., I mean.

About Irv. Seems that the more I become involved in Bobby's story the less I want to see him. It isn't only what I just said, either. It's a lot more, when I give it some serious thought. It feels like whatever closeness we had at first has begun to recede, to dry out. It doesn't seem so important to me to free up time every Friday night to eat a meal and share a bed with someone, when I'm only interested in that time with him.

Funny how that got started. I met Ol' Irv in Ellsworth the Tuesday morning before last Thanksgiving. We were standing in one of seven interminable lines at the Shop 'n' Save, as seven harried checkout women and seven overburdened packers tended to long lines of impatient people, their carts overflowing with cranberries, squash, potatoes and apples, not to mention the ever-present frozen turkeys. They probably wondered why we all rushed in like lemmings at the last minute, sweeping up the traditional fixings for our dinners and funneling through the narrow checkout aisles, causing ourselves yet another supreme lesson in patience. No, that wasn't it at all; they didn't wonder-- they had come to expect this behavior. After all, it happened every holiday, and probably the same idiots waited until the last minute each time.

I was there because there was a monumental sale on turkeys. I had come to buy a new tablecloth and napkins for Leena, a gift for having us for Thanksgiving dinner. I stopped at the Shop 'n' Save as I was leaving town. Figured I'd freeze a turkey for later. I was thinking of leaving, rather than waste time in line with one item, when I noticed the guy in front of me.

He was kind of good looking, short and compact, good hands and forearms. Forearms are a real turn-on for me. B.S. had great ones. He had most of his hair, black with interesting white wings at his temples. He was perusing the latest edition of The Inquirer, no doubt informing himself of some poor soul's descent into drug addiction and misery. I was considering a small book that, for a couple of bucks, would give me the latest expert info on how to keep cellulite from creeping into my thighs. Not that it hadn't already, but I could always use some advice to keep it from getting any worse. I must have sighed out loud, thinking about my deep-seated cellulite, because he looked up from his reading and cocked an eyebrow at me.

"This is a bitch, isn't it?" He offered. "The lines, I mean," he clarified as he jerked his head toward the long queues. He smiled. His teeth were straight, square and white, and the smile reached his eyes, which were kind of greenish gold. Nice. I'm still pretty picky about looks. Maybe when I need a man more than I need a man to be good-looking, it will be different. Maybe not. "I do it every year; wait 'til the last minute to get my dinner stuff, I mean," he continued. "Don't know why. Sometimes I think I actually like the last minute crush. Makes me feel more festive, y'know? Or, maybe it just makes me feel less depressed."

Well. This was quite a mouthful from some guy who didn't even know me. No guy I had ever known actually had expressed a real emotion, a *feeling*, for godssake. And he was getting *his* dinner stuff, not his family's dinner stuff. That buried my impatience enough to allow me to shove the cellulite issue to the back of my psyche, and to flirt outrageously with him for the half hour it took him to reach the register, cash out and prepare to leave. I paid for my food and wheeled my cart toward my car, still smiling inside. He was waiting for me in the parking lot.

"My name is Irv Spenser, like the poet and the detective, and I'm a podiatrist in Sullivan. What's yours?"

"Jackie. Jacqueline Gianni. I live in Quoddy, and basically do odd jobs and take care of my two rugrats."

"I'm not married right now, but I have been. It was hell, and I won't ever do it again. How 'bout you?"

"Ditto, at least today. I don't know how I'll feel next week."

"That's an interesting answer. Wanna go out for dinner sometime? We could go to Armando's. Great pasta."

"Dinner's okay, but it would have to be a place closer to me. I can't afford the long babysitter hours."

"I'll take you to dinner and add the babysitter. The pasta is worth it. I won't pick you up, though."

Well, that's how it started. I met him at the restaurant the following Friday night, and I have to admit, it was great. We drank a lot of Chianti and talked until I didn't think I had another word in me. Then we drank coffee and sobered up, and I drove the 42 miles to Quoddy. It was great, and I have been doing it on a regular basis, until recently.

You'd think, the way I talk about him, that Irv is this really special guy. He is okay, and he's good-looking, and definitely good between the sheets, but I soon discovered that he has faults. Major faults. For one, he loves to talk about himself. Constantly. And you'd think he was the only one in the entire world who ever had problems. Work, ex-wife, mother, yata-yata-yata. I don't think there has been one time he ever asked how I was doing, or wanted to know anything about my kids. He'll listen for a while if I need to bitch, but I see his eyes glaze over when he's had enough.

And there is the one biggest thing. He doesn't care about kids. Doesn't care that I had them, or who they are as people, or if they're healthy, or anything. He pays the babysitter every week, because he doesn't want to travel to Quoddy, but he just forks over money without any need to know who he's paying for. As I said, it's about him. He is a bit anal, too. Keeps a neat, extremely well organized house. Nice taste and all, but boy, would he hate to live with me full time.

I was always aware that some day it would end, and now, I can see the time coming up quickly. I see myself in flux with a lot of things in my life. In some ways, I know these changes will be good for me. When I'm ready to stop seeing Irv, it'll be sad to give up the sex, but I'll be ready.

Bobby 's the one who's really changing. Or maybe the two years spent with Emma had already changed him. I still don't really know what made him keep going back to her, but he certainly felt driven to finish whatever he had started. The Bobby Parker I knew had been a hard worker, but kind of shy, didn't ever talk much, seemed to be in love with Debra, as messed up as she was, and we all knew she was something different. He couldn't have been happy with her, bitchy and surly as she was, and his kids must have been miserable. You'd never know it, though, from meeting Bobby on the street. He always asked after your family, always a kind word. But never a word about himself. Didn't ever seem happy, nor unhappy. Hard to read.

I see a different man when we have our meetings. He laughs more, is openly affectionate with his wife, even lets Sharky the wolf-dog (yes, we became friends after a time or two) settle in with them on the large living room sofa. The four of us have spent many pleasant Sunday afternoons in front of a warm woodstove, me in a deep recliner taking incessant notes, Bobby and the dog on the sofa, Doreen putting together one of her great feeds.

I've often thought it would have been great to have met Emma, since I'm so involved in her story. But I've gotten to know her through Bobby. Turns out Doreen didn't even know her very well; they had been together only once or twice. She said Emma was sweet to her, but didn't talk about the things she and Bobby did together. Their meetings were brief, and Doreen came away with the impression that Emma was a very old, very quiet woman, used to being by herself, not familiar with a lot of human company.

Bobby confirmed that Emma had lived most of her life alone, and as far as he knew, she had no close female friends. Her social life consisted of visits from one or two women from the Baptist church, which she rarely attended, or bridge with a group of local ladies twice a month. She was also taken to market, to her physician and to luncheon regularly. She always seemed relieved when people left, or she returned from an outing. These visits tired her, she told Bobby, because she couldn't ever really communicate with those women. They did not know who she was, nor, she felt, did they give a sweet damn. And neither, she admitted, did she.

While I'm on the subject of change, I need to mention the writer part of me. That certainly has changed. After spending hours each week hammering away at Bobby's story, instead of tapping out short inane articles for the weekly paper or the quarterly newsletter, I am learning to put words together in a way that pleases me. When I first started on the project, I would thump out everything that was rattling around in my head into my computer, and frankly, I thought it was the greatest writing since Hemingway.

After I had hammered out a number of pages, I would print it out, and for some reason, the writing was awful. The printed word on the white page read so differently from the writing on the screen. I still cannot fathom why that is, but I have learned that I need to print out my work every ten to fifteen pages, read it carefully and re-write where it's needed. Once I began doing that, the writing improved tenfold. I also bought books about novel writing, and subscribed to a couple of literary magazines. Now, after six months, it is beginning to come together for me. If I never publish this novel, it will at least have been a damn fine learning experience.

2

The Breakup

ONE

By eight the following morning, Bobby was sitting in Emma's kitchen on an antique carved straight-backed oak chair, drinking a hot cup of Lemon Zinger tea. He felt extremely energetic, definitely ready to tear the shingles off a roof. Emma noticed the change in him right away.

"Who put the bee in your bonnet, Bobby Parker?" she asked. The old lady was perched on the edge of her chair, holding her tea in both bony hands. She looked nice, he thought, dressed in a yellow flowered print dress with a crisp white collar, small pearls in her ears and a thin strand at her neck, a large white ruffled apron tied securely around her diminutive waist.

"Oh, I guess you could say I got a shot of life from a certain pizza lady," he replied as he leaned back and took a huge bite from the hunk of raspberry and cinnamon coffee cake on the plate before him. "Mmmm, this is great. Who's been cookin' for you this time?"

"I bough it at the school bake sale they had at the IGA last week," she replied. "I knew you'd like it; kept it in the freezer against your return. Want another piece?" She cut him a large wedge from the cake, and returned to her perch.

"Enough about food, my dear. I am much more interested in your 'shot of life' from the pizza lady. You must fill in all the wonderful details. I know they are wonderful," she added, "because you look wonderful. All rested and youthful and relaxed."

"I don't mind tellin' you about it, but seems like you're on edge about somethin'," Bobby said. "Skittery. You got somewhere to go today?"

"Oh, you're good, Bobby. You don't miss a trick, as they say. I did gussy myself up a bit this morning, both in celebration of your return, and because I need to go to the market in Ellsworth today. Millie Broward is coming by about nine to take me shopping and out to Frankie's for a bit of lunch. A real outing, and one I am somewhat looking forward to, because I rather like Millie." She smiled wryly. "I often go with a neighbor or a woman from my church, but I don't often enjoy the outing. I don't know if I have shared this with you, my friend, but I am not fond of many people."

Bobby was surprised, and told her so. He remembered the treatment she had received in the hospital emergency room. Everyone there seemed to genuinely like her. He shared this with her.

"I am acquainted with many people, and I am polite, even civil to most of them, but I must confess that I put up with society for the most part. If one lives in a place all of one's life, and minds one's manners, one is probably accepted quite readily everywhere. Whether I am liked, I do not know. I have never thought about it. But I am accepted, as an old lady whom everyone has always known, and who has never caused trouble.

"Probably, no one realizes that I do not like them. They may not recognize the difference between civility and friendship. And I do like a few, very few, people. Millie, for one, Thomas, my dear husband of course, and Ralph Ohlstead, a lovely old school friend. Then there is Jonathan Brimmer, the man with whom Thomas sailed. He lives in Portland. Ralph lives in Rhode Island, and we correspond a few times yearly. And, of course, there is you." She looked at him as she talked, and began to snicker, then to laugh out loud, her head thrown back. "Your face indicates absolutely everything you feel," she said when she calmed down. "You think I am daft."

Bobby scowled at her. It was difficult for him to be read so easily. "Not daft, Emma; you just constantly s'prise me. Jest when I think I'm beginnin' to know you, you're different. Keeps me guessin', for sure," he said.

"Oh, there is much to me that you may never know," Emma countered. "And much to me that I may tell you, some day." With that, she rose spryly, put her cup in the sink and exchanged her apron for the thick white cotton sweater that hung from a hook behind the door. "Millie will be here very shortly, and you need to get to it. I will wait for her on my bench in the yard, and you and I will see each other after lunch. Your lunch is in the refrigerator--ham, cheese and cucumber sandwiches, some potato soup you can warm on the stove if you'd like, and feel free to finish the coffee cake for your dessert." She took her purse and sweater and left the room.

"Whew! I can't figger that old gal for nothin'." Bobby shook his head, pushing his cap back on his thick hair, rose slowly, put his cup and plate in the deep porcelain sink beside Emma's and geared himself up to work on the roof.

TWO

Emma was back before two. Bobby had finished his lunch, and was standing atop a ladder just outside her back stoop, nailing grey asphalt shingles neatly on the top row. Emma stood looking up at him, shading her eyes from the strong afternoon sun. "Such a beautiful day, isn't it?" she called. "How is it going?"

"Comin' right along," Bobby replied. "Finishin' up on this side, then plannin' to get a leg on the other side 'fore I finish up f'r th'day. Mebbe work another hour or two. That okay with you? The bangin' gonna bother you any?"

"It's fine, Bobby. I am petered out, going to lie down for a while. I should be up by the time you are done. Please have a cup of tea with me before you leave. Do you have time? I am ever so curious about your pizza lady."

"Sure. Don't want to climb right in the truck after workin' all day anyhow. Ride's too long for that," he answered. "Mebbe I'd rather have a beer, if you got any."

"Yes, of course. I'll refrigerate it now. See you in a while." She waved a bony hand in his direction, then picked her way in gingerly beside his ladder. He noticed she was walking more firmly up the mended stairs. Good thing he had completed that job first. Weary as she was, she may have tripped on those old broken steps.

Having finished the north side of the roof, he laid fresh tarpaper on half of the other side. At four-fifteen, he quit. Enough for today, he thought. Only a couple more days work to finish the roof.

He dropped his tool belt and crowbar into the cab of his truck and stepped gratefully into Emma's cool kitchen, creaking the door shut behind him. He decided that would be the next project. He didn't know about Emma, but the squeaking of the old door certainly bothered him.

She was sitting at the table, her headphones firmly on, stitching on a piece of white cloth. Her head was rocking back and forth to the rhythm of the CD. He tapped her shoulder gently, as she had asked. The old lady started a bit, then turned and smiled. She removed the headphones, put down her sewing and rose to get the cold beer from the refrigerator. "Frankie, today," she said in a soft voice. "Just love that CD. Only the Lonely. Do you know it?"

"I know Frankie, I guess y'mean Sinatra; but I'm not familiar with that CD."

"Some of the songs on it were favorites of my Thomas," she said. "He so loved Frankie."

She poured his beer into a glass, made a large cup of fragrant tea, and sat opposite him at the table. "This is getting to be a regular thing to do," Emma said. "I, for one, like it."

"Me, too," answered Bobby. "It feels real homey t'me. There ain't many places in this world make me feel this good." He grinned. Emma grinned back. He found himself wanting to give her a hug, but he refrained, sipping his beer instead.

"So you wanna hear about the pizza queen?" he asked. He proceeded to tell her about his evening with Doreen Shanahan. They had driven to the lake in East Machias, where they sat in his truck and talked for hours. Bobby realized after he left her off at her mother's small cottage that he had not once given Debra a thought.

"I really like that woman," he said. "She's comfortable, she's easy, she's fun and she's beautiful. I also feel as guilty as shit for likin' her. I ain't never gone out on Deb as long as we been together. Today, all them feelins are mixed up in me. I don't know as I'm comin' or goin'." Bobby smiled sheepishly at Emma, who had listened to him with her alert, bright blue eyes on his face throughout his story. At some point, she had finished her tea, poured herself a second cup and fetched another beer for Bobby.

"Whatta y'think, Miss Emma? Am I an adulterous fool?"

Emma smiled. "I am not the one to judge you, Bobby Parker. I am one who believes that everyone needs to find his or her own brand of contentment and happiness. Only God, if in fact He exists, can ever tell you if you are doing something wrong by looking for happiness in your particular way. And I have always had a deep feeling that God smiles on the person who finally finds what he has been searching for. We humans set the rules for being together and apart; God only stands back and roots for us to find our own way. I feel that being happy means being in God's light. And, "she added, smiling, "a good love makes us happy."

Bobby grinned. "Well, next time I'm feelin' guilty for feelin' so good, I'll remember every word y'jest said." He looked at her intently. "Maybe it's time I let myself feel good a mite more than I have so far," he stated. "God and me ain't been buddies for a while, though I kin remember back t'times when we was. I still feel spirit when I'm workin', like on y'r roof today. But mostly, 'specially with the people I'm s'posed to love, like Debra and Dicky and Bess and all, I feel like God ain't really doin' much f'r us."

Then, "Mebbe, it's me ain't doin' much for God. Or for myself, even. Or my kids. Debra, she's a different thing. I'm wore out doin' for her. Seems no matter what I do, it don't count. She's like a black hole, always empty, can't be ever filled up no matter what you throw into it, even love. And I ain't thrown a lot of love into it for a long time, tell the truth. Maybe it's time to give it up."

Bobby put the empty bottle on the sink. "Lord, Emma, you sure get me goin'. That's enough mulin' on my part for the day. I gotta go, it's gettin' real late and I have a strong feelin' Debra's comin' back real soon. The house looks like lightnin' struck it, and that ain't gonna set well by her." He gave Emma a quick kiss on the cheek and pushed his hat back on his head. "I'll be back in the mornin', all things bein' okay," he said. "If they ain't, I'll call."

Emma touched her cheek where he had kissed it. "Thank you, Bobby Parker, for that, and for your company. I was worn out when I returned from my outing, but your presence has rejuvenated me. No one other than Thomas has ever been able to do that for me." She shook her head slightly and looked off into the distance, smiling gently. "No, not a one," she whispered.

Then, aloud, "I will see you tomorrow, Bobby. There will be fresh tea, but I have no more treats in the house. The church ladies have not graced me with any goodies this week. Would you bring whatever you like, including some more beer? I will reimburse you for it. I would also like to talk about Thomas some time. It has been many years since he passed, and I have not spoken aloud about him very much. Maybe, with you, I will be able to do that. Would you mind?"

"Geez, Emma, here I go on like there's nothin' but me and my life for hours. What makes you think I'd mind if you do a little talkin'? Feel free, any time, t'bend my big old ear." He grinned again, grabbed the small piece of cake which remained in a plate on the sideboard, saying, "This's for the road," as he bounded out the door.

THREE

Bobby's heart leaped to his throat as he pulled into the driveway. Debra's small battered Colt was backed up to the door, its hatch still open. "Shit." It was all he could think of to say.

He parked the truck and went in through the kitchen, hanging his worn denim jacket and battered cap on their customary metal hook behind the door. Debra didn't like his hat on in the house. "Debra? You home?" He stepped gingerly into the living room. She was on her hands and knees in front of the tall bookcase in the corner, pulling books and magazines onto the floor in a jumbled pile. She stopped, but did not turn. Her back was taut; he could feel her energy across the room. A cat caught in a trap.

"What's it look like, Asshole?" She snapped, still not turning to look at him. "It's me, all right. Who the hell else would it be?"

He sank into his worn recliner, suddenly bone tired. "C'mon, Deb, you been gone for days. Din't your trip take some of the piss outta you?" He looked at her back, which was tightening more as he spoke. He also noticed a jumble of empty cartons strewn around the room.

"What the fuck's goin' on here, Deb?" He suddenly felt frightened, his stomach in a knot, his throat tight and sore. "What the hell you doin, here? What're all them boxes?"

She jumped up so suddenly it startled him. She turned and came toward him, shaking her small hard fist. "I'm gettin' outta here for good, Bobby. I'm so freakin' sick of this place. I hate everything about it. I hate this house, I hate your mumma always keepin' her eye on me, I hate the people in this freakin' town, I hate bein' a wife and freakin' mother, my kids always in trouble and you not able to do anything for 'em.

"But mostly, I hate you, for makin' me stay here and keepin' me in this freakin' prison. I need to be where I can breathe, for Godsake. I need *things*, I need to dance and have fun and wear nice clothes and not worry that my house is clean all the time, and that my kid is so whacked out on drugs she never calls me, or thinkin' one of them kids could turn up dead any time! I don't need you mulin' after me, wantin' sex suddenly after you don't come near me for weeks because you're always freakin' workin' your ass to the bone." Her eyes blazed, her fists looked ready for action.

"I am almost forty years old, for Lord's sake. Pretty soon I'll be too old to do anything I want to do. God knows if any other man besides you would ever want me--ever. I need to know that, Bobby. I need to know what the hell's out there for me besides all this crap I've always lived with." She began to pace the room as she ranted, randomly throwing objects into the boxes.

"Part of me's scared there ain't nothin', that this is all there is and I'm stuck with it. I figure I need to go now, before all of me believes that. Tell you the truth, if that ever happens, I might just kill myself."

She continued to circle the room, pulling things haphazardly from shelves and windowsills. When she finished, she sank into the worn sofa across from him, suddenly shrunken and drawn in. She began to sob loudly, her hands quiet now, caught between her bony knees. She looks like a little kid, Bobby thought. His fear suddenly dissipated, and he found himself wanting to comfort her. He couldn't, though. He felt rooted to the chair like an oak, his hands glued to his thighs, his body numb and immovable.

Debra suddenly leaned back into the sofa, her hands over her eyes. "I don't really hate you, Bobby--I don't," she wailed. "I jest can't live this life any more. I don't hate my kids, neither, but I can't raise 'em right. I don't know how. I have never known how." She was crying quietly now, her black glittering eyes peering at him from beneath lowered black brows, her body soft and small.

"Geez, Deb, this is a bunch of crap to hit me with all of a sudden," Bobby replied tersely. "What the hell's really goin' on? Where you been, and what gives you the notion to come back and willy-nilly decide to throw everything away we had all this time?"

"It don't matter where I been, Bobby. And I am not jest deciding to throw things away. Things got thrown away a long time ago. And don't you tell me you don't know that. We ain't been close for years. Oh, we do hit the sheets once in a while, and it is still good, you was always good, Bobby. But that ain't a marriage. That's jest good sex."

She shrugged. "I don't know what a marriage is, t'tell the truth. But one thing I do know, and I know it deep down in my self, we ain't got one. You're an okay guy, you never hit me or kept your paycheck from me or prob'ly you never cheated on me for all I know, though to tell the truth I don't care. All your farty friends think you're damn near perfect, you never do anything wrong. And they're prob'ly right. But we ain't got a marriage, still.

"I want something for me. You and the kids and your mumma prob'ly think I'm the most selfish bitch in the county, but I need what I need. I need to be special, to be noticed. And I have decided to get it." She took a deep breath, rose and walked to the kitchen. "I'm gettin' a beer; want one?"

"I guess." Bobby followed her to the kitchen. Debra opened two beers and set them on the table with a bag of taco chips, a jar of salsa and a package of cream cheese. She must have stopped to get groceries, Bobby thought. Strange. "This is the best meal I make," she said wryly. "You got your veggies, your fats, even your proteins in the cheese. A truly balanced meal." She laughed, the sound between a cackle and a cough. She put the opened cheese on a paper plate, dumped the jar of salsa on it and sat, opening the chips and digging into the mess with a handful. "Sit and eat, you gotta be hungry, it must be after eight."

"I don't much feel like eatin'," Bobby said. "I'll jest suck on the beer for a while." He leaned back in his chair and stared at his wife. "So where d'you think you're goin, anyways? You plannin' to go with Sissa? And what about your kids? You jest plan to leave 'em, not be their mumma any more?"

"Not that it's your business, really, but yes, I am goin' to stay with Sissa for a time, till I get a job and enough money together to get my own place. She's fine with it. Her roommate moved out last week and she needs someone to share rent for a while. I got a little money I put away from that last spell I worked at Flo's, enough t'pay my rent for a couple months." She leaned toward him, elbows on the table.

"Kids? My kids? Whose kids are they, anyways? You always spent more time takin' care of 'em than I did. They probably won't even notice I'm gone. Maybe Becka, but I'll call her and let her know where I'm at. Dicky and you are thick anyways. He never has listened to me. Bess is such a mess she don't know what month it is most of the time. I don't even know where she is now--do you?"

Bobby recalled that he had promised Bess he wouldn't tell Deb where she was. Forget that; he'd take the consequences.

Deb needed to know. So he filled her in on the last few months of their daughter's life.

"Well I can't say any of that surprises me," Debra said when he had finished. "Except the part where you let her make the decision where to go to have the kid. How come you did that?"

"I'm not sure," Bobby replied. "I guess I din't know what to do m'self, and she seemed t'know a lot about the place, so I was of a mind t'let her decide." He ran his fingers through his thick hair. "Turns out she was right; the place is akch'lly decent." He smiled. "She was pretty good with it, Deb," he said. "She was almost actin' like an adult. It was nice." He couldn't sit and look at her any longer, so he rose and paced the kitchen with his beer. "I'm takin' her Sunday. You interested in comin' with us?"

Debra snorted. "Oh, sure, like Bess is gonna be fine with that," she retorted. "I can see it now. She'd need to smoke four or five joints before she could even get in the truck with me. Then the place would throw her out because she'd be stoned. That'd be a cool scene!"

Taking her beer into the living room, Debra sank again into the sofa. "No, Bobby, I think I'll skip that one. I won't be here, anyways. I'm goin' tomorrow. Give me a little time to settle in, then I'll look for work startin' Monday."

"So y' really got your mind set on all this." Bobby looked at her, finally beginning to feel his body. Beneath the fear lay relief, he noticed. And some guilt, probably because he felt relieved. He thought of Emma and her parting words. Taking a deep breath, he sat beside Debra.

"You're prob'ly right about Bess," he said. "She is pretty pissed at you. But y'gotta know she loves you, too. I know that, and y'gotta know that, even if Bess don't know it jest now. She will, and she will need you some time. After all, you are her mumma. And I think you're right about us. We ain't got much between us any more, except a good roll once in a while. I see it as we jest ain't never had enough in common. We can't enjoy the same things. I can't party with you, or dance and listen to the music you like, and you can't stay home and watch TV or ride around in the truck in the summer and sit by th' lake with kids runnin' all over and eat ice cream. We don't wanna talk about the same things. I want someone who's at home when I get here, and cooks me good food once in a while. You wanna go out every night and eat junk food. Sex jest ain't never been enough to keep us together." Bobby reached over to give her a quick hug.

"I did love you though, Deb, an awful lot when we was young. You was the most electric, beautiful thing in my life. Y'know that?"

Debra smiled. "I know that, Bobby. You were a rock for me. You were there when I had no one, and you never left. I liked that best about you." She turned to look at him. "I'll miss that, the knowin'," she said, "but I can't stay. This life with you's got me all dried up. I feel like I'm in a cage, nowhere to go, all brittle and dry. If I stay I'll just ruin our lives more than I have already. It'll kill me, Bobby, it really will, I was serious when I said that before." Her body had relaxed and was leaning in to his. "I will miss you, Mr. Rock," she said softly.

"You said you was leavin' in the mornin'?" Bobby asked.

"Well, some time tomorrow. I'm leavin' myself enough time to get to Portland by tomorrow night. I'll go through the house and pack what I need. I won't take much, Bobby, I can't fit it in my car. Only my clothes, some books and stuff, some blankets and towels, some of the pictures. If I need more later,

I'll talk with you about it and maybe take it in a little trailer. Like maybe one of the beds and the little couch in our bedroom. But I don't know about any of it right now, so I'll let it be."

As he listened to Debra talk about leaving, Bobby wondered why he was so calm. He had thought about this time for years. Every time Debra slammed out of the door, he wondered what would happen when she returned. Would things be the same, or would she decide she could not live with him any longer, and leave for good? He had agonized over the leaving, in his thoughts. How could he go on, if the only woman he had ever loved left him with three children to raise? How could he live his life without her?

But Deb had left too many times, and two of the children had moved out, the third fairly self-sufficient. Bobby realized he had numbed himself to her leavings, and was quickly realizing that Debra was indeed right, that any marriage they had was dead and gone, and this permanent separation may indeed not make a great difference in his life. In fact, life could even improve without her presence. His day to day existence certainly would not be so frustrating if Debra, with her constant whining about her unfulfilled needs, was not there to remind him of his inability to please another person.

He felt more than calm, almost loving toward her. Relief was making him feel lighter every moment. He pulled gently away from her and stood, stretching. "I'm bone tired, Deb. And I guess I'm gettin' hungry, finally. I'm gonna eat somethin' and take a long shower and bed down. You comin' to bed with me?"

"After all this, you want me in the bed?" She asked shakily.

"Deb, you been away lots of times. Every time, when you git home, you climb in our bed like you never been gone. You never ask if it's okay, or how I did while you wasn't here, or nothin'. I guess I'm used to it, by now. Sure, it's okay. Where else was you plannin' on sleepin?"

"I didn't think about it, tell you the truth," Debra stated. She looked at her nails, chewed thoughtfully on a cuticle. "But it seems weird to me, after I just let you know I'm goin' for good. I guess I want to sleep down here, on the couch. I'll finish packin' anything I plan on takin' down here before I go to sleep, then I'll finish packin' the stuff in the bedroom after you go to work. You are workin' tomorrow, ain't you?"

"I had planned on it. I'm finishin' up Emma's roof."

Debra jerked her finger out of her mouth and glared at him. "I mighta known it was the old lady. She is an old lady, ain't she? For all I know she's a young broad and you been screwin' her all this time. You sure spent more time with her than you have with me for the past few months."

Bobby roared at the thought of himself in bed with little Emma. "Oh, right, Debra. I been beddin' down an eighty-some year old woman. I may be bad off for female company lately, but I ain't stooped to that!" He headed for the kitchen and a large can of beans, shaking his head and chuckling. "You sleep where y'want. It's okay with me if you wanna come to bed, or not. Right now I'm so goldarn tired I prob'ly wouldn't even know if you was there or not."

After the beans and several slices of half-stale bread had been washed down with two more beers, Bobby thought he could sleep. While he was eating, he remembered a note from Dicky informing him that he planned to go bowling with Sam after work, and would probably stay at his house. Good thing, Bobby thought. This mess between him and

Debra must have affected the kids over the years. Bad enough they had to live with the day-to-day fights, without one of them being there to witness the final scene.

At least, Bobby thought, it might be the final scene. Debra had left him many times, but this was the first time she threatened to leave for good. He believed she meant it. The prospect of living without her did relieve him, but it also made him sad. They had spent a lot of years together. Most of them had not been good, and he knew that Debra had not been any happier than he had. Except for the good times with the kids and his work, married life, to now, had frankly sucked.

Twenty plus years he had spent with Debra, and only now was he fully aware of the truth of tall the things his friends had told him about her before and after they had married, things he had vehemently denied for years. She was selfish, whiny, childish, anti-social, demanding and a downright pain in the butt. But she was his pain in the butt, and the mother of their kids, and there was a part of him that thought once you married a woman, you should plan on growing old with her. Now she had taken that privilege away from him, along with his peace of mind and most of his ego.

He guessed he should be jumping up and down angry at her. He should be shaking her until her teeth rattled, reminding her that she had ruined his life for over twenty years, and now she was leaving him to fend for himself with two teenage kids, one of whom was about to have a kid. He should be asking her how could she do this, how could she leave her whole life for something she wasn't even sure was out there? How could she leave him?

But he wasn't angry. He was simply exhausted, and relieved that the whole thing was almost over. He would deal with the kids. Debra would do whatever she wanted, just as she always had. But from here on, her doings did not need to involve him. That was the relief. He washed his fork and plate, put the empty bean can in the trash, and dragged his weary body to bed, barely aware of the slight, sleeping figure of his wife, wrapped in a thick wool blanket on the sofa in the darkened parlor.

FOUR

Bobby barely heard the buzz of the alarm from a deep well of sleep. He rolled onto his back and stretched his muscled brown arms over his head, yawning mightily. The memory of last night rolled over him like Quoddy Bay's morning tide, swamping him in its largess. "Damn," he whispered. "Deb said she's leavin' today." As he mouthed the words, he wondered if it could be true. Would she really leave him for good? He was too curious to lie in bed; he needed to find out if she meant what she had said the night before.

Debra was up, dressed and packing things from the kitchen, a mug of fresh-brewed coffee next to her on the counter. "You made coffee?" he asked, sniffing deeply as he stood in the doorway of the kitchen watching his wife wrapping cups and glasses in newspaper and tucking them into a box on the floor. She moves like a dancer in one of them ballets, he thought, graceful and lithe, a cat who wastes no motion. He would miss watching her, he realized.

"Yeh, I am capable of a miracle once in a while," Debra quipped. "I got a long day, gotta get my energy up to par. Pot's still half full--help yourself," she added.

"You use'ta make the best coffee, way back when," Bobby recalled. He crossed the kitchen and took his cracked blue cup from the hook under the cupboard. He helped himself to coffee, adding a couple of teaspoons of sugar and a generous amount of evaporated milk from the can beside the coffee pot. He routed through the breadbox and located a couple of week-old molasses donuts, reviving them by sticking them into the microwave for a few seconds. Sitting at the table, he dunked a dark, sweet donut liberally into the coffee. "Gaw, that's good," he sighed. "Ain't had good coffee for weeks."

"I use'ta do lots of things not so bad," Debra said softly. "I cook pretty good, when I want to. I made you a few good meals when we was first married." She paused with a small cream pitcher in her hand. "I don't like to cook, or keep a house or nothin', but that didn't mean I couldn't do it when I put my mind to it." She laughed. "I didn't put much of my mind to it, did I?"

Bobby chuckled as he dunked the second donut. "Nope, Deb, can't say's you did. Once you got it in your mind that Mumma was better'n you at that kinda thing, you sorta quit on all of it. Guess you wasn't made for all of that, don'cha think?" He glanced at her quickly as he rose to refill his cup. She looked good, this morning. Rested and calm, her face not so scrunched up. Softer, was the word. Rummaging through the cabinets, he located one of those packaged sweet rolls that were never destined to become stale, and sat to dunk it. "You're happy to be goin', ain't you?" He said.

"I have to say it, Bobby-- yes I am," she returned. "I ain't happy to leave us and what good we have, but I want the city so bad. I want it like you want to be by the lake, eatin' ice cream. It's a gnawin' in my gut, and I gotta see what it's all about." She closed the box and taped it, labeling it with a fat black marker. "I'm through with packin' downstair', I'll get to upstair' as soon's you get to work. That okay with you?"

"I guess. What do I have to say about all this? It ain't my decision, but when I get to thinkin' about it, it seems right somehow. I think we'll both be th'better for it, some day. The kids will prob'ly be okay with it, too. They don't like all the fightin' and the way we been livin', that's f'r sure. Maybe after some time, we can get together in Portland, us and the kids, and all talk about it." As he said it, Bobby was positive that would never happen. He also realized that he would like it to happen.

"Sure, Bobby. That would be fine," Deb agreed. He could tell by her tone she believed as he did. He crossed to her and held her shoulders, her small, birdlike bones between his fingers. "I still got a lot of feelin's for you, Deb," he said. She came to him then, her small arms around him, her face buried in his large flanneled chest. He turned her face up and kissed her, long and hard. "Lots of feelin's," he whispered.

"Well, Bobby," she said softly, and began to cry. They hugged, crying together, for a long time.

Emma was waiting for Bobby in the kitchen, perched on the edge of her chair, her coat on and a bright scarf pulled around her thin neck. She rose as he burst in. "Sorry I'm late, Miss Emma, but things went on this mornin', and I couldn't get out in time."

"I thought you weren't coming, Bobby. You're usually so prompt. I need to go to my bridge game. Jane Crockett is taking me, and she is due at any moment." Emma looked at him closely, then. "What is wrong, my young friend? You do not seem yourself this morning; you're pale, and tired looking. Has something happened?"

"You ain't got time for my story, Emma. Go do your card-playin', I'll catch you up when you get back. Maybe your friends'll take you out for a big lunch, it'll do you some good. I'll git on with my work and we can talk this afternoon when you get back, after your nap."

"I must say, you know my schedule by now, Bobby Parker. That's Jane's horn now. I guess I will go, although I have a feeling that your story will be the highlight of my day. The ladies in that group are rather prissy, and their company does not always perk me up." She took her worn leather purse from the table and her cane from its hook beside the doorframe and left.

Bobby climbed the ladder and began to shingle the lower part of the south roof. The work went quickly, and he heard Emma's ride bring her back as he was finishing up. He put the ladder back in his truck and called in to her. "Emma, I'm goin' to get lunch at Burger King. Be back in a jif'."

"I can fix you something if you want to wait a few moments, Bobby," Emma replied. "I have plenty of supplies."

"You jest take your nap. I'll be back in a while, and tell you my story." Bobby left to feed himself lunch, and to pick up the lumber he would need to fix Emma's two doors, the next project they had agreed on. The frames of both entry doors had rotted, and the thresholds needed replacing. The doors would then be sanded and painted. Barn red, Emma said. They had always been black, and she had decided they needed some color. "I have always loved the color of a barn, a red barn," she had said. "I need to see that color on my house. Do you like the idea?" Bobby had, he agreed it was a fine color for her, and for her doors.

"Of course, then the blue of the shutters would be all wrong, and it would need to be changed to black. Can we do that?" Bobby thought there would be enough funds to enable him to fix and paint at least the front shutters. "Fine, then we have decided it. Isn't this fun?" Emma had asked. "Aren't we rascals together, changing my life and my house?"

Bobby had looked at her closely. Were they doing that? Changing her life by changing some of the color of her house? He guessed that was so. She was old, and she had been in that house all her life. Any change must be a big thing for her. He would never have thought that changing a house a bit would change a life, but for her, this was true. He guessed it was all a matter of which window of life you looked through. Her window wasn't his, but his wasn't hers, either. His life would probably scare her witless, he surmised, while hers most likely would bore him to the death.

When he returned, Emma, refreshed from her nap, was making a large pot of tea and setting out chocolate and jam-filled cookies on a plate. "Preparing for our chat," she said with a small smile. "We need to be fortified when we talk about important things. My morning with the ladies was not important. After bridge, Jane and I took a little drive, ate a little lunch, had a little conversation. She is a little person, if you catch my drift." Emma grinned then, a skeleton grin, her lips pulled back, her teeth and gums exposed.

"I am often not a nice person, Bobby," she said, shaking her head slowly. "I can be very petty and judgmental, and as I have stated before, I do not like most of the people in my life. They are often petty, also, and perhaps

I view myself in the mirror of their lives. I do not like it." She poured the tea and set a small plate of lemon wedges beside Bobby's cup. "Special treat today, Bobby. Lemon. Try a wedge with sugar in your tea. You'll like it."

Bobby did. He was feeling good. Emma, with her chatter and her face-making had cheered him. He felt lighter, more prepared to face life. "Debra left me today, for good," he announced brusquely.

"Oh." Emma sat silent, her lips pursed into a sharp thin line. "Oh, my word."

"That all you got to say?"

"I must admit you shocked me, Bobby. That was the absolutely last thing I would have expected you to tell me." Then, "How did this thing happen?" Concern showed in her bright eyes.

"I got home last night expectin' to clean house, as I said to you. Deb was there, boxes all over the livin' room, throwin' stuff everywhere, pullin' stuff off shelves and all. She told me she needs t'go t'Portland to live in the city, can't stand bein' here any more; wants to get a place and work in Portland.

"Threw me, I gotta tell you, for a time. But when I got to thinkin' about it, I started to feel almost good about her goin'. I'd only tell you that part of it, Miss Emma, you havin' heard about our bad times and all. I don't tell much to those I know about Deb's and my relationship. It's been between her and me. But since I met you, I been blattin' out all my feelin's, and I guess it's becomin' a mite more comfortable for me. I even told Deb I had hurt feelin's about her leavin'. I found myself cryin' over it, there, for a time."

Bobby finished telling Emma about his and Debra's last few hours together, in great detail. The old woman listened, sipping her tea and nodding from time to time. "I feel better now, bein' here and talkin' with you about it. Takes pounds o'weight off my chest. I hope my blattin' don't bother you too much, Miss Emma." This was a long speech for Bobby, and he was suddenly weary. He rested his chin in his big hands, his elbows on the table, and gazed apologetically at Emma, a slight smile on his open face.

"Bobby Parker, you are some piece of work," Emma said. "I have not met any soul quite as honest as you in my life. There I was, going on in my small way about my small life as if it contained some real importance, and you are sitting there with this monumental event taking place in your life, and sparing me the courtesy and time to listen to an obstreperous old bag like me.

"That is why I enjoy your company so much, Bobby. You expand my world immensely. You make me realize that there is so much out there other than my existence, my small mean cohorts from my church and my concerns about my old decrepit house and measly budget. I hurt for you, Bobby. I wish your life to be as good as you are. I want the best for you." She sighed and leaned toward him, offering her hand.

"It is as if I had suddenly borne a child, and know what it is to feel pain for the wrongful things which can happen to him. You do not deserve to have these things happen, Bobby Parker. You are a good person, a good man. This woman, this Debra person, does not realize how much she is throwing away, when she gives you up." Bobby reached for her hand and held it tightly. "You have brought me something special these past few weeks. I am almost happy that I fell from that curbing. It brought me your friendship, and that is something I will always be grateful for."

"I really like you, too, Miss Emma," Bobby said. "I ain't nothin' special, but you make me feel good, and I appreciate that. I guess you could say we're good friends. I don't mean t'cause you bad feelin's, though," he added hastily. "I kin take this stuff with me and Deb, honestly. I almost feel good about it, 'cause I know how bad things was gettin'.

"And I gotta add one thing before I finish shootin' off. I been thinkin' about Doreen Shanahan ever since I left the house. That's another thing I would never share with any person besides you. Havin' Deb out of my life, I don't feel so damn guilty for havin' a likin' for that woman."

Emma laughed, the sound like the tinkle of a slightly off-toned bell. "Well, good for you. The memory of the Debra person is not even cold and you are bringing a new woman into your life. I think that is simply wonderful. She seems to be someone whom you might deserve. I hope I am able to meet her, some day." Emma rose to clear the table as Bobby half-rose, offering to help. "Sit right there, I have a few more questions of you before we finish this important conversation." She sat again, folding her hands in front of her, leaning toward him.

"Now tell me, what of your children? What do they think of all of this?"

FIVE

The sun was setting when Bobby arrived at the house he and his family had shared for over twenty years. As he hung his jacket on its familiar hook behind the entry door, he was aware of an emptiness of the small place. Dicky was watching a video of his basketball coach teaching new moves on the court, taking notes in a large spiral book. "Hey," he said without looking up. "I see Ma's gone for good."

"I guess." Bobby sat heavily next to his son, hanging his hands wearily between his knees. "Did you see 'er?"

"Yeah, she was loadin' the car when I got home. Started cryin' when she saw me. Jeez."

"You need to talk or anything?" Bobby looked at the boy. He seemed calm enough.

"Nope. She's gone most of the time anyways. This don't seem much different." He rose, stretched. "I gotta get to work, Jimmy can't make it tonight and I'm takin' his shift. I'll eat there, see you prob'ly in the mornin'. You takin' Bess to that place tomorrow?"

Bobby started. "You know about that? How did you find out?"

"Ma told me. She said she's knocked up and sick, and she's gotta go away to have the kid. She also, in her huge wisdom, told me to behave myself and stay off drugs and not knock up any broads so I don't have to support lots of little bastards." He sighed. "Last words from a lovin' mother," he added wryly.

"Jeez." This time from Bobby. He leaned to his son, grabbed him around the shoulders. "Sorry about that, Dick'. She's just that way, y'know?"

Dicky pulled away. "Yeah, I know. Now I gotta go." He left, then stuck his head back through the door. "C'n I go with you and Bess tomorrow? You think Bess'd be okay with it?"

"Well, sure, if you want to. Hey, even if she ain't okay, I am. I'd like the company comin' back. We're leavin' about nine from Calais, so we gotta get outta here early. Want me t'wake you?"

"Sure; hey, could you make coffee before we go? I won't be in 'til after two."

"It's done. You better git before you're late."

Kids will always surprise you, Bobby thought as he heard Dicky's car squeal out into the street. He hadn't thought about the kids' reaction to Deb's leaving until Emma had asked him how they felt. He would call Becka after he had a couple of beers and some food. She was the one offspring who was close to Deb. He figured she might take it hard. Leave it to Debra to pull that on Dicky. She was just pissed that the boy didn't share his life with her. Poor Dicky never had much mothering, maybe even less than the girls. Bobby wondered why his son wanted to go with them to Portland.

"Dad? How are you? What's up?" Becka sounded rushed, breathy. "I just got in, we took the kids to McDonald's. I can't talk long, I gotta get them into bed, they're drivin' me bonkers."

"Why don't you call me back when you get them settled, honey. I gotta tell you somethin'."

"Just tell me, Daddy, I ain't got time to call back, we're goin' out to play cards with Ben and Susan; the sitter's comin' in fifteen minutes."

"Okay. Your mumma was back yesterday and she informed me she's leavin' for good, goin' to live with Sissa and have herself a life in the city." Bobby paused to let the information sink in. There was no reply. "She packed up and left with most of her stuff this mornin'." Complete silence on the other end. "Becka? You there?"

"Fuckin' bitch." Becka's voice was small and low. "Bitch."

"Becka--"

"I don't wanna hear any more, Daddy. I guess it was comin' sooner or later. How's Dicky and Bess?"

"That's the rest, Becka. Bess is pregnant from some guy with AIDS and she's goin' t'Portland tomorrow t'stay and have the kid. Dicky's comin with us; we're taken her in the mornin'." Bobby paused. "I hate to tell you all this so rushed, Becka, but it happened real quick, and I need you to know all of it. I really would've liked to see you, t'tell you, but I figgered you might find out from someone else, and I didn't want that to happen." He took a deep breath; Becka did not respond.

"We're basically okay, honey. I jest want you to know that. Dicky and me are okay, and your sister is clean for now, and seems to wanna take care of herself for this kid. Can I do anything for you?"

"Goddam it, my whole freakin' family is fallin' apart." Becka began to cry, long wailing sounds. Bobby waited. Finally, the sobs slowed and stopped. "You ain't goin' away, are you, Daddy?" She wavered.

"No way, Becka. I'm always here, you know that. You're always my girl, and I'm always your daddy. We just gotta get used to bein' without your mumma permanently. It's hard, but we can do it." He could, he realized as he said it.

"Yeah. It probably won't be much different, will it," she agreed. "I gotta go, Daddy, I'll call you Monday and we'll make time to see each other. You should see the kids more, you know, they're growin' older an' taller every day. You give Bess a hug for me and tell her to stay clean for that kid. She keepin' it?"

"She don't seem t' know just yet," Bobby replied.

"If she does, we could finally have somethin' in common." Becka chuckled wryly. "Gotta go, Dad--the sitter just came, and the kids are still runnin' around. See you soon. Love you."

"Love you too," Bobby said to the dead receiver. Two of his kids knew; now only Bess to tell. He could imagine her reaction, and he did not have enough energy to deal with any more tonight. He would tell her in the morning. For now, he couldn't think about anything but sleep.

SIX

Bobby was climbing the ladder to Emma's roof shortly before eight on Monday morning. The early weather report had warned him there was a long spell of rain due by the end of the day, and he figured he'd better get going as quickly as possible. If he worked fast enough he could finish the roof, and begin the work that was needed inside when the weather worsened.

He set new shingles until late morning with no sign of the old woman. He had not wanted to bother her when he arrived, thinking she may be sleeping. But when she had not come out to greet him by eleven, worry began to creep into his work. By noon, he could not staple another shingle into place until he had checked on her. "Prob'ly fine, I'm jest an old fart, worryin' about that lady", he muttered to himself as he tentatively tried her door.

"That lady" was busily sweeping her kitchen floor. "Bobby Parker, as I live and breathe", she exclaimed sprightly, grinning at him. "How are you today, Bobby?"

Bobby gaped at her. "Din't you hear me on the roof about the time the birds finished their wake-up calls?"

"Of course; how could one miss all of that consarned racket you make? That staple gun is enough to wake all the citizens of Roselawn Cemetery, two miles from here."

Bobby stared at his scuffed boots, suddenly a bit embarrassed. "Well, you us'ally pop out to say hey when I come. I was a bit worried you might be sick or somethin'."

Emma rested on the handle of her broom and peered up at him, her eyes bright with humor. "It's lovely of you to consider my health, Bobby. No, I heard the weather report this morning, and figured you might have arrived early to finish my roof before the rains come, so I decided not to bother you. I'm sorry if that worried you. As you can plainly see, my health is very good today. Better than usual, in fact. I have been feeling better every day. Perhaps it has something to do with the knowledge that I have an exceptionally good roof over my head." She smiled again. "Since you have taken the time to climb down to check on me, however, and since it is almost time for lunch, would you like to take a break? I just happen to have some particularly good haddock stew, a gift from the pastor and his wife. I could offer it to you with chowder crackers and a couple of frosted brownies."

"Well, Miss Emma, you know how puny my appetite is. I reckon I could only put down two or three large bowls of that *chowdah*, with only three or four brownies--if you could spare that small amount, I'd be most grateful." Bobby grinned back at his friend as he sighed deeply with the relief of knowing she was all right. He found himself all too willing to play along with her mischievous mood.

Emma served iced tea with the sumptuous lunch, telling Bobby she would not give him beer until he was finished climbing on high for the day, since she was not willing to take responsibility for his slipping off and breaking a precious bone, thereby rendering himself unable to enslave himself to her for a prolonged length of time. They laughed and joked for an hour, until Bobby stated that if he did not get back to work, it would be a week before the roof could be finished, since the wind was picking up and ominous-looking piled-up bluish clouds were beginning to scoot quickly in from the west, signaling the onset of bad weather.

Bobby stapled the last shingle into place at four fifteen, just as small droplets were beginning to darken the newer light grey shingles. Tired but satisfied, he stored the tall ladder in Emma's barn and slung his tools in the rear of the truck, covering them with a heavy blue protective tarp and securing it from wind and weather with bungee cords.

"All done," he announced loudly as he cracked open the door. "You hear me, Miss Emma?"

"Yes, Bobby, I'm in the sitting room. Come on in, sit a while with me. And," She added, "bring yourself a beer if you'd like."

He found his friend comfortably settled in the oversized wing chair, her feet propped on a brocade-covered ottoman, a large album of photographs opened on her lap. "Pull up that chair, rest and drink, and share my past with me for a few minutes before you toddle on home," she offered.

"Happy to, m'lady Emma," he retorted as he complied.

The photographs toward the front of the album were mainly filled with family groups attending gatherings in the warm sun, the women in Sunday finery, seated and holding shade parasols, the men posed stiffly in the rear, the children caught in the midst of wriggles seated at their parents' feet. Following these bucolic scenes were a number of sober formal portraits of men, women and couples, and a few candid photos of young children playing or seated in large fancy perambulators.

A number of the sepia-stained portraits were relatives of Emma's including her mother, father, maternal grandmother and grandfather, grand aunts and uncles. One of the children was Emma, another, surprisingly, a brother who had died of influenza when he was four. Bobby made a mental note to ask Emma about this brother, since he had been under the impression that she had been an only child. The groups were mainly made up of members of her father's church, celebrating warm-weather holidays at large picnics held at local lakes or on the church lawn.

On a page by itself was a large, lovely soft portrait of Emma as a young woman. Her hair was long and curling around her face, her eyes the same bright hue, full of humor and life, her mouth just turned up at the corners in a slight smile, as though she harbored a wonderful secret.

"You were a lovely woman, Miss Emma," Bobby said softly. "I would have paid some serious attention to you if I'd been in your life back then."

Emma blushed. Then Bobby blushed. They looked at each other and laughed. "That is interesting, Bobby Parker," Emma remarked when they had calmed down. "Here we are, me an old hag of eighty-seven, you a young buck of thirty-nine, and we're turning red thinking how it would have been to have had a relationship when we were in our teens."

"I guess it's because somewhere deep down, I still feel like a young buck, in my prime," Bobby mused. "I guess maybe you do, too. There's still th'teenage dude buried in there somewheres, complete with all them young feelin's. So here I am, bein' embarrassed for fallin' for a nice lookin' lady in a picture that's prob'ly sixty some years old."

"It will be sixty-nine years ago this April. That picture was taken just before my graduation from high school, when I was looking forward to my new-found freedom, before preparing to become whatever I was to become." Her eyes misted suddenly. "Of course, I did not become much, in the many years which followed."

Emma sat silently then, her hands quiet on the page. Bobby glanced at her, aware that something had suddenly made her sad and wishing to comfort her, but not knowing how. He wanted to bring back the lightness they had enjoyed earlier. "Gettin' late; maybe I should go, Miss Emma," he said quietly.

Emma started out of her reverie and looked intently at him. "No, Bobby, I would like it if you stayed for a few moments, if you wouldn't mind. I have had it in my head to tell you some things about my life for some time, and since I seem to have begun, I would like to continue. That is, of course, if it is all right with you. Am I keeping you from anything or anyone? Are your children needing you?"

Bobby realized he had not told Emma the details of his trip to Portland with Bess and Dicky yesterday. That would have to wait, although he knew Emma would want to know all about the trip. "Nope; the kids are all fine and dandy jest now", he replied. "Dicky's workin' tonight, Bess is all set, we moved her in yesterday, and I talked with Becka Saturday to catch 'er up on the goin's-on. So I'm all yours for now, Miss Emma."

"Oh my, Bobby. I completely forgot that yesterday was the day you and Bess went to Portland. How uncaring of me. I never thought to ask you how your day went.

Been thinking too much about myself again, I fear. I am sorry." She reached over to pat him gently on the arm, shaking her head in dismay.

"Think nothin' of it, Emma. I'll be sure t'fill you in on th'trip when you're up to hearin' about it. It's not that important, anyways, and everything went just fine, so's you don't need to worry yourself about it." It had, too, he realized as he reassured the old woman. He and Dicky had picked Bess up after a huge breakfast at Sadie's Diner in Calais. She was pale but scrubbed and her clean, freshly brushed hair had been colored a sedate light brown to cover the psychedelic pink. Although her nails still showed evidence of having been bitten down, they were pink and free of the chipped black polish. She wore a new navy blue sweatshirt over a neat white blouse, jeans that were faded but without holes, and used, clean Reeboks. She seemed excited about her new adventure, and he and Dicky found themselves being swept along with her mood. They joked and made light conversation during the four-hour trip, and there were very few tears when they finally dropped Bess off at her new digs.

The facility was clean and modern, and the director welcomed Bess and her family warmly. They were treated to a tour of the building, which consisted of a main area with two large wings. One wing contained small pastel-hued private rooms with shared baths. The main area contained a large common room with comfortable furniture and a huge TV, a smaller dining room with four or five round tables set for lunch, and a spacious, well-equipped kitchen. The other wing of the structure held classrooms for those young women who were still in school, rooms for birthing and parenting classes, a well-stocked library/computer space, and a number of small rooms for counseling.

Dicky and Bobby stayed until Bess was settled in, then left her with hugs, promising to visit her whenever they could. The return trip was long, and it was close to midnight when the two men fell into bed exhausted. Bobby was sorry his daughter would be forced to live in that situation for any length of time, but he was relieved that she was safe, clean of drugs at least for the present and not too unhappy to be there.

Dicky had surprised him by being more sociable than his father had seen him, and by tearing up when he hugged his sister as they were leaving. "Love you, Bess," he had said as he held her close. "Love you back, Bro'," Bess had replied quietly. They clung to each other for what seemed a very long time. Bobby had not realized that there was such affection between the two, and the sight gladdened him. He smiled now, remembering their closeness.

As he thought about his children, Bobby suddenly realized he had not told Doreen about Debra's leaving. Suddenly, he had a strong urge to be with her, to let her know he was free. He pushed his feelings down as quickly as they surfaced, realizing that Emma needed him now, more than he needed Doreen. There would be time to be with her later. This thought comforted him immensely.

"Well, I do want to hear every bit of it, but I am rather anxious to begin to tell you some of these things which presently weigh heavy on my mind. But again, only if you are all right with it. We shall have a cup of tea one of these days and you'll fill me in on Bess's journey really soon, I promise."

"Okay with me, Miss E. Let it all rip, I'm listenin'. I am goin' to get me another beer, though, if it's okay with you."

"Fine with me, Bobby. There is strong cheddar cheese in the refrigerator door, and a box of crackers that are not too stale in the cabinet next to the sink, if you'd like. Actually, you could bring me some of that, also, and a glass of juice. We'll have snacks and hunker down to enjoy the rain on my new, wonderful roof."

SEVEN

"I don't talk much about my Thomas," Emma began. "I like to hold him in a special place inside, just beside my heart. I feel if I let him out more often, he would go away after a time, and I would be left with no memories. This is something I could not bear. Do you understand that, Bobby?" She added wistfully.

He nodded, said he thought he did. This understanding was very recent, and only because he happened to be developing a similar warm place inside in which a new love was beginning to bloom. Doreen Shanahan's lovely dimpled smile was snuggling into that small spot a little more comfortably each day.

"I want to talk with you about him, however," the old lady continued. "I feel comfortable with you, and feel you are trustworthy. You will not make a mockery of my memories. At least, I have hopes that you will not." Bobby started to protest, but Emma quickly stopped him with a finger placed on her lips. "I don't need affirmation from you, Bobby. I do need you to hear me out, however. Do you have time for this, just now?"

"Sure, Miss Emma, I ain't got nowhere to go. The weather is lousy, it's warm and comfortable in here, and I'm full of food and beer. Go to it."

"Be sure to stop me if you become too bored or sleepy to continue listening," Emma added. "Sure", Bobby answered. Suddenly, he was becoming curious, even excited as she prepared him for her story. What was this all about, he wondered? Why was Emma suddenly being so mysterious?

Emma took a deep breath. "Thomas and I had just over twenty-three years together. He came into my life when I was certain I would never love a man, and had prepared myself for a life as a single woman, settling for living in this small town forever, taking care of my parents as they aged, perhaps volunteering at the library from time to time, or at the hospital.

I fully expected to live in this old wreck of a house, blooming and withering along with the seasons until it was time for me to pass from this earth. Leading a small life, you might say. I was not unhappy with this existence, mind you. I do not seem to need what some do, excitement and diversion in my days. I have always loved to read, watch a fire burn itself out in mid-winter, listen to music.

"I was not quite a candidate for a nunnery, however. I did have a few beaus, in my youth. They were mostly young men from town who would ask me to school or church dances or accompany me on my long walks. One brave young fellow even went so far as to escort me to church on Sundays for a while. But I'm afraid I may have bored them, after a short time. You see, I do not have much to say if I do not feel stimulated, and I am not flirtatious in the least. I have never been able to pretend to state or feel anything but what I know to be my truth. I could not tell them I liked their company, or that they were charming or handsome, if I did not feel they were. And frankly, none of them were. In fact, they all rather bored me," Emma admitted, with a chuckle.

"So, after a period of trying to get me to be what they expected, these supposedly eligible young men went on to marry young women who were, I am sure, much better suited to them. And I, I am afraid, became one of those young women of whom it was said, 'she is attractive enough, and rather sweet, but destined to be an old maid, I fear.' I was a reputed bore, I imagine.

"Thomas came to town in the early spring, thirty-six years ago. I was in my fifty-first year. My father had passed away that winter at the age of ninety, while my mother was in the nursing home on Water Street, unable to care for herself and with no memory of me or her long life with my father. Come to think of it, Mother was just my age, that year. Eighty-seven. My, my. I am certainly glad that I did not inherit her tendency to loss of memories." Emma smiled wistfully, gazing into the distance. "Memories are such an important part of my life, these days." The old woman fell silent. After some minutes, Bobby wondered if she was finished with the story of her meeting with Thomas. Maybe the telling of the story was too difficult for her.

"You c'n always catch me up on y'r life some other time," he ventured. "Is it hard f'r you to talk about this?"

Emma started, realizing Bobby's presence. "No. Of course not. My mind was beginning to take itself far beyond my mouth. I would like to tell you this story. It is important to me."

"Fine with me, Miss E. Git on with it," Bobby smiled, relaxing into the sofa.

"My days back then were much as they are now; filled with twice-weekly walks to visit Mother, trips to the market for groceries or to the library to seek out my weekly read, an occasional luncheon with a church friend or dinner with the pastor and his wife. I was able to attend concerts in Portland twice yearly with the church, and I took a bus trip to Ellsworth regularly to replenish clothing or shop for the few Christmas gifts I gave.

"That particular day, I was planning in my mind the changes I would make in the kitchen garden for the upcoming growing season. The garden needed turning over for the spring planting, and I thought I might put in a few new wild rose bushes on the south side of the house, and perhaps a pansy bed or two to line the front walk. Such an exciting life, don't you agree?" Here, Emma chuckled and paused for a moment. "Such a lonely life, as I see it now," she added wistfully.

"But never mind, it was my life, and I took a certain satisfaction in it. There was a definite daily schedule which almost never varied, there was certainly very little stress, and I was a healthy, able woman who never became ill, and who would never want for a bed or a meal. That seemed enough for me, then. I must admit, however, that if I woke late at night, and could not regain sleep immediately, I would entertain certain thoughts. These thoughts excited me.

"I traveled beyond my world in these fantasies. Perhaps I would take a trip as far as Boston on a train, or even sail on a ship to some completely foreign port, Hong Kong perhaps. Or, I would buy a lovely car, and drive it wherever I pleased, investigating towns I had never seen. My parents never owned an automobile, you see. The town is small and self-contained, so they felt we did not need to burden ourselves with the expense of a vehicle. If something was needed which we could not find here, there was always a Sears and Roebuck catalogue. This would bring them whatever they wished, delivering it right to our door. And, since I lived a life so like my parents, I did not see the need for an auto, either.

"Contained within my list of fantasies was the love of a special man. In my dream, this man would come to town, a man who would actually admire me just as I was, and who would find my company so fascinating that he would agree to live in and share my world. There would be no need for flirtation with this man, since he would not appreciate coyness. We would merely have wonderful, straightforward conversation, sharing our lives and experiences with each other. Our souls would meet, and we would love. Of course, I did not know how we would love physically, since I'm sure you realize I had retained my virginity, and certainly did not entertain thoughts of bearing children in my advanced years. Perhaps this man would love me on a higher, more spiritual level, content with looking deeply into my eyes as we shared a meal, or holding my hand as we walked out.

"As I continued to develop this fantasy, I began to include in my walks past Main Street a trip to the dock, where I would sit and watch the boats come and go. Of course, these boats were mostly for fishing, manned by those who make a living on the sea. I was not interested in any of these men, weathered and smelling of daily catch. The man in my nocturnal dream was tall, tanned, dressed in soft clothing, had a wonderful welcoming smile and perhaps sailed in on a ship from an exotic, faraway place. I realized I was drawn to the docks in the hope that he would sail in as I waited, knowing I searched only for him.

"Sounds like pure silly rubbish, doesn't it?" She smiled. "But it was my fantasy, and it was all I had, then."

"It's what you had, Miss Emma. Sounds more like the dream of every young girl, to me," Bobby answered softly. "And guy, prob'ly. I'd like t'think my girls've had their own version of your dream. Us'lly, we jest settle for someone, 'cause we're lonely, or gettin old, or tired of waitin' for jest the right person to come along. Kinda like me and Deb, actually. After a time, neither of us was really satisfied with each other. But I don't think we thought much about it from the first. Chemistry is awful strong when you're young. I think lots of us settle for that, and sort of give up on our real dream person."

"I guess I am different from most," Emma continued. "I could never settle, as you say. I could not live with someone who would not accept my ways, or with someone whose ways I could not accept. I would rather have lived alone, and as you see I have, most of my life."

She sighed deeply. "Now. I need to finish this part of my story."

"On this particular day in early April it was cold and sunny. I needed to pick up groceries, and to see Mother. I bundled in my old wool coat and a warm hat and gloves, and as a last thought, threw on a bright red scarf, a long-ago gift from me to Father. He had never worn it, being the staunch conservative he was, but he could not discard a new thing. The scarf had hung on the back of the kitchen door for years. I spied it under the other dull-colored scarves, and decided the day warranted something bright.

"Mother noticed the color. She said, 'Who is this little girl in red? She's pretty,' and smiled. I reminded her that I was merely her mid-aged offspring, but she took no notice, instead reached out and stroked the scarf. I decided I needed to wear it more often. Perhaps I should give it to her. But something selfish in me could not let it go.

"After our visit I walked to the docks, and sat for some time watching the sea, deep blue-green today, with slight, wind-tossed whitecaps. After an hour I became too cold to sit, and set off for the grocery store. I still felt fine, but I admit there lurked within a bit of sadness that I did not seem to be able to walk off. Never mind, I would buy the groceries I needed and fix myself something delicious for lunch, perhaps some baked eggs with pan-fried potatoes. In the afternoon, I would turn over one bed in the spring garden.

"I bought potatoes, and headed for the dairy department with eggs on my mind. I was reaching for a dozen when Thomas spoke to me. 'That is a lovely color with those curls of yours.'

"Needless to say, I started, nearly dropping the potatoes. I spun around to see who had startled me. A tall dark-haired man stood there, his bright green eyes crinkled with laughter, his grin wide. And, I thought instantly, welcoming. I felt the heat of a blush coming from my chest and flooding my entire face. I, who had never in my awareness ever blushed at anything, not being the type.

"Sorry, I didn't mean to embarrass you," he said, becoming suddenly serious. "I needed to remark on your scarf, since it's the first hint of color I have seen in this God-forsaken town.

"Needless to say, I bristled. 'This town is not God-forsaken in the least,' I retorted quickly. 'I have lived here for over forty-seven years, and I have not found it to be forsaken. There are some souls who may not be aware that God is present, but I for one see lots of evidence of Him.' This from me, who rarely attended church. But I resented his instant judgment of us, you see. Of me, since it was my place to live.

"Thomas actually bowed. 'Please forgive me, I didn't mean to offend. I'm a big-city fellow, and actually I've not been in too many small towns. I did not mean to judge, just to comment. And that comment was rather stupid, I see now.

"'I tell you what, let's start over. I like your scarf. I like your auburn curls tumbling over it in the back. My name is Thomas. Thomas Manchester, like the city in England. I arrived this morning in my motorized sailing rig, up from Portland. I'm here for a period of time to interview fishermen and possibly their families. I'm filming a documentary about those who make a living from the sea, especially those on the East Coast from Cape Cod to Nova Scotia. Are you by any chance the wife or daughter of a fisherman?'

"Well, I must say I was startled into silence for a few moments. This man, this tall, wonderful looking man, had sailed in on a boat, and was actually speaking with me?

I must have had my mouth open, because he laughed again.

"'You look like you've seen a ghost. Believe me, I am totally mortal, and totally here, now.'

"'Oh, of course you are,'" I finally stammered. 'There are so few strangers in my life. You'll have to forgive me my lack of manners. My name is Emma Colridge, and no, I am neither the wife nor daughter of a fisherman. My father, who passed over in January, was the head loan officer at our small branch of the Bank of Bangor before he retired.'

"'I see,' he replied. 'Well, since I won't be interviewing you as part of this documentary, and since I would not like to think that this would be our only meeting, perhaps you would be so kind as to show me around town, with the idea of supplying me with knowledge of local customs.'

"I laughed. 'Well, that might take all of an hour. But of course, I would be happy to show you the sights of our village.' I need to state now, Bobby, that I was truly surprising myself. I was talking with this man as if we were old friends, and I felt strangely comfortable about it. It was as if I had stumbled into a waking dream.

"But I digress. Thomas then informed me he was staying in the Homeport Inn a few doors away, and that he had brought his mate with him, a man named Jonathan Brimmer, from Portland. Jonathan would stay until tomorrow, then return by bus to his family in Boston until Thomas finished his interviews here, when he would bus back to continue their water journey northward to Nova Scotia. While Thomas was here, he planned to travel by rental car to interview fishermen in the Ellsworth, Bar Harbor and Machias areas.

"'Would Mr. Brimmer like to come with us to see the town's marvelous sights?' I wondered.

"'No, Jonathan is not one for sight-seeing, nor for socializing. He is a man of the sea, deep and quiet. He prefers to walk for a while to regain his land legs, and to spend time alone, resting, today. He's anxious to get back to his family, and plans to leave early tomorrow. That's why I'm here, poking around the local market, looking for a newspaper, something to snack on, and a guide. And, it seems I've at least found the latter,' he added with a grin.

"And here, I did something else that was entirely unlike me. 'I was about to make myself baked eggs and potatoes for lunch,' I blithely stated. 'It's not much of a meal, and I'm not much of a cook, but if you'd like, you may join me.'

"Amazingly enough, he did. He bought his supplies, I finished my shopping, and we walked to my house as if we had done this every day for years, talking and laughing all the way. We ate, then we walked around town, stopping briefly at the inn to allow him to place a call to a garage in Ellsworth to arrange for a rental car for the following morning. We then returned to my house and sat, drinking tea and chatting and rocking on the front porch. Sunset was upon us when he prepared to return to the inn to route out Mr. Brimmer for dinner.

"As he left, he grasped my hand and squeezed it, saying that the afternoon had been wonderful, and that he would call me soon, to arrange to repay me for my kindness and take me to Ellsworth for dinner. As he walked away, he said, 'Thanks for being there today, and for being you.'"

Emma looked wistfully at Bobby. Her eyes glistened with tears. "That was the most amazing thing that had happened to me in my whole fifty-plus years. I sat in the dark for hours after he left, unable to move. I was tempted to give myself a hard pinch. The experience was so unlike any other, so surreal. Nothing in my life to that day had prepared me for it. It was my fantasy, materialized. I knew that if I slept, I would wake and realize I had been living a dream.

"This man, his purpose for coming into town and into my life, had surely been manufactured by my needy unconscious self. Experiences like this did not happen to ordinary people, and I was certainly an ordinary person. I had never done anything to deserve this experience. It must, therefore, be a dream.

"I finally slept, and woke to the telephone about nine the next morning. 'Emma? It's Thomas Manchester. Jonathan has just left, and I am fully ready to get on the road. Would you like to come with me to retrieve my car?'

"Of course I went. This was the beginning of our friendship, and it continued for twenty-three years." Emma sighed. "Bobby, I need to stop now, for a while. This unburdening has been relieving but very emotional for me," she said wearily. "I am tired, but I would like to continue to fill you in on my story soon. It is important because it has never been finished, and I need to end it before I pass on. I have a strong feeling that you will help me to finish this tale, Bobby," she added wearily. "Frankly, I had thought I would die without real closure until I met you."

"Wow. That sounds heavy, Emma. I don't know about this. Sounds like a packet of responsibility." Bobby shook his head. "I guess I'm ready to listen, at least. Whether I can help or not, I guess we'll decide later. I can see you're pooped, Miss Emma. I've gotta go, too. Gettin' late, gotta get home and call Doreen."

"I hope I have not overwhelmed you, Bobby," Emma said. "I will take things a bit at a time, and you certainly will want to hear all of the facts in order to decide whether you can help me. I will talk with you soon, and you be sure to give your Doreen my regards." She rose slowly and walked with him to the door. "Thank you, Bobby Parker, for being you," she said as she squeezed his arm. "I am thankful each day that we met."

Bobby bent and kissed the old lady's pale withered cheek. "Me too, Miss Emma," he whispered. "You get yourself some sleep, now. I'll see you in a few days."

EIGHT

"How are you, Bobby?" Doreen asked warmly. "It's nice to hear from you."

Bobby grinned on the other end of the phone. He warmed and tingled with the sound of her voice. He had not waited to take off his coat before calling her at the restaurant. "You wouldn't believe me if I told you how good I feel now, Doreen, jest hearin' you," he said.

"Well." Doreen paused. "You certainly do sound excited," she continued finally.

"I'm sorry, Doreen," Bobby sputtered. "I had a strange kinda day, and I been thinkin' about you all the way from Milltown. Thinkin' about your smile, and your dimple," he added, grinning again. "I need to see you, Doreen, to tell you a bunch of things that are happening," he finished. "Would it be okay if I picked you up after work tonight?"

"I'm actually through in a few minutes, Bobby. I was going to take a long bath and watch a rented movie. I guess we could get together, if you don't mind that I'm kind of worn out. It's been that kind of day."

"I won't keep you late, Doreen. I've got a hankerin' t'be with you. How 'bout I pick you up and we go to the 'Claw for a beer and a fish sandwich? We could find a quiet booth and talk for a while. That be okay with you?"

"I am starving, and I cannot even look at pizza. Cooking doesn't appeal to me tonight, either. So, alright, if I shorten the bath to a quick shower, I can be ready in about an hour. See you then."

Slightly over an hour later, Bobby and Doreen were comfortably nestled in one of the restaurant's deep booths, and had been served two mugs of pale foaming beer. Bobby settled back and heaved a deep sigh. "Y'don't know how good it feels, bein' able to set back and relax my screamin' bones," he stated happily. "And t'be sittin' across from the prettiest girl in Quoddy, at that. Maybe even in Washington County."

Doreen blushed a deep crimson. "Bobby, knock it off. You really love to embarrass me, don't you?" She smiled as she objected, however. Then, "How's Bess, Bobby? Did Debra ever get home to help you with her?"

"I know you're changin' the subject, and I guess know why. So I'm about to tell you a bunch of happ'nin's that could change things between us, Doreen. That's why I been so excited about gettin' together with you. To start, yeah, Bess is fine, and no, Deb did not help me with her. Deb didn't help anyone with anything. Except for helpin' Deb with Deb. She's basically a pretty self-absorbed human bein', as anyone who knows 'er will tell you."

Bobby then proceeded to share the recent events concerning Debra, his children and Emma Manchester. Three beers, a fish sandwich with fries, two pieces of blueberry pie and a mug of coffee later, he rubbed his full belly and sighed deeply. "So, Doreen my lass, what do you think of all that?"

Doreen had been mostly silent throughout Bobby's narrative, stopping him only to clarify a point here and there. Bobby found himself appreciating her listening skills immensely, since Debra had not been fond of listening to anyone but herself, or perhaps her friend Sissa, whose word seemed to be akin to God's. She put her coffee cup down now, and patted her lips with her napkin.

"God, Bobby. You've had quite a time of it, haven't you? Frankly, I don't know what to think. I've known you for a long time, since we were kids, and I always considered you a strong person. I couldn't quite understand why you and Deb got together, but I figured you did okay. Seems, from what you say, you didn't do well most of the time you were together. Sounds like it's a good thing, her leaving. Seems kind of shitty for your kids, though, not to have their mom any more. Though from what you say, I guess they never did have much of her. I can't imagine not lovin' your kids like crazy. Never having had them, I always thought if I did, I could never stand to see 'em hurting.

"I'm puzzled, though. What does all of this have to do with us, Bobby?" She looked at him quizzically.

"Well, since I'm sorta free, I kinda thought we could see each other sometimes--maybe even after a while more than sometimes. You think?" Bobby smiled at her. "I feel so good when I'm with you, Doreen. Comfortable, y'know? Like I could say anything. I have said things I ain't told anyone, t'you. Did you know that?"

"No, and I am flattered. But, Bobby, I need to remind you that you haven't asked me once if I have a life, and what my life is about. Seems it's all about you, since we first talked with each other. You think?"

Bobby realized this was true. The dream of a relationship with Doreen had been his dream. He had not asked once what she did before she came to her mother's aid at the restaurant, or even if she was married or living with someone. During the time they had been together previously, they had talked about his problems, with a minimum of time spent discussing her dad's death, her mother's health, and her job at the restaurant. Maybe she was gay; what did he know? He had simply assumed that Doreen would be there for him if he needed her, that she would work for her mother only until she recovered, and that the woman would be delighted to simply hand her life over to him when her mother was well.

It was Bobby's turn to blush deep red. "Jeez, Doreen, I'm sure sorry," he said sheepishly. "My life has been so damn' complicated lately, with Deb leavin, kids fuckin' up and all, I ain't taken time to think about another soul. I didn't think about you, except to want to spend time with you. Come to it, I don't know a damn thing about your life out of this town. I guess, for me, you're workin' for your mom while she was gettin' well, and when you was through, I guess I figgered you'd be up for grabs. And I wanted to do some grabbin' before someone else got t'you." He shook his shaggy head. "I'm truly sorry for that, Doreen."

Doreen threw her head back and laughed, the sound pealing out for all to hear. Couples in the surrounding booths craned to see what the joke might be. "Bobby Parker, you are something else," she chuckled. "I don't think I have ever thought of myself as being 'up for grabs', as you say." She stared at him intently, suddenly serious. "And, Bobby, you may be the most honest person I have ever met. There's nothing hidden in you, is there?"

"Guess not," he replied, not knowing how to interpret her sudden change of mood. "Is that a good thing or not, s'far as you're concerned?"

"As far as I'm concerned, that's a very good thing. I haven't met many people in my life I can trust. And I think I can trust you, Bobby. That is definitely a very good thing.

"And because it's a good thing, I guess I could fill you in on my life outside of Washington County, Maine. It's not much of a life, really. I work hard, cooking, just as I have since I arrived to help Mom. I don't have much time for socializing, and what little I do no one would consider very exciting. I've dated a few times; I've taken a few trips, including a nice cruise to Alaska. I have a couple of woman friends I see movies with, or sometimes we bike for a day, or hike one of the trails in the area. Life isn't bad, but a bit boring, I must admit."

She sighed deeply and continued, "And, I was married for a time. It was years ago, and it was not a very long or satisfying marriage. His name was James, and we cooked together, and fought together, for just over two years. We were young, he was very handsome and charming, and we enjoyed drinking together and enjoying each other's bodies during the sex we squeezed into our hours off. On that basis alone, we decided we couldn't stand to be apart, and got married.

"Of course, it did not work out. We continued to fight, then he began to drink more each week; it got so we never spent time together away from the restaurant. So much for the sex; it disappeared in just a few months. Less than a year after we married, we ended it. He moved to the west coast and is still there, as far as I know. Or care.

"I need to say, I don't feel I make a good wife for any man. I love to work, and when I'm not working I like to read or walk or even cook sometimes. I'm quiet and not very exciting, and I like my life organized and comfortable, without the tangles most relationships can cause."

She paused then, sighed again, and stared intently at Bobby, sitting quietly with her hands in her lap. After a pause that seemed to Bobby to last for an overly long time, he began to feel uncomfortable with the silence. He didn't know what to say, and didn't want to interrupt her train of thought with words which might, God forbid, continue to make this all about him. He was, however, becoming uncomfortable with her scrutiny and her silence. He began to squirm in his seat, avoiding her gaze.

She laughed, watching him. "You just can't keep still, Mr. Parker, can you?" she teased. "I didn't mean to make you uncomfortable. I guess I don't know where to go, from here."

"Jest continue bein' yourself, bein' honest," Bobby replied, relieved. "I'm doin' fine with what you're sayin'. Makes lots of sense, t'me. And it's lettin' me know who you are, and what you need." He took a long drink from his beer. "We got time, Doreen. I ain't goin' nowhere. We can always take this up some other time, we don't need to finish discussin' this tonight."

Doreen smiled. "This--this whole thing about jumping into a relationship-- scares me about you, Bobby. You love to be tangled. You just re-connected with me days ago, and here you are, wanting to tangle. You know everyone in town, and from what I've observed, everyone's your friend." She paused again, sitting back and lacing her fingers behind her head. "Well, not everyone is my friend. I am a private person, and have never had many friends or acquaintances. How could you have someone like me in your life? You'd be bored with me in no time, I'm sure."

She stopped again, and resumed gazing intently at him. "You through?" He asked tentatively after a few moments. Doreen nodded gravely.

"I guess you're right, about me needin' to be 'tangled'. Never thought of it that way. I've always been part of a big family, and I've known jest about everyone in town all my life. This is where I live, never lived no other place. This is where I work, most of the time. And yeah, I am what you might call an outward person." He drummed the scarred table in front of him with his fingers, gathering his thoughts.

"But all that don't mean I'm happy. Or comf'table. "S True, I always got someone t'talk with, someplace t'go. I kin go to

Mumma's to eat any Sunday. I kin go t'my daughter's or any of my friends' homes on a Friday night for a meal, a game, a beer and a visit. But for a real long time, I been one lonely guy. I ain't got that person in my life t' *be* with, if y'know what I mean. Bein' with, that's different.

"Bein' with means that person is there, when I git home. She's got food for me, don't need to be fancy, but somethin' besides a can of beans and a couple dried up hot dogs, or a pizza in a package I need to nuke before I kin eat. She's put some of herself into the house, maybe some nice curtains, or a comf'table chair, and she don't leave crap all over the place so's I can't find a place to sit, or dirty clothes leakin' from the washer in the hall all the way to the middle of the kitchen linoleum 'cause she ain't interested in washin' 'em jest now.

"I like to spend time with a woman, Doreen. I like to eat with 'er, and watch some TV with 'er, and maybe take a long walk or build a big fiah and jest sit and have a beer in front of it. I work hard, sometimes six days a week. I'd be happy jest to be next to a woman for a few hours a day. Silence don't bother me."

Doreen leaned toward him, cocking her head. "And what if the woman wants to work as much as you do?" she asked. "What happens to 'being there when I get home'? What if the woman isn't there, even for a couple of days, or what if she's tired from all the work; as tired as you are?"

Bobby leaned back, a puzzled look on his broad face. "Well, come to think on it, never gave that a thought," he pondered. "Never was a woman in my life who worked like I do. Deb worked a little, when she wanted somethin' for herself we couldn't afford, but it was mostly mornin's, and there she was on the couch eatin' corn chips and watchin' soap operas when I got home, bitchin' she was bone tired after two, three hours of work, no food around, no laundry done and the house lookin' like a hurricane hit it." He grinned. "I don't have nothin' against a woman workin'," he added. "I guess it's a state of mind, of bein', even. Not all women wanna live in a sty, do they?"

The last comment elicited a giggle from Doreen. "Of course not," she quipped. 'But when both people in a couple decide to have full time careers, all that needs to be worked out. You never said a word about work around the house you'd be willing to do. What did you do when you were fed up with the mess, or there was no food around?"

"Seems you'd like me to say I pitched right in and helped Debra," Bobby replied. "Right?" Without waiting for an answer he continued, "Well, I din't. I guess the way Mumma raised me, I thought if the wife was home, and the husband out, it was her job to keep the house runnin' right. If it wasn't kept right, I could either bitch about it or keep my mouth shut and put up with it. I chose the keepin' quiet. It saved a lot of unneeded blackness in the house.

"But," he added quickly, "that don't mean I ain't open to change. If a woman I'm with works a full time job, she should be able t'count on havin' help from me. I'd be fine with that. Lord knows I done enough of it when Deb took her trips with Sissa over the years."

Bobby suddenly stopped talking and shook his head. He peered at the woman across from him for a few silent moments, then reached over and took Doreen's hand. "This is all crap, anyhow," he stated bluntly. "If we're meant to get to know each other better, we jest will, and never mind worryin' who's gonna take care of who, later. I feel real comfortable with you, Miss Shanahan, and I would like to spend a lot more time with you. I like your quiet self, and I respect your need to be private. It warms me to think about bein' in your company. So, whethah we end up livin' under the same roof or not, that's to be decided by both of us, when we're both ready. At least, that's the way I feel. I jest want to take it from today, to know you better. How 'bout you?"

Doreen's eyes were bright with unshed tears. "You are sweeter than any one person I have ever known, Bobby Parker. I like you a lot. And I guess I could get used to spending more time with you, if that's what you think you want. I don't really know what I want, today. But I do feel comfortable with you, also, and I could like looking forward to more time together, for now. I will be here for another two weeks, at least. Then, I need to make a decision. My job may not be waiting for me if I don't go back in two weeks. Mom wants me to stay here, to work full time for her. She's planning to cut her hours when she comes back, then maybe to retire in a year or so. I need to decide if it's what I want, moving back here. It wasn't the happiest place I ever lived."

Bobby was surprised. Doreen had never told him she was not happy to be back in

Quoddy. Then, he had monopolized all of her time with his problems, as she had pointed out. "You need to catch me up on all that sometime," he said. "I need t'know why you weren't happy, and if I can do anything to fix that. Meantime, we need to get some sleep, or neither of us is gonna be good for nothin' tomorrow. "I'm happy that we can be together more, even if it is for two weeks," he added as they prepared to leave.

Two weeks was not much time, but he would use it the best he could, he vowed. This woman had become important to him, important enough so he ached within at the thought of the loss of her, long before he needed to face it. He would not lose her, he promised himself.

NINE

Bobby woke on Tuesday with two important realizations; he had taken steps to be closer to Doreen Shanahan, and he had allowed his work to accumulate to an overwhelming load. There was a deck to construct and another to shore up, windows and screen doors to replace, two roofs to patch, and a bedroom to add for one needy family of four who were expecting twins in the next month. He felt warm and fuzzy with the first thought, and panicked with the second. He had enough work piled up to keep him from Doreen and Miss Emma for months.

He needed to squeeze time from his overwhelming workload to be with Doreen, and to visit Emma. Perhaps he and Doreen could make time on Sunday for a picnic in Acadia and a visit to Milltown. Bobby couldn't help grinning as he recalled that he must keep it in his mind that Doreen was also working hard, and that their time together needed to be negotiated. "Strong, sweet woman," he mused. "Great."

Over three sunny side up eggs with bacon and as many hotcakes at Nan's Diner on Water Street, he labored over his schedule and made calls from his cell phone. Not so long ago, Bobby had resented owning or even needing the machine, but he now realized that having the bloody thing may be good, especially if he wished to contact Doreen from work during the day. Doreen seemed happy to hear from him; she was getting ready for her long day at the restaurant, but she would be happy to arrange time to be with him on Sunday. She was also free on Thursday night for dinner.

He told her he would cook, for a change. "Didn't know you could cook, Bobby," she said lightly.

"I ain't the best, but I grill a mean burger," he replied jauntily. For him, dinner at his place meant they could be comfortable, without the stares of others. He thought she might appreciate that. She did.

Three jobs were then lined up, enough work to keep him busy until late Friday afternoon. If the work was not finished, he would work half of Saturday. He also needed to squeeze in an hour to meet Joey for a quick beer Saturday afternoon. His friend had left umpteen messages on his machine, angry that he had not kept in touch lately. It had been hard for Bobby to keep up a social life, what with trips to Milltown and seeing Doreen, never mind the work he needed to do to keep food on the table. He did decide that the least he could do was meet Joey at the 'Claw and do a quick catch-up. Joey must know about Deb by now; everyone else did. And if they didn't, the whole town was surely aware that Bobby Parker had escorted that good-looking Doreen Shanahan to the 'Claw last night.

After Joey had soundly cursed him for not returning his calls, his friend reluctantly agreed to their meeting. Bobby then called Emma, to ask if she would mind if he and Doreen came to see her Sunday afternoon. Emma would be delighted, and could she offer them supper? Bobby assured her they would be full of picnic, and that tea would be fine.

Emma seemed relieved, he realized as he sipped coffee, contemplating the dead phone. He realized that the old woman did not like to cook, or to clean for that matter. And she had never held even a part-time job. She did keep her home neat, he noted. And he felt comfortable in her kitchen, dusty as it was, with its worn old table and bright curtains and flowers. "Guess there's many kinds of women in the world," he mused. Maybe Doreen was right, it would take two people to work out the running of a house. And a relationship.

TEN

Following work on Thursday, Bobby picked up fresh-ground hamburger and buns from The IGA, along with two large potatoes, a bag of ready-made salad greens complete with dressing, a package of brownies, coffee ice cream, cola and beer. He had not checked with Dicky to see if he would be around for dinner, so he bought enough to include him.

The hope that his son would be there to meet Doreen took him by surprise. He could feel just the opposite, rather guilty because Deb had been gone for just a few days, and here he was, already dragging another woman into their lives. He and Debra had not loved each other for as long as he could remember. This woman he was bringing home tonight was the first for whom he had felt anything in many years. He really wanted Dicky and his daughters to meet her, perhaps to know her as they had never known their mother.

"Hey Dad," his son called from the recliner where he was listening to a rap CD with headphones. Bobby could hear the bass beat across the room. So much for his son's hearing. It would be shot by the time he was thirty. Dicky's legs draped over one arm of the chair, and a textbook was open casually on his lap, but his head was lolling back and forth with the music. "You got food? I'm starved."

"Hey yourself," Bobby replied, pulling the headset from his son's ears. "Yeah, got burgers and stuff, but we're not eatin' for about an hour. I'm gonna grill burgers and make some cheese baked potatoes, and we're havin' company."

Dicky bolted to his feet, unceremoniously dropping the book on the floor. He pranced around the room, finally clapping a friendly hand on his father's shoulder. "Cookin', hey? Makin' your famous cheese baked, hey? You bringin' a date to meet your kid? That great-lookin' blonde works at Shanahan's?" He grinned.

"How'd you know about Doreen?"

"DO-reeen," Dicky smirked. "Ain't that a sweet name for a sweet thing?"

"Shut it, Dicky. I mean it. How did you find out I was seeing her?"

"Oh, come on Dad. This town's atom-size. A couple guys from school were in the 'Claw last night, plus the waitress is a part-time teacher's aide. Lots of guys from school are over eighteen, they go there all the time. You really think you can keep a secret from anybody in Quoddy?" With that, he resumed prancing around the living room, chanting "Bobby's got a girl, Head's in a whirl, Bobby's in love, Puttin' on the move," in a rap beat.

Bobby watched his young son for a moment, then roared with laughter. "Mighta known," he gasped when he could speak. Then, "You okay with this?" he asked, serious now. "I need to know, Dicky. Been such a short time since your Mom left."

"It's your life, Dad," the boy replied. "Ain't mine. I ain't had a mother for a lot longer than a couple weeks. Kinda used to not havin' one by now. If you want to have a woman, that's your business. Is she a good cook?"

"Only had her pizza, so can't judge jest now," Bobby stated. "Says she is. Why?"

"Well, I figure if she moves in, it'd be good to have a decent meal now and then, somethin' other than hot dogs and corn chips and canned beans." Dicky shrugged. "But, if she can't, she's sure easy to look at, so I guess it don't matter."

Bobby explained that Doreen was just coming for dinner, she didn't even live in town, and far as he knew, she was planning to return home in a week or so. "I'd like it if she stayed a spell, even for good, and I'd like us to see each other a lot more. I've let her know all that, so now it's for her to decide," he added. "She's got a life outside of Washington County to live. She ain't decided if she'd like to come back here. And I ain't plannin' to leave. So that's where it is, for now."

Doreen arrived a short time later, bearing a six-pack of imported beer and a bottle of California red wine. Bobby grilled burgers, Dicky stayed to eat, then left with the carload of young people who honked and yelled for him shortly after dinner. Bobby and Doreen sat on the wide pine bench on the porch, sharing a voluminous wool blanket as they watched stars emerge by the millions in the clear blue-black sky, drinking good dark beer and musty Cabernet and talking long into the night.

It was close to midnight when Doreen rose and stretched. "I need to get back. It's been a long day...nice, though." She turned and smiled. Bobby rose to meet her. He reached out to touch her hair. "Lovely. You are just plain lovely." He leaned into her, wanting her sweetness. Doreen stiffened.

"Not yet, Bobby Parker. I'm not quite ready for that much closeness. It scares me a little...you scare me. I need to get used to your way of being with me." She gave him a quick peck on the cheek and ran to her car. "I'll think a lot about us tonight," she said as she opened her car door. "And I will also give some consideration to moving back to the county. We can talk some more tomorrow". She drove off quickly, spraying small rocks in her wake.

Bobby grinned as he dropped his jeans and shoes beside his bed and pulled the covers over his head. Before he drifted off to sleep, he pictured Doreen humming and smiling as she drove carefully back to town, perhaps making plans for packing and moving into his life.

ELEVEN

Sunday dawned clear and barely warm enough to consider an outside picnic. Bobby decided they could chance it if they were able to locate a thoroughly sunny spot, and if the wind was kind, and remained a light breeze. He picked Doreen up at ten, and they followed Route One through Machias, Harrington and Cherryfield, and finally turned into Acadia National Park in Winter Harbor. Since it was mid-spring and the trees were not even considering leafing out until late May or even mid-June unless the weather was fully cooperative, the traffic in the park was sparse. Small mounds of snow were still visible in shaded areas, and small patches of ice were still mirrored in wet spots by the side of the road.

The bay was deep azure and fairly calm, sporting small whitecaps offshore. Although they spotted a sail or a small fishing boat as they rode, the water seemed as sparsely populated as the land. As they slowly traveled the narrow road that circled the park, they stopped now and then to exclaim at a spectacular ocean view. They finally parked the truck in a bare clearing beside the road, and hiked until they found a relatively warm, sheltered clearing a short distance from the water.

An hour later, after packing up the remains of lunch and leaving it in the cab of the truck, they wandered leisurely on one of the paths beside the ocean, holding hands and rubbing their shoulders together, enjoying the crisp air, the beautiful sights around each bend and each other's company.

Bobby had not been happier in his life, he thought as he watched this beautiful woman bending to pick a spiny pinecone souvenir from its nest of brown needles, or reaching to retrieve a large withered oak leaf which had clung tenaciously to its dried branch through the long winter. Doreen was wearing faded jeans and a bright red wooly jacket, with a striped cap pulled over her red-blonde curls and comfortable walking boots. Bobby had never seen anyone so lovely.

He needed to pull her close, to kiss her, tell her how he felt. He found he couldn't. He turned her gently to him, stroking her smooth cheek, running his finger along the line of her dimple. "I can't find words t'tell you what I feel," he whispered. "Dunno why that is."

"I know. It's too—big right now, isn't it. I feel larger, wider inside, like there's light in me, and it's expanded somehow. And it's so good to be with you, Bobby. I have never felt so comfortable with another soul, I swear." Doreen pulled his beard playfully. "I love your beard, and your shaggy head," she giggled.

"I could shave it if y'want," Bobby said. "I don't take very good care of m'self these days. I prob'ly need a haircut bad, and at least a trim on this thing," he added, tugging on his beard.

"You are just fine, the way you are, Bobby Parker," she retorted. "Don't change a hair for me, not if you care for me..." she smiled as she mouthed the words to the old song. "Wish I could sing, but I can't worth a damn," she finished.

Bobby gave her a quick hug. "Hate to break up this great party, but it's startin' t'get cloudy and too cold to be out much more, and we gotta get to Emma's soon if we're gonna have time enough for a decent visit. That all right with you?" He kissed her then, on the tip of her nose. "Yep. Gettin' cool. Your cute little nose is fast becomin' a cute little ice cube."

Doreen laughed. "Race you to the car!" She cried as she trotted off, Bobby jogging behind her. When they climbed into the truck, she was panting. "I'm out of breath, and out of shape, for sure," she wheezed. "I need to find me a gym."

"You're in great shape, far as I can see," Bobby said, reaching over to squeeze her hand. "Thanks for this, Doreen," he added. "I ain't had such a good time in don't know how long. Maybe never," he mused as he started the truck.

Doreen turned to him. "Okay, now I'm ready for that kiss, Bobby Parker." She leaned over to kiss his cheek, and Bobby turned to her mouth. "You really take my breath away," he murmured into her soft hair. "Me, too", she answered. Then she took a deep breath.

"About four o'clock this morning I made a decision," she stated. "I'm going to take over Mom's restaurant. It's what she wants, and it's probably what I want. I hope it is, at least. It will take me about three months to make the move and the change. I'm scared to death, but I don't want to leave you here, alone. I like your company. I know it's been such a short time since we've been seeing each other, but that doesn't seem to matter, at least today. I feel like more when we're together—and I like that feeling.." She hugged Bobby hard.

"One more thing.' she added. "And it's an important one. I don't want to hear any talk about bedding down with you until you and Deb are final. I won't sleep with a married man, no matter how far gone that marriage is. I won't change my mind about that, so don't be tempting me, 'cause it won't work. Understand?"

Bobby nodded. "Yep; I hear you, loud n' clear. I will warn you, though, I'm gonna try t'change y'r mind."

"You can go for it, but I'm pretty stubborn." Doreen grinned. "Whew; I'm glad that's off my chest. Let's go to Emma's."

Emma welcomed them with cookies and tea. They visited for over an hour, filling the old woman in on the good time they had on their picnic, and the plans they had begun for their future, all of which delighted her. Conversation on the return trip was devoted entirely to Emma, with Doreen chatting about her quickness of mind, her spirit and her agility for her age.

"No wonder you like to spend so much time with her, Bobby," she remarked at one point. "She loves you, that's clear as glass, and she appreciates so much all you do for her." And, a few minutes later, "Isn't it wonderful you came along to rescue her last winter? Imagine, you never would have met if she hadn't fallen. I think that's so special, so serendipitous." Of course, Bobby then needed to know what 'serendipitous' meant. When she explained, he agreed. "She is pretty special to me, I know that. I don't think I woulda had the courage to run after you, hadn't been for her," he added.

"Well, then, I have something to thank her for, too," Doreen stated. "I hope I get a chance to do that, some day."

"Of course you will, hon. When you git back, we kin go see her regular'."

"She's so old, Bobby. When you're that old, who knows how many days and months you'll be around. Every day must be a gift, for her."

"That's what she says, exactly," Bobby answered. "But she's pretty healthy. I 'spect she'll be around for a good long time yet."

"She says she needs to be around until your work together is finished," Doreen mused. "What's that about? Is she talking about her house?"

"That, and another project she keeps hintin' she wants me to do for her, involvin' her dead husband. Don't know what is yet, but I'll keep you posted."

"Mys-terious." Doreen teased. "Very mys-terious."

"Hmm. Only mystery at th'present is how I get home after I drop you off. I'm so beat I could park by the roadside and sleep till mornin'." He yawned widely.

"If I could make it home Thursday night with all that good wine in me, you can make it home tonight," She quipped.

INTERLUDE: The Author

Mothering is different when you have two children in school full time. So many hours to myself; I feel like a large cat suddenly released from its cage into the wild. It hesitantly pokes its nose out into the vast space beyond its confinement, picking its way along, sniffing new aromas, feeling the firm earth under its feet. Finally, there is the unbelievably expansive feeling of finally being unfettered, and it bounds gleefully into the forest.

There is also an underlying fear of the unknown, so it probably bounds for a few seconds, then stops to take stock of its surroundings again, to assure itself that it is safe. There is, for a time, a certain yearning to return to the small protected place it left, but it knows deep in its intuitive mind that this is no longer a possibility.

As a single parent, my children were constantly in my life for all those years before Stevie started school. Now, I have seven hours each day--seven precious hours to use exactly as I wish. I love it. I have used the time to re-connect with Gramma

Gianni and other woman friends at long, conversational lunches, or to walk leisurely around town, alone, enjoying the crisp fall weather and noticing any changes which have taken place while I was involved with diapers, playground time and supplying constant amusement and structure to my offspring.

Of course, I have also taken advantage of this opportunity to increase my writing. I am now meeting every two weeks with a small group of aspiring authors from the county. We bring our work to share and critique each other. I hope it's making me a better writer, although I sometimes feel I've begun to write more for other eyes than mine. Need for approval is never far away.

Lately, I have been thinking that it might be best for me to just write the words roiling around inside, and keep them safe for myself rather than exposing them to the criticism of others. I like the group, and they all seem to be pretty good writers, but I am faced with the dilemma of absorbing their styles, and losing my own. So I haven't brought any of Bobby's story to the group. I've stuck instead to some journal writing, or attempts at short stories.

This writing of Bobby Parker's story is so new for me, so different from any project I have taken on in the past. It feels private and vulnerable-- a small, sheltered bird about to venture from its safe nest. I guess I'd like it to have its own, unique experience as it discovers the world. And now that Bobby has shared his complete story with me, it is especially important that I write it well, in my own voice.

I do enjoy sharing the process with Bobby and Doreen (and of course, Sharkey). Our times together continue to be great, and the two of them have never failed to appreciate any progress I might have made, no matter how small. I know Bobby gets impatient to have me finish, but patience and restraint are two of his virtues, so he continues to put up with the interference of the bullshit that's part of my life.

After I've caught them up with the new pages I feel like Hemingway, with the feedback I get from them. There were times I couldn't write more than a few pages a month, what with kid problems and other work, the kind that actually paid. And after I broke up with Irv in late August, I was kind of out of it for a few weeks.

I didn't realize how much energy I had invested in that relationship until I didn't have it any more. After all, I had shlepped down to meet him somewhere in Hancock County almost every Friday night for eighteen months. It left a hole in my social life, let me tell you. And of course, not a small amount of frustration over the lack of good sex.

But it's been a couple of months now and I'm over it, and thinking it's going to be better that I stay home on those early winter or spring Friday nights when the temperature dips down suddenly, and the roads are covered with a thin coat of ice after a spell of Maine's famous freezing rain. There were some nights I didn't know if my kids would be half-orphaned as their mother slid around that curve in Black's Woods into Tunk's Lake at four a.m. That would leave B.S as their surviving parent. We can't have that, for sure.

I actually had a date last week. One of my old high school buddies, Sam Cardiff, got divorced recently. We met up at the park on a glorious October Saturday. He was doing the divorced-dad thing, taking his daughter for play and ice cream on his day off. He looked cold and miserable, sitting on a bench, trying too hard to keep his attention riveted on an over-active three-year-old.

I plunked myself down beside him and told Stevie to keep an eye on little Chelsee (what's with that name, anyway?). I promised him pizza and a rented movie if he left us alone for a half hour and if he returned Chelsee in one piece. After a couple of "Jeez, Ma's", he actually took her hand and off they went to the slide and climbing gym the Elks had built for the kids two years ago. It was near enough so we could keep an eye on him when he put Chelsee on the tot's slide and swing.

Sam shot me such a grateful-puppy look, it would have broken your heart. We chatted, catching up on the years it had been since we'd seen each other. Sam had gone to college in Massachusetts for an MBA, thinking to join his dad and two brothers, managing the financial end of their plumbing business. While he was completing his degree, he balanced the books for a law firm in the city. He met and married Claudia, a Boston woman and made the grave mistake of bringing her here. She hated it. Period. And, she never let Sam forget it. After untold arguments and one kid who was supposed to fix everything, she went back to Boston.

I told Sam it reminded me of someone I was writing about.

"I didn't know you were a writer," he said.

"I didn't either, until a year or so ago," I replied. "I've always kept journals and noted ideas for short stories, but never took myself seriously. I was banging out a couple of articles a month for the paper and a newsletter for the extra cash, when this person asked me to write this story for him. It intrigued me, so I decided to do it."

"Wow, I'm impressed. Anyone I know?"

"Probably. I'm not talking about it until it's finished. The person may get it published if it's good enough, or not. He hasn't decided yet. He just has this need to see it written."

"Oh. Well, if his story is as miserable as mine, I'd like to meet him sometime. Maybe we could get soused together and commiserate."

"He doesn't need to get soused over his problem any more. You won't either, some day. I know you feel like hell now, but it doesn't last. You'll be fine; it just takes time. I recently broke up with a guy I've been seeing for a while, too. It sucks, but life goes on.

"Thinking on it, maybe I'll get soused with you." I gave him a little punch on the shoulder. "Just kidding; getting soused isn't my thing any more, either.

"By the way, if Claudia's back in Boston, what are you doing with Chelsee?"

"She didn't take her daughter with her, loving mother that she is. Felt a kid would interfere with her career. She's a paralegal; we met at the firm I worked for," he added. "My mom usually takes care of her. I relieve her on Saturdays and Sundays. She's in a pre-school program at the Congo Church two mornings a week, so Mom gets a small break there. I feel guilty for dumping a small kid on her at her age, but she keeps telling me she's okay with it.

"Claudia's only called the poor kid twice since she left", he added sadly. "Whatta gal."

"Sounds just like ol' B.S.," I returned. That led to our continuing to share our woes regarding lousy ex-spouses until Stevie came back with Chelsee.

"This was good", Sam said. "I haven't had anyone to vent to. Hope I didn't bend your psyche too much."

"Fine with me," I answered. Then I did something entirely out of character. My character, that is. "Would you like to come over for dinner some night?" I almost choked on the words before I got them out. "I write

Monday, Wednesday and Friday mornings, so that's out, but Thursday's okay, or Saturday. And it'll be real casual, probably involve kids," I hastened to add.

"Sounds nice, but why don't we just go out for a meal instead. Less trouble." He grinned at me.

"Whew. I don't usually feed someone I hardly know, expose them to my kids and all," I said. "Sure, let's go out. It'll be fun. And a relief", I added, grinning back. Sam plopped his tired daughter on his shoulders, I grabbed Stevie's hand, and, waving at each other with our free hands, off we went in opposite directions.

We saw a fairly good movie in Calais, then had a great meal at the Chandler house. As dates go, it was better than average. We found things to talk about that didn't involve ruined marriages or the burdens of single parenting. We even laughed a lot. Turns out he has a sense of humor, likes kids, *and* talks about something besides him. Nice. We agreed to do it again, soon. Maybe I would get the courage up again and offer to feed him, the next time.

3

The Opus

ONE

Doreen left for New Hampshire in mid-July, a couple of weeks after her mom was able to prove to her that she had recovered enough to run her business full time, and Bobby found himself buried in local work for almost a month. There was no time for travel to Milltown to continue the work at Emma's. If Bobby let jobs slide too long he would lose money, and his clients might search for someone else. There were too many good carpenters in Washington County to allow him that freedom, especially during the summer, when exterior work must be completed before it became too cold to be outside for sustained periods of time.

Bobby called the old lady often, both to make sure she was all right, and to assure her that he would be back soon. He was worried he may not be able to keep his promise to finish her house before the cold returned. The roof repair was completed, the front door and stoop replaced, the front shutters repaired, sanded and painted. He had chipped the many coats of paint from most of her windows, allowing her to open them to summer breezes for the first time in years. He hoped to sand and paint the south and west sides of the house before going inside for the winter. When that task was completed, he could concentrate on interior repairs.

Before Doreen left, she and Bobby had spent some of their time together acquainting themselves with family. Doreen's mother invited them for an evening playing pinochle and introducing Bobby to Chianti wine and real lasagna, both of which he loved. Debra had always served lasagna as she served all entrees, from frozen boxes. Bobby had never experienced alcohol other than light beer. They also visited Bobby's family for barbeque on the Fourth, where Doreen re-acquainted herself with Bobby's mother and his siblings, complete with spouses and offspring, and met his daughter Becka and her small family.

"Whew", she sighed when that day was over. "You have a huge family. Hard to get to know in one afternoon. It'll probably take me years to learn all their names."

"That's okay, we only get together once or twice a year", Bobby countered. "I don't even get to see Becka much. She and Jared are plannin' to move to Portland one of these days, so I'll prob'ly see her even less."

"I heard. She told me they're almost ready to go. Another couple of months and they'll have enough saved to rent either a two-bedroom apartment or a little house. She's real excited to get out of here, isn't she?"

"She told you that? Wow, she doesn't talk about stuff like that to anyone. Even Mumma doesn't know her business. She musta liked you a lot." He grinned. "Of course she did. I do."

His mother had liked Doreen, also. She actually pulled him aside during the gathering, dragging him into the kitchen where they could be alone. "She's a nice girl, Bobby," Mumma observed. "You gonna divorce Deb?"

"Jeez, Mumma, I dunno, it's kinda soon to be thinkin' about that. Deb's jest outa the house."

"She ain't comin' back, Bobby. You know that. You better do somethin' about it soon, 'fore you lose that one. She's a keeper." Mumma cuffed him playfully on the arm. "I mean it, y'know. You deserve better than that bitch you been puttin' up with all these years."

Bobby was stunned into silence. That speech was more than he had ever heard from his quiet mother. Finally, "I'll give it some thought, Mumma," he sputtered. "But I gotta wait a while 'til Deb gets settled."

"Always thinkin' about the other, never take care of yourself," Helen muttered almost to herself as she fished another bowl of potato salad from the refrigerator. "Take after your mumma." She grinned at him as she scurried from the kitchen. Bobby stood rooted to the floor, amazed by his mother's remarks for a few moments, then took a deep breath and followed her to the yard to re-join the crowd.

The Sunday before she left, Bobby and Doreen traveled to South Portland to see Bess. Bobby could now talk with her by phone, and she was anxious to see him. She knew about Debra's relocation to the area, but had not tried to contact her since she had arrived in the city. Said she was not ready for the confrontation she was sure would ensue when her mother and she finally connected.

"She'll blast me out for a couple hours for the drugs and gettin' prego, then I'll blast her out for leavin'. It's not worth it", she decided. "I'm a pregnant woman, I need to keep my stress level low." Bobby smiled at her phrasing. She must be taking in some of the teaching she was receiving at the home.

Bess liked Doreen, as Bobby knew she would. She had seen her at the restaurant once after Doreen had taken over for her mother. "You make better pizza than your mom", Bess offered shyly. Doreen laughed. "She uses her same old recipe every time. I need change, so I switch it around some days, use three or four recipes I found in books stashed away in her kitchen. We brought some uncooked for you. I hope you can eat them. We brought enough to share. Just freeze them until you're ready for them, then follow the directions on the wrapping."

"Can I eat pizza?" Bess grinned. "I'd eat it every meal if I could. They're always forcin' salad and fruit and stuff on us here. I'm gettin' used to it, but I miss my junk food bad." She grinned. "I am gettin' more healthy, though," she added. "And I know it's good for the kid when I eat good.

"I'm also real fa-at," she added as she stuck out her rounded belly. Over four months pregnant now, Bess was just beginning to show. She did look more healthy, Bobby admitted. Her face had filled out, her color was good and her hair was finally her own color, a soft auburn. She smelled clean and young when they hugged. He was pleased that she had chosen to come here to make her decision about her baby. She seemed content, the place was clean and attractive, her roommate Kath, a very pregnant teen from Skowhegan, was friendly and outgoing. Here was one kid he didn't need to worry about for a while, at least.

"What's she going to do with her baby?" Doreen asked on the trip home.

"Dunno," Bobby replied. "We're not s'posed to talk with her about it, she's gettin' counselin' and they say that'll take care of it."

"What if she chooses to keep it?"

Bobby looked hard at Doreen. "I don't wanna think about it, or talk about it now, if you don't mind, hon," he said. "It feels far away for now. I just wanna enjoy it that she's safe. Okay?"

"Okay. But we will talk when it's time, right?"

"Right."

TWO

Emma met him at the door early on a hot, cloudy Monday morning in middle August. "Well, it's about time, Bobby Parker. You've been gone much too long, in my opinion." She frowned at him, but he saw at once the sparkle in her bright eyes.

"Well, I was chasin' othah wimmen for a time," my deah," he countered, broadening his already heavy accent. "One wanted a new porch, anothah needed me to replace her roof, the third one jest needed me to replace a couple soffits and shore up her foundation. I was busy to the max," he finished as he leaned down to plant a light kiss on her cheek. "Missed you, though, I gotta say," he added.

They peered intently at each other. Emma sensed a certain lightness she had not been aware of in Bobby. Bobby noticed a frailty he had not seen before in Emma. Neither commented on their findings. It was enough for now that they were together again.

"So where d'you want me t'start?" Bobby wondered. "I thought mebbe I'd paint today, since it's not sunny. Ain't s'posed to rain, neither. Too hot in the sun, paint dries too fast and don't go on right. We still gonna go for white?"

"White will be fine, Bobby, but I really need to talk with you, also. I have another job I would like you to do, aside from the work on the house. I know the house is important, and I also know you have a need to finish outside before the snow flies, but this other thing is of much greater importance to me." She smiled, rather sadly, Bobby noticed. "Would you mind if we discussed it later?"

Bobby was silent for a few moments, considering Emma's proposition. "I wanna talk with you too, Emma, but your house is really needin' some paint. And the day is jest right to paint it. How 'bout this? I do one side before three, then we talk. I ain't got nothin' to be home for, so we kin take our time. But I really need to do your paintin' today."

"I hear you, Bobby. I have spent the past month sitting and thinking, ruminating in my own juices really, while you have been working your buns off making life better for those other 'wimmen' of yours. I must realize that you have my best interests at heart, and that it is a very large heart. We will meet then, at three."

Bobby looked more closely at the old woman. "You really okay with this?" he said.

"Yes, of course, I am just a stubborn old bird and I saw things my way. But I now see the situation from your perspective, and I fully understand what needs to be done. Go, purchase white paint, Bobby. I will read and nap and have some lunch with you, and we will talk later. Go now," she insisted, shooing him out with impatient fingers. "Get paint."

Bobby went, wondering how their banter had suddenly turned so serious. Something was going on with his friend. He wondered what the "other job" entailed. That made him a little nervous. However, whatever she needed from him would have to wait, because he did need to get paint onto the west side of the house.

It was just three when Bobby came into the kitchen after storing his ladder in Emma's barn. Because the weather was cooperative and there were only four windows to contend with, he postponed lunch, and managed to scrape and paint the entire side of the house in just six hours.

Emma sat at the table, drinking tea. "You must be starved, Bobby," she said. "Lunch is in the fridge, along with your beer."

After wolfing down two thick ham sandwiches, a bag of potato chips and two bottles of beer, Bobby refused dessert and declared that he was sated enough to talk. "You're chompin' at the bit over somethin', Miss Emma. I did get that side finished, so we got time to catch up."

"Let's go into the parlor where we will be more comfortable," Emma suggested. Bobby chose the large leather side chair with the ottoman and Emma settled into her wing chair, propping her small feet on the embroidered hassock. "I am so sorry to drag you into this now," she began. "But the time has come to do something about it before it is too late."

Emma sighed deeply. "Let me preface the explanation of my needs with the fact that I visited my physician last Friday for a yearly examination. His news was not the best. He states that my heart is not giving its all to this ancient body, and that I need to be more careful in my comings and goings. He then supplied me with a very expensive medicine, which I must take, appalling though it is. He says that without it, my time on this mortal soil might be severely limited.

"I have decided to take his advice, but only because of the unsolved dilemma in my life. It is a problem I have put on the back burner since shortly after my Thomas passed."

The old lady paused and peered intently at Bobby, who was clearly undone by her news. "I see from your totally revealing demeanor that I've upset you, Bobby. I am sorry, but you need to come to terms with it. I am, after all, very old. I have lived much longer than I expected. My father passed in his late seventies, and although my mother was over ninety when she died, she had been in nursing care for a number of years. I am grateful for the extension of my life, since I have retained my mind and some of my energy. But I am not under the delusion that I will live forever. I was not surprised by the news I received.

"I hope you have set aside enough time to hear me out on this," she said, suddenly changing the subject. "It may take me some time to plow through the information."

"Sure," I replied. "I got no where to go tonight. But yeah, your news upset me. I always get freaked out when someone I like gets sick. And this someone's tellin' me she is about to cash in. Not only that, but that she's all right with it. First person in my life ever told me that. So, yeah. I don't want you gone yet, Miss Emma. I ain't ready for that."

Emma threw back her head and laughed heartily, startling her friend. "I don't intend to "cash in" as you say, tomorrow, Bobby Parker. I fully intend to stay around at least until my dilemma is resolved. And that," she added with a wry grin,"could take a while. Years, perhaps."

Bobby sighed, visibly relieved. "Okay, then. Let's git to it."

THREE

"I spoke the last time about the meeting between Thomas and me. I would like to continue where we left off, if it is all right with you. Gives the tale some continuity."

Bobby nodded. "Fine with me."

Emma then continued her tale of her relationship with the man who traveled the Atlantic coast interviewing men who made their living at sea. She and Thomas rode the length of Washington County, searching out those who would agree to speak with him. Late every afternoon, they would return to Miltown, ending up either at Emma's where they would rest and drink tea and talk over the day's events, or at the old Inn, where they would sit in the lounge, sipping a glass of sherry and enjoying an evening meal.

"We never, never ran out of things to converse about," she said wistfully. "We were immersed in each other's lives."

Thomas had spent most of his life in Portland. His father was a banker, and he was an only child. His frail mother was from a wealthy eastern Maine family. She died of influenza when Thomas was very young.

After Thomas learned to sail at fourteen, he yearned to captain a small ship, but his father wouldn't hear of it. He would go to Harvard to receive a degree in business, and would follow his father into banking. (That was the way it was done back then, Emma mused. One followed the wishes of parents.)

Father and son shared a career, and the love of the sea. Thomas received his own skiff when he graduated from Exeter Academy at eighteen. He never missed an opportunity to be on the water, spending each summer sailing from the dock at their summer cottage in York. Although he was successful at work, in his heart he harbored a wish to one day give up banking and return to the sea. He would sail the world, writing about and taking photos of his experiences.

In his mid thirties, Thomas finally decided not to continue working with his father, and he purchased a large schooner, which he outfitted with sails and an engine, the best photographic equipment he could find and an updated typewriter. He then began a search for a first-rate mate, someone truly dedicated to the sea, who would travel with him for as long as he was needed.

He discovered Jonathan Brimmer in South Portland. He was fishing for lobster then, single and in love with travel but unable to afford it. Jonathan was deep, silent and honest, like a calm sea. They liked each other right off, and Jonathan remained in his employ until Thomas died.

"Jonathan is still alive, I think. Last time I heard from him he lived in the Portland area with another retired seaman," Emma offered. "I need to stop talking for a short while. Could we have a bit of supper, then continue? Are you able to stay into the evening?"

Bobby agreed, reassuring her that he was hers for the duration of her story. They prepared soup and toast, followed by coffee and lemon tarts from Emma's baking friend, and returned to their comfortable chairs shortly after six.

Bobby noticed that Emma seemed less fragile this evening. When he commented on her returned energy, she replied, "I am feeling better. Either it is the medicine prescribed by the good doctor taking hold, or it is the relief of finally being able to tell my tale and reveal my dilemma." She sighed as she settled more deeply into her chair. "So, to return," she said.

When Thomas Manchester reached Milltown, Maine, he had been traveling the northern Atlantic coast for more than two years. He had spent almost twenty years sailing the seas of the world, and he now wished to explore the coast near his home. Most of this present journey had been spent in Portsmouth, New Hampshire and Belfast, Maine, two of the larger ports on the eastern seaboard. He had also spent three months in Bar Harbor, and a month in Ellsworth. He expected to be in Milltown for only two or three weeks. From that base he planned to travel to Eastport and Calais.

As the second week drew to a close, Thomas and Emma sat in her parlor, reminiscing about their wanderings and the men that Thomas had interviewed. It had been a fascinating experience for Emma, who rarely left Milltown. She would be forever grateful for this opportunity, she stated.

"It doesn't need to end, you know," Thomas stated.

"What do you mean?" Emma replied.

"You could travel the sea with me, I go to Nova Scotia next week. I would love and appreciate the company. Jonathan is an excellent seaman and captain, but he is not the greatest conversationalist I have ever encountered." He leaned toward her, smiling, his green eyes sparkling. "I really like you, Miss Emma," he added. "I hope you realize that."

Emma turned crimson for the second time in her life. "Well. I must say you have completely surprised me. I do not like surprises as a rule. I don't know how I feel about this one." Thomas opened his mouth to reply, but she stopped him with a finger on his lips. "Please. Just let us sit silently for a time, while I think. I am feeling very befuzzled just now."

They sat for what must have seemed an interminable time to Thomas. Finally, Emma broke the silence. "I must say I do enjoy your company immensely, and the past two weeks have been the most exciting of my poor boring life. But I find I cannot even consider living on the sea. I cannot even consider leaving Milltown. My mother, my home, my life are here. I have never known any other. My past fantasies may have included a journey or two, but they were simply fantasies. I never expected them to be realized, and now, as I think of it, I really did not wish them to be realized.

"I'm afraid you are the dreamer, the traveler, while I am the obedient daughter. I do not create my life, I live it. I have filled it with small offerings, for over fifty years.

I walk, I garden, I read, I volunteer at the church, the library and the nursing home, I visit my mother three days weekly. Granted, I do like an outing from time to time, to Portland or Ellsworth. But to sail the seas to Canada? I don't think so. Sitting by the sea, contemplating life as you live it seems to satisfy my need to travel.

"I will miss your company, however," she added, smiling wistfully into his eyes. "Our conversations and outings have buoyed me up. Any time you wish to sail in and motor me around for a week or two you may feel free to do so." This last was stated in a small, barely audible voice.

"Well, you are something different," Thomas replied. "Here I offer you my company, my ship, my life, and you prefer to stay in this insignificant town, living what you see as an insignificant life." He grinned, taking her hand. "And you are one of the most significant souls I have ever encountered.

"You are so thoroughly who you are," he continued. "I am amazed at you. I am thrilled by your company, you never bore me. I have kept company with highly educated intellectuals in the largest cities in the world, both male and female. Most of them bore me silly. They are, with few exceptions, pretentious, overfed and unhappy. You are, in contrast, real, content and rather beautiful, both inside and out." Emma blushed for the third time.

"If you are serious concerning your invitation, I intend to hold you to it," he said. "I would like to reserve the right to motor you out whenever I can find the time to come back to this area. And I fully intend to return as soon as possible." He leaned over and kissed her cheek. "Is that all right with you?"

Emma put a hand to her cheek. "That would be just fine with me, Thomas Manchester," she replied softly.

FOUR

It was approaching eight o'clock. "Although I am tired, I would sorely love to finish this tale tonight," Emma stated wearily. "But I am afraid it is impossible. I do have a suggestion, however. Could you stay in my guest room? We could have an early breakfast and you could paint the south side of the house by noon. Then we could finish my tale in the afternoon. What do you think?"

"I guess that'd be okay," Bobby replied. "I need to get my body movin' for a bit. I'd like to take a walk out, get a paper mebbe. Somethin' to read, since you ain't got TV."

"Oh, but I do have a television. The church donated it to me when I broke my leg. It's in my guest room. Of course it only receives two channels, but it does work."

"I think I'll skip that and go for the paper and the walk if y'don't mind," he retorted. "Can't git sports on them two channels."

"There are clean sheets and blankets in the linen closet at the top of the stairs. Help yourself when you're ready. I will leave lights on for you, but I'll probably be asleep when you return. I will make coffee for you early, since I don't sleep many hours, these days, I will probably be up before dawn."

It took five days for Emma to finish telling her tale. Bobby finished painting the south wall just before noon on Tuesday so Emma conceivably could finish telling him about her project. After she had talked for two hours, she found she needed to nap. She was able to continue for an hour more after she woke, but they concluded then that much more time would be required to complete her saga.

"Before I began, I truly thought I could tell you all I needed to in one afternoon, Bobby," she said. "It seems I have so much more to say than I had ever imagined."

When Bobby realized she could not possibly finish relating all she needed to tell him that day, he decided that he was due to take vacation time. He called the two clients he had lined up. They both agreed to have him move the work back a week. He then called Becka, Dicky, Bess and Doreen to let them know that since he had decided to finish the work in Emma's house, he would not be in town until the following Sunday; they could reach him at Emma's on his cell.

His kids thought it a bit strange, him spending all that time with some old lady. Doreen was worried. "Is Emma okay?" she wondered.

"Oh, sure, she's fine, a little tired is all, she's on some new meds for her ticker. She's got some project she wants to have me do for her, and it's gonna take some time for her to make it all clear to me. Plus," he added, "I can use the rest. Been pushin' myself bigtime. I'm okay, though," he added. "Jest a mite tired m'self."

"Well, all right. I'm hoping to get back by the first of September. I'm packing and selling things, winding down the job and all. Looking forward to seeing you again, I must say."

"Me too, for sure."

For the next three days, Bobby worked on the house in the morning and shared meals with Emma. Early each afternoon they carried large glasses of iced tea to the parlor, where, with spurts of dialoguing interspersed with long naps, Emma continued to release the burden she had held in for years. She needed to relate to someone the story of Emma and Thomas Manchester's life together, and the legacy he had left to his wife when he had suddenly been taken from her.

FIVE

Thomas Manchester returned every five or six weeks, arriving by car and staying at the Inn for three nights. His ship remained docked in the harbor in Halifax. He and Emma would take long drives into the country or along the shore, returning to share sherry and conversation, or long walks in the evening. They never tired of each other's company. When he was away, they communicated by phone and through Emma's long letters. After Thomas read her letters, he would call, and they would talk for hours.

Following a number of short visits, Thomas announced that his work with the fishermen on the northern Atlantic coast was complete. He now needed to return to Portland to compose his notes and photographs into book form, and to arrange for its publication. He was excited about it, stating that he planned it to be another large, coffee-table type book.

He told Emma he would certainly miss her, but he was not about to suggest that she join him after the rejection he had received when he last suggested a journey together. He did have a suggestion, however. Why couldn't they marry? He would come and stay in her house whenever he could, and they would be able to correspond often while he traveled.

Thomas had no intention of giving up his travels. Traveling was as important to him as remaining in Milltown was to Emma. Their union would not be a common one, but Thomas thought it might work, since they seemed to share such intimate closeness whether they were physically together or not.

Emma agreed, much to her own amazement, and to Thomas' delight. She had never much cared what others thought about her or her comings and goings, and she could not think of anything that would make her more happy than to be the wife of this wonderful man who had appeared rather late in her mundane life. He would be missed when absent, but enjoyed thoroughly when he appeared. Being a solitary soul, she would spend the time between savoring their last meeting, and in anticipation of the next. For these two, this seemed a proper joining.

The couple married on a beautiful afternoon in early October, six months after they met. They spent a brief time in Bar Harbor, then returned to prepare Emma's house for Thomas' occupation. Her new husband would need a space to write, and a private phone installed in that space. The second parlor was considered, but Thomas did not approve of the lack of privacy; he also thought that, because the furnishings were so quaint and even humorous, he did not want to disturb them.

He preferred the large, finished but little-used attic, with its deep eaves and long windows at either end. An electrician was engaged to modernize the power in the loft, and to prepare for the telephone. A large desk, a small drafting table and several other tables of varying sizes were hefted up the narrow, steep stairs, along with comfortable leather chairs. Mahogany bookcases were built into the low walls under the eaves. Soft oriental rugs, two Homer Winslow prints and a large framed map of the Atlantic coast completed the space.

Thomas was enchanted with the room. Stating that it had a nautical feel, he declared it his "ship away from ship", and spent hours setting it up to his exact specifications.

He then informed Emma that although he loved her dearly, he wished her only to enter this inner sanctum when invited, and that he intended to keep it locked while he was away. This was because he required a space which would ensure him complete privacy, where he could plot and plan wicked things if he so desired. Being a creature who also appreciated her privacy, Emma readily agreed to her new husband's terms. After all, she had the privilege of setting up the remainder of the house exactly as she wished it. Why shouldn't Thomas have his space?

With the office finally completed, they moved on together to their next project--the bedroom they would share. Emma grew sad as she recalled the purchase of the carved oak bedstead, the large armoire and long dresser for their clothing and personal possessions, the silk draperies and thick rugs to soften the floor, the two upholstered chairs where they enjoyed nightly conversation with large cups of tea.

"I adored that room," she sighed. Suddenly her mood shifted. "We had a wonderful time in that bed," she added mischievously. "I know, I told you before that I would have been happy having an intellectual relationship, walking out with a nice man and having long conversations with him over tea or a glass of wine. But there is much to be said for good physical love, also." She grinned.

"I gleefully surrendered my virginity in that bed," she added. ""And that is all I have to say on that subject."

Bobby interrupted. "That's not what your room looks like now," he mused.

"No, it is not. I decided to sell all of the pieces of furniture a year after Thomas died. I could not sleep in that bed, or look at those furnishings another night; they made me too sad. I bought a simple iron bed and a wardrobe in which to keep my personal things, and, except for one small ornate side table, I gave Thomas's small possessions to the church charity bazaar." She sighed. "There are times, I must admit, when I regret giving up that part of our life together," she said.

"I kin understand why y'did it, though," Bobby stated. "I wanna throw all of th' furniture outta my house every time I think of Deb." He shook his shaggy head. "But I don't, instead, I crawl into the bed or sit on that saggy ol' chair and eat at the crappy

Formica table and use the ol' chipped plates and cups, and feel like shit."

"I think it's not the things, per se," Emma offered. "I think it is more the energy one feels while using them. Somehow, the person is still living in those pieces, those things." She smiled sadly. "And we are angry at that person for leaving us, so we take it out on the things that remind us of them.

"Problem is, when we stop being angry, we often want the things back in our lives, and it is too late. Perhaps you need to hang on to your possessions until your anger has subsided. Perhaps then, you will be able to make a more rational decision regarding them."

"Well, I'll sure give that some thought, Miss Emma. Seems t'make sense. But sometimes I think all it is, is old crap, and I've hated it f'r years. Anyways, t'change the subject—let's get back t'your story. Mine kin wait. I don't wanna talk about Deb jest now."

SIX

Life was good for Emma and Thomas Manchester. Thomas continued his travels, returning to their shared home four or five times yearly to stay for two to three weeks. While he was away, Emma continued to maintain the house and her life. She was sustained by his visits, and as she had hoped, was able to keep herself content with the knowledge that they would see each other soon. While he was home, they spent the days together, walking, cooking, conversing and continuing to enjoy each other's company.

Two years passed. During that time, Emma's mother grew more mentally distant and frail each month. She and Thomas paid her a visit twice weekly each time her husband was home. At one point Emma's mother decided that her husband, Emma's father, had returned, and she would welcome Thomas warmly, asking if his work at the bank went well, or if he had planted the roses he wished to see on the south side of the house.

Thomas played along with her fantasies, pleasing her and Emma. One day, when she seemed exceptionally clear, the old woman sat bolt upright when Thomas walked in. He had come alone, since Emma was afraid to pass on the cold she was battling to her fragile mother. "Francis, is that you?" she asked.

Thomas was puzzled. Emma's father's name was Michael. He hesitated. Finally, "No, it's Michael, Irma," he said.

"Well you don't look like Michael. You look like Frank. I thought the war took you, Francis." Irma began to cry. "I have missed you so, my dear," she began. "It has been so long since we have been together."

Thomas made a quick decision, to go along with this new fantasy. In what strange direction was the old woman taking him, he wondered? "Tell me about our last meeting, Irma," he said softly.

"You were going to war," she moaned softly. "We were going to tell Michael about our love, but we decided we could not until you came home. We couldn't leave each other, that night. We did something we never should have.

"It was almost six months later when I received news from your brother that you were missing. You never returned. Why have you been away for so long?"

"I'm here now, my dear. And everything is fine. You had a good life with Michael, and you have a beautiful daughter. Perhaps life with me would not have been so good."

"Perhaps, And yes, Emma is a joy. She is a good, quiet girl. Not like her brother, James. He was dark, and lovely and boisterous. He was your son, you know. Our son."

Irma sighed, looking at Thomas with sadness. "I think Michael knew, but he never spoke to me of it. He loved me, he really did. Even when I did not love him, he loved me. I think I was good to him, finally. I hope I was good to him. He deserved for me to be good." She began to sob.

"James died, Francis. He contracted the influenza when he was four. I couldn't save him. I stayed with him day and night, hoping I could make him live, give him my life. I wanted to follow him on that terrible night he went. I lost you, then I lost him. I could not bear that.

"I was not the same after James died. He took such a large part of me with him. You took, then he took. Emma was deprived of me, after James went. I could not fully be there for her, ever. Or for Michael." Irma lifted a wrinkled, bony hand and gazed thoughtfully at it. "And here I am, old and dying, and I am still less than half of myself. How did I come to be so ancient?

"I want to leave soon, Francis. It is my time. Will you be there when I go? Will you bring James with you?"

"I'll do that, Irma. I promise I will be there whenever you go."

The old woman sighed deeply and smiled. "Good. I am almost ready to go." Suddenly, "Where is Emma? Has she left me?"

"Not at all. Emma stayed home with a slight cold. She did not wish to pass it to you. She will be here tomorrow, if she's better."

"She needs to come tomorrow. Please tell her she needs to come. It will be too late after tomorrow."

"I will be sure to tell her. You get some sleep now," Thomas said. He sat by her bed, holding her hand until she drifted into sleep.

As Thomas returned to Emma, he wondered what he was supposed to do with the story the old woman had shared with him. More importantly, what would Irma want him to do? After some thought, Thomas decided she would wish him to share her story with Emma. It would make his wife unhappy, he was certain of that, but Irma was Emma's mother, not his, and he was certain that she was close to death. Emma needed to hear about this part of her mother's life.

"I often wondered about James," Emma mused after Thomas had related his strange meeting with her mother. "He did not look like mother, or father. He was so full of energy, so handsome and dark. My parents were fair-skinned, and Father had chestnut hair like mine, while Mother was a reddish-blonde. Mother doted on James--we all loved him dearly.

"And Mother did change after James died," she agreed. "She was more quiet, yet somehow less content. I attributed it to her loss. I was twelve at the time, and somewhat aware of the feelings parents had for their offspring. I thought I could imagine how terrible it would be to lose a child.

"But to have lost a lover, and then his child, that I cannot imagine." Emma was quiet for a few moments. "I loved my father deeply. Now I know that my mother did not love him," she said. "That will be hard to live with. That will be hard to forgive."

Irma Colridge died peacefully in her sleep early the next morning. Emma did not pay a final visit to her mother. She made arrangements for Irma's burial next to her father, and for a small service to be held at the church. Only Thomas was aware that she grieved not only for her mother's death, but for a marriage which was never what she supposed it to be, and a brother who did not belong to that marriage. Only Thomas was there to hold her through the many nights that followed, nights when Emma could not contain her grief.

"From the time Thomas told me of my mother's transgression, I have considered myself an only child," Emma offered. "James was in my life briefly, but I was my father's child. His only child. I have forgiven Mother; after all, she was human, as am I. But I have not forgotten that she never shared her unhappiness with me. If she had, I would have known the reason for her distance. I might have been assured that it was not only James' death, or my survival which had caused her misery.

"It was, instead, her survival. She was left to mourn. I was left without my mother's care." Emma sighed. "Perhaps not care, so much as her presence."

SEVEN

On a late autumn day twenty years into their marriage, Thomas returned after a three-month absence. Emma noticed that he seemed to have aged during his recent hiatus. She was no youngster, since she had been over fifty when they met. She had passed her seventieth birthday, but she felt as fit and young as she had in her thirties. Thomas, however, was now seventy-three, and looking pale and tired.

Thomas, with Jonathan as his mate and traveling companion, had traveled the world during those years. He had sailed to South America, flown to Japan and China, traveled by plane and ship to Australia and New Zealand. Each time he planned a trip, he invited his wife to accompany him. Each time, she refused.

Thomas had been able to cajole Emma into one journey by water. A year after their wedding, he suggested a short sail to Bar Harbor. It would be an anniversary celebration. Emma reluctantly agreed. After all, how uncomfortable could she be, traveling for less than one day? They left from

Ellsworth early one calm morning, docking in Bar Harbor by late afternoon. Thomas had reserved a room for them at a large hotel on the island, and had ordered a special meal to be served. After they had toasted their year together with champagne, he asked Emma how she had fared on the sea.

"I hated it. I will return to Ellsworth on the ship, but please do not ever suggest that I set foot on a sailing vessel again."

"I was so put off by that trip" Emma told Bobby. "I felt I was on another planet. Being on water, with land so inaccessible, was horrifying. I guess I was meant to be a stodgy old stick-at-home,"

Deciding that her husband's pallor was due to lack of rest and good food, she decided not to mention her concern to Thomas. After they had shared a good bottle of burgundy from France, eaten a light meal and finished the evening with a small glass of brandy, Thomas sat back and sighed.

"I felt a need to visit my physician while I was in Portland a month ago," he began. "My old friend recommended I put this old body through what they are calling a battery of tests." Emma sat quietly, her stomach suddenly in a knot.

"Now Emma my love, not to worry," he added. "I see those frown lines forming on your brow." He laughed. "No, it's only that my heart is not beating quite as it should; not keeping its rhythm correctly. After all, it has been working quite hard, serving me well all of these years."

"The whole story, Thomas. I need to hear it all," Emma replied tersely. "What, exactly, is wrong?"

"I will most likely need to have a pacemaker inserted in my chest to regulate my heartbeat," he replied. "This is a fairly new, but well-documented procedure. One does not need to expect a long hospital stay, or any side effects from the insertion. It will, I am told, do a fine job of regulating my old ticker." He smiled, squeezing his wife's hand. "You must not worry about this, my dear. I will have the procedure performed by the finest surgeon in Portland." But Emma was upset, to say the least. She had retained excellent health her entire life, and she had, perhaps foolishly, assumed that Thomas was as healthy as she.

"How serious is this procedure, and when, where and how will you have this done?"

"Two, three days in hospital, a week's convalescence, and it's over," he replied a bit too briskly. "As to when? I am not too sure. The problem is not very serious now, so I may decide to put it off for a few months. Have it done in the spring, when the poor weather clears away. I don't fancy being an invalid of any sort during a Maine winter."

EIGHT

Thomas did not have the operation. He and Jonathan traveled to Mexico that winter, where he assured her that the pleasant weather and relaxed lifestyle of Mexico City revived him, Indeed, he did look much improved when he next returned to his wife. That year, they spent four comfortable months together, and the condition of his heart was not mentioned.

Life as they had set it up for themselves continued for the Manchesters. Jonathan had now completed four large books, and never seemed to tire of photographing and interviewing people with diverse careers. Following his book about the men who fished the northern Atlantic, he wrote a book about manufacturing in the Far East. This was followed by a tome dealing with men who farmed in Australia, and finally a book about those women and men who served others in hotels and in private homes in South America.

In the introduction contained within each book, Thomas would state that the themes for his writings grew from conversations that he and Emma had shared as they sat and conversed in the evenings. They would begin to wonder how others felt as they went about their daily lives. For hours on end, they would discuss what might be contained in the minds and hearts of these people. Finally, Thomas would become so curious that he would decide that he needed to set off to discover these facts firsthand. As he worked, he continued to share his experiences with his wife through long letters and phone conversations.

Emma never missed the experience of meeting the hundreds of people Thomas interviewed. His second-hand narratives satisfied her completely. She did miss his presence when his journeys seemed to last forever, as when he was in Australia. That endeavor took him away for almost a year. Their reunion was very emotional. Emma was happy to have him back, but angry at him for having remained away for so many months. They walked gingerly around each other for some weeks following his return. Finally, however, Emma decided that Thomas' company must take precedent over her peevishness, and they resumed their content lives.

Early in the spring of their twenty-third year together, Thomas returned from a trip through the southern United States, where he was developing his next project, a book which would chronicle those who had retained the belief that the South should have remained forever separated from the North, and who resented the influx of those northerners who continued to invade their territory, migrating south to live in their midst. He and Emma had discussed this concept in great depth, fascinated by the thought that there was probably a group of southerners who had never accepted the union of the two factions following the Civil War.

Thomas had in fact discovered many families in Mississippi, Alabama and Georgia who retained these beliefs, and he was excited to share his notes with his wife. They spent their first night together in lively discussion long after their usual retirement time.

"We literally fell into bed that night," Emma recalled. "We were elated, yet really exhausted. We had eaten well and sipped some good brandy after our meal.

"The strange sound woke me near dawn. I was deeply asleep, and dreaming that someone was choking and I could not find the person. I slowly woke and realized it was in fact my Thomas. He was thrashing around in the bed, choking and moaning. When I asked him what was wrong, he gasped, 'pain...heart,' then he passed out. I called the doctor immediately, but by the time he arrived, Thomas was gone.

"Just like that...gone," Emma sighed deeply. "The rest of our lives together, taken away. His heart had only grown more weak, and he had not cared enough to do what was necessary to mend it."

"Prob'ly figgered it would be okay," Bobby offered. "Men do that, y'know. We ignore what don't bother us, figgerin' it'll go away. Called denial, I guess, but it's what we do."

"I guess. It certainly changed my life," Emma continued sadly. "I went through those stages of mourning I had only read about. I took to my bed for weeks, severely depressed. During that terrible time I gave his possessions away, and sold our bedroom furniture. I would have dismantled his attic room, but I could not bring myself to go there. I have not entered that room since Thomas' death.

"I did not know what to do about Thomas' burial. I decided to call Jonathan. He rushed to help me with the preparations for his funeral and interment. A small service was held, and he was laid to rest in the Milltown cemetery in my family plot, which also has a place for me. While Jonathan was here, he searched Thomas' room, looking for a will, or a list of people he could contact. He found nothing. I gave him the key to the room, told him he could do what he wanted with it."

"So his family came from Portland?" Bobby asked.

"I did think it strange at the time, but Jonathan convinced me that I had done what I could, since Thomas had left no information to tell us what to do if he should pass. I was in no condition to disagree with him. He informed me that he would place notice in the newspapers of Thomas' death, and that he would call or write to any family to whom notice would matter.

"I did nothing to help him. I was unable to function in any manner during that entire process. Thank God for Jonathan, he took care of everything. I don't know what would have been done if he had not come to my aid." Emma smiled sadly.

"The minister and people of the church were also wonderful," she said. "They made sure I bathed and took in food on a regular basis, cleaned my home and filled my larder. Each day for three months, some good woman would show up on my doorstep, ready to do my bidding. I'm afraid I was very rude to them, for the most part. I wanted to die; how dare they presume to keep me alive." She chuckled.

"They put up with me, however, as they had all of my life. I've been blessed with good people around me, Bobby Parker. You certainly are one of them."

"It was over a year before I was able to thank them. I finally crept from the dark hole that had been my existence, and looked around me. My body was skinny and unkempt, my house was disheveled, my garden was non-existent. I took a deep breath and plunged back into my life.

"And, here I am," she added. "Chipper and raring to go." She laughed heartily. "Well, maybe a mite less chipper, and not so raring, these days," she mused. "Certainly a touch sadder than I was back then. I miss my Thomas every day. I still expect him to walk in one crisp fall day, laden with bottles of good wine and brandy, smelling of tobacco and a mixture of leather and musk and other things foreign. His scent was so familiar to me. I sometimes think I still get a whiff of it in the air.

"He would load the table with his purchases, then pick me up and hold me for what seemed forever. We would prepare a meal together, drink wine and talk into the night. Not until I met you, Bobby, have I been with another soul who could inspire such long, interesting and absorbing conversations."

"And I've allus considered m'self the quiet type," Bobby said. "You seem to bring out the talker in me, Miss Emma."

"And you in me, my friend," Emma returned. "It's wonderful, isn't it?"

"Sure makes me feel good," Bobby returned.

NINE

Bobby and Emma had retired before ten the previous night. It was Thursday, and Bobby informed his friend that he really needed to leave by four that afternoon. His life contained too many unfinished projects demanding his attention. He wanted to touch in with his daughters and he needed to make some decisions regarding his wilted marriage. His carpentry projects were on hold, and Doreen was due back in a few weeks. It was important that he complete enough work so he could make permanent adjustments to his weekly schedule, in order to ensure regular time with her.

The two rose before dawn, allowing Bobby enough time to complete his last repair project--applying fresh white paint and new hardware to the cabinets in Emma's pantry. When these were finished, her kitchen would be in good shape, with its new inlaid flooring, repaired cabinets and new refrigerator. Bobby had convinced Emma that her food would stay much fresher with a new appliance, rather than in her ancient fridge. They were able to locate a slightly used bargain, and it had been delivered the previous week.

Emma's stove was also very old, but she balked at replacing two appliances. "The old thing will still boil my water for tea and heat up those soups my friends from the church bring around, and I do not need it for much more than that," she argued. Bobby agreed she had a point there, so the equally ancient stove remained.

When he had finished, Emma asked Bobby if he would retrieve her mail while she prepared a meal. As he was removing the letters from her box, he noticed an official envelope from Portland addressed to Miss Emma Colridge. "Wonder who would send her mail in her maiden name," he wondered in passing. He dropped the mail on the table and went to wash his hands.

"Now that you have heard my saga, I need to finish by proposing the project which I mentioned at the onset of my recitation," Emma began as they sat to enjoy their final lunch. "I have thoroughly enjoyed your company, and am truly grateful that you have set aside this time to hear me out to date. But I am not quite through, and our final day has arrived. I am aware that you need to return to your life today, so I must complete unburdening myself rather quickly." As she spoke, she leafed through her mail distractedly. When she came to the letter from Portland, she pulled it from the pile and placed it between them.

"Strange, that this should have come today. It usually comes on the first of the month," she mused, indicating the letter. "I say strange, because it is a part of the mystery which is included in my relationship with Thomas.

"Yes, there is some mystery," Emma replied to Bobby's quizzical glance. "Much mystery, as a matter of fact. Our joining was unusual, you will agree. And the life we led together was not what one would expect to see in a normal marriage. Thomas and I were fine with it--we never expected it to be any more or less than it was. But with this eccentric agreement came certain conditions that were set up by Thomas, and by me.

"I would not travel with him. He would live here, with me when he could, and must consider himself free to live wherever he needed when we were apart. He would not interfere with my comings and goings in this community at any time. While we were together, he would not communicate with any of his friends or relatives from away on our shared telephone, nor would he receive mail from these people in our shared mailbox. He must instead maintain a separate telephone in his loft office, and receive his mail at a post office box. We would spend our time together, with no interference from the outside world. While he was living in this house, he and I formed a sanctuary which was essentially unspoiled by outside contact.

"Those were my conditions. These conditions were established for a very good reason. They were needed to protect my fragile ego. This, because it was my fear that while he was away, he would be taken from me by those who demanded or enjoyed his company. Especially, those women he encountered on his journeys. After all, he traveled extensively, and met so many people as he journeyed. Yes, Bobby Parker. I was jealous. Not envious, since I had been invited many times to travel the world with him. I did not wish his life while he was away. I only wished his complete attention while we were together.

"Perhaps this was wrong of me, but it was the only way I felt that I could survive our separations. And as I have stated to you many times, Bobby, I am not very nice, nor am I always good. I consider myself rather selfish, and because of this, I desired my life to be comfortable, and suited to me.

"Thomas agreed to my conditions. In fact, he was delighted, stating that he appreciated my independent nature above many of my wonderful qualities." Emma paused, smiling to herself. "He was the only person in my life who ever considered me wonderful. Have you ever thought about that word, Bobby? Full of wonder. Thomas saw me in my ordinary small life, and found it full of wonder. And because he saw that, I began to see it for myself. Life with him, whether we were together or apart, was full of wonder. I developed appreciation for so many small events in my life. The coming of spring, the wonder of the open sea, the beauty always present in this area, flowing and changing with each season.

"Since he has gone, my sense of wonder has tarnished somewhat. That is," she added, "until I came in contact with a certain carpenter who is also a great philosopher. Bobby Parker, by name."

Bobby reddened. He was about to object when Emma stopped him with a raised finger. "No time for your objections, Bobby. I have only time to finish my story so you can have it to mull over, to consider whether you will help me."

TEN

"We have now come to those conditions which Thomas outlined when we married," Emma continued. "These were not so numerous or so self-serving as mine, I must admit. However, they were somewhat difficult for me to understand, and even more difficult to agree to.

"There were actually only two conditions. One, I was not to enter his attic office unless invited. And the second? This is the condition which is causing my consternation. Thomas asked that I not legally change my surname after we were married. I would use his name for correspondence to friends or family, and the community would know me as Emma Manchester. But legally, I was to remain Colridge. This condition was connected with a financial arrangement he set up for me shortly after we met.

"Thomas was aware that my family did not have much in the way of financial resources. My father had been an administrator in our local bank, but his salary while he lived, and later, the pension he left my mother, barely covered our basic expenses. Thankfully there was a good insurance policy for Mother. This paid for her care at the nursing facility. After she was placed in permanent nursing care, I obtained Mother's power of attorney and accessed my father's pension to eke out a living, using those funds that remained after paying Mother's monthly expenses. My needs were very simple, as you can imagine, and I was able to make out fine so long as I remained healthy. If my health were to deteriorate, there would definitely have been a problem. I did not have insurance to cover expenses should I need extended care for chronic illness, or hospitalization.

"Dr. Hoffman had cared for my parents for as long as I could remember. When he discovered that I did not have a medical plan, he offered to treat me pro bono, making sure that I had a yearly exam, and supplying medicine for any illness that might require it. In this small community one is, thankfully, able to find that spirit which assures that those who need care receive it. Although I did appreciate the good doctor's offer, I did not like to owe anyone, so I have been very careful with my health.

"During one of our long conversations I mentioned these facts to Thomas. He was appalled to hear that I was, as he termed it, 'just short of destitute'. I laughed. I did not think of myself as poor. I had a warm home, clothing for all seasons, good shoes for walking, a good book from the local library any time I cared to borrow one, and friends who were happy to ferry me to a concert or a movie from time to time. I had my garden, my music, my sewing and an old television set with which to catch up on local news each night. What else could a body want or need?

"Apparently a lot, according to Thomas. I might need emergency health care above and beyond that which Dr. Hoffman could supply, or a special meal at a nice restaurant, or a short journey somewhere on my own. If my home burned down, or if it needed repairs, what would I do? What if my stove ceased to work, or my refrigerator burned out, or my bathroom plumbing stopped working? What would I do to replace or repair these expensive things?

"I realized that I really had not given any of those matters any thought at all. I supposed that people from the church, or those in the community who knew me and my parents would come to my aid. There were a few dollars left after expenses, and these were in a small savings account. I could make arrangements to pay for emergencies by taking out some sort of loan, I supposed, although I had never needed anything like that.

"This did not comfort Thomas. He was still upset that I had no emergency financial resources. To take care of this, he set up a fund in my name, which was Colridge at the time. The terms of this fund allowed me a certain stipend monthly, and would continue until my death. Then, I thought that Thomas' offer was more than generous. He wished to add insurance to the stipend, but I would have none of that. He was too generous. My doctor took good care of me, and the medical people in the area have continued to do so. They did not send me a bill for that little incident I suffered through—if you remember; the fall which brought us together.

"I knew my Thomas was wealthy, but I never gave it thought, and his wealth did not enter into our relationship. He never mentioned money, but he certainly was able to afford an elaborate lifestyle. His clothing was expensive, he always drove a new luxurious automobile, and he owned at least one large sailing vessel, perhaps more, for all I knew. He traveled by plane or train with no thought to expense, and he maintained the employ of Jonathan Brimmer, and most likely many others.

"He furnished his attic office with wonderful, costly antiques and Oriental rugs. He also offered to embellish this house, but I refused. I was perfectly satisfied with my furnishings. They were older, granted, but they had belonged to my parents, and therefore to my life. They were, and still are, serviceable and comfortable. I did agree to his purchasing the two comfortable chairs for the sitting room which we have enjoyed this week, and of course he furnished our shared bedroom.

"Thomas died very unexpectedly, as I have stated. When Jonathan came to help me with arrangements for his funeral, he said something which seemed strange to me at the time. He asked if Thomas had made arrangements for my share of his inheritance. I had to admit that I had no knowledge of this. Jonathan then spent much time in Thomas' office, going through his papers. This upset me, but he informed me that he and Thomas had made an agreement that if anything should happen to him, he wished Jonathan to take care of any unfinished project concerning the business he had conducted from Milltown. When Jonathan was finished, he took his key to the loft with him. I had no need to go there, and wished to continue to honor Thomas' wishes to maintain his privacy. I had no use for any of his material things, and his business was not my business.

"I was suffering such grief at the time, I simply allowed Jonathan to do what he needed to do, and to finish the business as quickly as possible, so I could be left alone. He did tell me, after spending a few days with Thomas' belongings, that he could not locate any information which indicated that I was entitled to his inheritance. He asked if Thomas had a safe in his room. To tell you the truth, I did not know. I had been in that office only a handful of times in the twenty-three years I knew my husband. I was usually invited to look at an acquisition, a rug or a new picture. He would tell me its origin, we would admire it for a short while then return to our sitting room.

"I continued to receive my usual stipend, which seemed fine to me. Thomas increased the monthly amount after Mother died, since I no longer received Father's pension. It has been enough to take care of my basic living needs. Of course, it is now thirteen years since Jonathan has passed, and everything is more dear. Food, electricity and taxes have all increased. This check, however, has not increased." She picked up the envelope. "Thomas' gift to me," she said sadly. "He so wanted me to be well taken care of. I am afraid, however," she continued, "it will soon not be enough. I did not qualify for Social Security since I have never earned a salary, and I will not accept charity of any sort while there is breath in my body.

"For quite some time, the things that Jonathan said concerning an inheritance have come back to me. I did not want or need it for many years. It was of absolutely no consequence to me, and would not have changed my life one whit. But now, I see that if my finances were to improve a bit, I could look forward to a more comfortable old age." Emma looked at Bobby. She saw that he was trying hard to stifle a laugh. She laughed, he immediately joined in. "We needed that, Bobby Parker," she said, wiping her eyes when they finally stopped.

"Yes, I am already old, and have been for years. But I have not felt old until recently. I have been able to live life fully, with relatively little ache or pain. It is becoming more difficult for me to get around as quickly, and

I have recently developed a fear of falling. I think it stems from that fall when we met. What if you had not found me just then? I might have laid there for hours, even frozen to death. Or even worse, needed care for my remaining years.

"I plan to die at home. I would like to know that if I should become bed-ridden before I pass, I could pay someone to provide care for me. It would need to be someone with whom I could feel comfortable. Wouldn't you love to do it, Bobby?" She glanced up at him, laughing again. "Your face says it all, dear boy. Of course, I would never ask you to do that. You are not the type to enjoy bathing and feeding an old bird like me. I am sure that one of the more tolerable ladies from the church would be happy to have the money. Most of us in this area are poor, are we not?

"To come to the bottom line, I would like to have my stipend increased if it is at all possible. I trust I have made it clear that I have no desire to be rich. But I am selfish enough to desire safety and comfort in my last years. There are not many of them remaining, I am certain of that. So there would not be a great financial burden on the person or persons who are in charge of

Thomas' estate. As you see, I receive my stipend from a firm in Portland. Perhaps it is his duty to care for the funds. I don't know, nor do I care, I simply wish a larger amount of money each month.

"Tell me, Bobby, do you think this is too much to ask? After all, Thomas has been gone for thirteen years. Would my request be ridiculous? I do value your opinion."

Bobby was silent for what seemed forever. Emma finally began to fidget, waiting for him to speak. "Don't you have an answer for me, Bobby?" she asked.

"Well. I gotta say, I'm flummoxed, Miss Emma. That's quite a story. Seems to me," he mused, "that since you was married to the man, and that joinin' was on the up n' up, you must be legal heir to his estate. That's what I'd assume. If 'twas m'self I'd git in touch with the guy who sends you the check. How come you ain't done that?"

"Of course you would wonder about that. And with good reason. I wish I could give you a solid answer to your question. I suppose I just have not cared to, when I think of it. I have not cared to remind myself of the life Thomas led when he was not with me, and I have not wished to involve myself in any tangle of legality. I also have not needed money until recently.

"I do not like the world out there. I am a reclusive, crotchety old woman who wants to be left alone to do exactly what I desire, every day. That is the truth. And if I were not in the financial state I find myself, I would die without investigating my options. But," she sighed, "it seems I have no choice at this point." Emma sighed, clasping her hands tightly together. She looked up at Bobby.

"So it comes to this, Bobby Parker. I need a favor of you. Would you be willing to carry out my investigation? Would you do what it will take to solve my dilemma?"

"Jeez. Me? What d'you think that involves?"

"The best scenario for me would be that I hear nothing. Denial is what this is about, after all. You would contact the person who is in charge of my account, his name is John Chambers. His firm is Chambers and Slater, and as I understand it, he attended college with Thomas. I would think the best scenario would be for you to travel to Portland to meet with mister Chambers. Jonathan Brimmer may also have some information that would prove valuable, if he is still with us. He is also in Portland. He is getting on in years, as are we all, but I have heard from him two to three times yearly. Our last correspondence was less than a year ago.

"I have set aside funds for this project each month for over a year. There is not much in the account, but it should cover the costs of some travel, hotels and meals. Actually, I began to save just before we met. I did not know who I would ask to complete this work; I had hope that the right person would come along.

"I have thought of this project as my opus. That means a large work, an important project, usually having to do with something creative or artistic. To my way of thinking, we will need to be very creative to solve my problem. Don't you agree? It could be our opus, our last work together, if you are willing to help."

"Oh, sure. Sounds great to me. And you do re'lize, I'm bein' sarcastic here. So, like when d'you want this done?"

"Tomorrow, if you could," Emma replied. "And you realize I am shooting sarcasm back at you. No, I know your life is rather full these days, Bobby. If you agreed to take this on, you must name a time when it would be best for you. Taking into consideration that I am very old, of course, and might croak before you begin." She grinned as Bobby began to look anxious. "I am fairly healthy still, especially since I have begun to take medicine for my heart. So we could put it off for a while, say a few months, if that's what you need."

"How long d'you think all this business will take? I mean, if I do agree to take it on, I do have a business to worry about. I can't be trottin' off f'r months. I'd prob'ly lose lots of work."

"I really cannot even guess at that. I don't suppose it would take more than one or two trips to Portland, so perhaps you could figure on two long weekends. Sounds reasonable to me. How long could it take to look up a few records such as the legality of our joining, and to adjust my monthly stipend? That is," she added, "if the estate has the funds to accommodate my needs. It could be severely depleted, after all. I have no idea."

Bobby shook his head. "I dunno, Miss Emma. That's a lot for me. I don't much like travelin' neither. And hotels? I jest dunno. I need time for thinkin' on this. And I really gotta go, soon.

"How 'bout this? Let me do what I gotta do this next month. I need to reorganize my life so's it fits Doreen. I gotta do somethin' about Debra. I dunno if she has plans to file for divorce, but if she don't I gotta do it. I also I gotta check on my kids, make sure they're okay, 'specially Bess. And, I definitely gotta git back to the kinda work that makes me some real bread. Doin' this project for you ain't gonna pay my bills. You barely got enough for your own.

"Somewheres between all them things, I'll see if I kin figure out somethin' to help you solve your problem. But I prob'ly won't be callin' you for some time. That be okay?"

"That, Bobby Parker, would be just fine. Just to know that you are giving the opus some consideration is all I can ask. Thank you."

"Hey, don't thank me yet. We may go nowheres. This--opus, you call it may jest flush itself down the hopper, when all's said and done." Bobby rose and stretched. "For now, I'm outta here."

Emma leaned forward to place her hand on her friend's arm. "I will look forward to our next connection. And again, I have appreciated all you have accomplished this week. I will hear from you whenever, and will not push you into this too soon, I promise."

They walked together to Bobby's truck. As he climbed in, Emma added, "I do want to know why I needed to keep my maiden name. That is part of the mystery."

She stood in the driveway looking after her friend long after he had driven off, her arms held close to her chest against the cool breeze, wispy white strands of hair blowing around her small, sad face.

INTERLUDE: The Author

Here it is, winter again. Of course it's almost always winter in this neck of the state. Winter starts creeping in by late October, if we're lucky. If we're really lucky, it's over by late April. I guess I'm used to the cold, although I could never say I love it. I love lots of things about living here; the people, the slow pace of life, the cost of living and the woods, lakes and fingers of ocean around me. But the weather can truly suck. We sometimes go through more than two weeks when we don't see the sun, for fog or thin clouds. It can rain consistently, either cold drizzle or sheets of the stuff, for days on end. We have ice storms, Northeasters that blow in over 2 feet of snow at a whack, and damp heat waves in the summer. We have blackflies and green flies whose bite can swell your ears and ankles so no one recognizes you. Seems like we just finish with one thing, another comes along.

It's the in-betweens that keep us here. Those glorious, hushed, sparkling days just after snowstorms. The foliage, aflame for three weeks in October. Crisp dry spring and fall days with glorious deep-blue sky. Cool summer days with puffy marshmallow clouds in the clear sky, and the most gorgeous sunsets. These days are our payoff for living with horrid weather for weeks, sometimes months. Large parties are thrown to celebrate the temperature finally reaching sixty degrees. Forget California; you just get used to plain old perfect weather 300 days a year. Give me a super warm sunny day in Washington County, so I can dance and drink a good bottle of red. If I lived in California I'd most likely be drunk every day of the year—a raging alcoholic with nothing to celebrate.

I've actually been to California. Ol' BS has a cousin who lives in Camarillo. We drove out there two years after we were married. One baby, another in the oven, and BS didn't believe in stopping a car until it ran out of fuel. Never mind that I had to pee every 200 miles. I finally was forced to fashion a makeshift potty seat from an empty gallon water bottle, using a pair of lawn shears Steve had in the trunk.

We had fun, though. I was through with my morning sickness stuff, and Steve's cousin was a nice kid and had great friends. We had lots of red on that trip. Good thing

Stevie wasn't born with FAS. I wasn't taking very good care of myself during that time of my life. (Obviously wasn't taking very good care of my kid, either). But I watched my booze intake most of the time, and I didn't smoke, so he came out just fine. At least, so far. But I've been over that guilt trip forever. Single parenthood wiped it right out.

So that's how I know about the weather in California. It was great, but after a week I forgot to notice it. I figured if I lived there, I'd get too used to the perfection. I'd rather opt for celebrating those rare perfect days. It feels better if we earn them.

I'm still deep into the writing. Coming down the home stretch with Bobby's book, and I am now writing more short stories in my down time. I can't concentrate on the book for more than a few days at a whack; then, I need a break. I don't get those writers who can sit and write for eight hours a day, five days a week, like it's a regular job. This book might take me years. I don't think so, but sometimes I get stuck and don't know where to go with it. After a down time, the computer calls me back, and I'm right there again.

I'm mailing out short stories to a bunch of magazines and contests. Maybe one of them will make me some money. I have no expectations concerning the book. After all, it's my first, and it may stink for all I know. It does feel good that I can put so many words together which seem to fit. I thought I'd take a writing course at the college, but I think the only way I'll learn is to do it. I read lots, always have, and I don't like bad writing. When mine looks bad, I know it. So I'll keep on plugging until it's done, then see where I go from there.

Am I still seeing Sam, my old high school buddy? You bet. We have a good time together. I love his daughter Chelsee, although I would never have saddled a kid of mine with that name. It took some time, but Stevie and Kristen are finally accepting the fact that I have a person in my life. They never really lived with Big Steve; even when he was home, he was usually out. And of course they were never aware of Irv, since I saw him far, far away from any thought of little people.

Sam is, frankly, a sweet, nice man. I truly never thought that I could be with a sweet, nice man. The thought of it bored me, when I gave it any thought at all. My mother-in-law has urged me on a regular basis to forget guys like Steve and seek out a sweet, nice guy. (And Steve is her son!) Even my sister Jen, who can't seem to hold on to a guy more than three dates, wants me to find a nice guy. She knows I like to have a partner. And she's right. Some of us need a partner, while some of us want to go through life free and independent. I find freedom and independence fine for a time, but I really want someone to go skin-to-skin with after the sun goes down. Jen met Irv once, and pronounced him "cute, but ego-bound". That about summed it up.

Sam's not as cute as Irv or Steve. He's tall and rangy and craggy. And, he does not have much left of his hair. But all of that doesn't seem to matter when we're together. He's funny, quiet and patient. Now that I've been with Steve and Irv, that feels comfortable. We are actually friends. We share kids, politics, values and a love of great Italian food. Looks are way down on the ladder, with this one. We're taking life together one day at a time, but I'm beginning to think I'll keep him.

We spend lots of time with Bobby and Doreen. They, like everyone else who's met him, love Sam. Bobby seems much happier now that he knows the book is sure to be finished. I know he had some doubts when we began, although not as many as I did. We're both relieved that it's going as well as it is. We got together with them last weekend, along with Bobby's son Dickie and his girl Marcie, who waits table at the Lobsta Claw. She seems like a nice kid, a bit older than he, but who am I to judge. I hear she was married for a time, has a kid. Dickie graduated, and he's moved up from busboy to full-time cook at the 'Claw. He takes courses at the tech college in Calais; wants to be a real chef. Doreen's been a big influence in his life. She's the reason he loves to cook. They got to know each other when she invited him to make meals with her after she and Bobby moved in together.

Speaking of moving in, Sam has hinted at that particular shift in our relationship. Part of me really would like to pack my things tomorrow and hike myself and my kids over to his big white house in the center of town, while a bigger part of me is holding back, and not because I am so fond of our little old cottage with the roof and plumbing which could use serious attention. What if Sam turns out to be a bore, being so nice and all? Right now I can't see it, but you never know. Plus, we have not had our first fight. And I can't see living with someone if you don't know what he's like in a fight. When I get angry, I'm likely to come out with it, have my tantrum, stomp and yell—then the sun comes out. Anger just sweeps through me and leaves me feeling clean and fresh.

Steve was different. He seethed. Rage would seep slowly and quietly down into his bones, deep, before I was even aware it was there. Then it would fester in him until he couldn't take the pressure any more, and he would erupt, sometimes for hours. If it got too bad, he sometimes lashed out physically. This only happened a couple of times, but I wouldn't want to live with it again. Usually, he would leave. He'd stomp and yell and sometimes punch a wall for a while, then he'd slam out the door, off to get drunk. After he had slept it off, he was usually okay. Quiet and surly for a couple of days, but not dangerous. We never talked it out. That was the most frustrating thing, for me.

It wasn't much fun, since I never knew what would trigger it. Could be no work for a couple of weeks, or me bringing the wrong beer home on Friday night. Kristen has demonstrated the same rage. She's prone to long sulks and extended temper tantrums. I can only hope she learns to control it. Leena Gianni, my mother-in-law, says Kristen and

Steve are like her father. Maybe it's in the genes. Thank God Stevie isn't like that. He's just like his mom; it's in, it's out, it's over.

I'm waiting for my first fight with Sam. Then I'll make up my mind. I firmly believe that fighting is inevitable in any relationship. If you don't have a good go-round once in a while, nothing seems to resolve or change. Getting out the kinks clears the air. And there's always the making up. Clear air makes for great sex, in my book. But I won't live with another volcano.

Not that sex with Sam isn't great already. It certainly is. We fit together like a hand in a chamois glove, despite our difference in size. It's often, it's long, it's sweet and it's satisfying. But good sex doesn't guarantee a good relationship. Look at Irv. That says it all.

For now, it's enough that we're seeing each other exclusively, and that our kids like us, and that our life together is comfortable and fairly low-stress. Perhaps when the book is finished I will consider taking on the added stress of blending our lives. I can't give the relationship the attention it deserves while I am working on resolving Bobby Parker's problems.

4

The Resolution

ONE

"Aw, Jeez. Jest what I need. Debra." Bobby spotted the Colt nestled up to the front entrance as he rounded the corner to home. "She prob'ly wants to move back in. Outta bread, ready to come back. Shit." Bobby had spent the last hour sifting the projects he needed to attend to when he reached Quoddy in order of their importance. Suddenly, priorities had shifted. He slowly climbed from the truck's cab, retrieved two bags of groceries from the bed and walked into the living room, his shoulders hunched against the expected impending attack.

"Hey, Bobby." Debra lounged on the sofa, feet up, sipping a coke.

"Hey, yourself. What's up?"

"I'm not comin' back, in case you was gettin' worried. I jest wanted to do this in person." She handed him a large manila envelope with a lawyer's logo embossed on its front. "It's papers for a divorce. I didn't want you to get 'em in the mail. Not that I'm bein' nice about it; it's actually a big inconvenience. I want 'em signed quick so's I kin get on with my life. I figured if I sent 'em you'd sit on them or somethin' and I'd have to come anyway."

Bobby looked at his wife. She looked good. Debra had colored her normally brunette hair with various shades of reddish blonde, darker red and an eggplant color. She wore a mauve silk blouse under a black pant suit, cut to flatter her lithe body. Her mauve suede pointed-toe shoes looked very expensive, as did her gold hoop earrings and bracelet. Her perfume hadn't come from CVS, either.

"I gotta sit for a minute," Bobby said. "I had a tough week."

"Yeah, tough. I heard you was at the old lady's. I also heard you been seein' that Irish cow, Doreen Shanahan. What's with that anyhow, Bobby? You like 'em fat now?"

"Jeez Deb, shut the fuck up, will you." Bobby was getting riled. "You sure look fancy, but your mouth is as foul as ever, I kin see that.

"I ain't said nothin' about the way you been leadin' your life lately," he continued. "I don't appreciate you tellin' me how to live mine." He went to the kitchen to put away the groceries. "I'll go where I want, and see who I want. The way I see it, you got no right to comment on any of it." He returned with two tall cans of beer and a glass. "Now that you're so uppity, I figure you don't drink your brew from the can no more." He handed her the can and the glass, and sank into the cracked leather chair.

After he had finished the beer in three long swallows, Bobby sighed. "There. That's doin' it. So you want me to sign them papers? What's in 'em?"

Debra paced as she sipped. "The usual stuff, I figure it's no-fault all the way. I only want my stuff, and half the equity in the house. Nothin' else. I had an appraisal on the house while you was with the old broad. It's worth forty-five thou. My half is twenty-two five, less any money we owe the realty."

"And what's your "stuff" include?"

"Well. You know I bought the bedroom suite, and this couch and the coffee table," she returned, indicating the living room furnishings. "And there's the microwave and the toaster oven, and all my rose cups and saucers. And I figure the car is mine, 'cause even if you bought it, you don't drive it at all. I paid the insurance on it last month. It's on its last legs, anyways. I plan to get somethin' better soon."

Bobby was suddenly so tired he could hardly hear Debra rattle on. The small amount of energy he had when he arrived had drained through his toes. He looked at her as she paced nervously from the stairs to the kitchen as she spoke.

"I don't know why I asked you. I really don't give a damn, Deb," he said wearily. "Take it all if you want. I hate everythin' in this dump. I can't even think right now. Can we talk about this in the mornin'?"

"I'm afraid not, Bobby. I'm leavin' tonight. I gotta be somewhere first thing in the mornin'. I won't take nothin' more than I've said, I mean it." She waved the envelope in his face. "Come on, Bobby, sign it. Let's git this thing over with so's we both kin do what we want with our lives."

Bobby wearily reached for the papers, opened the envelope and briefly scanned its contents. Debra was right; the agreement was a simple one. It granted her the items she had mentioned and half the equity in their home after the necessary expenses. He grabbed a ballpoint from the end table and quickly signed the papers.

"Do I hafta go to court?" he asked as he passed them to her.

"Not unless you decide to change your mind. You want me back?" Debra smiled wryly.

"Nope." Bobby had nothing more to say.

"Then I'm outta here. I'll come back in a couple weeks to get my stuff. You got three months after the divorce is final to come up with the money from the house. It should be final in six months, if it all goes smooth." She grinned. "Then you kin marry the cow. You must have some hots for her to agree to all this so quick. I figured on a couple of hours and a battle."

Debra grabbed an expensive black leather bag which had been by the door, took the papers and headed for the door. "Have a great life, Bobby; I mean to," she tossed back breezily as she slammed the door behind her.

Bobby sat staring at the closed door. After what seemed forever, he whispered, "Well, that's that. At least she ain't gettin' any cash. Not that I got much. And I still got my sanity, whatever that's worth."

As he stared out of the window, Bobby realized that it was still light. His fatigue told him it was bedtime, not early evening. He turned on the TV, searching for something to keep him awake for a couple of hours. If he went to bed now, he would be up at three. He sighed deeply and turned the set off after a fruitless search. He was snoring loudly when Dickie came thumping down the stairs, startling him awake.

"Hey, Pop."

"Hey. I didn't' know you was here, Dick'."

"Yep. I got to be here when Ma came in. That was real fun. She spent an hour tryin' to get everything you was doin' outta me."

"I kin imagine. So that's how she knew about Doreen. And where I been this week."

"Did she get you to sign them papers?"

"Yep."

"If she wants to be shed of you so quick, why is she so pissed about you and Doreen?"

"I dunno. I guess it's the old thing about her not havin' me, so no one should." Bobby chuckled. "She ain't had me for years, I don't know why she'd be pissed at that." He shook his head. "It's wimmen stuff, Dick'.

"I'm beat. Don't even feel like eatin', but I brought home some stuff; help yourself. Gotta get some zz's. We'll talk tomorrow, okay?" Bobby rose, gave his son a brief hug and dragged his exhausted body up the stairs.

TWO

Bobby woke after ten to a clear, perfect late spring Downeast day. He lazed in bed, watching doves feed from the seed, honey and peanut butter balls he had hung and kept filled in the large fir whose branches draped across his window. Impossibly white clouds danced across a deep blue sky as the women in his life scampered across his mind.

There had not been many. Darlene and Corrinne, two girls he dated briefly in high school. His sisters, of course. There were three, and the youngest was four years older than he. They were one year apart, and had been close to each other and mostly ignorant of their younger brother's comings and goings. His quiet, efficient mother, who also seemed unaware of her son's inner workings, aside from knowing that he needed his large appetite satisfied at least three times daily and his clothes replaced regularly as he outgrew them. His wife of more than twenty years, who knew only that Bobby could not satisfy her ever-present desires. Then recently, Emma Manchester, and Doreen Shanahan.

Only the latter were the least aware of the person who was really Bobby Parker. Why was this, he wondered, although he knew the answer even as he put the question to himself. They were the women who had been interested enough in him to question him about the person who lived within.

Corrinne and Darlene were young and shy, and only spoke when spoken to; his mother had no clue about any person in her life, probably because it had never occurred to her to wonder. Perhaps she had communicated intimately with his father, but if so he had not been aware of it. Bunn had been even more silent than Helen. He had always figured their sex life must be very satisfactory, since they seemed content enough with each other, and the babies had come thick and fast for years. In addition to his sisters, Bobby had one older and two younger brothers.

Deb and he had their share of conversations, but they mostly concerned her complaints, needs and wants. Sometimes they talked over problems they were having with the kids, or whether to buy a new appliance, or where they would go on

Saturday night. They usually went to dinner or to a lounge for drinks on Saturday nights. Debra did not consider a night alone with her husband her favorite form of entertainment. She preferred drinking and dancing until the 'Claw or Moore's Bar and Grill in Calais closed. They had little to say to each other on a daily basis.

Emma was the first woman who had probed deeply enough to discover him. During the times they had shared tea and good food she had questioned him relentlessly, gently paring away the long-hidden layers of his psyche, exposing parts of him that had been hidden even from himself. Her questions had led to his questioning himself, wondering how and why he had come to be the person he was. It was during this inner discovery that he had befriended Doreen, who was also interested in the depths of Bobby Parker.

It felt good to be able to talk intimately with someone; to express feelings so long buried. He felt younger, lighter. And yes, more content-- and sometimes, even happy. A new experience for him, he had to admit. Bobby had always been somewhat satisfied with life, had felt that he could deal with whatever each day brought him. Even when things with Deb were at their worst he could find solace in his work, or with his family. He enjoyed being with Becka and her small family, or sharing Sunday dinners with his mother and siblings. He felt good when he and his buddies watched sports, shared beers and pizza. Life was what it was supposed to be, he had decided. Not the most wonderful life in the world, but enough for him.

Emma and Doreen had certainly introduced a number of new dimensions into his existence. Most of them were great, but some were not so wonderful. He had found a wonderful love in Doreen, and a warm motherly comfort and acceptance from Emma. He was also being asked to extend himself further than he ever had, to venture into unknown territory, severely stretching the limits of his physical and emotional comfort zones.

This thought brought him to Emma and her request. He did not know if he was capable of doing what Emma was asking from him. He was a country man, accustomed to country ways. He was rough and coarse, not smooth and refined. How would he deal with big city financial people? He might need to buy a suit, or at least good trousers and a dress shirt. Probably would need a tie to go with it. And, decent shoes. He did not own any of these things. The last time he had dressed for anything was his daughter's wedding. He had worn his best work pants, a clean plaid flannel shirt and his new work boots. He had consented to wearing a tie, which was loaned to him by the minister.

How would he approach these people? What would he say to them? New people did not often appear in Bobby's life. He had rarely left the small town in which he was born and raised, except for a rare visit to a doctor in Bangor, or the occasional short trip to Milltown, Calais or Machias to buy work supplies when he could not find them locally. He had been to Portland many times, but not for formal reasons. His youngest sister lived there, as did a couple of cousins, and he and Deb had brought the kids for occasional family gatherings. They had attended a few movies and had done some shopping, but that certainly was not the same as presenting himself to a big prestigious law firm to conduct business.

Bobby sighed. Enough. Time to get up and out. For now, he had more important problems in his life. He would deal with Emma's opus after he had finished with the other matters that were picking at him.

There were messages on his machine that needed attention. Checking on Bess and calling Doreen were on his agenda. Then, there was the house. He had to clean it out, get rid of anything which reminded him of Debra, organize his stuff and prepare for Doreen's moving in. Next, he needed to call Becka and find Dicky to inform them about his and Doreen's plans. Finally, he wanted to call the four people whose names he had written in his work book before he had left for Emma's, to set up times to estimate their projects. One would be a long one, building a large garage to house three boats. That was sure to take a while, so it was necessary to plan his time carefully.

Also, he would like to have Becka and her family for dinner soon. He realized he had not spent enough time with his older daughter since he had become involved with Emma. He did not know whether she missed him, but he was very aware that he did miss her and her sweet kids.

Attending to all of those projects was sure to take at least a month. He would spend time organizing his life, settle in with Doreen for a week or two. After all had been tended to, he would give Emma's project some thought. Of course, he would talk it over with Doreen. He wondered what her take on it would be.

The thought of Doreen made him smile. As he headed for the shower, he knew what his first task would be.

THREE

Three weeks later, on a cool grey afternoon in early June, Doreen Shanahan drove into Bobby's yard in her red Chevy SUV, towing a rented U-Haul container. Bobby had just finished the second week of work on Rich Woodworth's garage, and was showering off the day's grime.

"Any chance I can get a hand unloading my earthly possessions?" Doreen called as she opened the front door. Then, "Wow," she said softly as she stepped into the living room.

Bobby had been busy. After Debra had removed the pieces she wanted the week before, he had painted the walls a soft yellow, and had removed the carpet and refinished the underlying wide pine floors. Doreen walked through the house, taking in the changes. The worn, second-rate appliances in the kitchen had been replaced with new. A new round oak table with four chairs replaced the former much-scarred chrome and Formica set. In the living room, Bobby had installed a new sectional sofa and two large recliners.

"You're finally here," Bobby whooped as he clambered over the stairs wrapped in a large towel, and excitedly enveloped Doreen in a huge hug. "Seems forever," he breathed into her hair. "You smell great. You look great. I'm so glad you're back in my life."

"The place looks amazing," Doreen said as she stepped back to look at him. "So do you," she added as she took in Bobby's strong exposed upper body, his clean damp hair and beard, his glowing face, his bright blue eyes. She smiled broadly, then suddenly looked serious, "I hope you remembered our agreement about our sleepin' arrangements."

"Yep. Got two rooms upstair' fixed up. Dicky's in the third room. You got the girls' old room."

"Doreen beamed. "I'm so glad you remembered. However, during our long separation, I have been re-thinking my position regarding our original agreement. That is, if you don't mind," Doreen added coyly.

"Y'think? That'd be great with me." Bobby put his arm around her shoulders, leading her toward the freshly sanded, newly carpeted stairs. "So what happened to the 'Let's not git tangled up too soon' thing?"

"If you remember, I also said to you that for me, things take more time," Doreen answered. "A month ago, I felt that way. A month can be a looong time," she added, giggling.

"Too long in my book. Hell, let's go upstair' and see what we kin do about re-arrangin' things."

Three hours later, they had snuggled for a few minutes on the new king-sized bed in Bobby's room to determine whether it was comfortable, settled on combined furnishings for their now shared room and unloaded and combined the new furnishings with Delores' possessions. They decided to settle in and have dinner, promising themselves a much longer welcoming later. After Doreen had unpacked, they prepared a salad and put steaks in a bowl to marinate, and settled on the new sofa with a bottle of merlot and two glasses, exhausted but comfortable.

Bobby groaned as he propped his feet on his old cracked leather ottoman. Doreen plopped one foot beside his, draped the other over his leg. "Could you please massage my ankle and foot?" she pleaded. "I sprained that ankle years ago, and when I spend too much time on my feet, it starts to ache."

"Be happy to, Love, once I git up enough energy to lift my arm." He grinned and began to gently rub her ankle and foot while Doreen poured the wine. "Seems we're gonna learn all kinds of new things about each other," he remarked. "We got the rest of our lives to investigate our aches, pains, eccentricities and bad habits. Sounds good to me," he finished, taking a large swig of merlot.

"Ah, yes," Doreen replied softly. "Like the habit you have of drinking wine like it's beer. That's bound to make you light-headed real quick."

"Whoa. It's workin' already. Gotta watch that one." He shook his head, grinning. "Feels good, howsomever. Prob'ly worked so quick because I'm so hungry. Ain't eaten since noon, and my body really wants some of that steak."

While Bobby grilled the steak on the deck, Doreen set the table with the colorful placemats and cloth napkins which she had brought. She added Bobby's contribution of new white dinner plates and stainless cutlery. A loaf of crusty bread in a basket and a slice of butter on a small plate complete with its own spreader came next. After she had added dressing to the salad and prepared fresh green beans, she lit two tall white candles and placed them in the center of the table.

"The table is ready when you are, sire", she announced.

"This is a new one for me, for sure," Bobby stated as he sat. "A real home-cooked meal, candles and napkins; and all that in a clean house. I don't know if I kin take it."

"You better get used to it, hon. It's the only way to live."

"Oh, I don't think it'll take me long," Bobby replied as he cut into the tender meat with a contented sigh.

After dinner Bobby and Doreen found enough energy to wash the dishes and take a short walk in the cool June night. When they returned, they settled on the sofa again, full and relaxed. "Wanna watch some TV?" Bobby asked.

"No, I'm not much of a TV watcher. I really want to find out what you've been up to since the last time we talked," Doreen answered. "That was almost a week ago, and if you remember, it was a short, very unsatisfactory conversation. You've been so busy, what with your week with Emma and all the projects you've taken on since you got home, and I've been straight out getting packed and re-arranging my life.

Communication has been too short. But sweet," she added.

"I need to talk about all that, I know," Bobby said. "But I jest can't, tonight. I got so much to tell you, but my brain ain't able to filter my thoughts through my mouth. I'm so happy you're here, I jest want to be quiet and hold you. Then I wanna take you upstair', feel every inch of you, then sleep a whole night with lots of your skin rubbin' up to my skin. I ain't workin' tomorrow, so we kin finish settlin' you in, then talk. That okay with you?"

Doreen leaned over to kiss him. "Sure. Especially the part where we do the every inch feelin' and sleepin' skin to skin bit."

FOUR

After a long busy day spent settling into their now combined home, Bobby and Doreen were nestled deeply in one of the old 'Claw's distressed wooden booths, beer and potato skins before them. Despite the many decisions they had to make, from placement of furniture (Doreen wanted it entirely changed), to arrangement of the kitchen (Bobby gave this completely over to her), the day had progressed smoothly. Dicky had come home some time during the early morning hours, slept until noon, then appeared to help with the re-arrangement. Fortunately for him they had finished moving the heavy pieces long before, so he offered to cook a late breakfast. Bobby and Doreen agreed heartily, having had only cereal and coffee at six a.m. By one o'clock, the three of them sat talking comfortably, polishing off sausage, scrambled eggs, cinnamon toast and a large pot of excellent French Roast coffee.

"How d'you like the way Dad fixed up the place?" Dicky offered.

"I love it," Doreen replied. "But right now, what I love more is this food. I didn't know you were such a good cook. Yum," she added as she helped herself to another sausage and a third slice of toast. "I could get used to bein' fed, from time to time. Your dad grills a mean steak, too," she added."

"Yeah, that's about it for his contribution in the culinary d'partment. I had to learn t' cook, bein' in this house. Ma never cooked, and Dad's never around. Plus, if you kin cook, there's always work around here. The restaurants in the county are always lookin' for someone who kin put together a decent meal. I jest got a cookin' job at the 'Claw, matter of fact."

All of this was news to Bobby. "How come you never cook for me?" he said. "When did you cook for yourself, come to think on it?"

"Been makin' my own meals since I's about twelve," Dicky answered. "When I wasn't eatin' at the 'Claw, that is. That was since I's fourteen. I started bussin' there then. I got my meals free, 'cause I bussed and fixed Harlin's car when it went wonky. "Harlin's my boss," he added for Doreen's benefit.

"But when I had days off, and you's workin', I cooked my own food. Mostly eggs and bacon or ham and beans, so I learned to make them good, first. Then I graduated to cheeseburgers and mac and cheese."

"How about vegetables and fruit?" Doreen asked.

"Hey. That's complicated cookin'. Ain't got there yet. They use canned at the 'Claw. And mostly, the veg is coleslaw. That comes in big tubs, don't need to make it. I'm learnin' fries and clams 'n' scallops and that, now."

"You mean if we go t'dinner tomorrow, you're gonna fry our clams?" Bobby asked.

"Yep. I'm on tonight 'n' tomorrow, doin' the fryin'."

"How would you like to learn how to cook fresh vegetables?" Doreen asked. "And maybe, to bake a great chocolate cake or a blueberry pie? Or make a decent salad?"

"That'd be okay," Dicky replied. "I'd be able to git a job in a real restaurant if I knew them things." He smiled broadly. "Maybe, even open my own in a couple years."

"Sounds great to me," Doreen replied. "Any time you're ready to learn, let me know. I'm sure your dad would appreciate us feeding him some home cookin'. He can be the live-in judge."

As Bobby listened to the comfortable banter between his son and his new love, he realized that this son he had never known continued to amaze him. He was capable of adult conversation; he had been a hard worker since he was fourteen; he wanted to own his own business, and he was willing to learn what it took to do that. What other qualities of Dicky's was he unaware of? He had to spend more time with the kid. Before he knew it, his son would move out to live with some girl, and they would never know each other. That thought brought tightness to his chest. No more kids at home. Now that would be something different.

"Nickel for your thoughts," Doreen said, reaching over to grasp Bobby's hand. "You were some far away just now."

"Thinkin' about last night and you and Dicky," Bobby offered. "That was great, what you said you'd do for him. I really appreciate it, Hon."

"No problem. He's such a nice kid. He'll probably make a great chef some day. It will be fun to have someone to teach. I don't ever plan to have a kid of my own, so I can pass on my legacy to Dicky."

"No kids, huh?" Bobby recalled his thoughts of the previous night. "How come?"

"Just don't see myself raising a kid at my age," Doreen mused. "If I'd had a baby when I was in my twenties, it might have been okay. But I didn't; now, the urge is entirely gone. Not that I don't like kids," she added. "I just don't want to raise one. I'm kind of lookin' forward to bein' a step-grandmumma to your daughter's kids, actually" she finished.

She peered at Bobby. "I know we haven't talked at all about this. But then, there's so much about each other we don't know. How d'you feel about it?"

"I'm okay, I guess. I jest realized how much I'd miss havin' a kid in the house. Been a dad lots of years. But then, I got you now. Gotta get used to havin' someone around to talk with," he grinned.

"Yep. I'm gonna be around lots of years, Bobby Parker. You'll get quite used to me. And by the way," she added, "How are your daughters? Have you been in contact with Bess? And has Becka made plans to move yet?

"And, last but far from least, how's little Emma? You need to fill me in on everyone." Doreen settled back in the booth as huge platters of fried clams, French fries and coleslaw were placed before them. "Oh, my. They never have skimped on portions here, have they." She laughed as she dug in.

After the couple had shoveled their way through most of their dinner and boxed the remainder to take home for lunch the next day, they drank coffee while they filled each other in on the events of the past weeks. Becka and her family were moving to South Portland the first week of October. She and Jared had been offered jobs in a large fish packing company that supplied affordable on-site day care for the its employees pre-school children. They continued to save money for the move, and Becka was keeping her promise to avoid another pregnancy. She was actually thinking she'd quit producing kids altogether, but Bobby confessed to being leery of her sticking to that resolution.

Bess was fine, due in the middle of October. She was eating well, had gained enough weight, and was still pleased with the place she had chosen. She had made friends, and seemed somewhat content. She had not decided yet whether to keep the baby, although she had discovered it was a boy.

Doreen shared her experiences around giving up her small home and quitting her long-time job. She felt fine about the changes, knowing that she was coming to a place where she would feel cherished and cared for. She could always work for her mother, and she was looking forward to making a home and a life with Bobby.

"I confess to one wish, however," she stated as she finished. "I know you have rid the house of Debra's belongings, but I think I will always know that it is Debra's house. Her presence was--is--strong, and I feel it in the rooms.

"I would like for us to have another house to live in," she mused. "Doesn't need to be new, just a different place for the two of us to be in, to have our new life. Would you be all right with that?" she asked anxiously.

"Sounds fine to me," Bobby replied. "This one'll sell faster, now that I've fixed it up. I gotta admit, Deb would be a hard person to git outta someplace. I see what you mean about her energy. Y'can't paint it out, or hammer boards over it. It's jest there. Kinda creepy, ain't it?" He shook his bushy head.

"One condition," he added hastily. "Would you mind livin' there for a few months, while I git this garage project done, plus a few others I can't put off? I wanna help Becka move, and there's Bess to worry about, and I need to git the divorce settled. Lawyer says it'll be over by some time in November. Can't be too soon for me. And then there's

Emma's project. Her opus. We gotta talk about that, too."

"No, I don't mind. So long as I know it will happen sooner than later. Maybe we could plan to be out by Christmas." Then, "Emma's opus? What's that all about?"

Bobby then filled Doreen in on the saga of his week with Emma, including her strange relationship with Thomas Manchester, the circumstances of his death and his legacy, and the problems she was experiencing living on the now meager pension he had provided for her. He finished with the opus she had outlined, the final, "grand work" which she wished Bobby' help complete.

"Wow." Doreen said after Bobby had finished his tale. "Wow. That's all I have to say." She sat for a few moments sipping coffee, taking in the information she had been given.

Finally, "So. What will you do? Have you thought about your next step?"

"Not really. I kinda thought I'd run it by you, see what was your take on it."

"Hmm. Frankly, I think you ought to do it. We'll get you a good suit, some fancy shoes and a silk tie, get your hair and beard trimmed out a bit, give you a couple of Valium and send you on your way."

Bobby stared at her incredulously. Then, "Oh, you're kiddin' me," he said. "Scared me there, for a minute."

"Well, about the Valium," Doreen giggled. "But the rest, actually, no. I really do think something like this would be good for you. You're such a smart guy, and you've been livin' in one place all your life, livin' one kind of life. Might be good to see how the other side does it up.

"Plus, I really think you can do it; solve her problem, I mean. And you know how much it would mean to her."

"Jeez. You really think I'm up to all that?"

"Better believe it."

"I dunno. I don't think I'm up t'talkin' to all them bigwigs about Emma's business."

"You don't know who you'll need to talk with. Maybe the first thing you need to do is have Emma write the firm a letter containing all of the information she has. I don't believe she hasn't tried that already. What's with her and this project, anyway?"

"For some reason, she don't seem to want to do anything about it herself. She told me it's denial. There's somethin' she don't want to know, I think."

"Certainly seems that way. What d'you think it may be?"

"Ain't got clue one. From what she tells me about this Thomas guy, he was one strange bird. Came and went more or less as he pleased, whole time they's together. And she seemed t'be okay with it. Didn't want t'go with him, so felt she wasn't free to question where he'd been or where he was goin'.

"Mebbe he was involved in some not so legal doin's, for all I know. I think mebbe Emma thinks about stuff like that, too, and gets scared of what she'd find out if she went deeper into his life."

"Maybe," Doreen said slowly. "But I think, after sharing his life for so many years, and being a smart old bird, she knows what the answers are, deep inside. And that's what she's afraid of. That she's right."

"So why's she wantin' me to uncover all of it jest now.? You'd think she'd be content to live out the rest of her life as it is. It's pretty stress free, as I see it."

"Perhaps that's exactly the reason she is ready to discover the truth. She may know that her life is limited, and sometimes we want to finish any business we feel is not complete, before we leave this life."

"Mebbe so. One thing I forgot to mention. She tells me she's takin' pills for her heart.

Mebbe it's worse than she makes it out, and she's not lettin' me in on it." Bobby sighed.

"I really got m'self in for a passel of stuff when I took on that old lady," he said. "But then," he added, "she took on quite a package when she met me.

"I guess we both made out okay in the deal," he mused. "She kept probin' deeper and deeper into me, so I learned a lot about myself, and while we was spendin' time together, she got her house put together a bit. So, I guess I'm gonna help her out. Seems right, somehow, since I think I made out better in our arrangement."

"How do you figure that?"

"If I'd never met Emma and decided to go to Milltown to work for her, I wouldn't have gotten to know you. I'm pretty convinced of that. I woulda listened to Debra and let her continue to beat me down, while she did what she pleased. I wasn't too aware of what was goin' on in my life, until Miss Emma started pointin' stuff out.

"She made me think. And once my brain got jump-started, I started t' change things. The way I was with my kids, distant and not aware of what was goin' on in their lives. Not that I din't care, I jest din't spend enough time thinkin' about 'em. Also the way Deb and me was livin'. It had purely sucked for more years than I care t' think about. It wasn't too hard to let her go. For her, or for me. It was what needed to be. Emma helped me see that, and get through it.

"Yep, I sure owe her more than I've given. So that settles it. Soon's I finish that garage for Rich I'll go down and have a talk with her. Find out if she'll write that letter."

"If she won't write it herself, maybe she would let me write it. I would be happy to contribute what I can to the solution of Emma's problem. After all, I also made out in all of this. I feel I owe her too, big time." Doreen leaned over the booth and kissed Bobby soundly. "Right now, let's go home to our re-arranged room and mess up the covers." She sat back, looking at him intently. "If I didn't make it clear last night, Bobby Parker, I wish to tell you now. Coming home to you, loving you, being close to you, is the best move I have ever made in my entire life."

Bobby took her hand. "Thanks for that, Love. Now, let's go. I'm followin' jest after you, Miss Sweet Doreen."

FIVE

The following morning, Doreen came up with another good suggestion. A former high school friend was a lawyer in Milltown. Perhaps Bobby would benefit from talking with him about Emma's situation. Bobby made an appointment with Carlton Hendricks for the following Friday. He would finish the garage project on Thursday, and this would free him to spend time preparing himself for his role in Emma's opus. He arranged to meet with Emma in the morning; he and attorney Hendricks would get together after noon.

Friday dawned rainy and cool, typical for mid June in Washington County. If warm summer weather were to appear, it would not begin until after the 4th of July. Sweatshirts were usually a necessity at the popular Eastport parade. If the sun made its appearance you might get away with short sleeves until after four. Then, a cover-up was definitely needed. The weather warmed for two or three weeks, then cooled again after the first week in August. Natives were fond of telling the tourists that summer might appear between the twenty-fifth and twenty-eighth of July--don't blink, you might miss it.

Bobby spent twenty minutes at Red Crawford's garage before he began his trek to Milltown, installing new wipers on his truck. Ten minutes was spent on the installation, the other ten being thoroughly grilled regarding his new live-in guest. He didn't remember telling anyone except his kids and his mother about Doreen's arrival, but apparently the whole town already knew.

This was no surprise, of course. Nothing happened in Quoddy that was not known by everyone in town within a week; usually it was much less. It did no good to try to keep a secret. Share it with one person, and the whole town was soon aware of your every move. Bobby was fine with this, since he had never known anything different. He had been on the grilling side of many a rumor, and was more than happy to share his news. He figured that most everyone in the county knew that Deb was about to divorce him days, maybe even weeks before he did.

Emma was obviously happy to see him. She strained up to plant a kiss on his cheek and led him into the bright kitchen, where she had set a table with donuts, pastries and a large pot of tea. "I have missed you terribly, Bobby Parker," she sighed. "No one to philosophize with for weeks."

Emma looked pale and even more thin than usual. "You been all right, Miss Emma?" Bobby asked.

"Now, don't get your nerves askew, Bobby. I am fine. I am just old. And feeling it more every week. I am over eighty-eight, now, you know. Had another birthday last week. Oh, don't look at me like that, I didn't tell you or anyone else. When you're my age, every birthday is another toll of the bell, another step toward the final passage.

"For an ancient hag, I'm actually quite healthy, according to my good doctor.

"And, of course I have awaited your decision concerning my finances with bated breath. Have you given any thought to our final discussion before you returned home?"

"Matter of fact, I have, Miss Emma," Bobby replied. "Been thinkin' on it a lot. And I decided I'm gonna try to git you some more money. But," he added as Emma's face lit up with relief, "you gotta come out of that denial of yours and talk about this some. I can't do it all alone."

The old woman's eyes filled. "I guess I am able to do that. I am aware that you will need my help to some extent, and I am so grateful that you have agreed to come to my aid. What is it that I can do for you?"

Hesitantly, Bobby said, "I need to know how come you ain't already asked them lawyers for more money when back when you knew you'd be needin' it. And, if you ain't, Doreen suggested you write them a letter to that effect as soon as possible."

Emma sat forward in her chair, her hands clasped tightly before her. "This is very difficult for me, Bobby. I certainly had given that some thought. But writing to ask for a raise in my allotment seemed as if I was begging. I abhor charity, as you know. Sending a hale young man like you to represent me seems more appropriate, somehow. Perhaps it is just foolish pride, but there it is.

"As to your other request, it also makes sense, but I don't wish to do it. Do you think Doreen would agree to write a letter in my stead? She seems such an intelligent, articulate soul. I would be happy to supply her with any information she might require."

"She's already covered that," Bobby said. "She wanted me to ask you if she could write the letter, if you didn't want to. You gals think alike, I guess." Bobby looked quizzically at the old woman. "I guess I don't git it. Seems to me that it'd be far easier if you write your letter, wait to see what they got to say, then go from there. The way you're goin' about it seems pretty complicated, to my mind."

"I can understand your confusion, my friend. It is a conundrum, even to me. But there it is, and it will not change. I am far more willing to pay you to travel to Portland, and to have Doreen write a letter representing me, than I am to do it on my own." She sighed deeply. "Fear is at the root of this, Bobby. Fear of the unknown." She placed a gnarled hand over her eyes. "I really cannot talk about this any more," she said softly. "There is too much pain."

"Okay, Emma. Me and Doreen'll do it. We'll do it for you," Bobby said gently. He sat with her for a few minutes while she regained her composure, then they went to the sitting room where Emma opened her small roll top desk and handed Bobby a manila envelope. Contained within were complete records of her allotment checks dating back to the month following Thomas Manchester's death, and all of the correspondence from her late husband's lawyer. The envelope also contained correspondence Emma had received from Jonathan Brimmer.

"As you can see, I have spent some time in preparation for your return. I hope everything is in order. I have included the last letter I received from Jonathan, along with his address and telephone number, thinking that perhaps you would want to talk with him. He might be of some help in the project.

"I have also included my marriage license in the package. One thing I wish to know," Emma said quietly. "As I have said, I wish to know why I have needed to use my maiden name in all of the transactions with Thomas' law firm. The answer Thomas gave me when I asked him has never seemed right to me. I need to know this, before I prepare to meet with him again."

Bobby took the envelope and gently kissed his friend, assuring her again that everything would be done according to her wishes. He hated to eat and leave, he said, but he had another appointment in town in a few minutes. Promising Emma to be in touch soon, he left the tiny woman sitting in Thomas's large chair, seeming suddenly ancient and forlorn, and more alone than he could remember seeing her.

SIX

July and August were Bobby Parker's busiest work months. Once he had finished building Rich Woodward's garage, he found himself overwhelmed with new projects which needed completion as soon as possible, according to the homeowners. The weather was warmer and periods of rain fewer, so doors and windows could more easily be replaced, and decks and porches built or roofs repaired without worrying about a cold spell to subside or ice buildup to melt. Clients also wanted him to complete work in kitchens and bathrooms, but they knew that they would need to be patient until the weather cooled and he was no longer able to work outside.

Doreen was at least as busy as Bobby. Summer brought tourists to the county, and tourists ate pizza. Shanahan's provided delivery service in July and August, so pizzas were shipped daily to the summer camps and motels nestled in the trees surrounding the area's lakes. Reliable delivery people were hard to find, so Doreen often found herself traveling rut-laden dirt roads at odd hours with hot boxes in the back of her SUV. She was often needed in the kitchen, also, since her mother's energy was not quite what it had been prior to her heart attack.

Emma understood that the couple were not able to deal with her opus until after Labor Day, at least. Doreen had informed the old lady that Bobby's meeting with her lawyer friend had gone smoothly, and that he had stated that her paperwork seemed in order, so she could proceed with her written request for increased funds. She needed only a brief statement from Emma with her signature, stating that she was allowing Doreen and Bobby to represent her.

Emma seemed pleased, agreed to send the statement immediately, and asked that Doreen please write the initial letter as soon as she received it. She had also decided to give Bobby full power of attorney over her affairs. She promised to be patient if that one task was accomplished. Doreen agreed and mailed the letter shortly after she had received Emma's correspondence.

For the remainder of the summer, Bobby called Emma each Sunday afternoon to make sure she was all right. He was still concerned about her emotional outburst, and her apparent weight loss. Each time he called, she sounded chipper and assured him that she continued to enjoy good health. She was spending time in the garden every day that weather would allow, and that was energizing her.

The reply to Doreen's letter arrived from the Portland firm in early September, as Bobby and Doreen were winding down and planning a much-needed week off in mid-September. Eager to be away, they loaded Doreen's vehicle with camping gear and food and, leaving cell phones and business concerns behind, pitched a tent on a high bluff beside the bay in Cobscook National Park in Edmunds. They spent the week sleeping, eating and hiking, and, most importantly, re-connecting. On the last day of their vacation, they drove to Bangor to make certain that Bobby was fitted out properly for his journey to Portland.

At Filene's, they purchased a pair of black dress trousers with a proper leather belt, good black loafers and matching trouser socks. A white dress shirt with a red cardigan topped off the outfit, since Bobby had balked at a tie and jacket. The sweater would do nicely; he could see himself wearing it on cool nights, and the dress pants and shoes would do if they had to attend a funeral or a wedding. Doreen also dragged him into one of the many unisex salons in the mall, where she supervised the trimming of his hair and beard.

Doreen also urged him to buy two pairs of new jeans and three other dress shirts. Finally, she took him to dinner at the Pilots' Grille, a local favorite, where they dined royally on Caesar salad, lobster bisque and a bottle of good chardonnay.

"You do clean up good," she purred as she sipped the wine. "I'm lovin' your hair."

"It still smells of that sissy crap they sprayed on it," Bobby moaned. "But it's okay. Especially since you like it. I don't see me that often, but you do."

"Mm, yes. And you're a juicy sight." She grinned. "Tell me again what the Portland accounting firm had to say regarding Emma's situation. I must confess I don't remember you reading it to me. Maybe I wasn't paying as much attention to you as I might have. I had camping under the stars and making you over on my mind at the time."

"Oh, yeah. I don't remember readin' it t' you, either. I brought it with me." Bobby produced the single sheet of paper from the pocket of his new striped shirt, and read it aloud. Simply stated, Emma's papers seemed perfectly legal. It was agreed that the stipend she was receiving could be reviewed and probably updated. Included was a paragraph inquiring why she felt she needed legal representation. The firm did not seem to find this necessary, since the procedure would most likely be a simple, straightforward one.

"Seems to me, all these legal folks agree with us," Bobby added after he had replaced the letter in his pocket. "She coulda' done this pretty simply. Her excuse seems som'at feeble, t'me.

"She sure gits emotional when I bring it all up to her, though," he added. "Says there's too much pain to talk about it."

"I do think she knows all of the answers, my love," Doreen replied. "And she has simply decided she wants them from you."

"Mebbe so."

"I am so glad you're not as nervous about the trip as you seemed. I wish I could go with you, but Mom still needs me for a few weeks. Tourists are trickling out, but the restaurant is still going great guns. And Jami, that twit she hired to make pizza is not working out. She's lazy and doesn't show up half the time. I think she's supplyin' half the high school with free pizza, too. Mom can't prove it, but the groceries seem some depleted lately." She sighed. "So, I need to supervise for a couple of weeks, or at least until things quiet down some more.

"Besides, I'd rather go to Portland with you when we can have fun," she added. "Then you can wear your spiffy new duds just for me."

"I' gotta go to Portland in October for a couple of things, Hon. I promised Becka and Jared I'd help 'em move, and if things go the way they should, I promised Bess I'd be there when she pops the kid."

"You kin come with me each time, if you want," he added. "Matter of fact, I'd really love it if you was there."

"Things should be quiet enough at Mom's by then," Doreen said. "Sure. Count me in. I'd love to be there when Bess delivers her baby. She wrinkled her nose. "'Pop the kid, indeed'; how crass." Then, "Has she decided what she'll do when he comes?"

"Not so's she's let me in on. I think she'll decide after he's here. A kid inside and a kid outside's two different things. I know I would never've given up one of my kids after they come. But before? Deb was such a bitch durin' pregnancies, I woulda shipped the whole package to Canada, if I coulda'."

Bobby left for Portland early the following Monday morning. As he drove Route Nine, the shorter route to the city, he grinned as he thought of his new love, and how happy he was when they were able to spend time together. And although he would miss her, he realized that he would feel less nervous if he could just get there and have the whole mess over with.

The five hour trip passed quickly enough, and Bobby checked into a Comfort Inn in South Portland just after noon. Fortified with a large coke and two double cheeseburgers from Burger King, a short nap and a shower, Bobby was dressed and prepared for his two o'clock meeting with D. H. Sanderson, an attorney for Chambers and Slater.

SEVEN

"Nice to meet you-- Bobby, is it?" David Sanderson rose from behind his huge mahogany desk to offer a long thin hand to his visitor. "Or perhaps you'd prefer Robert."

"Bobby's m'name. Never been no Robert," Bobby replied. This smooth, impeccably dressed young man was already making him nervous. Maybe he should have let Doreen talk him into buying a jacket.

"Have a seat then, Bobby. And please, call me Dave. I have Ms. Colridge's file right here. Would you like coffee before we begin? A beer, perhaps?"

"You drink beer in your office?" Bobby was perched gingerly on the edge of the leather and walnut chair, Emma's folder on his lap.

"Love it. Most lawyers prefer scotch or Irish whiskey, or a good wine. Give me a good brew any day. There's a great micro-brewery in town; I'm the first one there when they're trying a new ale or beer. Got a great dark ale in my fridge." Of course, I don't drink all day, every day. Certainly wouldn't be very effective at my job. But I enjoy a good cold glass once or twice during the day. Relaxes me, you know? Also, usually helps to relax my clients. Care to experience it?"

"Nope, but jest the offer relaxed me some. Beer's certainly my drink a'choice," Bobby replied with a smile. "Don't us'lly choose it 'til after five, howsomever," he added.

Sanderson opened the thin folder and said, "I understand Ms. Colridge would like to have us review her stipend with the idea of a monthly increase to ease expenses," he began. "It's a pretty simple process. We'll need an account of her monthly expenses, her last three bank statements and her most recent income tax return."

"It's all in here," Bobby said as he handed Dave the folder.

After Dave had spent some minutes looking through the information Emma had sent, he nodded and said, "Looks fine. Should be no problem. Seems Mr. Manchester established a trust in her name some years ago, and it contains the stipulation that her income be increased at any time she wishes. All she needed to do was to send us this information and it would all have been pretty automatic."

He sat back in his chair and looked quizzically at Bobby. "Just to satisfy my curiosity, could you share with me why Ms. Colridge sent you to do this paltry bit of business? Obviously she doesn't have much money. Funding this trip of yours must have set her back a few pennies. So what's going on?"

"Can't say rightly as I know m'self," Bobby answered. "Miss Emma has her own way of dealin' with things in her life. She told me she hasn't needed more funds until recently, and she seemed to know she could've written or called you to take care of things, but she admitted she's been puttin' it off for months. She says she's in denial, and also admitted she's scared she might find out somethin' she don't wanna know."

"What do you suppose that may be?"

"I kinda thought you might be able to tell me. How much d'you know about Miss Emma and Thomas Manchester?"

"Actually, nothing. I've been with the firm just over three years. When Mr. Manchester dealt with us, old J.R. Chambers headed the firm, along with Chet Slater. Both of them passed on years ago. Slater's son and daughter head up the firm these days. Slater senior had stipulated in his will that Chambers' name be kept, in deference to his old partner. Chambers had no relatives, far as I know.

"Manchester set things up with Chambers. The trust is pretty simple, contains plenty of funding that's supplemented with investments negotiated by a local trusted brokerage firm, and will expire when Ms Colridge dies. The trust then stipulates that any remaining funds be transferred into Manchester's estate, to be distributed according to his will. If this will states that monies are to be transferred to Ms. Colridge's heirs, that will be a different matter. According to the terms of this particular trust, monies are not to be passed on without permission from Manchester to change the distribution. Are you aware of a will?"

"Nope. Miss Emma said she searched for it after he passed, but it wasn't found." Bobby shook his head. "Tell me, does Miss Emma have any say in how much she can draw from the funds?"

"Sure. She can take out up to forty thousand a year."

"How much does she take out now?"

"Only about eighteen thousand."

"Jeez. That's hardly enough to buy groceries, these days."

Sanderson nodded. "Right. And at this point, may I bring something to your attention. I'm not obligated to tell you this, Bobby, but for some reason I trust you. Probably for the same reason Emma Colridge trusts you.

"Ms. Colridge has given you complete power of attorney over her estate. That means you are able to conduct business for her. Perhaps, since she has such difficulty dealing with a large sum of money, you could withdraw funds in her name, to assure that she is taken care of in her last years. She's getting on, isn't she?"

"She's eighty-eight. She's got a bit of money left from her Daddy's estate, but that's almost gone. She ain't got health insurance, neither. Her doctor's been treatin' her gratis, for the most part.

Sanderson smiled. "There's a clause in the trust that states that if Ms. Colridge should require medical care at any time, it will be completely taken care of. We would just need correspondence and the bills from the medical personnel who treat her."

"Is your firm in charge of Manchester's estate?"

"I'm afraid not. This trust is the only thing we ever handled for Mr. Manchester. I have no idea where his estate is based; it isn't in Portland. In fact," he added, "it isn't in Maine."

"How d'you know that?"

"All estate information for any of our clients in the state would be in our files. We have no information about the man other than that in this file," he stated, indicating the thin file before him.

"So, how would you know where to send any leftovers after Miss Emma passes?"

"We wouldn't. His will would conceivably indicate where his other monies are located, and any heirs would apply to us to transfer the funds."

"Well, Jeez." Bobby shook his head. "More I know about this man, more I'm flummoxed." He sat back, fully relaxed now. "Emma tells me he's from Portland. That's what he told her. He also married her; was you aware of that?"

"Absolutely not. We were never informed that she had changed her name, or that they had married. Does she have proof of that?"

"That unmarked white envelope in her file, the one you didn't open, that's her marriage certificate. They's married over twenty-two years.

"And that's another thing. He was hardly ever with 'er all that time. He'd travel a lot, bring her back things from all over the world, spend a few weeks or maybe a couple months with her, then off he'd go again."

Bobby's story concerning Thomas and Emma fascinated Sanders. So much so that he convinced Bobby to share a dark ale, then a second, while Bobby told him the complete story of Emma Manchester, nee Colridge, and how he happened to be in Portland conducting her business. When he had finished David Sanderson sat, saying nothing, for some moments.

Finally, "Amazing. Simply amazing. Never heard anything like it. You should really write a book."

"Mebbe I will, some day. Or have it done, at least."

"Well. The question is, where do we go from here?" The attorney thought for some seconds. "My suggestion, should you care to hear it, is that you remove enough funds to make up forty thou from the trust as soon as possible. It's almost October, and Emma can take another forty on the first of January. That will ensure her about sixty thou after taxes, and she won't need to pay the taxes on the forty until April of the following year. "That should take care of any needs she might have at least for the next fifteen months."

"Emma'd kill me if she thought I'd taken out all that. She's got such a thing about spendin' money she feels ain't hers."

"No problem. We'll arrange for the two of you to have an account through our firm with the bank we use for the trust. We will continue to send Emma a modestly increased amount of money, albeit from yours and Emma's joint account rather than from the original trust. We'll also arrange for forty thou to be transferred to your joint account each January one, for as long as Emma lives. If she wants to pass monies on, those funds will be in her estate, not tied up in Manchester's. As for you informing her of all of these events, it would be your call.

"By the by," he added, "are you sure their marriage is legal?"

"Jeez. Why wouldn't it be?"

"I don't know. Perhaps there is some kind of hanky panky going on here. She may not have been the only woman in Manchester's life. He may have trotted around the world, "marrying" women he took a fancy to, and leaving them with trusts. He wouldn't be the first asshole to do that to a woman.

"For that matter," he added, "Manchester may not even be Manchester. Could be an alias."

"Ah, crap. What'f you're right. Poor Emma. It'd kill her." Bobby sighed. "How'd I ever find out, d'you think?"

"Good question. Do you know anyone who knew the two of them? Preferably, who knew anything more than she did about Manchester?"

"Matter of fact, I do," Bobby replied. "Name's Jonathan Brimmer. He s'posedly worked for Manchester 'til he died. "Sailed under 'im." Bobby thought a minute. "But, if you're right, he may also be a phony. Jeez."

"True. My next step, if I were you, would be to get in touch with this man as soon as possible, With the old gal so frail, and getting to the end of her days, you've no time to waste."

"Good thinkin'. He is supposed to live in South Portland. And I gotta see my daughter tomorrow. I'll see if I kin find him. Emma included his phone number in her folder, but I ain't sure he's still alive. She ain't heard from him for a while."

Sanderson pulled a recent phone book from his desk drawer. "Save you some steps if I can," he said. A moment later, he wrote an address on a slip of paper. "He's on Vine Ave. I'm giving you the address and directions. It's not hard to find, from your hotel.

"When you finish your business in the city, drop by. I'll prepare transfer papers for you to sign, and we can issue a check to Emma within a couple of days."

He rose. "Great talking with you, Bobby Parker. You made my day." They shook hands vigorously. "By the by, did you like the ale?"

"It was great. I gotta go talk with my girl, fill her in on the day's doin's. She's gonna be as gollywagged as I am over this whole thing."

"Nice; you have a girl. I wouldn't mind teaming up with someone, but don't have much time for the search. Keep thinking I"ll meet Ms. Right without trying. Had a few somewhat serious trysts, but they don't stay long. I work too hard. Seems women want their men to be around at least some of the time." He smiled wryly.

"Some of th'time is all I'm us'lly around. But she works as hard as I do, so we're doin' okay, so far. She's a keeper, so if she wants me around more, I guess I'll be around." The two new acquaintances shook hands vigorously. "Good talkin' with you, Dave. And drinkin'. See you tomorrow."

EIGHT

At precisely nine the next morning, Bobby was sitting with his enormously pregnant daughter on the sprawling screened-in veranda at the Freedom House for Women. Bess was trying her best to get comfortable in a wooden rocker, while Bobby chose one of the deep cushioned wicker chairs.

When he had arrived an hour earlier to join his daughter for breakfast, the receptionist informed him that his daughter was not dressed, so he walked to a diner a short distance away and returned after downing four blueberry pancakes and two cups of coffee. When he tried to hug her, Bess pulled back, giving him a quick peck on the cheek.

"Too far along to fit y'self into one of these, I guess," he grinned as he watched her struggle to sit upright.

"Two more weeks; seems like two years," his daughter whined.

"You're doin' fine, Bess. Be over in no time." Bobby noted that Bess looked more mature. Her hair was still short, but had regained its natural chestnut color. She looked healthy for the first time in years. "You're lookin' real good," he offered.

"Sure, you'd say that. Y'prob'ly like fat wimmen. Like that Doreen you're with."

"Wait jest a minute, girl," Bobby retorted. "You're soundin' jest like your Mumma. She been here givin' you her version of my life?"

"She comes every Friday, takes me out t' dinner. More'n you done," Bess sulked.

"I s'pose she's tellin' you what to do about the kid, too," Bobby said.

"That's between Mumma and me."

"Fine. You still want me and Doreen t'be here when you have the kid?"

"Okay if you come, but Mumma says she won't help me out at all if you bring the cow."

Bobby rose. "Guess you've chose your side, Bess. You know how your mumma and me feel about each other. Y'also know how I feel about Doreen Shanahan. We're livin' t'gether, and mebbe some day we're gonna marry.

"Doreen'd sure like t'be here with me when you have the kid. If y'don't want her, then y'don't want me. That's the deal. Take it or leave it."

"Mumma and Sissa promised they'd be there. Guess that's all I need," Bess offered. "Besides, I think I'm gonna keep the kid, collect some welfare, live with them for a bit." Bess glared at Bobby. "Mumma's got a new boyfriend. Rich guy, gives her lots of stuff. She's plannin' t' live with him real soon, too."

"You ain't changed much, Bess. Always lookin' for an opportunity t' goof off. Gonna live off the state, off your mumma, off her boyfriend. They call wimmen like you opportunists, or gold diggers. You'd rather suck off others than work."

Bobby sighed. "I love you, Bess. I'm always gonna be your dad. But I ain't gonna support your lousy choices. So I guess I'll be goin'. I would like to see the kid if you decide to keep 'im. If you call me when you're ready to, I'll come. But I'll most likely bring Doreen. You gotta know that." Bess shrugged, tried unsuccessfully to rise gracefully from the rocker.

"I'll be goin, then," Bobby said tersely.

"Shit," he muttered as he stomped off the porch, leaving his daughter to finally make it to her feet and waddle into the building.

Bobby strode heavily down the city street, breathing hard, working to restrain his seething rage. When he had walked long and far enough to calm himself, he hailed a cab to take him to Jonathan Brimmer's. His frustration with the choices Bess had made was really anger at Debra, and he knew it. Deb had been working hard to drag their vulnerable daughter to her with her old manipulative tricks. She was good, he had to admit. And it didn't hurt her cause to know that Bess was more like her than her father.

What he couldn't figure out was that Bess and Debra had always been on opposite sides of an argument. They fought like two alley cats going for the same fishhead. All he could figure was that Deb was doing it to get back at him. But why would she want to, if she'd met the rich man she'd always dreamt of? Just maybe, that man wasn't all Deb or Bess made him out to be. Or maybe Deb just couldn't stand to lose any man in her life. "That's prob'ly it," he reasoned.

"Hope I ain't lost her for good," he mused as he rode. He knew, however, that he could not allow the confrontation with his daughter to interfere with the meeting he was about to attend. He had called Jonathan, who warmly welcomed him, asking only that he come after eleven, since it took him some time to get going in his declining years.

By the time Bobby arrived at the small house on Vine he had taken time to breathe deeply, and to push his issues with Bess and his soon to be ex-wife into the nether recesses of his mind, to be dealt with at a later date.

NINE

Jonathan Brimmer was working to balance a plastic pitcher of iced tea in one hand and a silver-headed cane in the other. "No. Don't get up. I'm used to this," he said as Bobby rose to help him. "Need to keep moving, or I'll freeze right up like the Tin Man," he quipped as he set the container on the coffee table and returned to the kitchen for glasses and napkins.

"Now, Mr. Parker," he said as he settled into the rocker across from Bobby. "What can I do for you, besides pouring you some tea?"

Jonathan Brimmer was slight and wiry, with the appearance of a man who had been very strong and agile in his youth. He looked to be in his early eighties. His hands were deformed with arthritis, and he obviously had trouble walking on his right leg. His mind, however, seemed fine, and his clear green eyes lit up as he welcomed Bobby into his small, well-kept home. Bobby warmed instantly to the old man.

"Well, like I said when I called, I'm here on business for Miss Emma Manchester. Been to 'er lawyers to straighten out a couple things for her. Jest b'fore I left Milltown, she suggested I drop by to see 'f you're still here, check up on you, I guess."

"Miss Emma. I always called her that, also. She's quite a woman. Mr. Thomas was very fond of her. Very fond. And I couldn't say that about all of the women he was involved with. I used to call her often and visit once in a while, but I've drawn in these past few years, you might say," he continued. "So many aches and pains, doesn't seem worth my while to go out any more than I need.

"Nice to have a bit of company, though," he added. "I used to bunk with another retired sailor, but Mike passed away over a year ago. Now it's just me, rattling around in the house." Jonathan peered intently at Bobby over his rimless glasses. "She told you about her Thomas yet?"

"She's told me what she knows about Thomas Manchester. I guess that's why I'm really here. I got a need t'know 'im from some other source, someone who knew 'im when he wasn't with her.

"The lawyer, Dave Sanderson, tells me that the only info they have on him is the trust he set up for Emma. They don't know where his money come from, nor whether there's any more than they're respons'ble for. Seems Manchester told Emma he's from Portland, but he ain't, Ain't any money in his name in another bank in Maine."

He went on to tell Jonathan about Emma's financial predicament, and how he and Sanderson had arranged to free up extra funds in her name without Emma's permission. Jonathan agreed that she would probably not approve of the arrangement if she were aware of it. "Some stubborn, that woman is," Bobby added. Then, "You worked for the guy for a lot of years. How well did you know 'im, if y'don't mind my askin'?"

Jonathan nodded. "Yep. Worked with him, traveled with him, ate and drank and smoked good cigars with him. In all that time, we never became close. He paid me well, provided for me, made it possible for me to have all this, along with good insurance for myself for this time of life. He surely was a good boss.

"When we met, Thomas did live in Portland. At least, he kept a small apartment by the water. But he gave that up a short time after we decided that I would be his permanent mate. Seems that before me, he would hire out someone different for each trip he took. He owned a smaller ship then, and hadn't taken the long voyages in the large schooner we sailed on in later years. That was his home until he moved his things in with Emma." Jonathan fell silent, remembering.

Finally, "Thomas was a man with secrets. Never knew what he'd done with his life before we met; he never offered that information. What I do know is, he lost his mother when he was young, was raised by a grandmother. Her name, I don't know. He said only one thing regarding his father; that they didn't want anything to do with each other. He told me he took his mother's maiden name, which was Manchester, when he left home at eighteen to go to sea the first time. Whether that was true, I don't know. Never revealed his father's name to me.

"His mother's family had money, he said. Educated and supported him well. I think they were originally from Boston. He wanted for nothing, went everywhere he wished, purchased any possessions he wanted or needed, no regard as to cost."

Johnathan paused. "You ready for more tea?" he asked. Bobby shook his head. "Nope. I'm fine; more int'rested in y'r story."

The older man smiled. "Must say, this is the most I have talked in years." He looked at Bobby. "Feels good, remembering again."

Then, "The man loved the sea. He signed on as crew to go to China right out of school, never was really comfortable on dry land from then on. He would spend short times exploring foreign lands, or staying with Emma, but he wasn't ever in one place very long." Jonathan paused again.

"Must say, I'm enjoying your company, Bobby. Say, would you like some lunch? I've got ham and cheese in the fridge. I need to eat at regular hours, I find; my stomach is informing me that it's time." Bobby was about to protest, but Jonathan stopped him. "Please stay, Bobby. I don't get much chance to talk with anyone about the old days. Think about them a lot, but it sure feels good to remember times when my body was whole, out on the sea. I loved it as much as Mr. Thomas did," he added wistfully.

Bobby agreed to join him for lunch, which they shared at the small kitchen table, conversing only about the weather and goings-on in the city. After the plates were cleaned, large mugs of coffee were taken to the sitting room, and the recall of Jonathan Brimmer's time with Thomas Manchester resumed with a question from Bobby.

"What d'you know about their marriage?"

"I know that Thomas loved Emma. I also know that they had a ceremony at the small church in Milltown, and that a license was purchased and signed legally. I did see that paper after he died, when I went through his things looking for his will. Whether it was Thomas' only marriage, or whether he was married to another when he joined with Emma, I can only speculate." Jonathan paused. "Never did find that damn will," he added.

"If you know Emma, you are aware that she would not travel with him. She would not share his greatest passion aside from his love for her. Because of that, he was lonely much of the time. And due to that loneliness, I would like to think, he often sought out the company of women.

"I did not meet all of these women, but I was invited to dine on occasion with him and one of his female friends. They were always lovely, mannered women who seemed to be thoroughly smitten with Mr. Thomas. The color of their skin, their hair, or their ages varied, but they all shared a great fondness for him and a certain air of the cultured and educated.

"I know that there were a chosen few that he spent an inordinate amount of time with,"

Jonathan continued. "There was a woman in Japan, a lovely young woman in France, and another in Australia. The relationship with the one in Australia consumed almost a whole year of his life.

"Whether he married any of these women, I am not aware. But I am certain that he did provide for them if or when they required provision." Jonathan smiled wryly. "Thomas was very good to all of his women. But," he added, "I am also as certain that he loved Miss Emma. And that he always wished to return to her.

"He did, after all, die while he was with her. I have a feeling he chose to be with her at that time, knowing that his days were limited. He did realize that his condition was terminal, you know."

"No I din't, and neither did Emma."

"He would never have shared that information with her. He considered her too fragile. He had been informed a year earlier that he was living with a fraction of his heart muscle. He apparently had suffered two or three of what the medics called 'silent heart attacks' during his life. He said they told him he probably experienced them as bouts of indigestion, possibly coupled with a certain soreness in his arms or back, so he took a handful of antacids and aspirin and went on with his life.

"He laughed when he related that to me. 'Guess that's about right, wouldn't you say, old man?' he said." I agreed; that's exactly what Mr. Thomas would do. During those last years he carried a bottle of nitro pills in his pocket, and got on with his life. Told Emma he had a problem a pacemaker would fix, to placate her. Worked, too."

"And that's about all I know concerning Mr. Thomas Manchester," he said. "Does it help with your solution of Miss Emma's problem?"

"Dunno. I guess I'm wonderin' if I could ever tell her any of this," Bobby said, shaking his head. "Don't know as I consider her too fragile to hear it. Jest don't know.

"I ain't doin' too well with it m'self, you wanna know," he continued. "All this is hard t'hear, thinkin' how much that old woman loved him, and how here he was, trottin' around the world, keepin' company with any woman who fell in his path.

"And mebbe you thought you could trust him, but he told Miss Emma many things that don't line up, that is if your version of his life is true. Like the banker stuff. He told her he went to college and trained to be a banker.

Then he joined his father's bank and they shared a career until he was somewhere in his thirties.

"So what's the real story? The one he told you, or the story Emma told me?"

Jonathan was silent for some moments. "Tell you the truth, Bobby, I don't know. I did meet him when he was in his early forties, but he never mentioned a career aside from his journeys on the seas." Jonathan shook his head sadly. "Don't know what to make of your story," he finished. "I'd hate to think Mr. Thomas was not trustworthy. That would not have been the man I worked with all of those years."

"He's pissin' me off, and I never even knew 'im." Bobby offered.

"He would probably not have angered you if you had known him," Jonathan offered. "Mr. Thomas was a charming, charismatic man, and I have a feeling that everyone he knew forgave him his weaknesses. Including me," he smiled. "He had little guile, and would probably have shared his experiences, all of them, with Emma, if he had felt she could bear them. He did not like to lie, and I am sure that the women he left were very aware of his feelings. He may have hidden truths concerning his personal past, but he never told me anything that couldn't be backed up. Even though I knew he was hiding facts from me, even if I thought he had not been called Thomas Manchester all of his life, I trusted him.

"And regarding Miss Emma, I know that because he could not tell her all, he told her what she needed to hear; he simply left out the rest. Whatever he chose to share with her was the truth.

"I considered him one of the most amazing men I have had the pleasure to meet. I will always be grateful to him for the time we worked together." Jonathan sighed. "And, I wish you luck if you choose to pursue the remainder of his biography. I tried to locate a final will while I was in Milltown, but I failed. I think it is there, however; I just could not locate it." The older man shrugged. "If it does exist, it would certainly fill in many of the parts of the puzzle which was Thomas Manchester. Perhaps you will find it."

"Mebbe so. I had it in my mind when I came here that you and Sanderson would supply all the missing' parts. Hoo, boy, was I wrong. I'm still in limbo with all this." Bobby sighed loudly. "And I don't know if I want to take it another step," he said. "Mebbe limbo's gonna lead to hell. At least for Miss Emma."

TEN

Bobby woke to rain on the roof and Doreen's voice on the phone. "If you'll hold on a minute, I'll see if he's awake. He got in real late last night," she stated. "Bobby?" she called up to him. "You awake yet?"

"Yep, I'm up," he answered sleepily.

"Emma's on the phone. You ready to talk with her?"

"Sure, I'll be right down."

The old lady must be real anxious to find out what happened in Portland, he thought as he pulled on jeans and a sweatshirt. "Do I smell coffee?" he asked as he took the phone from Doreen, planting a kiss on her cheek.

"I'll bring you a cup. I'm on my way out. Mom wants me at the restaurant right away. Big order just came in for the campground. Bunch of bikers staying' there." As she dashed to the kitchen, she added, "I should be back late afternoon; we can catch up then."

"Good; see you later, Love." Then, "Hey Miss Emma, how are you this mornin'? I don't often git phone calls from you. I'm honored, I must say,"

"I don't usually make them, Mr. Parker," Emma retorted. "I could not manage to wait another minute to find out how you made out in the big metropolis of Portland." He could hear the lilt of laughter in her voice. "I am sorry to have pulled you from your bed, however," she added.

"It's okay, gittin' late anyhow, I need t'git goin'."

"Were you able to connect with Chambers?"

"Not exactly, seein' as how he's been dead for years. I did git to speak with Dave Sanderson, one of their lawyers. Our interaction was quite straightforward, I gotta say. Turns out there's still lots of moolah in your trust, and we made arrangements to increase your monthly check.

"Sanderson also says there's enough in the till to take care of you should you need extra medical care, or more expensive heart meds or whatever."

"Good, That certainly relieves me. You did not request too much of an increase, did you? I do not want to remove any more monies than I will need."

"Nope. We figgered out a decent monthly budget increase, and that's what you'll be gittin'." Bobby squirmed with discomfort as he talked with the old woman, aware that he was keeping facts from her. He had definitely decided that it was necessary to keep most of the information he had obtained from Sanderson and Jonathan Brimmer secret from his friend. He considered her condition too fragile to have her exposed to her deceased husband's transgressions. "You sh'd have a check in a week or so," he added.

"You cannot know how relieved that information makes me," Emma said. "Tell me, were you also able to connect with Jonathan?"

"Yep, he sends his best. He's pretty healthy save for a lot of aches and pains, 'specially in his hip. Says he's due for a replacement of the joint, but he ain't got the courage for it yet. He says he'll try to git up to see you when he feels better."

"I am glad you were able to meet. Jonathan is a sweet man." Emma paused. Then, "And tell me, were you able to discover why it is that I receive checks in my maiden name?"

"Not really. Seems Thomas set it up that way, and never requested a change after you two joined. Sanderson wasn't aware that you'd ever married."

"Hmm. I don't know why that should bother me, but it does. It's not that Thomas did not provide well for me. It was probably an oversight in his busy life." She sighed, "It does not change the fact that it continues to bother me, however.

"But the job is finished, Bobby, so far as you are concerned. Our opus is complete. I am certain I will feel satisfied with whatever you and this Sanderson have decided is a good sum for me. The maiden name thing is strictly my problem, and must be resolved by me. I am so grateful to have enough to live on, so that my life can be comfortable until the end."

"Wasn't nothin', Miss Emma. I had a good time, act'lly. Jonathan and me got on quite fine, and the lawyer was easy to talk with. Stretched my world a bit, and nothin' wrong with that. Got me into some new duds, too, which pleased Miss Doreen no end." He laughed. "Say, how you been feelin', Emma?" he asked.

"I am fine, Bobby. Missing your company, now that the work is completed on my house. I have had many positive comments on its new appearance, I must say. When do you plan to be in my area again?"

"Frankly, it'll be a while, Miss Emma. Both Doreen and me got lots of work to catch up on. She's settin' up the pizza place to suit herself, since her mumma plans to retire next month. She means t' organize the business better, so's she won't need to work so hard. Hire good help, for one. Mebbe even a manager to work part-time. She'd like t'work four days a week instead of six.

"And me, I got jobs lined up 'round the block. Could go every day for a year, but I'm tryin' to organize my work so I kin work five days, have weekends off. Now that I got someone t'spend my weekends with," he added briskly. "We're also movin' Becka and Jared and the kids t' Portland next week, and Bess is due to have her kid in two weeks. Makes for one busy life, as you kin see," he finished.

"But," he added, "I'll try t'git out there a couple times a month if I can; how's that? We kin have tea and goodies and catch up on things."

"That would be fine with me," Emma said. "Even a phone call once in a blue moon would please me. I can see that your life has become much more complex since your love moved into it," she added. "I am very happy for you. Hearing about your life brings back thoughts of my youth. Oh, to be fifty again," she said, and laughed. "Enjoy these days, Bobby. Don't work too hard. Life passes too quickly to waste it doing those things which do not matter to you. Remember that."

'And I got somethin' for you to remember, Emma. Jonathan Brimmer told me that he was certain that you were Thomas Manchester's true love."

ELEVEN

A preview of winter hit Washington County the following week. The temperature plummeted below freezing, and three inches of snow covered the ground overnight. Doreen and Bobby moved Becka's family during the early hard frost. And Bess delivered an eight-pound healthy boy on the last morning of October. Bobby wondered if they would name him after some ghoul, since he had arrived on Halloween. He was not present for the delivery, since Bess had remained firm in her resolve to have only her mother and Sissa present. Doreen sent Bess a large box filled with baby clothes, toys and blankets; the gift was never acknowledged. "Prob'ly gave it to the Salvation Army, or even worse, never opened it," Bobby remarked with some sarcasm.

He called Deb in early November to find out haw Bess had made out. "She's fine, jest fine," Deb spit out. "Big boy, name's Dustin. Not my choice, b'lieve me; you can't talk that kid outta nothin'; but you know that already, Bobby. Y'always said she was jest like her mumma.

"She ain't doin' too well, though. Kinda depressed. Don't wanna breast feed, and don't wanna even think about gittin' a job somewhere. I can't support her the rest of her life, y'know. Welfare don't half give her enough to live on. As good as that baby is, we don't wanna raise it, neither.

"Oh, and by the by. I got notice yesterday that our divorce is final. So you got three months to sell the house or get up my twenty-two thou'."

Bobby didn't miss the reference to "we". He decided not to pursue it. "I'll chip in a bit for a couple months," he said, "but I got no intention of supportin' her neither. Tell her I'll send a check next week." He sighed. "Tell her I miss her, and I'd like t'see Dustin sometime soon, if it's okay with her."

"It'd be fine with her, if you'd take her back. But she won't live with the cow, and she won't call so long's you're with her," Debra retorted.

"That's enough for me. I'll send the check." Bobby hung up. He sat for a moment, teeth clenched, then went to get coffee. Doreen found him at the kitchen table. "Somethin' wrong?"

Bobby sat at the table, dropping his head into his hands. He began to sob. "Oh my,"

Doreen said as she held him. When he could speak, he told her about the conversation. Doreen said nothing. "I feel like I lost her for good," he said finally.

"I'm so sorry you're hurting, Love," Doreen murmured. "And sorry I can't make it go away." She sat, holding his hands. "Havin' kids is never easy, is it," she offered.

"Havin' that one sure wasn't," he replied. He then told Doreen about the divorce being final, and the house needing to be put on the market.

"Good, That will get both of us out from under that bitch," Doreen muttered. "Can't be soon enough for me."

Emma crept into Bobby's thoughts on a regular basis. When he thought of her he called, or took time from his busy schedule to visit. Doreen asked her to join them for Christmas Eve, but Emma declined, stating that her church friend Wilma had entertained her each Christmas Eve since Thomas had died, and that was fine with her. Having no close relations, she never went out on Christmas Day, preferring to build a fire and listen to her crooners' renditions of Christmas carols.

Doreen and Bobby had joined Bobby's family for Thanksgiving, along with Doreen's mother. Following that day, Doreen confessed that holidays with Bobby's huge family were a bit overwhelming, and had stated that if he didn't mind, she would rather have dinner on Christmas with him, Dicky and perhaps Emma if she wished to come. Bobby was fine with that. When Dicky chose to have dinner at Helen's and Emma declined, they spent a lovely quiet afternoon, watching light snowdrift down and dining on duck l'orange, sweet potato and apple cobbler.

"Thought I'd miss turkey, but that dinner beat the hell outta the bird," Bobby offered as he poured merlot into two glasses by the bed. "I'm even learnin' t'like this wine. And I'm definitely learnin' to like you, Miss Doreen." He nudged her over and lay with her. "More and more each day," he added softly.

INTERLUDE: The Author

It's been a year since Sam and I met in the park. Did I decide to move in with him? Yes, I did. Made the big move three months ago, just after the holidays. And yes, we finally did have a fight. It was a doozy. Had to do with Kristen.

As I have stated, Kris can often be very sullen, and very stubborn. My way of dealing with her is to ignore her for the most part, but there are times when she really gets to me with her whining and complaining when the world is not going according to her interpretation of it. Which can be often. Just before Thanksgiving, Kris came to me one Saturday morning after having perused the Sears Christmas catalogue thoroughly and having decided that she wanted at least half of the age-appropriate items contained within. (I must interject that this is no different from every year since she was three).

I responded to her mile-long list as I always had. "Ask Santa, Kris; he's the one to decide what you'll find under the tree."

"That old Santa must be pretty poor," she responded. "I never get more than a couple things on my list. How come all my friends get piles of stuff and I get crap?"

I was about to respond with my usual smart remark, when, "Maybe crap is what you deserve," Sam said softly, looking sternly at Kris over the morning paper he supposedly had been immersed in. My reaction surprised even me. "What's that supposed to mean?" I snapped. Then I turned to Kris. "Get out of here, Kris. Go finish your homework. I'll call you when dinner's ready."

"Jeez, Ma, I haven't done nothin'," Kris whined. "I don't have any homework, anyways."

"Do as your mother says," Sam said tersely, teeth clenched. "Just go."

Kris huffed off, list in tow. As soon as her bedroom door slammed, I lost it. What did he mean, all she deserved was crap? Where was he coming from? How dared he think he could talk to my daughter that way? And on and on, defending this kid who could drive me crazy.

Sam listened as I ranted. Then he told me that he was having a hard time with Kris's lack of discipline. He thought she got away with far too much, because I either became involved in long battles with her that ended with my giving in or giving up, or I gave in to stop her whining. He even said that there were times he did not like my daughter.

Through with ranting, I commenced to the next step. I cried. Sam sat with me until I finished. Then we talked about Kris. Turns out, I was about to respond to her with my version of the same words Sam used. I defended her because she was mine, not his, and I didn't feel he had the right to feel that way about her. Only I had that right, because I could love her even if I didn't like the things she did.

We actually worked it out. Sam rode my emotional roller coaster with me, and helped solve the problem. We agreed that I would basically ignore Kris's complaints, and that either Sam or I would tell her to do something once, then supply a punishment if she didn't do what she was told. "That'll be really hard," I said. "Can I leave if I want to get into it with her? Maybe I need to go to my room and stuff my fingers in my ears." Sam laughed, and agreed to stay and see it out if I needed to escape.

That episode did it, for me. Any guy who could argue like that and come through it unscathed, even laughing, was all right in my book. We celebrated our first negative interaction with a glass of red and decided we would give the new plan a try for three months, and if we could make it work, we would move in together.

With a pile of hard work all around, we made it. And Kris is a much nicer person to be with, I must admit. I thought her temper was something she couldn't shake—blamed it all on her resemblance to Big Steve. But it turned out to be a combo of that and my lack of parental structuring. Who knew.

Bobby and Doreen invited us for New Year's dinner, along with Gramma and Grampa Gianni. Their little house was bursting with family and friends. Helen Parker and her Calais friend Dwayne came, along with Bess and Jared and their kids. Dicky was spending the day with his new wife's parents. He had married Marcie in September, and planned to adopt her son Tory. Mary Shanahan, now completely retired, was also there, and contributed Irish bread in lieu of her usual pizza.

Bess was invited, but didn't show. Word was that she was living with another "scumbag", as Bobby put it, and that Debra and her new husband Vinnie were caring for her small son. I knew that it continued to be difficult for Bobby to admit that his wayward child was probably not going to reform. I thought it to his credit that although he loved her, he refused to support her self-destruction. I was aware of too many parents who were not willing to give up, and allowed their grown offspring to drain them financially and emotionally.

The book is not yet completed. I am still working on the final section. Our original intent was to finish it with the fourth part. After all, a "resolution" implies that everything is resolved, right? Well, wrong, as it turned out. So we're going for a fifth part, which is the truth. Because Emma wanted it that way, Bobby said.

Turns out that Emma never was satisfied with the information Bobby brought her after his visit to Portland. She told him she was, probably to placate him, and maybe because for a short while, she figured she could live with it. It was a resolution of sorts, but it did not end Emma's story. The truth was, she spent many a sleepless night not knowing who Thomas was when he was not with her. So the "resolution" was not the truth. And the truth needed to be told. Bobby chose to name the last part because he thought that's what Emma would have wanted.

That was fine with me, because I knew from our discussions that the full truth took some time to emerge. We could have changed the titles around, I suppose, but that didn't seem to fit, either. So, it is what it is. We're all satisfied with it.

Life has become more complicated, trying to finish the book, and adjust to my new life. I love our house, but it's large, and needs care that I'm not able to give it while I work. I'm strung out enough trying to be there for three kids and Sam. Sam does most of his work from home, so we're sharing an office. It's not easy finding quiet time to let words flow. As a result, the writing has slowed. Bobby doesn't seem to mind; he's been up to his nose in work himself. He's adding a second floor to Brittny and Brud's little cabin. Brittny's pregnant with twins, and driving Bobby around the bend with her demands. Some things never change.

Leena Gianni is here twice a week, cleaning and cooking for us. She says she loves it; her life at home was boring her. Not enough company to feed, and Grampa spends all of his time in the basement with his various whittling projects. We certainly appreciate her help. I wouldn't mind if she moved right in; the kids love her. She sings and plays with them, and is teaching them basic Italian. Sam is especially happy because Leena loves to be with Chelsee, and she won't be ready for preschool for another year. It leaves him with more time to work or even better, to be with me. That's definitely a good thing.

5

The Truth

ONE

Bobby was slathering plaster on Pat McBrine's living room wall when his cell rang. "What?" he answered, balancing it while he set his flat tool on the top of the ladder. "Hey. Hope you're on the ground," Doreen said.

"Nope, but I ain't gonna fall; what's up?"

"Emma's in the hospital. She's had a heart attack."

"Shit. Where is she?"

"In Ellsworth. Her shopping buddy found her this morning. She was sitting in a chair, holding her arm. Said she'd had indigestion all night, and her arm was a bit numb. Woman rushed her to the local clinic, and they sent her to Ellsworth in an ambulance. She told her friend to call you."

"I gotta clean up here, then I'll go down; can you go with me?"

"Sorry, hon, I can't. Mom doesn't work today, and it's slow so no one else is on the schedule to come in. I'm stuck here 'til nine. Give her my love, Bobby. And you drive carefully. One person in the hospital is more than enough for me."

It's been nearly a year since I found the old lady on the ground, Bobby mused as he drove as quickly as he dared through the early February cold. The roads were slippery in spots where "black ice", that coating of frozen water over macadam which often endangered drivers until the spring thaw. He knew that as safe and dry as the roads seemed, there could be a patch of black ice around the next corner, and driving through it too fast could send him careening into the nearest tree.

He reached the small hospital by late afternoon, and was directed to Emma's bed in the IC unit. He gasped as he saw his friend hooked up to what seemed like dozens of tubes leading from her nose, chest, arm and god only knew where else to various machinery which was placed around the bed. She was sheet-white, and looked to be barely breathing. Her eyes were closed, but opened slowly as he took her small, frail hand.

"Good. They found you. I'm sorry to drag you away from your work, Bobby Parker," she whispered.

"Wasn't much of a drag, Miss Emma; more like a zip," Bobby quipped. "What're you doin' in bed this time a day?"

"Thought I might take an extra little nap," Emma returned with a hint of a smile. "Almost took the last nap, they tell me," she added softly. "But I think I fooled the old devil this time." She smiled fully then, and closed her eyes. "I need to sleep some more now," she said.

Bobby sat with her, watching her light breaths. He was afraid if he left, her old heart would give up. When a nurse came to check on her, she told Bobby that Emma was basically out of the woods for now. Her heart was worn and weak, but it had survived the damage and would heal.

"This attack is bound to leave her pretty worn out," she added. "She might want to think about livin' with a relative when she's dismissed, rather than goin' home alone. These attacks are harder on people as elderly as she is. If it was you or me, we'd be up and runnin' in a month or so. It'll take a lot longer, with Emma."

"Ain't got no relatives," Bobby offered. "I guess you c'd say I'm her only family at this point." He sighed. "And bein' the stubborn old bird that she is, no way would she come t'live with me." He rose, stretched. "Mebbe I kin find her someone to take care of her before she gits out."

"Good luck with that, then," the nurse replied. "She ought to be ready to leave in about a week, if all goes accordin' to Hoyle."

"Alls I kin say is, Hoyle better be on my side right now," Bobby replied tersely.

Following calls to Emma's doctor, a home care service and the pastor of Emma's church, Bobby located a woman whose niece had recently divorced her abusive mate, and had accepted Millie Hayward's invitation to recoup with her. Nora Corcoran would meet with Bobby the next day to discuss the possibility of becoming a live-in companion to the old woman for as long as she was needed.

Bobby stayed at Emma's that night so he would be in town early enough to meet with Nora. She knocked on the kitchen door just after eight. "Mr. Parker? You home? It's Nora."

He opened the door to a large-boned, fresh-faced young woman with short, bouncy red curls. "Hey. I'm Bobby. Forget the Mr. stuff."

Nora and Bobby liked each other immediately. The young woman had traveled from Ireland five years before to marry a man from Calais that she met on the Internet. She realized that planning to marry a man she didn't know was foolhardy, but she did not have the funds to come to the states, and she wanted to become a nurse. He promised to pay her way and to fund her training. He kept the promise, and she had received a degree as a registered nurse a year ago. The man was pleasant enough to live with, and Nora felt she had made a good decision.

Following the completion of her training, her husband informed her that she had better plan to use the degree to nurse him, because no way was she going to work. Her job was to care for him, and only him. He feared her working in a hospital, since he was certain that she would leave him "for some doctor". Nora attempted to argue with him to no avail, then decided he might change his mind if she agreed to stay home for a time. Three months later, she applied for a job in a small regional hospital. When her husband discovered that she planned to work without his permission, he beat her thoroughly, stating that she was a disobedient wife, and deserved to be punished.

Nora left. Fortunately, her husband had an aunt in Milltown who loved his wife, but did not think much of him. Millie was happy to offer the young woman a home. "Ain't plannin' to stay here forever, though," she offered. "Plan to get meself together, then work me career in Bangor."

The young woman agreed to meet with Emma and Bobby at the hospital the day before she was due to return home, to decide whether they could work out an arrangement which would benefit both. Bobby felt he needed to be there, since a mediator might help Emma to make a decision.

Fortunately, there was no need for mediation. Emma's physician had made it very clear to her that if she did not find someone to care for her on a daily basis he would send her straight from the hospital to a nursing facility. He outlined her problem thoroughly with her, making certain that she knew how deteriorated her heart muscle was, and that if she overworked it, it would surely die.

Emma also took to Nora immediately. "Cute accent," she remarked. "Thank you, but I'm workin' hard t'rid meself of it," Nora responded.

"A shame," Emma remarked. "My parents trained me to drop my local accent at a very young age. They were overly proud, and somewhat ashamed of their roots. I hope you don't feel that way."

Nora shrugged. "P'raps oi do. Interestin' observation."

Emma grinned up at her, the twinkle apparent in her eyes. "We'll get along just fine, Miss Nora."

"Guess my work's done here," Bobby stated. "I'm off to see if I kin finish up a job I started yesterday." He bent to kiss the old woman on the cheek. "I need to talk with you after I am settled in, Bobby," Emma whispered. "There is another part to our opus that I find needs completion."

"I'll call you next week, then, and we'll git t'gether soon's you're feelin' a bit more chipper."

TWO

Nora let Bobby in and led him to the sitting room, where Emma's wing chair had been replaced with a rented hospital bed. The remainder of the room had been left intact. Nora had cranked up the bed, allowing the old woman to be erect.

"Oh, Bobby Parker, I am happy to see you. As you see, I am pretending I'm in my chair," she said jauntily. "Please, make yourself comfortable. It feels like the old days, doesn't it," she remarked as Bobby sank into the remaining wing chair.

"Nora will bring us some goodies. She bakes them, these days. Does a fine job of it, too," she added.

The young woman bustled in just then, bearing a tray with two cups of tea and a plate of lemon squares. "She's lookin' right foyne, don't'ya think?" Nora remarked. "We've got her up and walkin' three toimes daily. Hopin' to git her out th' door as weather permits."

"I am planning to run up the stairs to my own room within weeks," Emma added.

"Sure, sure," Nora giggled. "We'll cross that bridge whin we coom to it." She adjusted Emma's covers and left.

"I love that girl," Emma whispered. "She refuses to treat me like an invalid."

"Good f'her. Y'are lookin' pert," Bobby observed. Emma's color was back, and a modicum of flesh had appeared on her face and arms. "Y'll be up and about in no time."

"No, I won't," Emma said, suddenly serious. "I am a dying old woman. I feel it, deep inside. The life is draining slowly out of my body.

"Not only am I dying, I am enraged. I am very grateful that I did not die when I suffered that attack. I am also convinced that I suffered the attack because I finally became very angry with Thomas Manchester. I have read articles stating that anger is an integral part of one's grieving process. I never suffered through that part of the process. For me, there was only deep depression and tears which never seemed to cease. Following that, an all-consuming loneliness. But never, never... anger.

"I am certain that I was containing the rage in some unconscious part of myself, but it never presented its ugly self until you returned from Portland with your news.

Thomas and I had wed, but he had never shared it with others. Jonathan knew of our union, but those with whom my husband conducted business were never informed.

"Why was this? Why was I never allowed the privilege of being Mrs. Thomas Manchester? Why did he not announce it to the world, if he loved me so dearly? That, Bobby, is why I am angry. I am a selfish, self-absorbed old woman, and I want satisfaction for this before I go. I wish to know what my true place was in that man's life. Where did I belong?" She paused, then continued tersely, "I must confess, my worst fear has been that I was but one in a string of women. I was never unaware of Thomas' effect on women. He turned heads wherever we went. I was always aware of my plainness, my roughness, next to him. I was the poor little country girl, he the urban charmer.

"He never ceased to let me know that he loved me, while I never ceased to doubt his faithfulness. I was very good at hiding these feelings, even from myself. 'Denial is not just a river in Egypt', Nora tells me." She smiled wryly. "Well, I happen to be a master at it," she said.

Emma sighed and closed her eyes. "I am so tired," she whispered.

"You're not exactly back t' great shape," Bobby said anxiously. "Mebbe I should go, come back some other time. Y'don't want to upset y'rself too much."

"The physical fatigue is here to stay, Bobby," Emma continued. "I must become accustomed to that. But my inner fatigue is something else. I am weary from carrying this burden of rage and shame. I need to unload it. You need to help me release it," she added.

"I had planned to meet Thomas on the other side, where we would lie together, enjoying our young, enlightened bodies and sharing our most intimate thoughts into eternity, while drinking in the nectar of the gods. There was only love and satisfaction in that fantasy, Bobby. That was Heaven, for me. Now, there is doubt and rage. I find I want to beat him with my fists until he tells me every small detail of his life without me.

"There are secrets I need to know before I go. And to that end, I have every intention of following young Nora's bidding to the letter, including eating ten times each day and being dragged from my bed to walk every hour on the hour, if it will enable me to remain here until I do. I wish to know everything about the Thomas Manchester who traveled the world with only Jonathan for company. I wish to know if the stories he shared about his childhood were real, or merely fabricated for my benefit.

"I must know that he loved me, really loved me, or we must never meet." She looked intently at Bobby. "That would be my idea of hell."

Bobby was silent for some moments. Finally, "What is it y'want me t'do?" he asked quietly.

Emma sipped cold tea for a few moments, gathering her thoughts. Then, "As you know, I am now receiving more money each month. My nursing and medical expenses are also completely covered by Thomas' estate. Since I am spending so little on my day-to-day comings and goings, I have a bit more money to lend to this part of my quest.

"I would like you to do detective work for me. Find out everything you can concerning Thomas Manchester. Rout any skeletons from his closet, document any good deeds.

"In order to do this, you will need to go through his personal things. I have never been able to enter his office, his inner sanctum. But I do own a key. Before Jonathan left, he had a copy made and left it in my desk in a small envelope. I never opened that envelope. I am now providing you with this key.

"Jonathan swore to me that Thomas had concealed a final will in that room. He searched for hours, but was unable to find it. If it is there, I wish it found. And I wish it found by you, if at all possible. I do not wish to share my shame with anyone else." Tears coursed down her withered cheeks. She sighed deeply.

"Do you think you could do this for me?" She asked hesitantly. "I hate to interrupt your lovely life. I know you are happy with your new love. But I am running very short of time, and I fear I will die without the truth."

"You sure know how to strain my nerves, Miss Emma," Bobby said. "You know me enough by now to re'lize I gotta have time to let all this sink in." He sat, looking at his friend, for a few moments. "I also re'lize we're talkin' short-timin' it, here.

"All's I kin say is, I'll try to git back with you as soon as I'm able. As usual, I'm busy. But winter's still with us, and I don't have so much work I can't take a few days off now and again. But this seems to be a lot more compl'cated than the last part of our opus. It looks like it'll take more time off, and mebbe more travel. I gotta talk it over with Doreen, then git back t'you."

Emma sighed again. "I have an idea; why don't we include Doreen in the opus. She might be able to write some letters, or take care of any telephone correspondence which may be required. I would even consent to her accompanying you while you search Thomas' study, if it would help you to make a decision."

"I know that'd be hard on you, Emma. Why'n't we jest say I will promise t' talk with her, and git back t'you soon's I kin. If her help's needed, so be it."

Emma reached over to an ornate cherry wood table beside her bed. She handed Bobby the small sealed envelope on which was written in neat script, "Manchester's Study". "Take this, Bobby. I do not want it back. If you decide you cannot help me, destroy it. I do not want that loft entered by anyone I know aside from you, and Doreen if you decide to include her."

THREE

It was fine with Doreen that Bobby continue to work with Emma to complete their opus. However, she was not able to help him with the work. Her mother worked only one day a week now, helping her daughter through the process of learning how to run Shanahan's Pizza. Although business was slow during late winter, there was much to do to prepare the restaurant for summer. Doreen was familiar with the cooking and hiring end of the eatery, but Mary had continued to advertise the place, and to keep the books.

Doreen planned to modernize Shanahan's to attract a younger crowd. She would hire a manager and cook, and do any paper work and advertisement from home. She also intended to computerize all transactions, allowing her to supervise from either the pizza place or her home office. There was much to do, and Doreen was working six days a week.

Brud and Brittny's upstairs addition was consuming much of Bobby's time. He would pause in his work to think of a way to solve

Emma's dilemma, but he needed to complete the work on the young couple's upper story rooms before the first of May, when Brittny's twins were due. Bobby and Doreen had promised each other that they would never work on Sundays; these days, they both found it difficult to keep that promise.

In addition to their work lives, it was imperative that they find a new house as soon as possible. Bobby sold the small place he had shared with Debra at the end of January. The family who planned to live there was re-locating from Massachusetts, and thankfully did not intend to occupy the property until after the first of April. So, the couple spent their Sundays house hunting. Unfortunately, Emma's project took a back seat to the couple's busy lives.

They discovered the small house on the river one Sunday afternoon in mid-March, after having looked at three houses that neither cared for. Needing some quiet time, they decided to take a ride to the river to park and sit for an hour. Doreen spotted the small "For Sale by Owner" sign in the window of the white cottage.

"Boy, that's a nice location," she offered. "Wonder why we haven't looked at that one.

I thought we'd covered every house for sale in the county." She sighed. "It's waterfront. They probably want a mint for it."

"Y're prob'ly right. But let's see if they're home. We kin always look, right?"

Doreen smiled wearily. "Right." They tramped to the rear door and knocked. The old man peered through the kitchen window at them. "Jest a minute, I'll letcha in," he yelled through the glass. "Whatcha want?" he asked as he opened the door a crack.

"You have a 'For Sale' sign in your window. We wondered if we could see the house," Doreen offered hesitantly.

"Oh, yeah, almost forgot," the man said. "Wife died in November, it's gittin' too much for me t'care for. Needs a lot of work, I'm afraid. Couple people looked at it, thought it was too much of a project for them." He paused. "Jim Nichols", he added, sticking out a gnarled hand. "Gotta sell it soon. My son's comin' to take me t'Augusta. Goin' to assisted livin' there, first of April."

Emma's house was a piece of cake compared to this one, Bobby thought as he looked around. The wallpaper was hanging in strips, the wide pine floors had shifted, the linoleum in the kitchen was ancient, the plumbing was outdated, the windows needed to be replaced. There was very little insulation, and the place needed scraping, cleaning and painting inside and out. To top it off, the furnace was on its last legs and the house needed a new roof. It was a handyman's nightmare.

Doreen loved it. She pointed out the large bay window overlooking the river, the garden plot just outside the kitchen, the spacious combination living/dining room, the two large bedrooms upstairs with their deep eaves and window seats, the small storage room tucked behind the kitchen which could serve as a home office. "This would be perfect with a little work," she said enthusiastically.

Bobby roared. "Little work? This place needs a complete renovation," he said. "Can't move in 'til the wirin' and plumbin' is fixed and it's insulated. That's the beginnin'; then, we'd haveta work all our spare time t'git it in good shape."

"You promise t' put it t'gether proper, I'll give y'a deal on it," the old man offered. "We loved th'place, Gert and me. Hate t'see it abandoned f'good."

Doreen looked at Bobby, her eyes sparkling. "What d'you think, hon? Can we do it? The way I feel, we're young and have lots of energy. We'll only find a place like this once in our lives. I'll help as much as I can, and we can put the place together one step at a time."

Bobby shook his head. "I can't b'lieve I'm agreein' t'this. It's a year's work, jest in itself." He sighed. "But I gotta say, I like what you like. Plus, the foundation's sound, and the riverbank's high enough here so's the basement keeps dry. House's got good bones, as they say." He turned to Mr. Nichols. "Y'got a deal," he said. "I'll make sure it's done proper."

Jim Nichols son offered to have his dad stay with him in Augusta so the couple could renovate the small house. As soon as it was empty, Bobby hired the electrician and the plumber he used for his jobs, and arranged to replace the windows and insulate the house. While that necessary work was being completed, the couple covered the roof with tarp, cleaned, stripped wallpaper, painted and installed appliances so they could move in on the last day of April. On the first of April, their furnishings were stored in Helen Parker's basement, and they slept either at Mary Shanahan's or at his mother's.

Dicky had moved in with his grandmother in February, taking over his uncle's room. Her last son had finally left home, and Helen gladly welcomed her grandson's company. In exchange for rent, Dicky agreed to be her handyman. Dwayne, Helen's friend from Calais, spent Saturday nights, but they had no plans to live together. "We like each other's company enough, but we're too old t'share closets," she stated bluntly.

Shortly after the first of May, Bobby completed Brud's addition. Two days after he gunned the final staple into the new roof, Brittny delivered identical twin boys. "Hope they got their mumma's looks and their daddy's disposition, " Bobby observed wryly as he related the story to Doreen. "Otherwise, that pair is in for nothin' but trouble."

He thought about Bess as he spoke. According to Debra, their daughter had moved to Tucson after the holidays to be with some guy she had met online, and Deb had not heard from her all winter. She and her new beau were not willing to care for the little boy. Debra asked Bobby if he could take the child in.

"Nope. Much as I'm sure I'd love the kid, I got too much on my plate to take care of anyone more than I'm already committed to.

"Why don'tcha ask Becka? She might go for it."

Debra had followed Bobby's suggestion, and Dustin was now living with Becka and Jared. Bobby and Debra agreed to pay for his care. Doreen suggested that they might think of taking the child after they had completed work on their house and Bobby was finished with Emma's opus.

"Take in a kid? You crazy, woman? We're getting' too old for kids—ain't we?"

"I for one am nowhere near thinking of myself as old, Mr. Parker," Doreen retorted tersely. "As for kids, I'm only saying maybe; I need to live with the idea, after our life gets calmer. Let's just say we'll put it on the back burner for now."

"Fine with me, m'love. The stove's full to burstin' now, as it is. Dunno if there's room on th' back burner." He grinned. "I love you for even suggestin' we take th'kid in, but frankly I dunno if I want Becka's problems in my life. And her kid is likely to bring her." Bobby sighed. "It's always something, with that girl. Deb and me never knew what would appear from around the corner with her. There were accidents, a bad gang of kids, drugs, booze, sex; and all that by the time she was fourteen. Seems if there was a puddle or a pile of shit around, she'd wade through one or fall into the other. Jest when we'd think she was gittin' it together, she'd be in trouble all over again. Never stopped."

"Some kids are like that, I guess," Doreen mused." Doesn't seem to be anything you can do about it. Love her and let her go. But we can do something about her son. And some day, maybe we will."

FOUR

Toward the end of April, guilt overtook Bobby. He had promised Emma he would begin her project as soon as possible, and the energy involved in his moving project had pushed her plight to the bottom of his priority list. Now that he and Doreen were living in the small cottage, and his work schedule involved only the work needed on their new home, Emma invaded his waking hours on a regular basis. As he covered the roof with tile, he thought of Emma's new roof; as he replaced doors on kitchen cabinets, he recalled mending the old woman's cabinet doors. Now, she was confined to bed, hoping he could solve her dilemma so she could feel free to die. Finally, he was no longer able to concentrate on the projects in the new house.

Bobby and Doreen were now living in the three finished downstairs rooms of their new home. "Gotta go to Emma's this weekend," he announced to Doreen one early May Thursday morning as he poured a large mug of fragrant coffee, adding a healthy dollop of cream. The young woman smiled and nodded. "Figured you'd be ready to start on her project sometime soon," she answered.

"You sure you can't help me with it?" he asked.

"Nope. As I said, I'll be busy with the business for months. Plus, we have added this giant remodeling project which will take up any spare time I might be able to scrape off my schedule. But I wish you luck, hon." Doreen added as she dished three scrambled eggs onto a plate, added three strips of crisp bacon and a side plate containing four biscuits. She placed the meal in front of him. "Think this'll be enough?"

"Yep. For me and at least one more. You sure feed me good. I put an inch on my gut since we got together."

Doreen grinned and reached for the plate. "All right, Chubs, I'll dump it out."

"No y'don't, woman; I kin handle it." He snatched the hand from the plate and kissed it, then chewed thoughtfully for a moment. "I'm kinda pissed at Emma, you want to know.

"Oh? Why?"

"Well, Geez. I do all this work for her, then go and get all this money for her, then after all that she says I'm the only one who kin finish off her project. She tells me she's got a short time before she croaks, and she's gotta find out all the facts about her husband who's been dead for fourteen years, for godsakes. She had fourteen healthy years to delve into all that stuff. Plus all them years she was waitin' for him to finish all that world travelin' and come home to her. Why's she doin' it now?" He returned to his breakfast, shaking his head as he smeared jam and butter on a biscuit. "I don't git it."

"Sounds like you feel she's layin' a guilt trip on you, Bobby. And maybe she is. But sometimes we don't know we need something for ourselves until it's too late. Seems to me, she sees it as bein' almost too late.

"From what you told me, I think she's right. She's been pushing the facts about Thomas Manchester's life way back in her mind, hoping that he was only the person who spent time with her. Sure," Doreen added, "That doesn't make much sense. But people often don't make much sense. You stayed married to Deb for all those years. Did that make sense?"

Bobby peered at her over his coffee. "Got me there, you vixen." He sighed. "Okay, I'm goin' to Emma's on Sat'dy. I think I'm gonna need help, though. Mebbe I'll call Jonathan."

Doreen nodded. "That sounds like a good plan. He's been in Manchester's study, and he probably knows him as well as anyone. You think he'd do it?"

"Dunno. All's I kin do is give it a go." Bobby rose and stretched. "For now, I gotta work off all this food. I'm rippin' up the upstair' floorboards this mornin'. Half of 'em are rotted. Puttin' in some wide pine I saved from another job. If you need stuff from there, better git it out."

"I never did store anything up there. I knew we'd need to pull the whole thing apart. So, go to it. I'm off to the restaurant." She gave Bobby a quick hug. "Love you, Babe. See you for supper. I'll bring one of the new pizzas. Chicken and Alfredo sauce.'

"Geez, you're gonna kill me. Chicken ain't s'posed to be in a pizza."

"It's the newest thing. Not everyone wants red sauce. You'll love it." She grinned as she left.

Jonathan was very pleased to hear from Bobby. Due to a series of acupuncture treatments for arthritis, he was getting around in quite a spry fashion, and had been itching for a project to keep him interested and busy. He had attempted to volunteer in a local hospital, but it bored him, and he found he really did not like to work around people who were ill. He agreed to meet Bobby at Emma's on Saturday, stating that it was about time the stubborn woman opened the Book of Thomas.

When Bobby informed Emma that he had contacted Jonathan, she was delighted. She offered to connect with him to determine if he would like to stay at her home for the duration of the investigation of Thomas' study.

"How long d'you think this'll take?" Bobby asked Emma.

"There is a raft of material in that space," Emma replied. "Since we don't really know what we're looking for, there's bound to be a lot of wading through his things." She paused. "Perhaps you could work at the job whenever you are able, and Jonathan could fill in, if he is willing to stay with me."

"Sounds like a plan, if we all kin agree on it," Bobby replied. "I'm up t'my armpits in remod'lin' the new place, and we gotta git to finished by end of June, 'cause my summer work starts pilin' up. Even if I am roomin' with a lady who makes a livin', I still gotta hold up my end."

After they had enjoyed a long chat to catch up with their lives, Bobby agreed to meet with Emma and Jonathan early Saturday morning.

FIVE

The small key turned easily in the lock, unlike the door, which resisted with a loud groan when opened. "Whew, musty in here," Jonathan remarked, rubbing a hand over his nose.

"Ain't surprised; room's been sealed up over 14 years. Let's open up them windows and find out if any of them lights have workin' bulbs."

The two men made their way to the windows at each end and parted the heavy velvet drapes. A shaft of light shot into the room through the east window, illuminating one side of the large lofted space. Dust danced through the air, coating the massive mahogany furnishings with its ghostly presence. Jonathan found a light switch, and an enormous crystal chandelier illuminated more of the room. When they replaced bulbs in two floor lamps and a cut-glass desk lamp, the room offered enough light to afford a full view.

Despite more than a decade of grime and dust, the room was magnificent. Large mahogany beams interspersed with white plaster defined the lofted ceiling. The walls had also been plastered and painted white, and mahogany wainscoting surrounded three walls. The fourth wall boasted shelves above and built-in closed cabinets below. The furnishings were obvious antiques, and the oak floors gleamed with deeply fringed, patterned oriental rugs in shades of burgundy, blue, gold, green and cream. Burgundy velvet drapes hung at the windows, with gossamer lace panels over the glass. A collection of brass ship's bells was displayed on a long table under one window, and various small framed photos of sailing ships adorned the walls. Comfortable leather chairs with stout ottomans were abundant, and surrounded a small, red-lacquered wood-burning stove, vented through the roof in the center of the room.

"Geez," Bobby said as he took in his surroundings. "Guy didn't spare no expense in this place, did he?"

"Whoever Thomas Manchester is, or was, he was never stingy," Jonathan offered. "He had plenty, and he spent plenty. Where it came from, he never offered to tell me. Of course, I never asked. I was his employee, and although we spent many years in each other's company we were not close, as I have said, but I considered him a good friend."

"How's that?"

"If I needed anything, he was happy to oblige me. If I was lonely, he supplied me with funds to return to my family for a visit. He was comfortable to be with, and he never made negative judgments about those with whom he did business. And, we could spend hours on end, talking about almost everything." Jonathan poked through a collection of antique pipes on a long table under the window as he spoke. "I love to smoke a good pipe now and then; how about you?" Bobby shook his head vigorously.

"However, he would not talk about his private life," Jonathan continued. "He liked women, and bedded quite a few, but whatever he knew of them stayed with him. He loved Emma dearly, and I know he received letters from her almost daily, and called when he could. But he never talked of her. He wrote letters to others, and made other calls, but never shared with me who or what they were.

"Since I didn't know for certain, I must confess that I would fantasize his untold life. The money, for example. It flowed so freely, he had to have an unending supply.

I imagined that, since he loved the sea, he had past relations who had been pirates. They had plundered ships bearing treasure, and their survivors had stored the gold and jewels in vaults in New York, Chicago, Boston. As for family, as a young buck he had feuded with his father, abandoned a decent job in a thriving business to live a rebellious life alone. He left a wife, one he was forced to marry for social reasons, two children, a large mansion and many uncles, aunts and distant cousins to roam the earth, searching out true friendship and love. He chose me as a traveling companion, not wanting to be completely without human company. Then, after years, he finally discovered his true love, in Emma Colridge.

"But even after he met and married the fair Emma, he could not reveal his past, nor could he settle down. So he continued to sail the seas, and to write his flashy books, and to live his chosen life of deceit. Finally, life left him, and he passed on in this place, close to his love."

"Yeah, and now that love is pissed off at him, and wants to rout out his secrets. Boy, that's quite a tale. Make a great book. Y'think any of it c'd be true?"

"Why not? It makes as much sense as anything. Perhaps if we never discover the real truth, we could tell that story to Emma. Think she'd buy it?" Jonathan had brushed off a large leather wing chair, and was settled into it, clutching a dusty meerschaum pipe. He grinned, obviously enjoying the discussion.

"Dunno. It's for sure, she needs t'know somethin', and pretty soon. I gotta say, though, that's pretty far-fetched." Bobby smiled, nodding toward the pipe. "You gonna smoke that thing?"

"I assume a pipe which has not been smoked or cleaned for fourteen years would probably taste pretty gamey," Jonathan answered. "Looks good, though; in my hand, I mean."

Their light banter was clearing the air both between the men and in the long-abandoned room. However, they needed to begin their task. They decided that any material regarding Thomas Manchester's private life would most likely be stored in a book, a drawer or a sheaf of papers. The room did not contain a computer, nor was there outward evidence of a machine which would have recorded his words. He did own two typewriters, one of which was on his huge desk, the other on a small wheeled table against a wall. Most of the books in the shelves were stories or biographies of men who followed the sea. Other books, obviously purchased for investment purposes, included uncut sets of the complete works of Shakespeare and Dickens, and many original books of poetry, including those of Blake, Shelley and Coleridge. The desk was clear, making sense since Thomas had not actually used it the last night he was home. Any papers had been stored away or piled neatly on the desk, and the desk itself was locked.

The men decided it would be best to search the room in sections. Today's task was to unearth any written material, and comb through it thoroughly, with a special eye out for his will. Bobby suggested that Manchester may have stored private documents in a bank safe deposit box; if this was the case, they might want to look for a key. "Good thinking, man," Jonathan offered. "Add that to the list."

"What about th' desk? How do we get into it?" Bobby wondered.

"He probably stored the key somewhere in the room. He used the desk only when he was here, so he probably wouldn't have found the need to take it on his travels." Jonathan replied. "Why don't you try under the desk, and I'll check out the drawers."

Besides three or four small tables, drawers had been built in under the bookcases. Jonathan discovered two small keys in a drawer beside Thomas' large wing chair. "Strange that he'd lock it at all," he mused. "Emma never came up here alone, and no one else would have any need to go through his desk."

"I spent a couple of days going through the room after Manchester died, but I never found a key to the desk. I felt I was trespassing, and I needed to leave the room exactly as I found it." Jonathan sighed. "His energy was still in the room, back then. I'm afraid I may have been so upset by his death that I did not completely search the place."

"Can't say's I blame you," Bobby countered. "Turns out the guy had more secrets than a priest after Sat'dy confessions." Bobby chuckled. "I'm kinda lookin' forward t' the secrets in the desk."

Only one key fit the lock in the desk. "Wonder what the other key is for," Jonathan mused thoughtfully. He dropped the remaining key in his pocket. The desk contained folders with notes regarding the books Thomas had published, and large envelopes stuffed with the photos he had taken. Among them were many lovely pictures of Emma. There were also dozens of photos of other strikingly beautiful young women. The women were photographed by the sea, their hair blowing naturally. Most were brunette, although there were two blondes and one redhead. They were all tall and slim and healthy. Some were white, but there were also many Chinese, African and Spanish beauties.

"Man sure loved wimmen," Bobby remarked. "Good thing Emma never saw these. No wonder he kept th'desk locked." He frowned. "At least, he took more shots of her than the others. Guess that says somethin'."

"I recognize a few of those women,' Jonathan offered. "Thomas introduced them to me during our travels." He shook his head gravely. "I didn't realize there were so many. I don't know what to make of it. I don't."

"I got no problem with what to make of it; guy was a gigolo, plain and simple. Married our Emma, then ran around with anyone else who took his fancy. A regular shitheel, you ask me." Bobby put the pictures back, except for the ones of Emma. "Feel like burnin' these; pisses me off." He paced the room, shaking the large folder.

"Too late to be pissed off, I'd say. Nothing we can do about it. They're part of the man. Let them be."

"Well, ain't you the philosopher." Bobby slammed the folder on the desk. "I'll be as pissed as I like. Ain't fair to Emma."

Jonathan sighed. "Fair or not, this is one part of her husband she doesn't need to know about," he offered. "She'll never be strong enough to climb the stairs to this room. Whatever we find here needs to stay where it is, unless it helps the old woman. Agreed?"

"Yeah, sure. I ain't gonna do or say anything to hurt her; but th'man still pisses me off, alive or dead." Bobby sighed. "Let's git on with it."

It was late afternoon when the men decided to end their search. They had rifled through all of the drawers, the books and the few sheaves of paper on the surface of the desk to no avail. They unearthed only documents and paperwork pertaining to the man's writings, his travels, his local finances. There was no will, or any other written document pertaining to his demise or in fact, his future.

"I'm bushed. And I gotta tell you, I'm not lookin' forward to tellin' Emma we ain't found nothin'," Bobby said.

"Well, there are the pictures of her. She might like to have them."

"Yep. Let's lock up and git outta here. I'm ready for a shower. Th'place is dirty in more ways'n'one."

"Speaking of locking up. I think we need to take along this other key. Put it in the folder with the pictures, would you?" He handed the small key to Bobby, who dropped it into the folder containing Emma's photos. Exhausted, the men made their way back down the narrow stairs.

Nora met them in the kitchen with two large white towels. "Emma's nappin', me dirty-boys. See that you shower, then I'll serve tea and scones in her sittin' room. Leave y'r dusty things outsoide the bath, and oi'll brush 'em off for ye."

The men smiled wearily. "Yes'm; right away," Bobby saluted. Realizing from her stern tone that they had no other choice, they went to do Nora's bidding.

SIX

Emma was awake and drinking a large cup of ginger tea when the two men, clean enough to meet Nora's tough standards, finally settled themselves into the two large chairs at the foot of her bed.

"Well. Here are my two warriors, back from the fray," she remarked wryly. "Help yourselves to Nora's wonderful scones and tea. With homemade strawberry jam, to boot. Now, tell me, how did you fare?"

"You prob'ly ain't gonna like this, Emma," Bobby began. "We din't find no will, nor any other sign of Thomas's life outside of right here."

"We did, however, find a folder of lovely photographs of you, "Jonathan added.

"Ah, yes. A thorn among the roses; one of many women by the sea."

The men looked at each other. Women? They looked askance at each other. "Women?" Jonathan asked aloud.

"Following his book about the people of the southern states, he planned to write another; *Women by the Sea*. He loved the look of beautiful women from around the world. Each time he returned from a long journey, we would share the photos he took. Among them were always many pictures of beautiful women. They were always taken by the sea." She smiled. "He never did finish the book about the south. Following his demise, I sent all of the materials to his publisher, who planned to have it finished. I don't know if he did, now that I think of it. Probably not, since he would have sent me some copies if it had been published.

"Ah.' Emma smiled as she noticed the curious looks on the two men's faces. "You thought the photos might mean something else. Well, you can be certain that I have thought of that, also. And I am not sure that some of them were not. In the beginning, Thomas asked me to accompany him on every journey. He gave up only when I had finally convinced him that travel to that extent would never happen, for me. Each time he showed me the photographs of those lovelies, he reminded me that if I had been with him, I would have met them all, and would have been assured that he wanted only to capture their 'fleeting beauty' on film.

"I never doubted my Thomas," Emma continued, "until very recently. Perhaps I never knew the man I loved for so many years." She sighed deeply. "I do hope the two of you are able to put my doubts to rest."

"Interesting, Miss Emma," Jonathan interjected. "I wonder about something, however. We found copious notes in his office regarding books he had written and published, but there were no notes concerning a book about women of the sea. Do you know where those notes might be?"

"Can't say I do, Jonathan. He often wrote the text to 'surround' the pictures after he had collected the photos he wished to use in each book. The pictures were the important component, to him; text was always secondary. Perhaps he had not finished taking his pictures."

"Mmm. Perhaps." Was there any other place in the house that Thomas considered private? A place in which he might store things you were not privy to?"

"How 'bout that oak chest in the room I slept in while I was here?" Bobby interjected. "The one you covered with the shawl Thomas brought you from India. Did that have a lock on it?"

"Oh. That chest. He kept his sea-going clothing in that chest. He would have his things cleaned immediately after his arrival, then pack them away until his next trip. While he was here, he wore work clothing most of the time. You know, denim overalls and heavy boots and cotton shirts. For mending things, or working in the garden. We did not venture out much, as I have said. Yes, when I think of it, the chest did have a lock. I could not allow myself to get rid of it after he passed. I also couldn't allow myself to open it. I don't know where the key is, to tell you the truth."

Jonathan fished into the folder containing Emma's photos. "Is this it?" he asked, holding up the key.

"I truly do not know," Emma replied. "Perhaps it is. Perhaps, not." She pulled her robe close around her and lay back on her pillows. "I am very tired, suddenly," she said. "I think I must sleep now."

Nora, who was never very far from her employer, bustled in, stating brusquely, "Miss Emma must have a nap before her dinner, or she won't eat. She has had quoite enough excitement for one day, if ye don't moind. Toime for you t'be out of here, Mr. Bobby, and for you to take a nice walk for yourself, Mr. Jonathan. Dinner won't be fer another two hours." She adjusted the covers around her charge, then pulled the heavy drapes shut against the late afternoon sun.

"I will be fine tomorrow, I'm sure. I do feel a bit better each day," Emma whispered. "But for now, I must sleep."

Nora stopped the men as they were leaving. "She keeps sayin' she's getting' better, but to moi oiyes, she is still one very sick pairson. She is havin' a very hard toime regainin' her energy. Sure, she does have a good day once in a while, but most are spent sleepin' more than she's awake. I worry about her; she seems very sad, t'me.

"Oi was thinkin' oi'd be out of here by now, but now, oi think it'll be a while."

"Will that be all right with you?" Jonathan asked anxiously. "You've done such a wonderful job with her. And you know she loves you," he added.

"Oi have no plans to leave until she is ready to let me go," Nora stated firmly.

Both men sighed with relief. "Good. 'Cause I gotta work for a few days up north," Bobby stated.

"I'm fine with that, Bobby," Jonathan replied. "I'll try the key in the trunk, and if I find something I'll let you know. When will you be able to come back?"

"D'pends on the importance of any find. I kin be here in a flash if you find somethin' worth the trip." Bobby smiled as he shook the older man's hand. "Good workin' with you, man," he added.

"We're all on the same track; helping Miss Emma," Jonathan replied.

SEVEN

Three days later, Jonathan called. "I think we've got it," he announced gleefully.

"The will? Y'found it?" Bobby said eagerly.

"Nope, not yet. But the small key did fit the trunk's lock, and there were diaries in the trunk. Took me a couple of days to discover them. At first, I thought the thing contained only musty clothing. Smelled like mothballs mixed with mold. The mothballs sure weren't doing their job. Lots of wool in there, so they enjoyed a hearty feast. I hated the smell; needed a mask to go through the stuff, so I was not able to stay at the task for long; had to return three or four times. It's a large trunk, and there was a lot to pile through. I found the diaries in an oilcloth packet under almost all of the clothing. Apparently, Thomas only made entries in them while he was at sea."

"You read any of 'em yet? What'd they say?" Bobby urged.

"Thought I'd wait for you. This is something we need to do together. I need to return to Portland for a few days, take care of some business and see the acupuncturist. All of this stair climbing and walking is making the old hip creaky." He paused. "It's Tuesday. I should make it back by late Friday evening. How about Saturday?"

"Jest right. I'll finish the job I'm on Friday; then, I kin allow m'self a couple days off. So, if we need t'act on whatever we find, I'll have some time. I should be workin' on my own place, but I got a respite from the lovely Doreen."

"That woman of yours sounds like a gem. I hope I have a chance to meet her some day."

"You can be sure of that; she'd like to meet you, too. When we finish this project, this opus as Emma prefers t'call it, we'll have you for a visit." Bobby sighed. "House might even be finished by then."

"I'll look forward to it."

Jonathan and Nora greeted Bobby in Emma's kitchen early the following Saturday morning. Bobby joined them for coffee and bran muffins after greeting Emma, who had eaten earlier, and was reading the local news. "How is she today?" he asked Nora.

"Not bad, not bad," the young woman replied. "Had a good noight, she did, and took herself a five minute walk before her breakfast. Oi think she's feelin' better since the two of you began your work."

"Speakin' of that, where're th' journals?" Bobby asked.

Nora put a finger to her lips. "Shhh," she whispered.

"Yes. Regarding those; Nora and I agreed that Emma need not know about them unless they contain material that will benefit her," Jonathan whispered.

"Fine with me. My lips is sealed."

The men agreed to read the diaries in the bedroom where Jonathan was staying. Nora agreed to supply them with periodic coffee and nourishment. They set up a small table and two chairs and opened the first of the four leather-bound books.

The men, supplied with paper and sharp pencils, selected two journals each. They decided to read through them and share any information they considered pertinent at regular intervals. Each of the journals covered a period of approximately four years. As they read Thomas' small neat script, they discovered that most of the entries were impersonal, documenting the ship's progress, problems with the ship or crew, descriptions of ports of call. There were lists of the supplies needed for each journey, people who needed to be contacted, and cities and towns he had visited, alone or with Jonathan.

Interspersed among the business entries were brief comments about people he had met, and those to whom he wrote notes or longer letters. Most of these entries dealt with the places he photographed for his numerous books, women whom he befriended, and the ongoing communication with his wife. There were notes regarding the text he needed for each book, small bits of information he wished to share with Emma, and descriptions of the places he had been when he met each of the women he photographed.

The two men did discovered one thing that piqued their curiosity. Each journal contained the same note, entered at different intervals: "Contact Kurzman following arrival in Maine." There was no further indication of Kurzman's relationship to Thomas, or an address or number at which he could be reached.

The beginning of the fourth and final journal, which Bobby chose to read, contained notes regarding a book Thomas Manchester considered his "final work". It would be called "Women by the Sea", and would be dedicated to his darling wife, Emma.

"Guess the old lady knew him better'n we thought," Bobby mused as he poured fresh coffee and took a huge bite from one of Nora's famous cinnamon buns, dripping with butter. He leaned back in his chair and stretched his arms over his head. "Time for a break, I'd say." He yawned largely and rubbed his eyes vigorously. "This ain't the easiest work I ever done," he added.

"Nor the most interesting," Jonathan noted. "At least, in the first and third diaries. Ninety per cent of the entries in these don't give us a clue toward the information we need." He paced the room, favoring his hip, which was still a bit sore.

"Maybe the last one'll give us somethin'," Bobby remarked. "Why don't we read it together? I'll take a few pages, then you kin take over. How's that? That way we kin each git a break."

"I have a better idea," Robert replied. "Let's remove the pages from this journal. That way, we can split them up and read them much faster. We can always replace them if needed, in another folder. Although, I don't know why we would want to do that. I don't know of any soul who would be interested in them for any reason. The ship is sold, the man has been dead for all these years, and Emma's in such a state of denial, she'll never want to read them. What say?"

Bobby agreed. After a short break during which they fortified themselves with more food and a short walk, they cut the pages from the journal and settled in to read.

More than an hour later, Jonathan yelped. "Aha; I think we're near the mother-lode."

"What is it?"

"These entries begin about a year before Thomas died. Jonathan pushed the pages over so Bobby could share them. "He says the doctor tells him he doesn't have long to live. His heart is not receiving enough blood, and there's nothing they can do. They can't install a pacemaker, since his heart is too weak to support it. He's seventy-six, but has the heart of a very old man." Jonathan took a deep breath, then continued.

"He plans to end this voyage soon, and to live out his days with Emma. He'll continue to make notes in Maine for that last book about the women, and hopefully, finish it before he goes.

"He will tell her, but has decided to break the news after he has made arrangements for her future." Jonathan and Bobby now held the pages together, reading through the last few carefully. "Here's Kurzman again," Jonathan said. "Call Kerman in Boston when I arrive in Maine. Inform him of my condition and terms of the will.'"

Bobby sighed. "So, the damn thing does exist," he said softly. "But where in hell is it?"

"Maybe, it's with this Kerman, whoever he is," Jonathan replied.

"There are two entries on the last page," Jonathan offered. "'Inform Emma of will's location,' and, 'will be glad to return tomorrow. Very tired. Need to be with darling Emma.'"

"Whoa. That's heavy," Bobby interjected. "Especially seein' as he died the next night."

"My guess is, he didn't have time to 'inform Kurzman' of anything," Jonathan added. "Nor to tell Emma where the will is."

"Wonder where the blame thing is, then. We looked through every paper in that room. Y'think he might've stashed it somewhere on the lower two floors?"

Jonathan shrugged. "There's no mention of when he wrote it. Could have been years ago. Perhaps he stored it in a safe deposit box."

"If that's what he did, ain't no way we're gonna find it." Bobby paced the small room. "He died before he told Kurzman, so even if we find out who the guy is, he won't know anything about it. I'll bet it's somewhere in the house. He didn't want Emma to find it before he told her about it, so he made sure she wouldn't.

"But why wouldn't he have locked it in his desk?" Jonathan countered.

"Mmm. Well, Emma'd been in that room a number of times. She coulda gone in there while he was away, found the key to the desk and opened it."

Jonathan chuckled. "We both know she would not have done that."

"Yep; but maybe ol' Thomas din't."

"True. Perhaps we need to stop trying to be members of Scotland Yard, and get to work finding that will. Time and continued search is what it will take, not two fools playing at being detectives."

It was now late afternoon, and Bobby needed to leave. The men parted, with Bobby promising to think of places where a will might be hidden, and Jonathan deciding he would spend the next day covertly searching the second floor. He then needed to return to Portland for the week, but could meet Bobby again the following Sunday, if nothing had been found. They could search the bottom level of the house together. If the will was not uncovered by then, the barn and the basement could be searched.

EIGHT

Jonathan's search of the two bedrooms and the bath on the second level of the house proved unsuccessful. Bobby started to build a porch onto Mike Severson's small cottage in Machiasport, and continued work on his own home each evening. With Doreen's help, they had readied the lower level for final painting. New windows, new appliances and counter-tops in the kitchen, and a new inlaid floor in the mudroom, pantry and kitchen had been completed before their move, and the wide pine floors in the large living/dining room had been sanded and covered with three coats of polyurethane. All that remained was to paint the interior, and move in the remainder of the furnishings to the newly completed second level.

Because the couple was anxious to put the finishing touches on their renovated digs, Bobby was not able to meet Jonathan on the day they had agreed to return to Emma's. When he informed his friend that he was not able to get away for another week, Jonathan decided to put off his return until he and Bobby could work together. "We've worked well together so far, my man, and I feel we need to finish this thing the same way," he said.

Nora greeted them the following Sunday morning. Urging the men to sit, she poured coffee and supplied fresh baked corn muffins. After helping herself to tea, she began: "Y'll not believe it, Miss Emma has taken herself to church. Oi know, oi'm havin' a difficult toim believin' it meself," she said, noticing the amazed look on the faces of the two men. "She's been on me for weeks, wantin' me to foind someone who'll take her to church. Oi ain't carryin' her out, and she won't hear of a chair.

"So, since she was not about t'change her moind, oi finally called up th'preacher, and told him of her plight. The good man said he'd be happy to oblige. Half hour ago, himself came in a large van, picked her up bodily, plunked her down on his front seat and took her off. Wouldn't let me coom, told me oi needed time off, he'd take perfectly good care of her."

The young woman smiled. "She wanted to gussie up, did Emma. We got her dressed in all her finery. Dressed her early, so's she could nap a bit before she left."

"What do you think that's all about?" Jonathan asked.

"Dunno," Bobby mused. "She ain't been one t'go to church since I've known her. Mebbe she thinks she's not long f'r the world, and wants to make peace with her maker?"

"That's not it," Nora offered. "She says she needs to give thanks fer the two of you, for all you've done t'help 'er. Also, f'r me, she says." She blushed. "Says without me, she'd be pushin' daisies."

"Well. That's all I have to say," Jonathan offered. "No, there's something else. This is a good thing. Means we're able to search the rooms on this floor without causing her any undue anxiety. And I say, let's get to it without delay." He rose and put his cup and plate in the sink. "Nora, how long do we have before she's due back?" he asked.

"Oi'd say, about two hours. Preacher said he needed to do a few things after the sairvice before he could deliver her home. Miss Emma said that was quite fine with her."

"That should be enough time to search her room, at least," Bobby stated. "We prob'ly kin do the whole floor, if there ain't too many drawers and such to go through."

They divided the chore. Jonathan would search the kitchen, the mudroom, the formal parlor and the front entry. Bobby opted for the dining room and the informal sitting room, now Emma's combination bed-sitting space.

The search of the dining room proved fruitless, since the drawers in the sideboard contained only Emma's parents' ancient silver service, and a number of musty, long-abandoned linen tablecloths and napkins. The small closet in the space contained glassware and out-dated china. The room obviously had not been used as a dining room for decades. Emma, and now Nora, obviously used the large ornate table mainly as a catchall for the piles of clothing which needed mending, folding and ironing an ancient upright piano stood in one corner, closed and collecting dust. The bench contained a musty, discolored collection of old songs, mostly hymns.

Bobby moved on to Emma's room. He looked around. The only papers in evidence were on her small desk. He quickly riffled through these, finding nothing of value. The drawers were not locked, but they offered up no information. Emma had filled them with old Christmas cards, stationery and envelopes, crossword puzzles she meant to complete and ledgers pertaining to the running and maintenance of the house.

After rifling through her magazine rack and the local newspapers piled beside her bed, Bobby sat in the large chair at the foot of the bed, suddenly discouraged. He and Jonathan were getting nowhere, it seemed. Jonathan had not found anything yet, since he would surely have yelled for his partner if he had.

He looked around the room carefully. Where to look next? If he were Thomas, where would he hide a document so his wife would never discover it? Emma was not known for her obsessive housekeeping. Maybe he'd hide it in a place she would not think to look, or clean. Under something, perhaps; but what?

He looked around the room once more. Most of the furnishings had been there before Emma had taken ill. But there was one piece that had not. The small, oval ornate table which now stood beside Emma's bed and contained her medicines and the pencils with which to complete her puzzles was new. He remembered seeing it in Emma's room, and her telling him that she had sold almost all of the furnishings in the room after Thomas died. She had kept only the trunk, and that table. She told Bobby that Thomas placed it there to hold his ever-present book and a pipe; notes regarding his current books were sometimes kept in its drawer. Bobby could hear her mournful tone: "The smell of him, of his pipe, was in it, you know. So I allowed myself to keep it."

But Emma kept small things in its drawer, now. No place to hide a lost will. He couldn't let it go, however. He went to the little table and removed the bottles and writing implements, and emptied the drawer. When he turned the table on end, he saw it.

A long manila envelope had been securely taped to the underside of the small table's lower shelf. Bobby yelled to Jonathan as he freed the document from its hiding place. "Hey partner! I found it!" They met in the hallway as Jonathan ran from the formal parlor. Bobby waved the envelope as he danced up and down the hall. Jonathan grinned as he grabbed the envelope from his friend. "Last Will and Testament of Manning Thomas IIIrd" was printed in block letters on the envelope.

Jonathan scratched his head as he noted the name. "Manning Thomas? What's this?"

Bobby halted. "Y'know what it is. Manchester wasn't Manchester. He changed 'is name. No wonder he didn't want Emma to take his name. Wasn't his." The men looked at the envelope again. "Geez." Bobby said. "Wonder what's in it?"

"I suggest that before we settle in to read it, we make sure that there's no evidence of our search. At least, none that Emma is able to notice."

"Yeah. I gotta straighten up her room. Made a mess."

"We also might not want Emma to know that we discovered the will just yet; we need to read it thoroughly, then decide how to tell her what we find."

The two men decided to take the document to a local coffee shop, leaving a note for Nora stating that they needed some fresh air, and would feed themselves while they were out. Nora had left for the market while the men searched, so she had not heard the hoopla over the discovery of Manchester's will.

After carefully placing the envelope on the table between them, the two men ordered coffee, and ham and cheese sandwiches. "We could wait, but I gotta admit, I'm starved. My stomach's all'es come first." Bobby grinned. "Who's gonna open it?"

"I don't know if I want to read it, now that it's a reality," Jonathan replied

"Oh, 'course y'do," Bobby retorted. "We're jest spooked, is all. We need t'know what th' guy wanted f'r Emma, and we need t' find out who he really is. We agreed, and we can't go back now, it'd kill Miss Emma if we stopped now."

"I realize that. We also need to realize that the truth may do her in."

"True. But neverth'less, we need t'open that envelope." Bobby grabbed it and opened the seal. "Here goes nothin'."

Although the document was not long, they decided to finish their lunches before reading through it, agreeing that no news, good or bad, would be well received by their empty stomachs. They ate hastily, both fully aware of the importance of the piece of paper before them.

The table was cleared and fresh coffee was poured. "Okay, it's time," Bobby announced. "I'm as ready as I'm gonna be." He sighed. "You read it, Jonathan."

"Fine. Give me the dreadful task." It was Jonathan's turn to sigh. "Oh, all right, here we go."

LAST WILL AND TESTAMENT
Of
Manning Chester Thomas, III

October fifteenth, 19--.

This is my final will and testament. This document is intended to cancel out any and all previous wills. I have asked a local attorney to read and notarize the final document, so there will be no doubt of its validity.

I have decided to amend my previous will at this time because I have recently been informed that I may not have long to live. I fully intended to tell Emma about my past at some time, but this recent news has hastened my need to supply her with this information. I intend to make this will available to her, and to inform her concerning my legal name and the conditions surrounding our marriage when I return from Mexico, I will travel there to see a recommended specialist, hoping he will be able to do something about my failing heart. If for some reason I am not able to share this with Emma, I do have the hope that it will be discovered while Emma still lives.

To my knowledge at this time, these are my assets:

Here, the will listed the properties and monies contained in Thomas's estate. Following this list, it continued:

My darling wife, Emma Colridge, believes she is legally married to Thomas Manchester. This marriage, although entered into with my whole heart, and, for me, as real and binding as any joining which has ever been recorded, may not be a legal contract. It is not legal due to the fact that I was legally married to another at that time

I became Thomas Manchester thirty-nine years ago, when I left my home and family in Boston, Massachusetts. I left Manny Thomas behind, never intending to use that name again. The only person who knows of my whereabouts is my financial consultant in Boston, Leonard Kurzman. He has sworn not to reveal my name or my whereabouts, unless he is approached after my demise with a formal document such as this. Any legal or financial arrangements I have made during the years that I have been Thomas Manchester were made in that name only.

When I left my father's firm in Boston in 19--I was married to Sara Helene Thomas, nee Breckenridge. I did not divorce Sara, although we shared a loveless marriage with no children. Sara was a fragile, proud woman, and a legal divorce would have devastated her. I left my life to go to sea, but did not inform her of that fact. She was told that I was taking a voyage to London to conduct business for the firm with which I was employed. I left ship in London and was never seen again by any person who knew me. When I did not reach my supposed destination, she investigated my disappearance for a time, and then she must have assumed that I disappeared at sea, since she never heard from me again, and no person of whom she was aware could prove otherwise.

When the law declared me dead after seven years, Sara was entitled to her inheritance under the terms of a will filed in our safe deposit box under my original name. And all records involving Manchester Thomas were closed, I may have been able to marry again, legally. I had some doubts regarding investigating this possibility, since it may have emotionally harmed my Emma, so decided against it. Sara did not inherit my entire estate, but is well provided for until her demise. The terms of that will stated that Sara is not able to pass on the remainder of her inheritance to another when she dies. All remaining monies must revert to the original estate, and will then be added to my various "charities", as explained below. Sara is alive at this writing, since, according to Kurzman, there are still accounts bearing her name in the estate.

The bulk of my original estate was to be distributed to a number of charities of my choice. These charities were, in reality, accounts that reverted to Thomas Manchester. These accounts, along with any other monies, have been managed by Kurzman and Becker's brokerage in Boston. At this point, according to Kurzman, investments are doing well, enabling me to continue my affluent lifestyle.

On this day, I bequeath my entire estate, as it stands, to the wife of my heart, Miss Emma Colridge of Milltown, Maine. This inheritance will include any and all properties and/or monies in the names of Manning C. Thomas III, and/or Thomas Manchester.

Upon the demise of Sara Helene Thomas, the remainder of that portion of my estate will be added to the bequest to Miss Emma Colridge.

To date. This is the sole copy of my will. After I have informed my love Emma of its existence, and have apologized for deceiving her, I shall place a copy of this document in Kurzman's hands, so he may be informed of any changes in my life. The original shall remain with Emma.

Signed on this fifteenth day of October, 19—by

Manning Chester Thomas, III.

(Read and notarized on the twentieth day of October, 19—by the Hon. Arthur Wellman, atty.)

On a separate page, Thomas had added this note:

Emma, my only love,

I have no excuse for myself. I found I could not work out a plan for my life that would not have seriously harmed another, without necessity to deceive. You who are so strong, and know me so well, must surely understand.

I realize that I may have been free to marry you legally for many years. I have not taken advantage of this situation, because I did not wish to inform you that our original agreement was not legal. We have been so happy in our lives together. I thought that, if you discovered my deceit, you would leave me. And I do not ever want to be without you, my love.

I look forward to our lives together, both here, and wherever one's soul travels when the body can be here no more. I will wait for you to finally make that long journey to join me. Have no fear, my love; I am certain that the destination will be well worth the travel.

Ever yours,

Thomas

NINE

"Geez." Bobby finally broke the silence. "Too bad ol' Thomas croaked before he had a chance to let Miss Emma in on all that stuff that went on with him before he met 'er."

"Mmm. I was with the man for over thirty years." Jonathan shook his head in disbelief. "It's all news to me. Amazing. How did he maintain this secret identity? It must have taken some pretty complex planning.

"For example, why didn't this Kurzman get in touch with Emma when Thomas stopped contacting him? Does Kurzman even know the man's dead, or that Emma exists? And for that matter, how did they stay in contact? We know he phoned the man, but did Manchester have a secret mailing address? If he did, it must be stuffed with unclaimed mail, after all these years." The list of unsolved problems seemed endless." He shook his head in disbelief.

"One thing's for sure; we're not going to find answers with Emma, or in this document. We may need to travel to Boston one of these days," Jonathan finished.

"Guess we might. I ain't lookin' for'ard to that trip," Bobby groaned. "I hate gittin' through them cities. Be better if I go with you, though," he mused. "Problem now is, what d'we tell Emma?" Bobby looked at his friend.

"You are asking me?" Jonathan returned his stare. "I have no idea." He paused. Then, "I have a pretty good idea that if she reads this document, she will not take it well. It may not be the best thing for her, in her present state.

"Perhaps we could edit it somehow; leave out the part about Thomas' past."

"We do need t'tell her we found somethin'," Bobby added. "We can't keep it all from 'er. It's hers, and she needs t'know about it." He made a face as he sipped his cold coffee. Then, "Man, I need t'git outta here; let's walk."

As they walked back to Emma's, the men agreed to tell her that a document had been discovered, but it was in disrepair and needed to be gone over carefully, so that facts would not be distorted. They would ask Emma's permission to take the document with them so it could be closely analyzed. When that had been accomplished, they would meet with her and let her know the gist of any information they uncovered.

"We're tellin' a bald lie," Bobby mused as they neared the house. "Those papers's in perfect condition.'

"True," Jonathan agreed. "Can you think of any other way to break the news to her?"

"Guess not. I don't want her croakin' on us when she finds out her marriage ain't legal, that's for sure."

"Keep in mind that Thomas did consider it a marriage, and that he was really in love with our Emma. That, she needs to know," Jonathan stated adamantly.

"Yep. I agree t'that. She told me she knows she's dyin'. Says she feels life leavin' her. So I guess it's all right to tell her only the good stuff. She's not gonna want to read the original, I'll make book on that. She ain't keen on bringin' the past too close. Says it makes her unhappy." Bobby paused as they reached Emma's door. "We're doin' this to keep an old lady happy in her last days, is what I gotta tell m'self. Otherwise, I'm gonna have a hard time livin' with the guilt."

"Agreed. Now, it's time to tell her. I need to get back to Portland tonight, and you need to go home to your Doreen.

"I would prefer you keep the document with you, Bobby," Jonathan added. "I'll phone you in a few days, and we'll decide how to present the information to her."

Emma was still alert. Nora had helped her change and fed her a light lunch, and she was back in her bed, waiting their return. "She wouldn't close her eyes until you come back," Nora declared as she met them at the door. "She knows somethin's afoot; is she right?"

Jonathan smiled. "She is."

"You found something, didn't you." Emma's eyes were misted over and bright as her gaze darted from Bobby to Jonathan. "You found a note, or a will. I know it in my bones." She smiled. "Where was it?"

"Was under the little table, right there, next t'yr bed," Bobby replied. "Been there all the time."

"Thomas's table," Emma mused. "Might've known." Then, "What does it say?"

Jonathan cleared his throat. "It isn't in very good shape, Miss Emma. It has been there for a very long time. We tried to decipher the entire document, but we were unable to do that in such a short time." He looked to Bobby. "We wondered if you would allow Bobby to take it with him, to work on. Perhaps you would allow Doreen to help him. He and I will keep in touch, and when we have deciphered information, we will all meet to discuss what our next step must be."

Emma looked closely at Bobby. "Of course you can take it, my friend. I hope you and Doreen can make sense of it. But," she added, "before you leave, would it be all right if I hold it? I would like to have a part of Thomas near to me."

"'Course you can, Miss Emma." Bobby retrieved the envelope from his jacket pocket and held it out to her. "Why is this line on the envelope blacked out?" she asked. "Dunno. That's one of the facts we need t'investigate before we know what all's in it," Bobby answered. "We sealed it back up after we looked at it, too," he continued. "Paper's pretty fragile, and we din't want anythin' to happen to it."

Emma held the envelope over her heart. "Old and fragile, like me," she murmured. She handed it back to Bobby. "My eyes are so bad, I probably couldn't read it if I wanted to," she added. "These days, I need a magnifier to read a bit of the newspaper each morning. Perhaps I will want to read it as it is, some day. But not today." She lay back on the pillows. "I'm ready to rest now," she stated. "My soldiers have fought a good battle, and the war is almost won." She closed her eyes. "We'll meet, soon," she whispered as she fell asleep.

"Not all the news in that thing is good news, I reckon," Nora remarked as she saw the men out.

"Right." Jonathan returned. "We're forming a plan to tell her what she needs to hear," he continued. "The only lie is that it's not decipherable. We won't lie to her again, if we can help it."

"Except f'r the one sayin' y'don't know how a black loine came t'be on the envelope?"

"Except for that one."

"Oi'll go along with ye'. I love the old lady, y'know. Want only th'best f'her.'

"So d'we," Bobby agreed. "I feel like we're all in some big conspiracy or somethin'. I'm only doin' it because I know what'd happen if Emma reads that thing as it is."

The following evening, Bobby and Doreen brought a pad of paper to the table after their dinner, and read through Manning Thomas's Last Will and Testament. They then noted the facts that they were fairly sure Emma needed to know. The two things they omitted were Thomas's birth name and the fact that the marriage between Emma and Thomas may not have ever been legal. Doreen agreed that Emma did not need to know these facts, given her fragile health. She did make Bobby promise that if their friend improved, he would supply her with the remaining facts contained in the will. "I couldn't be a party to lying to her if I knew she was able to tolerate hearing all of it," Doreen stated. "After all, Thomas did want her to know."

Bobby agreed. Following the completion of the re-write, the information they agreed to share with Emma would consist of the bequest of all of Thomas's worldly goods to her, the location of the Boston brokerage, and the second paragraph of the note which Thomas had inserted. This information would be re-written by Doreen, and presented to Emma when Jonathan and Bobby were next able to meet. For safekeeping, the original will would be stored at Bobby's in a locked spare cashbox, which Doreen would supply from the restaurant.

Jonathan called toward the end of the week, and was delighted with the re-written document. They agreed to meet with Emma that Sunday afternoon. A message was relayed to the old woman through Nora, who stated that the time was fine with Emma, and that she looked forward to their return. "She's been right perky since you found the paper," Nora added. "Been walkin' out for ten minutes almost every day, she has."

TEN

Unfortunately, due to problems with Bobby's daughter Bess, the meeting with Emma was put off for a week. Bess had been roaming the country with a musician she hooked up with in California, and his schedule had brought him to Bangor for a gig at the "Country Club", a popular music spot. A friend of Debra's who saw the band play its first performance spotted Bess in the audience, and called her to let her know her daughter was in town.

Debra was able to trace Bess' whereabouts, and traveled to Bangor to meet with her daughter at the club. Early the next morning, she called Bobby. "Bess's around, Bobby", she began. "We talked. She's hangin' out with some drugged-out slob of a drummer in the band that's at the Country Club in Bangor. They been travelin' all over the country. I told her, her boy's with Becka. She told me she don't give a shit. She don't even want to see him."

Bobby sighed. "Geez. Whatta you want me t'do, Deb?" He asked.

"What're we gonna do with that kid?" Debra retorted. "If I hadn't gone to find her, she prob'ly never would have let either of us know she was around. She's obviously takin' drugs again, and now she's prob'ly got some STD or somethin'; the bum she's with looks a hundred years old, he's prob'ly been shootin' up for years. Who knows if his needles are clean; he sure ain't."

"How's Bess?" Bobby asked.

"Oh, you know Bess. She's got orange streaks in her hair, skirt's up to her navel, halter top down to meet it. She's wearin' so much makeup, I couldn't tell how she looked, tell the truth. It was dark, you know how it is. She is drinkin' a lot, though, I's well aware of that.

"Could you talk to her, Bobby? Sometimes, she listens to you. She's only in town a couple more days, then they're goin' up to Canada, to Quebec City. We may never see her again, she gets to another country for godsakes."

Bobby was sorely tempted to tell Debra that he didn't want anything to do with this daughter who obviously had decided never to contact her parents again. Neither Deb nor Bobby had heard from Bess in over six months. The last time she had called Debra, she slammed the phone down when her mother refused to send her money. Debra and Bobby agreed that any funds supplied from either of them would go to Becka, for Bess's daughter's support. They would no longer bail Bess out of the messes she continually found herself involved in.

However, Bobby was also Bess's dad, and he couldn't shut off the fact that he loved his errant daughter. "I guess I c'd take the day and look her up," he replied. "I ain't happy about it, but she's still our kid." He sighed again. "I'll give it one more try, see if I kin git her into rehab again. If it's no go with her, I'm lettin' it go, Deb. Maybe some day we gotta admit, she's lost to us."

"Shit, Bobby. How can you give up on your own kid?" Debra paused, then added, "I know you're right, though. She's never listened to nobody about nothin'. I thought I was bad; at least, I married you and stayed in one place for a while. Taught me a couple a lessons."

"Oh, really? That's a new one," Bobby chuckled.

"Yeah, I know. Maybe I'm finally growin' up. About time, huh?" Debra laughed. "I like Vinnie, he's a good guy; I like livin' in the city. I like havin' a little cash to do the things I wanna do. And I ain't gonna be a model.

I'm too old. And, I'm okay with that. So," she added, "I'm happier with myself. I guess that makes me more of a grownup." She paused. "How're things goin' with that Doreen, anyways? You guys gonna git married?"

"Things are fine with Doreen. We ain't talked marriage yet. And I'm glad things are better with you, Deb. You and me, we tried to make it for a while. And we do have two kids who turned out okay. That's gotta count for somethin'.

"How do I git hold of her?" he asked.

"Call the club and leave a message; they get it to her. Tell 'em it's for Kansas Gentry's girl."

"Kansas? That's 'is real name?"

"How do I know? It's what he uses for the band. Jest call her." Debra supplied Bobby with the number for the Country Club, then hung up.

Doreen came into the kitchen as Bobby put the phone down. "Trouble, hon?" She asked.

"Bess again," he replied. "She's in Bangor, she's drinkin' and druggin', travelin' with some musician named Kansas, don't wanna even see Dustin. Her own kid, for godsakes."

"That sucks," Doreen hugged him from behind and kissed the top of his head. "What're you gonna do?"

"Deb gave me a number I kin reach her at. I'm thinkin' of goin' to talk t'her about rehab again."

"You want company?" Doreen sat beside him with her coffee. "I think I can take a couple of days off, finally. I finished trainin' Ginnie last week, I think she'll do just fine. A little green yet, but she's got a good head.

"Mom's leavin' the restaurant for good a week from Thursday. Goin' to see her sister in Saco for a month. But we still have her for over a week, if Ginnie needs her. So maybe I can fly the coop and have some time with my sweetie."

"That'd be great," Bobby allowed. "It may not be a lot of fun, though," he added. "Dealin' with Bess is us'lly a bitch." He leaned over and kissed her. "Anything in my life's better if it involves you, though," he added. "Have I told you I love you, my lovely Doreen?"

"From time to time; but it's always good to hear," Doreen replied as she cleared the table. "You make the call; I'll pack."

Bess threaded through the small tables, making her way toward them in the crowded, dimly lit, smoke-filled club. Deb had described her to a tee; spiky, orange-streaked hair, miniscule black leather skirt, brief turquoise halter top, large silver hoops in her ears, dozens of bangles around her wrists and ankles, silver rings on every finger. She was clutching a half-full beer bottle in one hand, a cigarette in the other. At least she has some weight on her, Bobby noted. Last time he had seen her she looked anorectic.

"Hey." She perched gingerly on the rickety chair across from them. "So what's up?"

Bobby took a long pull from his bottle. "Jest thought we'd come see you; been a long time since we heard anythin' from you." He had to yell to hear himself. "Kin we go outside or somethin'? It's so loud I can't hear myself think, much less talk t' you."

Bess rose and motioned to them to follow her. She led them from the vast main room to a small private side room in the back of the club. There were two parties in there, drinking and playing cards, but it was comparatively quiet. They settled at a small table as far from the card players as they could get, and ordered another round of beer from a tired, under-dressed waitress.

"Great place y'got here," Bobby remarked wryly.

"I been in a bunch of places much worse'n this," Bess replied. "If Ma had given me money when I needed it that time, I mighta been able to git my own place and a good job," she added. "I met Kansas jest after that, and he's been pretty good t'me." She looked warily at Bobby. "Better'n you have."

"Hey, wait a minute, young lady," Bobby bristled. His face reddened and his knuckles whitened as he gripped his beer. "Your mumma and me, we done everything we know to git you to put y'self t'gether. None of it worked. You're still drinkin', druggin', hangin' with bums, even abandoned the only thing you done right, that sweet little boy of yours. You got no one to blame but yourself, now.

"Sure, your ma was not the best, and I was always workin' so I din't know what was goin' on half the time. We done things wrong, but we was young and we done what we knew. Now, you're a freakin' adult, and you continue to act like a stupid kid. That ain't our fault.

"Y'got choices to make in your life, Bess. You kin continue to blame your mumma and me for everything, or you kin git on with whatever your life has t'offer you. You ain't even outta your twenties yet. If drugs don't kill you, you prob'ly got fifty or sixty years to go. What're you gonna do with them years? You kin keep blamin' everyone includin' God for your sorry self, or you kin go make somethin' of that time."

As he spoke he noticed that Bess was fidgeting with her cigarette, looking at the ceiling and swinging her foot, tapping it incessantly against the table leg. Bobby knew the signs; she was getting restless, and she was not listening to a word he said. He rose.

"C'mon, Doreen. She don't give a shit about you, me, or herself. She's jest waitin' to see if I'm gonna give her money." He looked at Bess. "I ain't givin' you a cent," he said. "I come to see if you was far enough gone on drugs so's you might benefit from rehab again. But you act'lly look okay. You're jest an ornery kid who ain't grown up."

He looked down at her. "You called your sister? Mumma told me she let you know that Dustin's livin' with her. You got any plans to see your kid?"

"I figure she's doin' jest fine with my don't-never-do-nothin'-wrong sister. Why upset the kid when he's okay?" Bess replied tersely.

Doreen spoke. "I've been sitting here, looking at you, Bess. You're a beautiful young woman, under all that crap you put on your face and hair. You're young, still somewhat healthy, you'd think you had everything to live for." She sighed.

"Seems t'me, though, you're arranging things in your life so you've got nothing to live for. You're about to send the only daddy you got away mad. Your mumma doesn't know what to say to you, and you don't talk to her. You have a beautiful kid who would love you if he knew you. Kids love their mummas. It's just a fact of life. And kids mourn, when they find out their mummas don't want them. Doesn't make any difference how much the ones who care for them love them. They still want their mummas.

"You're throwing away those that love you, Bess. That may kill you, some day."

"Who asked you for your two cents?" Bess turned to Doreen. "What I do with my life ain't none of your goddam business. You're jest the whore my dad picked up after my no-good mumma took off." She turned to leave.

Bobby grabbed her arm. "You go now, and you and me are through," he hissed. "If you want anything to do with me, ever, you'll apologize to Doreen, right now."

"Lay off my arm, Daddy. You're hurtin' me." Bess started to whine.

"Don't pull that on me, Bess. I ain't fallin' for it. I mean what I said. Apologize, or we leave and you ain't never seein' or hearin' from me again."

Bess stood in front of Bobby rubbing her arm. "I ain't apologizin' to that cow," she spat. "I don't give a shit about any of you. I'm outta here." She grabbed her cigarettes and her half empty beer and stalked out of the room.

Stone-faced, Bobby sat in the passenger seat of the truck. Doreen had taken the keys from him, stating that he was not in any condition to drive. "Shit." He mumbled. "I really messed that up."

"She's very good at what she does," Doreen mused. "She knows exactly which buttons to push to get the strongest reaction she knows a person is capable of.

"You didn't mess it up; she did. You were absolutely right. She's makin' all the wrong choices. And nothing will change between you until she decides to change her interactions with the folks who care about her."

Bobby's jaw relaxed a bit. "D'you think we'll ever see her again?"

"Sure. I know you didn't mean it when you said you were through with her. And she's not stupid; somewhere inside, she knows it, too. But you both need some time and space; maybe years of it." Doreen grabbed Bobby's hand and kissed it. "Don't give up on her. Love her. It's all you can do, right now."

Bobby turned to her, his mouth and jaw relaxed. "How come you're such a wise woman?" he asked softly.

"Why d'you think I left Quoddy?" she said. "My parents and I never got along. I thought I hated them. It took my dad's death to bring me to my senses." She began to cry softly. "It took me a long time to forgive myself for not being there when he died. I had miles of fence to mend with my mother. I'd been away for over fifteen years. Never wrote, never called.

"I read about his death in the Bangor paper. If I hadn't picked up that paper after one of our guests left it on a table in the inn's coffee shop, and had the curiosity to poke through it to see what was going on in that part of Maine, I probably would not have known he died." She shook her head. "Don't know what would have happened to me, or my mother. Don't want to know. I'm grateful for what did happen.

"So, that's what made me wise. It's called life." She smiled wearily. "Let's go home, Love."

ELEVEN

Maine's short summer was in full bloom on the Saturday that Bobby, Jonathan and Emma decided the next step of the opus. Lilies and wild roses dressed the walkways of the houses along Main Street. The sky was true cerulean, with small puffs of white skittering across its vast expanse, urged on by a brisk, warm breeze. People were out in full force, the men in tees, the young women pushing strollers in halter tops they pulled from their closets only two to three weeks each year. Smiles and waves were in abundance; everyone was in celebration mode.

Nora had set up chairs in Emma's side yard. It was too lovely, she decided, to spend time inside. Emma was ensconced in her chair when the two men arrived. She wore a bright blue dress with a pert white collar, and a soft, multi-hued afghan was draped across her propped-up knees. Nora had washed and brushed her white hair to a sheen, putting it up with two engraved silver combs she had discovered in Emma's room.

"Oi'll put out a pitcher o' lemonade, then oi'll leave the passel of ye to do your dairty work," she quipped. "She had a birthday last week, y'know," Nora whispered to Bobby. "But we're not mentionin' it". Bobby smiled. "She sure don't make a deal outta them," he whispered back.

"You're looking well, and very pretty," Jonathan said as he bent to kiss the old woman's soft withered cheek.

"Oh, get on with you," Emma returned, smiling. "No one my age is pretty. Interesting or eccentric, or perhaps even attractive, but never pretty."

"Yep. The man is right. You're pretty. All them other things, too, but y'look downright cute sittin' there," Bobby added.

Emma blushed then, and the men laughed. "Sit yourselves down and have lemonade, and let's get on with it," Emma snorted. "Enough of this blatant flattery."

Bobby pulled the re-written will out of its folder and set it on the low table Nora had provided. "Do you want to read it, or shall one of us do the honors?" Jonathan asked.

Emma sighed, clutching the afghan with white-knuckled hands. "Why don't you read it, Jonathan," she said softly. "My eyes are not the best, and I must confess, I have been very nervous about this meeting." She sat up straight. "I almost cancelled it. After all, I am very comfortable now. I have enough money, I have Nora to care for me, my house is in very good condition, and I am feeling much better than I did a couple of months ago. Why should I want to disturb my life at this age?"

"Well, Miss Emma—" Bobby began.

Emma stopped him with a crooked finger. "I know exactly what you're going to say, Bobby Parker. You'll remind me that if I do not go ahead with my opus, I will remain always in denial. I may die never knowing the truth about my Thomas." She sighed. "And not knowing, I would die angry with him."

"So," she continued, "I am prepared to hear what he had to say." She looked at Jonathan. "Read on, McDuff," she finished wryly, waving a pale hand in Jonathan's direction.

"How much money do you suppose is in Thomas' estate?" Emma asked, when Jonathan had finished.

"Dunno." Bobby replied. "Must be a cartload. He's been supportin' you and God only knows how many others all these years." The three sat silently while Emma absorbed the information she had received.

"I think back to when he died," she said. "Remember, Jonathan?" Jonathan nodded solemnly. "You and I did not know what to do about his interment. We placed notices in all of the city papers in the state, wondering if anyone would call to say they had known him. He had placed a sum of money in an account in our local bank in both of our names, as he did each time he returned from one of his journeys, to cover the expenses we incurred while he was here. If we had not had access to those funds, I don't know how we would have found the money to bury him.

"Why didn't someone who handled, and most likely still handles, these monies, come forth?" Emma mused. Then, "Do you suppose they still think he's alive?"

Bobby and Jonathan looked at each other. Bobby shrugged. "Can't say as I got an answer for that one," he offered. "Got any ideas, Jonathan?"

Jonathan thought for a moment. "When Bobby contacted the lawyer in Bangor, he seemed to know that Thomas had died. Perhaps Thomas contacted someone that last night, before he went to bed."

"Thomas always went to his attic room directly after he had settled in, and before we sat to re-connect with each other," Emma said thoughtfully. "I think he did go upstairs for a few moments before we settled in for a glass of wine." She shook her head slowly. "Of course, Thomas had no idea he would not live to the next day," she added. "It's so difficult to recall all of the small details of that night. I remember only our lovely talk, and our late dinner.

"Thomas never complained of pain. I often think that perhaps he was in pain that evening, and hid it from me. He always wished our meetings to be joyous." She smiled. "They were...always."

"Well, if we suppose that he was uncomfortable, perhaps he wished to settle some business in case something did happen," Jonathan mused. "If that was so, he could have informed those in charge of his estate that if they did not hear from him within an ascertained time, they must assume that he had passed, and must go on conducting his business," he added. "Or, the firm read of his demise in the local papers. I did post notice in the Portland daily paper."

"And what of this will? Would he have informed those in charge of it?" Emma wondered.

"Perhaps; and, perhaps he had planned to mail it to them. He ran out of time, and it was never mailed. Of course, that did not affect your trust, since it had been established years before."

"We were married for over twenty-three years. He had that time in which to mail it." Emma stated through clenched teeth. "There is something wrong. I feel it in my soul. The Thomas I knew would not have left me without providing for me fully." She paused, looking into the distance. "Perhaps he is not the Thomas I knew. Perhaps he is someone else." Emma paused, her eyes brimming with tears. "I don't know if I could bear that."

She looked at Jonathan and frowned. "You traveled with Thomas for years. Did you ever know him as anyone but the Thomas I knew?"

"Absolutely not. He was always the same with me. He never told me anything about Boston, or life before we met. I knew what you know." Then, "Of course, Thomas and I were always Captain and Mate. We sailed together. In that capacity, we talked only of our trips, and the events at sea. He did not share his personal life with me."

"Mmm. So, perhaps Thomas was many things to many people," Emma replied. "It is very strange, to know of him in any other way than my dear husband."

Bobby shifted in his seat. "S'posin' there is somethin' goin' on that ain't right; how d'we find out the truth?" he asked nervously.

Emma glared at him. "I feel I must know the truth. No more denial. I would like you to go to Boston. That seems to be the root of his life. That is the first lie. He told me he was from Portland. He was not. I need to know this man, before I decide whether we will connect, wherever I go after I leave behind this bag of bones I call my body these days."

"We could do that if you'd like," Jonathan replied. "You need to know, however, that the people who were involved with Thomas' estate fourteen years ago may not be able to be contacted. You may need to settle for any pertinent information we can dig up." He turned to Bobby. "Agreed?"

"I'm in if you are," Bobby replied. "How 'bout it, Miss Emma? You willin' to hear anything we kin find out?"

"I am. I can only hope you discover the whole truth, so I can go knowing the real Thomas Manchester. But, I am willing to settle for whatever you are able to discover."

Jonathan and Bobby agreed to travel to Boston, but for the second time, Bobby needed to inform Emma that he could not make the trip until he had completed a number of outside jobs which could not be put off, since it was mid-summer, and the weather could not be counted on to remain fair for very long.

"You need to conduct your business, Bobby," Emma agreed. "I am well aware of that. I am fairly well now, and my life is fairly comfortable. Nora has offered to stay with me as long as she is needed; in fact," Emma dropped her voice to a loud whisper, "my plan is never to let her go. I plan to adopt her," She grinned.

"Seriously, I am in no danger of leaving this mortal coil in the next few weeks. Waking and living through each day is the basic chore of the fortunate souls who reach my ripe old age. Life drifts along, every day being whatever it is. And every day, I am grateful for three very good friends to pass time with as I wait to leave."

She smiled again. "Nora tell you I actually went to church to give thanks for the lot of you?" she asked.

"She did; we wondered if th'church'd caved in when you came through th'door."

Bobby returned her grin. It was good to be able to joke with the old lady again. Felt like the days in her kitchen when his work was completed, and they'd share stories while he drank a couple of beers. He told her as much.

"I feel good about that, also," the old lady replied. "When I was very ill, I lost the humorous aspect of living. The next time that happens, I don't plan to stay around. A world without humor is not worth living in."

Jonathan stopped Bobby as he was climbing into his truck. "I think we covered our butts very well in there," he commented. "You did an especially good job of covering up your inability to tell untruths."

"Hated every damn minute of it," Bobby retorted. "But I guess it's necessary, at least 'til we find out what's goin' on."

The two men agreed to stay in close touch, and to plan their trip sometime in October, following completion of Bobby's summer work. Because of the chance of worsening weather in northern Maine's late autumn, they wished to be done with Emma's opus before the start of the holiday season. Doreen had suggested to Bobby that Jonathan spend the holidays with them, and Jonathan was looking forward to Thanksgiving and Christmas in Washington County, an area of Maine he had never seen.

TWELVE

The brokerage offices of Kurzman and Becker were housed in an old, well-maintained brownstone near the courthouse, atop Chestnut Hill. Jonathan and Bobby arrived on a raw late October day, and were welcomed warmly in the reception area, where they were offered espresso in small, paper-thin porcelain cups. "Don't dare take it; I'm afraid I'd break th'cup," Bobby stated nervously. The Chanel-suited, perfectly coifed receptionist smiled warmly. "Please, Mr. Parker; we have plenty more where those came from."

Louis Kurzman greeted them in his vast office, indicating two deep leather chairs placed before his vast mahogany desk. "Have a seat; might as well be comfortable, we're bound to be here for awhile." Kurzman was obviously accustomed to comfort. His navy blue wool and cashmere jacket was open to an ecru silk shirt that had been tailored to fit his burgeoning paunch. His balding hair and manicured nails had been trimmed to perfection. Fashionable rimless half-glasses were positioned on the bridge of a nose whose pitted, bulbous appearance suggested access to aged scotch and rich food.

He opened a drawer as he sat, and brought out the slim folder Jonathan had mailed him. "Never thought I'd see this document," he began. "My father talked about the Thomas family every time we'd review our accounts. Family fascinated him." He paused. "Dad died last year; he was almost ninety. Crusty old guy. He would've loved to know that old Manny had come through." He smiled wryly. "Did a great job of setting up this business, however. I'm grateful for that. Jonathan Becker's been gone for years. Name's there because I'm too lazy to remove it. I'm it, for now, although I am seeking a partner."

"So, where are we going with this?" He removed the will from its folder and spread it before him. Bobby had never seen a platinum Rolex, but he knew Louis' watch had set him back a tidy sum.

"Emma don't know about Thomas Manchester's early life," Bobby began. "We," he added, indicating Jonathan, "decided not to tell her. She's pretty fragile, had a serious bout with her heart not too long ago, and we figured the news might do her in."

"Oh. How old is she?"

"Emma recently celebrated her eighty-ninth birthday," Jonathan answered. "Her mind is sharp, but her body is failing her. She feels she has little time remaining, and she wants to know about Manchester's, or Thomas's, past.

"We'd like to tell her whatever you know, but we're not sure she could take the piece about the wife." Jonathan smiled. "Emma says she wants to know it all, but she's been in denial since he died, and taking her from nothing to the complete truth may be more than she can handle."

"Well, I'll tell you what I know; how you present it to her is your problem." He cleared his throat. "Mind you, my information is mostly second-hand, since my father was the person Thomas confided in. But Dad and I were fairly close, and as I have said, he did share the family story with me.

"I will tell you before I begin, we were aware that Thomas had "married" Emma Colridge in a ceremony that was considered illegal. Since they never legalized the marriage, we were not able to contact Emma to inform her of his estate. We had no legal right to do that. If Manny Thomas had divorced Sara and married Emma legally, she would have been an enormously rich woman these past fourteen years."

"I think she considers herself pretty well off, despite her lack of monetary wealth," Jonathan commented dryly.

"Be that as it may, she sure lost out on a bundle of money." Kurzman shook his head. "Too bad. She's too old to use much of it, now." Then, "She have a will?" he asked.

"Dunno,' Bobby answered. "She's never mentioned it."

He shrugged. "Don't make much difference. She's got no relatives t'leave it to. It'll prob'ly go t'the church. People there've been good t'her."

"Whew. There's a bunch who'll have their prayers answered." Kurzman was obviously impressed with the size of Manchester's estate, Bobby mused.

The first Manning Thomas came to Boston from England in the late nineteenth century. His background was suspect, but his accent was charming. He was reputed to be quite a con man. Within a short time, he had connected with the families boasting of old money, and married the plain daughter of one of the richest bankers in the city. Using her money to set up various schemes, including the sale of phony stock and parcels of non-existent land, he amassed a decent fortune. Most of the people he had conned were from a society in which it was shameful to admit failure or defeat, so those who handed large chunks of their hard-earned family fortunes over to Thomas bit the bullet and kept their silence.

His son, Manning the Second, chose not to follow in his scheming father's footprints. He was educated at Harvard and became one of the city's most prominent lawyers. It was said that he married for love, but his wife was not poor, and the family fortune continued to grow. Manny Junior loved to play the stock market, and that contributed to their huge fortune.

Probably due to having little respect for his father's way of life, Junior became a religious fanatic, and any hours he was not practicing law were spent in prayer. When he was in his forties, he left his law firm to establish a brokerage, being aware that he could make more money and have more time to devote to his church if he managed the funds of others, rather than spending his time in the courts.

He and his wife bore one son. Junior and Doris were extremely strict parents. They structured every moment of the boy's young life, demanding that he follow their pious, Christian schedule. However, Manning Third was a rebellious youth. He decided early on that his father's fundamental beliefs did not suit him. Despite his rebellious nature, he did finish his education at Harvard with honors in the field of financial management. Knowing how to handle the family money was important to his lifestyle, and he wished to learn what he could about managing the huge estate which would some day belong to him.

He married Sara, one of his many youthful conquests, because she informed him she was pregnant, and because he was a decent man. It was rumored that she had lied to him in order to trap him into marriage, but the only story the public heard was that she lost the child in utero. During the years Manny and Sara were together, some say that more of his weekends were spent on the water, or at their cottage on Cape Cod than at their mansion in Wellesley.

When Manny Third began to rebel, his parents tried everything they knew to bring him back to God. He was forced to attend private fundamental Christian schools when he was young, but persuaded his parents to send him to Exeter Academy through high school. Manny's mother contacted Influenza, and died soon after the boy's sixteenth birthday. Following his graduation, the relationship between father and son grew more distant each year. Manny worked in his father's firm for a few years, but father and son fought continually. His father threatened to write him out of his will a number of times, but he knew his son's knowledge of financial law was excellent, and he would probably win if the will were contested.

In 19--, Manny planned a journey to Europe to conduct business for the firm. Before he left, he talked at great length with Leonard Kurzman, a colleague of his father's. He informed Kurzman that he was planning to go away forever, and he made arrangements for monies to be placed with Kurzman and Becker to be invested, both in his name and in a new name which he would inform them of in due time. His will indicated that his inheritance be distributed to his wife and to Kurzman's firm, for investment and dispersal to various charities. Those charities would actually exist as fronts for accounts that would revert to him in his new name. He was then in his mid-thirties. For a year, Kurzman and Becker heard nothing from him.

Finally, they received communication from Thomas Manchester. Manchester informed them that he had established residence in Portland, Maine, and that an investment firm there would be handling funds for him in that name only. This firm would not be informed of his earlier identity, but would handle only those monies that were entrusted to them.

Manning Junior had never been a particularly hale person. He died in his early sixties of tuberculosis contracted one brutal New England winter. Neither the Thomas money nor the fervent prayers of his congregation could save him.

Since his son's death had never been proven, Junior left the family fortune in his name, with the provision that, following proof of his son's demise, the funds would go to charity. Kurzman then stepped forward with proof of Manny's existence, and transferred the Thomas inheritance into his firm, to continue to be invested the transferences were perfectly legal, since Manny's partnership in the firm had never been dissolved. Three years after his father had died, Manny Third was declared legally dead. By that time, all of his father's investments were in the hands of Thomas Manchester.

"Brilliant man, that Manchester," Kurzman finished. "Never planned to do anything that would hurt anyone. He took care of his wife; he never took so much money that his father would even miss it. And, if he died before his dad, the terms of his original will returned the estate to him, except those monies with which Sara, and later Emma, would be supported.

"So he was able to have the life he dreamed of, live for years with his true love, and continue to make his money grow." Louis grinned. "Fucking brilliant."

"Yeah, except f'r one thing," Bobby put in. "He din't plan to die so quick. And 'cause he did, Emma was left without her legal marriage, and basically poor as a church mouse f'r all them years."

"Mom. True enough. Couldn't cover all the bases, I guess. Fate's a hard one to plan."

"One thing I need t'know," Bobby stated. "This Sara; she still around?"

"Sara is still alive. She suffers from Alzheimer's, and is now in a nursing home. All of her expenses are taken care of, of course She wants for nothing." He paused.

"She is in her eighties, and not well. She is not expected to live through the year."

"So if she passes before Emma goes, there's more money in Manchester's account." Bobby shook his head in disbelief. "All them funds, jest sittin' in banks and stuff, growin'. What good does it do anyone?"

Jonathan stood and stretched. "Question is," he added, "what do we tell Miss Emma?"

THIRTEEN

Following a number of phone meetings to decide the best approach for telling Manny Thomas's story to Emma, Jonathan and Bobby met in Milltown on a brisk Sunday morning in mid-November. Doreen had suggested that they invite Emma and Nora to Jonesboro the following Thursday for Thanksgiving dinner. Bobby replied that he'd ask his friend, but not to get her hopes up. Emma rarely left the house these days, never mind allowing herself to be dragged on a daylong outing. Shrugging, Doreen suggested he try his best; it would be her choice, after all. She thought Emma might like to meet Bobby's children. Becka and her family, Dickie and his girl, and Doreen's mother would be there, along with Jonathan. On Friday, they would all go to Helen Parker's to be with Bobby's siblings and their families.

"She certainly ain't gonna stay for that gatherin'," Bobby put in.

"Of course not; Jonathan can bring them home on Thursday evening. If he wants to go to your mumma's with us, he can come back on Friday. Stay through to Christmas, if he'd like."

Bobby chuckled. "Y'got th'whole thing planned jest right, eh?" He kissed the back of her neck as she peeled potatoes in front of the sink. "You're somethin' else, y'know?"

Emma greeted them at the door, frowning. "Well, it's about time the two of you arrived. I have not slept for over a week, waiting for your news." Nora stood behind her, shaking her head vigorously and mouthing, "She sleeps like a baby every night."

The three settled in the sitting room. Emma's hospital bed had been pushed to the far wall, and her customary chair and ottoman replaced it. Her friends noticed that although she walked with the aid of a cane, her step was livelier and her color was brighter.

'You're doin' right well, Miss Emma," Bobby remarked. "'Fore long, you'll be out galavantin' with your church ladies again."

"As a matter of fact, three of them plan to play bridge here just after the holiday," Emma retorted. "But we're not here to talk about those old geese, are we?" She settled in and placed her feet on the ottoman.

"What did you learn?" She leaned forward expectantly.

Jonathan and Bobby proceeded to inform their old friend of the information they had received from Boston, omitting only the presence of Manning Thomas's legal wife and the funds that Sara was still entitled to. They also informed her that they had made arrangements, using the power of attorney Emma's lawyer had drawn up for them, to transfer Manning Thomas's inheritance to her name.

Emma sat for some time after she had received the news, staring into the distance. Nora peeked in to see what was going on, since the three were so silent. Jonathan waved her away. Finally, "So. Was this fine, rich broker fellow able to supply a reason why Thomas, or Manny, neglected to amend the original will sooner? Or why Thomas—Manny—arranged to have monies sent to me in my maiden name, rather than acknowledging me as his wife?"

Jonathan cleared his throat. "Kurzman knew of your marriage, Miss Emma. But because the firm had only the original will on file, they could not acknowledge you as his beneficiary. No Boston lawyer had ever been engaged to change that will."

Bobby added, "We think Thomas was not givin' much thought to that money, Miss Emma. After all, he had transferred lots of money to Portland, and those funds was bein' invested and growin' all the time. We think that Thomas, or Manny, wanted outta that old life, and that he didn't give much of a hoot about the Boston investments. When he left the ship in London, he disappeared, and he wanted t'stay gone for good. He arranged for th'funds he needed to live a good life with you, and t'maintain his ship and take care of Jonathan. What else could he want?

"When you got married, he prob'ly thought of changin' the will, but like all of us, he mighta been lazy about it. So he had money sent to you in your maiden name even after you married. Didn't see that it made no difference. He din't know he's gonna die so quick. He only knew he's takin' care of you."

Emma bristled. "But didn't you say he kept in touch with this Kurzman?"

"He did," Jonathan replied. "But very sporadically. Apparently, he trusted that the firm would invest his funds wisely. He called perhaps once or twice yearly, to make certain that the firm knew he was still alive.

He had no need to draw more funds from those accounts."

"Mmm. Well, I must admit that what you tell me makes a certain kind of sense." She sighed. "This is a large parcel of information for my old mind to take in. First, I must accept that the man I loved all of these years deceived me to some extent. Before we met, he lived a life which he never shared with me. I was not aware of his fundamental background, or the circumstances surrounding his relationship with his parents.

"He was my Thomas. To his family, he was Manning the Third. He allowed his father to think that he was dead. Strange. I know he loved me. Of that, I am now certain. I think I would have sensed in him love for another. But the deep trust I had in him has been shaken. And that disturbs me greatly.

"I think I need to be alone with this, if the two of you don't mind. If you would like lunch, Nora would be happy to prepare something for you." Emma rose. "I know that all of this, the travel and the news you had to tell me, must have been very difficult for both of you. I am eternally grateful for your continued friendship and involvement in my affairs."

The men could see that Emma was agitated. They refused lunch, and Bobby decided to tell Nora about Doreen's invitation. Perhaps Emma would feel more like considering it after she had time to digest their information.

"Poor woman. No one wants bad news when they're old. Bad news is not well-received at any toime, but whin you're as fragile as our lady, it's worse." Nora agreed to pass on the invitation when she felt Emma could properly respond to it. "Oi'll give ye a call t'morrow," she added.

Emma decided to accept Bobby's invitation. "After all, it may be my last holiday season," she mused, "and most of the people I hold dear will be there, not here." She and Nora would arrive in the early afternoon. Nora would rent a car, so Jonathan did not need to bother himself with extra travel. "After all," Emma admitted, "I am a very rich woman now. I may as well take advantage of that fact before I go."

"Th'woman never ceases t'boggle my mind," Bobby said to Doreen as he replaced the phone. "She and Nora' are comin' on Thursday."

"You think she has accepted the news about her Thomas so quickly?" Doreen asked.

"Prob'ly not; but she's good at denyin'. Prob'ly shoved it into some non-conscious compartment in her brain. She'll take it out when she's ready t'deal with it."

Whatever Emma had done with the news, it did not interfere with her enjoyment of Thanksgiving with her friends. With Nora in tow, she arrived promptly at two, decked out in her best and walking slowly with the aid of a silver-headed cane which Nora had purchased for her. Nora brought along two pumpkin pies and two large bottles of red wine.

Everyone was in the mood for a celebration. For once, Becka's children were free of early winter colds or flu; Dickie, under Doreen's tutelage, prepared the turkey, the orange-cranberry sauce and the onion soup; Doreen's mother shared her feelings of contentment with her life, now that her daughter was successfully running the restaurant. After eating too much turkey, stuffing and pie, the adults spread out on chairs and sofas to digest their meal while

Dustin napped and the two older children bundled up and took Sharkey out to romp.

"I am exhausted, but I am so happy I decided to come," Emma said as Nora was bundling her frail body into an enveloping down coat. "Your family is wonderful, Bobby Parker, and you and Doreen have done wonders with your home. Makes me wish, with some small part of me, that I had produced a child. With Thomas, of course." She sighed. "And of course, that was never a possibility. I was much too old when we married.

"I enjoyed being with your young grandchildren, however. This is one holiday I will not soon forget."

FOURTEEN

Two weeks before Christmas, Nora called Bobby's house. Jonathan answered, since he had decided to accept their invitation to remain with his friends until the first of the year. He proved to be a great help around the house, cooking some of the meals, cleaning and helping Bobby with the finishing touches on their remodeled home. When Doreen and Bobby needed to work late, they arrived to lit candles, a fire blazing in the newly cleaned and refurbished stone fireplace, and the redolent aroma of beef stew or roast chicken emanating from the kitchen. If Jonathan had not been in residence, cans of soup or beans would have sufficed, Doreen stated as she sighed with satisfaction after tasting Jonathan's offerings.

"Oi'm afraid it's poor news, Mr. Jonathan," Nora said softly. "Our Emma's suffered another attack. 'Twasn't s'bad as the fairst, the doctors tell me, but they say she won't be out of her bed again."

"Oh, dear. Is she stabilized?"

"They say she is. She'll need to stay in hospital until they feel she's somewhat out of danger. She's already complainin'; want's to come t'her home. Says she won't leave for good from this sterile place." Nora chuckled. "Y'know Miss Emma; she most likely will have her way."

Jonathan and Bobby traveled to Ellsworth the next morning. Since snow was forecast for later that day, they planned to stay overnight, rather than attempt to travel back in unpleasant weather. Doreen offered to make reservations for them at a motel near the hospital.

Jonathan decided to drive Bobby's truck, realizing that his friend was very upset. "D'y think our news was th'cause of this one?" Bobby said mournfully as they traveled. "Or the trip she took down here for Thanksgiving?"

"The woman is eighty-nine, Bobby. Her heart is weak. At this point, any event in her life could have caused an attack. She probably should have stayed home Thanksgiving Day. But she chose to make the journey, because your place is where she wanted to be.

"And she wanted to know about Manchester. She sent us to Boston to get that news. What she does, or did with it is now up to her; not us." Jonathan shook his head. "Don't give yourself fits over this, Bobby. We'll do what we can for her, then we need to let her go."

"Y'r right. But I'm gonna miss that old woman some bad," Bobby replied. "Me, too." Jonathan nodded. The men completed the trip in silence, lost in their separate thoughts of Emma Manchester and her influence on their lives.

They found Emma in Intensive Care, wired to the usual machines. She was barely breathing, and her eyes were sunken deep within her emaciated face. "Looks like a skeleton," Bobby whispered sadly.

They met Nora in the small lounge adjacent to the IC ward. "I know, I know," the young woman said softly. "She looks like she ain't going to make it. But they say she is stable, they've reduced the fluid around the heart, and she should be showin' soigns o' loif shortly.

"She was doin' so well, these past weeks," she continued, dabbing at her eyes with a wrinkled tissue. "We thought she'd make spring. She was lookin' forward t'the plantin'. Creatin' new life, she said.

"Oi don't' think she'll be seein' the flowers bloom, this year," she said. "But I do think we'll be bringin' her home. Some of those who're leavin' us have strong ideas about how and when they want to go. And we all know, Miss Emma's one of the stronger ones."

Emma was stabilized enough to travel two days later. She was taking soup and other soft foods by mouth, and her vital signs, although very weak, were strong enough to allow the trip back to Milltown. Nora rode with her in the ambulance while Bobby and Jonathan readied Emma's house for their return.

"As you...are so fond...of saying...Bobby Parker; this... sucks," Emma wheezed, after she had been settled in her bed. Glad you're... here. Glad to be....home."

"We're sure glad you're home, too," Bobby replied. "Thought you's a goner there for a couple days." He held tight to his friend's skeletal hand. "You'll be up and whizzin' around in no time, though," he continued.

"I'm afraid...not," Emma replied. "I will... take the final journey... very soon. No wish to...stick around much longer." Bobby had no light quip left for her. He knew she was right.

The old woman was to rally slightly, though. Just before Christmas Day she was sitting, and Nora was feeding her solid food. She was able to breathe more easily, and to listen to her crooners through new headphones. Jonathan had stayed with her the week before the holiday, since Bobby needed to return to work. He was closing a hole in a roof which had been torn apart by a flying tree-branch during a recent windstorm. The family would freeze if he did not make immediate repairs.

Bobby's family gathered at Helen's for dinner with Jonathan, but Bobby was able to be sociable for only a few hours. No amount of holiday celebration could relieve a deep sense of foreboding. Finally, he told Doreen to stay at his mother's; he needed to walk and think, and he'd see her later at the house.

After he parked the truck, he grabbed Sharkey's leash and they strolled companionably in the brisk clear air. As they walked, Bobby re-ran the events of his friendship with Emma through his mind. He remembered their first meeting as clearly as if it had been yesterday. Emma's clear blue eyes, staring up from the slushy walk. The long conversations in her bright kitchen over beer and tea. The stories she had raveled out about her life, and her marriage. The love and deep friendship of a woman he originally passed off as just an old person, helpless and at the end of her life, most likely looking forward only to being a burden on others.

He was certain of one thing; Emma Manchester had never been a burden. Rather, she had helped him to lift burdens from his shoulders, and to discard many of them. For that, he would be forever in her debt. Contempt for her age had disappeared very shortly into their relationship; he often forgot that she was anything but sharp, intelligent, entertaining and helpful. And, loving. Most of all, loving. He would miss her smiles, her bright eyes, her jokes, her hugs.

"You've been a good friend, Miss Emma," he said to the breeze. "Next to Doreen, you're my best friend. And I gotta say good-bye to you. That's gonna hurt." He breathed a visible sigh into the cold. "C'mon, boy, let's git back; I'm freezin'. We gotta call Miss Emma, wish her Merry Christmas."

"Nice to hear from you, Bobby Parker," Emma whispered. "Are you...having a nice day?"

"Not partic'lly, Miss Emma. Too worried about you."

"Well, I am worried about...something else. My fate is sealed, I'm afraid. I am worried that you and the good Jonathan have...told me untruths."

Bobby blanched. Who had the old lady been talking with? "Whatta y'mean, Emma?" he asked hesitantly.

"I know that you...are trying to protect me from anything which might... make me more ill," she replied. "But I know there is more to Thomas Manchester's...story...than I have heard." She paused. "I need to hear the whole story, Bobby," she continued. "Every bit of it...nothing left out." She took three or four audible breaths. "And I need to hear it very...soon. I would like you to come alone, to see me, as soon as possible...and I would like you...to bring the will." She paused again. "The real, complete...will."

It was Bobby's turn to draw a deep breath. Then, "I'll be there tomorrow. I'll git the will from y'r lawyer first thing. We left it in his care so's he could help with the disbursement of th'finances into y'r accounts."

"Fine." Bobby heard relief in his friend's voice. "I look forward to seeing you in the morning."

"Wait'll I tell Jonathan about this development," Bobby moaned to Sharkey as he replaced the phone. "But I guess I gotta do it. She deserves t'hear it all, if she wants to."

FIFTEEN

When Doreen and Jonathan returned, Bobby filled them in on the latest development in Emma's opus. "I guess the opus is not complete until the truth is out," Janathan commented wryly.

"Poor Emma; I certainly would not want to hear the rest of Thomas's story, if I were her," Doreen put in. "You all right with this, Hon?"

"Nope. Y'r both right; she needs to have it finished, and she ain't gonna like it one bit." He sighed, then said, "But I"m gonna tell 'er, 'cause she's known all along that somethin' smelled bad in the pantry." He smiled slightly. "She sure ain't stupid. With all our plannin', we couldn't fool her."

Bobby looked closely at his friend. Emma was skeletal, and was breathing with some difficulty despite the aid of the oxygen beside her bed. However, Nora informed him that she had slept well, and had taken her medication and a bit of breakfast. Her eyes were closed as he approached her.

"I know you're...here, Bobby," she smiled slightly. "Takes too much...effort to open my eyes...unless I must." She did open them, and Bobby saw that they had lost their luster; their gaze was now focused on a point in the distance. "Would you mind...raising me up... so I can sit...instead of trying to...hear you flat on my back?"

Bobby complied, then sat beside her, clutching the retrieved will. "Y're right; Jonathan and me wanted t'keep somethin' from you," he began. "We thought it'd be okay if you never heard it, since y'r Thomas truly loved you." He paused. "I din't like it all along, but I din't want you unhappy, neither."

"I am well aware of that, Bobby," Emma said. "If I had not...been such a...what do you say...Wuss...I might have discovered...all of the facts years ago.

"Thomas was...so handsome. I...thought he might be a womanizer, doodling with every young thing he met...I am now convinced he was not." She took several deep breaths. "He truly loved me, and...for that I will be... forever grateful.

"However, I know there is...something. And I am prepared to hear whatever... it may be." She slowly turned to Bobby. "Read on, McDuff..." she said softly.

"Oh." Emma said when her friend had finished. "Oh, my." Silent tears slid down her cheeks. "That surprised me," she continued when she could speak. "I must say...I did not ever fantasize another wife." She paused again. Bobby had nothing to offer. He was too overcome with hurt, and guilt.

"Is she still...alive?" Emma said after a time. Her eyes had cleared somewhat, and she was looking directly at Bobby.

"Dunno. Haven't heard. She's got Alzheimer's; she's been in a nursing home for years. Kurzman said she's in the final stage, and wasn't s'posed to be around long."

"Oh. Poor thing. Thomas never...told her about me...did he?"

"Not so far's anyone knows. Don't think he ever saw or spoke with 'er after he left."

"That was...rather nasty...don't you think?" Emma said softly.

"I guess." Bobby was having a hard time knowing how to answer his friend. She seemed to be taking the news well, considering. But what if he said the wrong thing? Would that do her in?

Emma read his mind. "It's all right, Bobby...I can't explain why, but I feel rather... relieved to have everything out...in the open. Secrets are heavy things, don't you think?"

She smiled sadly. "I don't...like the things I have heard, but...I would rather have heard them than to...go not knowing them."

She reached out to him. "You need to go, now," she said. You and I...are square. We have only truth between us, now. And our opus...is finally finished.

"Go...be with your love. And promise me one thing..."she added. Bobby nodded. "Anythin', Emma."

"Tell Doreen the truth, no matter how... much it may hurt...don't keep secrets. Secrets will only...damage love and trust." She turned away from him, and slept.

Emma lived for two more weeks. Bobby was able to free up three mornings during that time to be with her; Doreen joined him for one visit, since she wanted to visit the old woman one last time. Jonathan stayed with Emma for a week, to give Nora some relief, then returned to Portland.

None of her friends were with her when she went. Nora called the following morning, to tell Bobby and Jonathan that she had gone quietly in her sleep. "T'was the way she wanted it, y'know," she told Bobby sadly. "Oi offered t'stay in her room, since she was havin' a divil of a time breathin'. But she sent me out.

"Before the lady left us, we talked a bit," she added tearfully. "She wanted me to thank you and Mr. Jonathan again, for everything y'all have done f'r her. I did get her t'take a bite or two of ice cream after her lunch, and I set her headphones so she could hear Frankie. He's her favorite, y'know. She did enjoy that.

"Last noight, whilst oi was seein' that she was as comfortable as she could be, she wanted me t'tell y' somethin' else pairsonally.

"She said t'tell ye she has takin' care of her friends. Oi know what that means, since she had 'er lawyer in the day before Christmas. Oi figgered she was drawin' up th'will.

"But then, she said somethin' made no sense. P'raps her moind was leavin' her. She said t'tell ye she was goin' t'keep th'date Thomas had set up f'r them. Tell me, Bobby; d'you know what she meant by them words?"

"I do," Bobby replied.

EPILOGUE: The Author

Two years and three months ago, Bobby Parker and I agreed to write his and Emma's story. The book is finished, and Sam is helping me to find an agent, or a publisher who will read manuscripts by new authors. Turns out, neither is an easy process. I loved writing the novel, but the marketing is throwing me for a loop. But that's another story, and I am far from the panic point over getting it published.

Due to the complexity of Manning Thomas's estate, the probate process was extended far beyond the normal time allotment. Following the transfer of funds to Emma's estate, her inheritance proceeded through a long process before her heirs could benefit. Sara Thomas died a month after Emma, complicating the whole affair. So, Bobby did not become uber-rich for almost two years after Emma Manchester's death. The Portland account was in his name, of course, and he was free to use that, but being Bobby, he wouldn't spend any on himself until he was absolutely positive that everything was settled.

However, he did use Emma's funds to pay me for writing the story. He said she would have wanted that. So, although the book has not been published yet, I feel pretty rich myself. The amount we settled on has left me free to utilize my time any way I please, which is a first, for me. So far, it's meant that I can spend time with Sam, and with the kids, and write whenever and whatever, for a couple of years, at least. The three short stories I submitted have been rejected, but that doesn't bother me, since I never felt I put my true self into them. Sam insists they are over the moon, and keeps re-submitting them, but I've given up any expectation that they'll be accepted. Bobby and I also agreed that if the novel was published, the royalties would be mine. I thought that mighty generous on Bobby's part, but he insisted, saying that if he finally inherited most of Emma's riches he would have no idea what to do with them, and dealing with a percentage of the royalties from my book would only add to his confusion.

He also dipped into Emma's account to supply Nora with enough money to support Emma's house. Emma left the house and a nice nest egg to Nora, but she wasn't actually able to take ownership until the monies were freed up. She made Bobby sign a document to the effect that whatever she borrowed would be completely paid back when the estate was settled. Nora obtained a part-time nursing position in the hospital in Ellsworth shortly after Emma's death, and has enjoyed living in the old lady's house. She was also bequeathed the furnishings in the attic, and plans to use them to completely re-furbish the old place.

Other than that, life went on about as usual until Bobby got what he calls "untold wealth" three months ago. Sam and I brought a couple of bottles of red over to celebrate shortly after the estate had been settled. Doreen cooked us one of her new French cuisine recipes, and she and Bobby shared their plans for the fortune.

"I'm completely flummoxed," Bobby began seriously, shaking his shaggy head. "Neither of us wants t'quit work or nothin'. We both love what we do. But we decided things could change a mite in our lives." He squeezed Doreen's hand. "You tell 'em what we've decided so far, hon."

Doreen smiled. "Bobby's a bit more confused than I about the funds," she said. "I definitely agree that our lives need to go on as they have. We're pretty satisfied with the status quo." Then, "But, we're also thinking we need to take some responsibility for using the funds wisely.

"Like the kids," she continued. "We could set them up to be super-rich for life. But where would it get them? Bess would probably drink herself into oblivion, and the others might not know how to handle all that wealth. We know Bess will find out about the money, and we expect her to try to wheedle it out of Bobby. So, we decided to offer her an allowance if she agrees to stay in Portland to raise her son near his cousins, since Dustin has been with them for so long."

"We kinda figure she'll take us up on it for a while, then take off again," Bobby added. "If she does, she's cut off." He sighed. "That'll be hard, but we gotta do it."

"Becka will also receive an allowance to take care of the kids, and supplement their income a bit," Doreen continued. "Like they need a bigger house, and we don't mind helping them with that. But we decided not to give them enough to tempt her hubby to quit his job. It's good if Becka can stay home, but work is too important to a young man to enable him to stop. What would he do for the rest of his life?" She shrugged.

"He's not used to money, so he might waste his life."

Bobby shrugged. "How d'we know? That's one of the things that's buggin' me. He may learn how t'do good things with the money. But we decided that, for now, we'll settle on this plan."

I couldn't keep my mouth shut. "So, how about Dicky? And you two?"

The pair beamed. "That's definitely the fun part of all of this," Doreen said. "Dicky's wanted to open his own restaurant ever since he graduated from his cooking classes in Calais. So," she added brightly, "We're planning to open one together."

They went on to explain that Doreen was in the process of hiring a full-time manager for the pizza place, and that they were purchasing a building on Main Street in Quoddy, with the intention of gutting it out and putting in a fine dining restaurant, the first in Washington County. It will feature fine wines and gourmet French and Italian cuisine, and Dicky and Doreen will be the chef and sous-chef. "Then, when Dickie has enough experience, he can take over and run it himself," she finished. When I asked her what she planned to do, she grinned.

"I'm thinking of a chain of pizza places, from here to Bucksport.

"You can begin thinking wide, when there's enough funding," she added with a chuckle.

The couple planned to allow themselves a generous allowance for lifestyle and household expenses, but the bulk of the estate would be turned over to a financial manager. They were searching for one, and would plan to sit down with him or her periodically, to assure that the funds were being invested and used wisely. "We'd like a lot of it t'go to eco-stuff," Bobby added. "Preservin' rain forests, fightin' clear-cuttin', that sorta stuff." He sighed, "This world's goin' bad, with all the resources bein' used up too fast. We been studyin' about it, 'cause it ain't so bad, here. Once y'find out how bad it is everywhere else, y'can't help but wantin' t'change it."

I had a couple more questions. "What about Jonathan? What is he doing with his life?"

Turns out Jonathan decided to keep his place in the city, but since he also loved Emma's house, he and Nora agreed that he would pay some of her expenses and take over the attic space for his own. He planned to spend weekends and holidays with his newfound friends. He would refurnish his new space simply, add a bathroom, and share Nora's kitchen. And, since he still loved the sea, but was not up to the rigors of boat maintenance, he planned to buy a small yacht, hire a crew, and spend summers traveling the New England coast,

I was dying to hear his answer to the next one. "So, Bobby—is Emma satisfied now? Is she still haunting you?"

Bobby nodded his head, perfectly serious. "Yep. She's been quiet for a spell now. Prob'ly spendin' time with her Thomas."

Riding home, Sam and I agreed that Emma would be delighted that she had entrusted Thomas's fortune to her friends. And, speaking of Sam, we're planning to marry next month, in plenty of time to keep the new addition to our family from being a bastard. The new rugrat's due in December. When I told Sam about the pregnancy, he was delighted, of course, being Sam. Said the new kid would be a perfect blend in the family; each of the kids could claim her, or him, as a real sibling. Lovely thought. Lovely man.